To Rexanne,
without whom this book would not be possible

Chapter 1

December 1820
London, England

LIBERTY OF THE PRESS is the Englishman's second most important privilege and should be preserved even when the results alarm us, for alarm induces reform, and the ability to reform society is the Englishman's *first* most important privilege.

LORD X, *THE EVENING GAZETTE*,
DECEMBER 5, 1820

Some fool was spreading rumors about him again.

Ian Lennard, the Viscount St. Clair, deduced that the moment he entered his gentleman's club and the butler greeted him with a knowing wink and a muttered, "Very good, milord," while taking his coat.

Brooks's somber butler had winked at him. *Winked* at him, for God's sake. Since congratulations were not in order, Ian could only assume the worst. He scowled as he strode down the carpeted halls to the Subscription Room where he was to meet his friend Jordan, the Earl of Blackmore. Then a reassuring thought occurred to him. Perhaps the butler had been tippling on duty again and had merely mistaken him for someone else.

1

Then a group of men he barely knew stopped their conversation to congratulate him. The comments—"Who is she?" and "So you've done it again, you sly dog"—were accompanied by more winks. They couldn't all be mistaking him for someone else.

With difficulty, he suppressed a groan. God only knows what the tale was this time. He'd heard most of them. His favorite had him rescuing the King of Spain's illegitimate daughter from a den of Barbary pirates whom he'd vanquished single-handedly, thus gaining the reward of a mansion in Madrid. Of course, the King of Spain had no daughter, illegitimate or otherwise, and Ian had never even met a Barbary pirate. The only truth to the tale was that Ian had once been presented to the King of Spain and that his mother's family owned a mansion in Madrid.

But rumors, by their very nature, required no basis in truth, so denying them was pointless. Why should anyone believe *him* when the gossip was so much more interesting? Thus he gave his usual response—a noncommittal answer and an ironic look meant to get the fools out of his bloody hair.

He'd nearly made it to the Subscription Room when the Duke of Pelham accosted him. "Good evening, old chap," the stout lord said with uncharacteristic joviality. "Wanted to invite you to a small dinner I'm having tomorrow, you and a few others with their inamoratas. Be sure to bring along your new paramour. Like to get a look at her."

Ian gazed down a good foot at the man he disliked. "My new paramour?"

Pelham nudged him smugly. "No point in trying to keep the woman a mystery now, St. Clair. The cat—or should I say, the kitten—is out of the bag, and everyone wants to know the color of her fur and how deep her claws are dug into you."

A paramour? *That* was the rumor? How disappointing. They could at least have made him into a highwayman. "I tell you what, Pelham. When I acquire this paramour of mine, I'll be sure to bring her to one of your dinners. Until then, I must decline the invitation. Now if you'll excuse me, I have an appointment."

Leaving the duke gaping after him, Ian strolled to the Subscription Room. A paramour—he couldn't remember the last time he'd had one. Certainly long before his return to England. Before he'd been forced into this search for a wife.

Not that he couldn't take a mistress if he wished, but he wanted to focus all his energies on courtship without some other female bedeviling him with jealous questions. Pelham wouldn't understand that, however, since his only aim in life was to debauch as many young virgins as he could lay his hands on. The man was a pig.

Entering the Subscription Room, Ian immediately spotted Jordan's auburn hair, like a beacon against the dark damask of a wing chair. Jordan lounged beside a mahogany console table, reading a newspaper. Ian dropped into the chair opposite him and chose a cigar from the humidor, looking forward to a companionable evening of smoking, reading the papers, and consulting with his closest friend.

As he snipped off the end of the cigar, Jordan glanced up. "There you are. I wondered what was keeping you. I've been impatient to hear what happened. Did she accept? Are congratulations in order?"

For a second, Ian thought Jordan alluded to the rumored paramour. Then he remembered. "Ah, you mean Katherine."

"Who else? Sir Richard Hastings' daughter. Did you propose to some other woman recently?"

He smiled. "No, only Katherine. One's enough, don't you think?"

"So when's the wedding?"

"It's not settled yet."

Jordan's eyes narrowed. "Surely she didn't refuse your offer."

"Not exactly." Lighting the cigar at a nearby candle flame, Ian drew hard on it. "She used that old female tactic of begging time to 'consider my proposal,' which was probably Lady Hastings' idea. The woman's a shark in skirts— hoping to get a higher settlement for Katherine by making her daughter play coy. Poor Katherine doesn't excel at playing coy, however. I felt sorry for her while she stammered about how she must consider my proposal further."

"Forgive me for saying this," Jordan put in, "but I don't understand what you see in the girl. She's plain and painfully shy. She wouldn't say two words to me when we met. And you're obviously not marrying her for her paltry fortune, or for her connections since her father is only a baronet."

"Your wife has no fortune and her father is only a rector, yet that didn't deter *you* from marrying and making her a countess."

At the mention of Emily, Jordan's face lit up. "Yes, but she has a number of other wonderful qualities that compensate for her lack of fortune and connections."

Ian chuckled. "Still in love, I see. Well, I'm not looking for love, Jordan—I'm looking for a wife. Despite your unusual experience, they rarely go together. All I require in a wife is respectability and good character."

In fact, a gorgeous, interesting young woman who could snag any man was the last thing Ian needed. He already despised himself for having to drag a woman into his troublesome situation. At least he could be assured that whoever married him would gain something she'd had no chance of gaining before.

"Well," Jordan remarked as he returned to reading his newspaper, "you know Miss Hastings won't refuse you in the end. She'd be a fool to do so."

"Yes." But he almost wished she would. He felt no enthusiasm for the marriage.

Enthusiasm isn't required, he reminded himself. *She suits my purposes.*

If only the woman didn't shy away when he looked at her. Or jump when he spoke. He knew why she did so—the rumors about him understandably made her edgy. But her skittishness irritated him all the same. Well, once they were married and she came to know him better, she'd relax. And he'd learn to deal with her timidity in time.

Jordan suddenly shook the newspaper and held it up to examine more closely. "I hope Miss Hastings isn't the jealous type, or you may find yourself refused after all."

"Why?" He blew a puff of smoke into the air.

"This column reports that you've kept a mistress for over a year."

"Column? In the newspaper? You must be joking."

"Not at all." Jordan held up the paper. "It's right here in *The Evening Gazette.*"

"My God, where do they get these things?" Ian's eyes narrowed. "Though that does explain why everyone's congratulating me tonight. Hand it here—let me look."

Jordan tossed the newspaper to Ian. "It's the 'Secrets of Society' column. You know, the one Lord X writes."

"I don't read Lord X's column." Ian barely had time to read the daily news, much less gossip written by anonymous rumormongers for third-rate newspapers. He picked up the paper, and added, "I'm surprised *you* read it."

Jordan shrugged. "The man's sense of humor appeals to me. Besides, some of the people he attacks need to be brought down a peg."

"Including me, I suppose," Ian said dryly as he scanned the page.

"Not at all. He compliments your good taste in women."

"This I have to see."

Discussion of private matters was nothing new in the

press, but Lord X was said to be particularly adept at it. No misstep escaped his attention; nothing was too private. Exposing the foibles of those highest in society seemed not only his profession, but his pleasure. Then again, it was easy to speak one's mind when writing under a nom de plume.

With growing impatience, Ian skimmed past the man's moralizing about the press, his accounts of a "scandalous to-do" at Lady Minnot's, and his criticism of the excesses of the Earl of Bentley, whose extravagant new house was an "abomination in an age when soldiers' widows go hungry." Then he caught sight of his name:

> Though rumors about the Viscount St. Clair's six-year absence from England abound, he keeps his love affairs so private that even rumor disguises his paramours. Thus your faithful correspondent was surprised to see the viscount enter a house on Waltham Street with a beautiful, mysterious woman. Further investigation revealed that the house belongs to the good viscount and the lady has resided there for over a year. Other men would flaunt such a treasure, but Lord St. Clair hides her away, which only proves that discretion is indeed the better part of valor.

He read it again, the words searing into his brain. Bloody hell. Waltham Street. He should have realized when everyone began discussing his "mistress" that they meant Miss Greenaway.

But how had Lord X found out about the woman and how much did he know? Had he questioned her? Although she wasn't likely to reveal anything, gossiping scribblers like Lord X could be very persuasive. Ian would have to speak to her at once, make sure she watched what she said to strangers.

He jerked his head up to find Jordan regarding him with undisguised curiosity. "Well? Who is she?"

Coolly, he tore the page from the newspaper, folded it in two, and slid it into his coat pocket. "I'll tell you who she's not. She's not my mistress. Lord X is mistaken."

And about to discover that not everyone would tolerate the man's loose tongue. If the man knew about Waltham Street, he might know other things, and before he revealed them all in his nasty column, Ian *would* put a stop to it.

"But you do have a house on Waltham Street?" Jordan asked.

Ian considered telling him it was none of his concern, but that was sure to rouse Jordan's curiosity further. "I have a house on Waltham Street, but not for the purpose Lord X implies. I lent it to a friend of the family fallen on hard times. Nothing more."

"Really?"

"Really," he said firmly. "No matter what that fool gossip says."

Jordan leaned back and folded his hands over his waistcoat. "Is this friend of the family as beautiful as Lord X claims?"

"Why do you ask?" he snapped.

Mischief sparkled in Jordan's eyes. "It would explain your lack of concern about Miss Hastings's physical attractions. If you have a beautiful mistress on the side—"

"Damn it, Jordan, you didn't listen to a word I said!"

"Sorry, old friend, but one doesn't help a beautiful woman who's fallen on hard times by providing her with a house in a very expensive part of town."

"I don't expect you to understand." Ian stubbed out his cigar in irritation. "You don't have a noble bone in your body."

"My wife would take exception to that statement," Jordan said, smirking.

"Would she? You nearly destroyed her reputation during

the first weeks you knew her, and over my objections, as I recall. It was only after you figured out what a fool you were being that you decided to marry her."

With a thunderous look, Jordan opened his mouth to retort. Then he snapped it shut and surveyed Ian a moment. "I see what you're doing: trying to get me off the subject of your mistress."

"Not at all." That was exactly what he'd been doing, and it usually worked with Jordan, whose temper erupted at the slightest provocation. Jordan had never been forced to learn the dangers of an ungoverned temper the way Ian had. "Besides, she's not my mistress."

"Lord X thinks so."

"Lord X is an ass. I'll have to talk to the bastard—make him stop maligning my friend publicly." His voice hardened. "I know exactly how to deal with his sort."

"If you can find him." Jordan hunted through the humidor. "No one knows his real identity."

"Someone does. There's generally a confidante or a servant or a relative to point the way. And surely there've been rumors—"

"There are always rumors." Jordan nudged a cigar aside, then picked up another. "Pollock was mentioned, though we both know he lacks the ballocks for it. Someone suggested Walter Scott. But no one really has a clue. Lord X keeps to himself."

"I'm sure he does," Ian remarked dryly. "Otherwise, one of his enemies might slice off his wagging tongue in a dark alley when he least expects it."

Jordan's gaze met his. "Is that what you mean to do?"

Ian laughed. "Slice off his tongue? And what would I do with it afterward? I doubt there's much of a market for gossip tongue at the butcher's." When Jordan's only response was a thin smile and a sudden absorption in his cigar, Ian stared at him. "My God, you were serious!"

Ever since Ian's return to England, the chasm between

Ian and his childhood friend had yawned wider and deeper with every day—and suddenly it angered him. "Did you really think I would cut out his tongue for printing gossip about me?"

"Of course not." Jordan shrugged. "It's all those stupid rumors about you and your bloodthirsty past . . . I keep forgetting it's nonsense—"

"Yes, it *is* nonsense." Some of it. He wasn't about to discuss his "bloodthirsty past" with his best friend. That really *would* widen the chasm. "You shouldn't listen to rumormongers."

"And you shouldn't do things that might stir up more gossip. Or prompt the man to write further columns about you."

"Don't worry about that," Ian retorted. "When I'm finished with him, he'll know better than to gossip about me or my friends again." When Jordan lifted an eyebrow, Ian growled, "I merely intend to *talk* to the man, Jordan. Bribery, manipulation, or threats should work, especially on the sort of sniveling coward who hides behind a pseudonym."

Jordan relaxed a little. "How will you find him?"

"Anybody can be found if one knows how to look." Ian rose and stared down at his friend. "I'll speak to his superior first—the publisher of *The Evening Gazette.*"

"John Pilkington? He'll give you no help. He delights in concealing the identity of his most popular correspondent."

Maybe, but even John Pilkington had vulnerabilities. And Ian excelled at using a man's vulnerabilities to find out what he wanted. "Then I'd best get started now, hadn't I?" he said, turning quickly toward the door.

"We'll see you next week at Sara's new country house, won't we? Emily's looking forward to it. We won't be staying at the house ourselves, since Emily hates to leave home for too long with the new baby, but we'll pop over for the ball. And you must come and see the baby."

"I'll be there. I promised to bring Katherine and her parents in my carriage."

Katherine. God only knows what *she* would make of this. It irked him that she might think him so callous as to flaunt a mistress while they were courting.

Well, Lord X wouldn't be mentioning Waltham Street in his column any more. Ian would make sure of that. First Ian would warn Miss Greenaway how to handle any inquiries; then he'd run this Lord X to ground. And when he did, the man would wish he'd kept to jibes about Bentley's excesses.

Chapter 2

The Countess of Blackmore recently provided her husband with an heir. Mother and child are thriving, so undoubtedly we shall soon see Lady Blackmore leaving her bed to renew her efforts for the poor. Such dedication in one so exalted must be commended, all the more because of its rarity.

LORD X, *THE EVENING GAZETTE,*
DECEMBER 8, 1820

The red missile dropping past the window of Miss Felicity Taylor's study strongly resembled a piece of fruit. At the sounds of a carriage screeching to a halt and a coachman spewing vile profanities, Felicity leapt from her chair and hurried into the hall.

"William, George, and Ansel, come out here at once!" she shouted up the stairs to the next floor.

A suspicious silence ensued. Then one by one, three identical towheaded six-year-olds peered over the railing at her, guilty expressions smudging their faces.

She glowered at her triplet brothers. "For the last time, you boys are not to bombard carriages with fruit. Do you hear me? Now, which one of you threw that apple?" When the boys muttered their usual protests, she added, "There

11

will be no pudding for anyone at dinner until someone confesses."

Two heads instantly swiveled to stare accusingly at a third. George. Of course it was Georgie. He was as troublesome as his namesakes—the late mad king and the reckless son who'd ascended to the throne this year.

His brothers' defection leached Georgie's face of color. "I didn't throw it, Lissy, honest. I was eating it, and it was real juicy, so when I leaned out the window—"

"Which you're also *not* supposed to do," she bit out. "I've told you before, only lowborn ruffians hang out of windows and throw things at unsuspecting passersby."

"I *didn't* throw it!" he protested. "It slipped!"

"I see. Like last night when your Latin grammar 'slipped' and nearly put a hole in a hackney's roof, or this morning when that snowball 'slipped' and hit the vicar."

Georgie's head bobbed up and down. "Uh-huh. Like that."

She glared at him. Unfortunately, glaring at Georgie made no impact whatsoever on the incorrigible scamp.

Nothing did, although that was understandable. The triplets were still reeling from Papa's death last year, as was she. They'd never known Mama, who'd died within hours of their births. But Papa had been their world. They considered their sister a poor substitute, since the debts their architect father had left behind kept her too busy trying to provide for them to spend much time parenting them.

Planting her hands on her hips, she stared at Ansel, the tattler among the triplets. "Where's James?"

"I'm here." Her fourth brother appeared behind the others, his gawky frame towering over their bent heads.

"I thought you were watching them for me," she said irritably.

She regretted her sharp tone the instant he flushed. "I-I'm sorry, Lissy. I was reading. I'm keeping up with my studies until I can return to Islington Academy."

His beloved Islington Academy, which they could no more afford than gold plate and silk suits. "It's all right, James. You *should* maintain your studies." Though God only knew when he'd be able to resume them, if ever.

A weary sigh escaped her lips. She shouldn't have put the eleven-year-old in charge anyway. Her studious brother had as much business playing nursemaid to three rapscallions as a puppy to three wolf cubs. But she couldn't afford a real nursemaid.

Nursemaid or no, Georgie needed the fear of God put into him before the other two began mimicking his antics. "Well, Georgie, I suppose we must call the doctor."

Georgie's jaw dropped. "What d'you mean?"

"You seem to have a problem with dropping things, so something must be wrong with your hands. Perhaps you have the shakes. I'll send for a doctor to examine you."

"I don't need a doctor, Lissy! Truly, I don't!" He held his hands out over the rail. "See? They're fine!"

She tapped her finger against her chin, feigning a look of deep speculation. "I don't know. A doctor might cure your sudden malady. He could suggest a physic—minced frog's eyes or some such."

Georgie went green. "F-frog's eyes?"

"Or cod liver oil. Three or four times a day." Georgie detested cod liver oil.

"Honest, Lissy," Georgie blurted out, "it won't ever happen again! I'll be very careful next time I lean out . . . I-I mean, next time I'm near a window."

"See that you are." She caught the other two looking smug, and added, "If the rest of you find yourself with shaky hands, I'll be happy to call the doctor for you, too."

That sobered them at once.

"Now go on with you. And play quietly, for pity's sake."

They didn't budge. Hanging on the rail, Ansel cast her a wistful look. "Maybe you could come tell us a story."

"About the peacock eating the dragon," William added

hopefully. Peacocks and fanciful creatures were William's current obsession.

"Not that one," Georgie piped up. "Tell us the one where the evil knight falls off his horse into the slime pit and his armor just sli-i-i-des off of him!"

His enthusiasm made her heart constrict. "I can't right now, moppet. I'm sorry, but I must finish this article. Mr. Pilkington is sending Mr. Winston over for it, and I can't keep him waiting."

"I don't like Mr. Winston," Ansel complained. "*He* should fall into a slime pit."

She daren't tell him, but Mr. Winston had indeed been the model for her tale.

"Mr. Winston is smelly and ugly," Georgie added. "When he looks at you, I want to punch his face. He's a bloody arse, that's what he is."

"George!" She tried to look shocked, but it was difficult when his word choice was so astonishingly accurate. "Watch your language, or I'll use that cod liver oil to rinse your mouth!" When he grimaced, she added, "Besides, much as we dislike Mr. Winston, we must be civil to him if I'm to keep writing for the paper."

"But I hate him!" Georgie cried. "We all hate him, don't we?"

"Uh-huh. If he were here, I'd punch him in the nose," Ansel said vehemently.

"I'd spit him on a sword," William added, as if he used one every day.

"I'd . . . I'd . . ." James hesitated, lacking his brothers' bloodthirsty instincts. "Well, I'd do something."

"No, you wouldn't. I wouldn't allow it." She bit back a smile at the thought of her little tin soldiers manhandling the oily-tongued Mr. Winston. "I tell you what. If you'll stay out of trouble in the nursery for the next hour, I promise I'll tell you *both* stories—the one about the peacock eating the dragon *and* the one about the evil knight."

"Hurrah! The peacock eating the dragon and the evil knight!" the triplets chorused as they ran back into the nursery.

Bless their hearts, they never walked anywhere.

James glanced down at her. "I'll look after them better this time, I promise."

"I know you will, sweetheart." She flashed him a maternal smile. "You're a good boy and a great help to me. Now go on with you."

James beamed as he hurried after his brothers. She must remember not to scold him unnecessarily. He was as sensitive as a poet, poor dear.

Though he'd not been half as sensitive with Papa.

A fit of anger seized her, and she scowled up into the heavens. "You see what you've done, God? Why did you let Papa fall into the Thames while he was drunk? You could have performed some miracle—parted the river or something. You certainly used to do enough of those. But no, you had to let Papa drown. Well, I hope he's giving you a time of it up there, gambling by the pearly gates and drinking in the streets of gold." Tears welled in her eyes. "I hope he's building your dratted mansions backwards."

She brought her head down to find a maid staring at her. The girl jerked her gaze away and began furiously sweeping the carpet again.

Curse it all, Felicity thought, embarrassed. Oh, well. By now the entire household must be accustomed to hearing her lecture the Deity—as if a house full of scamps wouldn't drive any normal person to rail at God. How could she accomplish anything with the boys underfoot? Thank heavens Mrs. Box would have them for the next few days while Felicity took her trip. She needed to escape her tin soldiers, especially the triplets.

But first, work. Hurrying into the drafty study that had once been her father's, she sat down at the desk by the window and examined a sheet of heavily inked foolscap.

Hmm, where was she? Ah, yes. *Finally, for advice concerning fashion, consider the Duke of Pelham's profound opinions: "What young girls need is that ancient apparel, the chastity belt, to restrain their passions. Then we won't have all these elopements."*

She dipped her quill in the ink bottle and crossed out the *s* on *opinions*. Of course, to be perfectly fair, the whole thing needed a drunken slur, but that was a trifle difficult to mimic in words.

Passions, indeed. It was the duke's passions the *young girls* must avoid, as she knew only too well. Fit *him* for a chastity belt, and every woman would cheer. Though to be truly effective, they'd have to bind his roving hands and gag his disgusting mouth.

The thought of that was so gratifying she sat back and savored the image of Pelham bound and harmless for once. Attach the lecher to a moving carriage and—

The sound of rumbling carriage wheels was so real, she jerked up out of her seat. Through her window she spotted a hackney lumbering up the snow-bordered street, its wheels knocking icy water out of every pothole. When it halted in front of the town house, an unladylike oath escaped her lips. The odious Mr. Winston had arrived.

She wrenched her attention back to her article. Drat. She hadn't finished reading it over for errors, and there was that troublesome phrase in the second paragraph that she had intended to amend . . .

Down in the street and out of Felicity's line of vision, Ian stood in the shadows watching Mr. Winston fumble through his pockets for the fare. Quickly Ian stepped forward and hailed the driver.

Producing a few coins, Ian paid him, and said, "Wait a minute, will you? The gentleman has somewhere else to go." Then he flashed the newspaperman a smile. "Pilkington will be relieved that I caught up to you."

Winston regarded him curiously. "Who the devil are you?"

"I'm the new man Pilkington hired this morning." Actually, Pilkington was still interviewing the applicants he'd advertised for, but Winston couldn't know that. "He needs you at Haymarket. Told me to come here and redirect you. He said since I'm new, I could handle the Lord X article." When Winston looked suspicious, he added, "There's a riot going on, and he wants you over there right away."

"A riot?" The sudden light in the man's gimlet eyes told Ian he'd judged his subject correctly. Winston was virtually licking his lips over the prospect of seeing violence in the streets. "I see. Well . . ." After a cursory assessment of Ian, he was apparently satisfied by the cheap wool greatcoat and beaver hat Ian had donned to make himself look less like a viscount and more like a workingman. "All right then. Just knock at the door and tell them who you are."

As Mr. Winston jumped in the hack and ordered the driver on, Ian smiled to himself. Three days of bribing clerks and following Mr. Winston around had finally paid off, thanks to techniques Ian had honed during the war. He didn't need Lord X's real name now. He'd located the man's house, and that was enough.

Carefully navigating the town house's icy steps, he noted the door's Gothic design and unusual griffin knocker. The knocker looked familiar. Where had he seen one like it? When the answer didn't immediately come to mind, he filed the information away for future consideration. Then he examined the town house façade through the steadily falling snow. The house was a superior example of the Gothic style, with pointed windows and excellent tracery work. A gentleman's house—but he'd expected that.

Lord X's poison pen was definitely aristocratic. Ian had studied the man's columns thoroughly, and though he still considered them gossip, he now understood why duchesses held back dinner to read them, and why every chambermaid and footman in London spent their hard-earned pence to buy *The Evening Gazette*. And why Pilkington protected his major resource so assiduously.

Lord X was any publisher's dream—sharp and witty, with an engaging style and an uncanny ability to discover the most hidden secrets. He provided both praise and censure in an entertaining manner. Like one of Ian's masters at Eton, who'd eschewed the usual canings for the subtleties of sarcasm, Lord X criticized with finesse. His subjects were principally those members of society exemplifying its worst traits—haughty disregard for the needs or feelings of others, misplaced arrogance, and love of licentious living.

No doubt that was why Ian had appeared in the column. Given the many misdeeds attributed to the Viscount St. Clair, Lord X probably considered him the son of the very devil. Ian shrugged. That might be half-true, but true or no, Lord X needed to learn more discretion in his choice of subject. And Ian intended to teach him that particular lesson.

A sharp rap with the iron knocker brought an instant response, although the snowy-haired woman who answered the door seemed perplexed by the sight of him. "Yes, sir? May I help you?"

He doffed his hat, sending snow flying off the brim. "I'm Mr. Lennard from the *Gazette*." Might as well use his real surname—Lord X probably knew him only by his title. "I'm here to pick up the article."

The woman wiped her damp and reddened hands on her skirts, then stood aside. "Do come in." As he entered, she added cheerily, "I'm Mrs. Box, the housekeeper. Where's Mr. Winston today?"

"He was called elsewhere. I'm taking his place."

"Oh. Well, you wait here, luv, and I'll fetch the article."

"Actually," he began as she started for the imposing oak staircase, "Mr. Pilkington wanted me to speak to your master in person."

"My master?" A bewildered expression deepened the lines on her forehead. Then she burst into laughter. "That Mr. Pilkington, he's so naughty. Didn't tell you, did he?"

"Tell me what?"

"Never mind. I won't spoil his little joke. I'll go tell the 'master' you're here." She lifted her skirts and took her time about ascending the stairs, all the while murmuring, "The master, eh?" between little fits of laughter.

He stared after her. Odd servant. She hadn't even taken his coat and hat. And was there no butler, no footman? What an eccentric household.

Crossing to a cast-iron hat rack, he set his coat and hat on it, then surveyed the marble foyer. Six years as a spy had taught him how to use observation to unearth a subject's secrets, but these surroundings were as enigmatic as their owner.

An understated room, devoid of the gimcrackery some preferred. A mahogany lowboy that held only a silver salver for letters. The tall mirror above it continued the griffin motif in small, delicate carvings. It was strange that a man who wrote so boldly about society's underbelly could have such refined tastes.

Perhaps the man's wife was responsible for the décor. That would explain the feminine touches—an edging of lace here, a softened line there. But if a woman was in the picture, why was the house so ill kept? The banister's brass fittings badly needed polish and the carpets needed sweeping. Where were the servants busily working at this time of the morning? The strong scent of tallow meant the man couldn't afford beeswax, but that wasn't so unusual.

As time dragged, Ian began to pace impatiently. He wanted this done, so he could go to Katherine's and settle this marriage business once and for all. He'd delayed seeing her since the column's appearance, telling himself she needed time to get over whatever pain the article had caused her. People already murmured behind her back, about her plain looks, timid manner, and poor chances of finding a husband. To have the allegedly beautiful mistress of her prospective fiancé lauded in the paper would torture Katherine, so he'd told himself his presence would only make it worse.

But he was a bloody liar, and he knew it. The truth was, when he was with her, he wanted to be somewhere else. It continually irked him the way she either agreed with his every word or remained utterly silent. When she did attempt conversation, her naïveté annoyed him.

Most men would be pleased to have a naïve docile wife. Indeed, he'd chosen her precisely because she would cause no trouble, especially in his fight against his uncle. So why did the thought of marrying her make his blood run cold?

He wouldn't think of that. He *would* marry her, no matter what his selfish impulses protested. She suited his requirements. Besides, indulging one's most powerful emotions inevitably led to ruin. One must think before one acted, ignoring the siren call of desire or even anger. He'd learned that most painfully ten years ago, and his efforts to banish such temptations had ensured his survival ever since. They would also be what won him this current battle, not only with Lord X, but with his bastard of an uncle.

He strode toward the stairs, then retraced his steps. That's when the ceiling caved in. A whoosh behind him made him whirl around in time to see a hunk of plaster hit the floor inches from where he'd been standing.

His eyes narrowed. No, not plaster. He kicked at it. When it crumbled, then clung stickily to his boot, he was surprised to discover that the misshapen blob was actually a pile of dirty snow, barely starting to melt on the marble floor.

Boyish voices wafted down the stairwell. " 'Ods fish, it's not him!" said one. A similar voice echoed, "It's some other gent." He glanced up to find himself the object of shocked scrutiny by three pairs of eyes. Identical eyes in identical heads that bobbed over the railing on the top floor like imps out of some farce. He blinked a couple of times, but there was no mistaking it. The three young urchins at the top of the stairs were identical. And one of them held an empty bucket in his hand.

"Hello there," he called up. "Do you greet all your guests with such hospitality?"

A new face appeared at the railing, an older boy whose alarmed expression directly contrasted with the curious ones of the other boys. "Oh, Georgie, what have you done now? Lissy will have our heads for this!"

Lissy? Their nursemaid, perhaps? For these must be Lord X's children. Hmm. Identical triplets, a rarity. He added that to his store of information, although for the life of him he couldn't think of any gentleman who'd bragged of siring identical triplets.

The boy who wasn't a triplet raced down the stairs, with the others tumbling after him. At closer examination, his resemblance to the triplets was obvious. "Please, sir," the older boy said as he skidded to a halt before Ian. "They didn't mean any harm."

"Didn't they?" Leaning down, Ian poked around in the filthy snow. "Coal dust. Three or four small rocks. Lump of ice." He picked out a roughly cylindrical shape and dangled it between thumb and forefinger. "An apple core? I'd say this lot would wreak quite a bit of harm on a man's head. And certainly his clothes."

"We weren't aiming for you, sir," one of the triplets said helpfully. "We thought you were Mr. Winston."

With great difficulty, he suppressed a smile. "Not a favorite of yours, I take it."

"He gawks at Lissy," the older boy muttered.

Ian straightened, drawing out his handkerchief to wipe his hand. "Who's Lissy?"

"Our sister," another triplet announced.

"I see." Four sons and a daughter. Lord X had quite a

family to care for. "Well, I thank God I'm not Mr. Winston. And that your aim is faulty."

"We're truly sorry, sir," the older boy said penitently. "We don't usually do this sort of thing. If we hadn't been expecting the gentleman from the newspaper—"

"I've come in his place," Ian broke in.

"Then you're a writer like Lissy?" one of the triplets asked.

"Not exactly." Inexplicably, he balked at lying to the child. "Your sister's a writer?"

"Oh, yes, she writes all sorts of things," the triplet continued eagerly, "but—"

"Be quiet," the older boy told his brother firmly. Then he cocked his head to stare at Ian. "I could tell you're not a writer."

"Could you?"

"All true writers have ink stains on their fingers. And you don't."

Ian examined his hands with mock solemnity. "I believe you're right."

"Lissy has ink stains on *her* fingers," one triplet offered. " 'Cause she writes—"

"I told you to hush, Georgie," the older boy said sternly. "We're not supposed to talk about it. Lissy says it's not ladylike for her to write stories."

Ian bit back a smile. He could easily imagine their sister, a budding novelist of fifteen or so, trying to imitate her father's profession while also clinging to her training in "proper" female behavior.

The housekeeper suddenly appeared at the top of the next floor. When she saw the children, she called out, "Stop bothering the gentleman, lads!" As she hurried down, she caught sight of the rapidly melting pile of snow, which they were ranged around like surgeons around a troublesome patient.

White brows furrowing, she shouldered the boys aside.

"I suppose you children got this from the balcony, eh? I swear, Father Christmas shall bring you naught but lumps of coal in your stockin's this year, 'specially if he has a word with your sister."

The panicky looks that the triplets cast each other roused Ian's rusty protective instincts. "Actually, one of the footmen came in and shook a great amount of snow off his coat," he remarked, hoping there *were* some footmen around somewhere. "I might have slipped in it if the boys hadn't hurried down to warn me." When their grimy faces lit up gratefully, he tempered his sudden burst of feeling with a stern glance. "I'm sure they'll clean it all up for you. They're very helpful lads."

"Yes, we'll do that, won't we, boys?" the older one ordered his brothers.

"Oh, yes, we want to help—"

"Let us do it—"

"We'll do it right away—"

"Very well, lads," Mrs. Box said, the edges of her thin lips twitching from the urge to smile. "You may clean it up. James, run and fetch a mop. Georgie, you can use that bucket you happen to have handy."

She faced Ian, her smile breaking out over her face. "Thank you, sir, for bein' so understandin'. They're wild boys sometimes, but they can be dears when they want."

He tried to imagine that and failed. "I gather they don't like Mr. Winston."

"To be honest, sir, none of us do. And speakin' of that, the article ain't quite ready, but you can go on up and wait for it." She glanced back to where the boys were spreading more snow than they picked up. "Do you mind findin' your way yourself, luv? If I don't keep an eye on them, they'll have the whole foyer slicker than a cow's spit by the time they're through."

"It's no trouble." It might give him a chance to glimpse Lord X unobserved.

"The first door to your right upstairs." Mrs. Box pointed up to the next floor. "Go on in. It's open."

"Thank you," he murmured, then hurriedly mounted the stairs.

When he found the room, he started to enter, then halted in the doorway. He must have misunderstood the house-keeper's directions. This room contained a woman, a petite young thing standing before a desk with her profile to him. He studied the profile with interest. She had a strong jaw-line and dramatic coloring, all russets and burnished ivory instead of the shell pink and alabaster so popular among young ladies these days.

She must be the boys' sister, Lissy. Judging from her size, she was probably only half his age, yet he couldn't tear his gaze away. Her hair was what drew him, a welter of cinnamon curls haphazardly piled atop her head and held in place by two crossed knitting needles. He'd never seen a female so unconcerned about her appearance. Indeed, the hem of her azure dress was soiled, and her shoes could use a cobbler's services.

Then she bent to open a desk drawer, and his mouth went dry. My God, what a derriere, its sweet curves perfectly outlined beneath the thin muslin of her gown. It was per-verse of him to look, but how could he not? She might be young, but she already possessed the well-proportioned fig-ure of a courtesan. No wonder Mr. Winston gawked.

It took all his self-control to wrench his gaze away and scan the hall for another open door. There was none. Think-ing to ask the young woman to direct him, he cleared his throat.

Just as he registered the fact that she was writing some-thing with the ink-stained fingers described by her brothers, she said without turning, "Come in, sir. I need only to make this one little correction, and then you can take it."

Two things hit him at once. One, her calm, assured voice

indicated that she wasn't as young as he'd thought. And two, she was obviously expecting a visitor.

Mr. Winston.

Bloody hell, he thought, cursing himself for his slow-wittedness. *Lord X is a woman.*

Chapter 3

A certain knight's lady should beware her husband's dalliance with an opera singer notorious for her open hands and closed heart. Rumor has it the thrush angles for a castle, and will not mind drowning the reigning peacock in the moat to get it.

LORD X, *THE EVENING GAZETTE*,
DECEMBER 8, 1820

Felicity scratched out a word, then scribbled another in the margin. "I'm sorry I'm so late with it," she said, still scanning the page for other errors. "It's been a frenzied morning."

A masculine voice, smooth as good French brandy, answered. "Take your time, madam. I'm enjoying the view."

The instant the man's insolent meaning registered, she whirled around, preparing to give this new employee of Mr. Pilkington's the same sharp setdown she'd given Mr. Winston on *his* first day. Then she froze. The man with the cool, collected gaze who stood outside the door to her study was definitely not from the *Gazette*.

The Viscount St. Clair. She would recognize him anywhere.

Drat, drat, and double-drat. What was *he* doing here?

Clearly Mrs. Box had mistaken him for Mr. Pilkington's man and sent him up. But that didn't explain why a titled lord would call on her.

He smiled, or rather his mouth did. The rest of his expressionless face didn't indicate why he'd come. He stepped into the room. "I take it you know who I am."

She certainly did. Though she'd never seen him this close, she'd noticed him at countless social occasions. Who wouldn't notice a man like that, nearly as tall as two of the triplets? Besides, few men filled out their coats and breeches so well in this age. And few men were so obviously *not* dandies. His face, with its sharp angles and rough lines, provoked comment wherever he went, especially when coupled with the olive complexion he'd inherited from his Spanish mother.

Not to mention those eyes . . . the exotic hue of India ink with pupils that seemed to spiral down into a black soul. They weren't called "devil's eyes" for nothing. Women either shrank from them or lost themselves in the depths. . . .

She shook herself. She wouldn't be losing herself in those depths. What was wrong with her?

Yes, she knew him, only too well after following him down Waltham Street last week. Could that be why he was here? Because of the mention in last week's column?

But he couldn't possibly know she was Lord X: Mr. Pilkington guarded her identity well. Nor had Lord St. Clair any reason to protest her article. Men of his ilk loved having their mistresses praised.

Still, it wouldn't do for him to discover the truth. Quickly, she shoved her article under some papers behind her, then pasted a smile to her face. "Good day, Lord St. Clair. You must excuse my surprise. I didn't think we'd ever been introduced."

"We haven't, madam." Reaching behind him, he closed the door, an action that substantially increased her unease. Then his gaze narrowed on her. "But I know who you are."

He said it as if surprised to discover it. "I've seen you at some of the balls. You're Miss Felicity Taylor. Your father was Algernon Taylor, the architect."

"Quite so." Good Lord, this was strange. He'd come to visit her, yet he'd only just now realized who she was?

"I was sorry to hear of your father's death last year." His words were suitably sympathetic, but his expression still impossible to read. "I saw his work at Worthing Manor and Somerset House. He was quite talented."

A lump choked her throat. "Yes, he was." Talented and foolish. His talent had led him into the company of men of rank; his foolishness and open temper had prevented him from recognizing the dangers of living beyond one's means. He'd died as he'd lived—recklessly. She had no illusions about the father she'd adored and despaired over. Or the men of rank he'd cultivated. Her voice hardened. "Thank you for your condolences, Lord St. Clair, but if you'll excuse me, I'm rather busy and—"

"I see he isn't the only talented member of the family," the viscount went on, as if she'd spoken to the wall. He gestured to her cluttered desk. "Apparently, you're equally talented with the pen . . . Lord X."

The blood drained from her face. He knew!

Or perhaps he only thought he did. She must tread cautiously. "You mean that dreadful man who writes articles in the newspaper? Surely you don't think I have anything to do with him."

He advanced on her like a threatening army. "Miss Taylor, don't assume I'm a fool merely because you think you know my secrets."

The agitation in her chest increased. She backed up, only to be halted by the unwelcome presence of her very solid desk. "Only a fool would believe me to be Lord X. Whoever gave you your information was grossly misinformed."

He halted within inches of her, much too close for propriety, and she cast him an outraged glance. She wished she could put him in his place and wipe that smug smile from his insolent mouth, but the top of her head barely cleared his chin, which made it impossible to look down her nose at him without seeming like a complete ninny.

"No one gave me any information," he said. "I did my own research. I unearthed Pilkington's minion, Winston. Then I followed him here, dispatched him elsewhere, and took his place." Angling his large frame around her small one, he rummaged among the papers on her desk. Bay rum spiked his heat with scent. "Your housekeeper was gracious enough to send me up to fetch your article." He suddenly stopped rummaging, a wicked smile touching his lips. Holding a sheet of foolscap up, he said, "This one."

No point in dissembling any longer, was there? She tilted her head up—way up—to stare at him. "Very well. You've discovered my secret."

"Yes, I have."

His eyes met hers, even more unreadable at close range. They were as mysterious as midnight . . . and just as seductive.

Jerking her gaze away, she fixed her eyes on a point somewhere beyond his broad left shoulder. "I can't imagine why you've gone to all this trouble to find me."

He tossed the paper onto the desk, but didn't move away. "Because you wrote lies about me in your column last week, and I dislike being the subject of false speculation."

Her gaze shot back to his. Had she written something other than those comments about his mistress? "Those are harsh words indeed, Lord St. Clair," she said flippantly. "I'll have to call you out for impugning my honor."

One jet-black eyebrow arched upward. "I warn you, Miss Taylor—you would lose any duel with me." His gaze drifted down her nose and cheeks to fasten on her mouth. "Although it would make for interesting sport until you did."

The devil—he was as much a philanderer as she'd suspected. Now she understood why some women found him fascinating. And why her timid friend, Katherine Hastings, found him terrifying.

"You said you came here to discuss my column," she remarked, annoyed by the rapid thudding of her heart. "I confess to being confused about which one offended you."

"Don't play games with me—you know which one I mean. The one about my supposed mistress on Waltham Street."

"*That* is the source of your objection? Please humor my stupidity a bit longer—precisely what in my comments gave you offense?"

"The fact that they are untrue," he said, enunciating every word with growing impatience, as if speaking to a child. "I already explained that."

He hovered so near she could see each neatly cropped strand of his hair, glossy as fine velvet. His proximity, coupled with an annoying glint of determination in his eyes, began to worry her. In times like these she would give a fortune to be taller. And possessed of a gift for fisticuffs.

Something about the man disturbed her . . . a dark purpose beneath the civilized appearance, like a falcon's hooded head. She suddenly had a profound desire to be near an exit before the hood came off and the bird of prey struck. Easing from between him and the desk, she edged toward the door.

"Don't even think of leaving before we're finished," he commanded in a steely voice, turning to follow her movements.

She halted in her tracks. "I-I wasn't."

Though she wanted to. She had dealt with stupid men. She had even handled furious men, who were merely larger versions of her petulant brothers. But this man, with his intelligence and eerie calm, was outside the realm of her experience. This man compelled obedience by his very manner. She didn't want to discover what would happen if obedience wasn't immediately forthcoming.

"What I wrote about you wasn't untrue." She attempted to match his calm. "It was a speculation, one I based on several facts."

"Such as?" Keeping his gaze fixed on her, he rested his hip on the desk. When he crossed his muscled arms over his chest, a shiver rippled over her skin. Being alone with him gave her an entirely new perspective on the man. When she'd seen him in public, surrounded by his peers, it had been easy to dismiss the air of danger he wore like cologne. But now that he stalked her in Papa's old study, it was anything but easy.

"Well, Miss Taylor?" he asked, jerking her back to the business at hand. "What are these facts?"

"Ah, yes." She ticked them off on her fingers. "The house in Waltham Street was taken by you over a year ago for the woman who resides there. She's beautiful, relatively young, and obviously enamored of you. And her name is Miss Greenaway."

Her one other point she kept in abeyance. She might need it later, if matters grew complicated. No need to provoke this fearsome viscount any more than necessary.

A moment of dead silence ensued. Then he shoved away from the desk and straightened to his full intimidating height. "Those are indeed the facts—for the most part." He paused, his gaze examining her with uncanny precision, as if to discover her weaknesses. "You did make one subjective statement: that she's 'obviously enamored of me.' What led you to that conclusion?"

"I spoke to her in person." Though that was stretching the truth a bit.

"In person?" An undercurrent of anger surfaced briefly in his voice before he mastered himself. "And Miss Greenaway told you she was enamored of me?"

A hot flush stole over her cheeks. "Well, not exactly . . .

I-I mean . . ." For a moment, the mad impulse to lie seized her. But she had the oddest feeling that he'd know if she did. "To be honest, she wouldn't speak of you at all. She confirmed her name and that the house belonged to you, nothing more." She'd only said *that* much because Felicity had flustered her by taking her by surprise in the street outside the house. But the moment Felicity had raised the subject of his lordship, the woman had blushed and fled back into her sanctuary. Surely that sufficiently proved the woman's status.

"How did you conclude she was 'enamored' of me?"

Her blush told me so, she thought. But he wouldn't take that as proof. "She was very secretive. She clearly wanted to protect you from—"

"Nosy gossips?" His voice rumbled with sarcasm. "I can't imagine why she'd want to do that."

She glared at him. "If her connection to you is innocent, then why should she hide anything?"

"Because she prefers her privacy perhaps?"

"Or because she feared your disapproval. You must admit you're known for your discretion, for not telling anyone, even your closest friends, about your activities."

Rubbing his chin, he circled her. "I suppose you're referring to all the rumors about what I did while I was abroad."

"Well . . . yes."

Thanks to his notorious reticence, discovering anything about him *but* rumor had been nigh on impossible. The few facts were that he'd disappeared from England at the age of nineteen, and he'd returned after the death of his father a few years ago. No one knew where he'd gone or what he'd done. Tales had ranged wildly from assertions that he'd been a spy for the French and the lover of a Spanish don's wife to one man's claim that he'd seen Lord St. Clair begging in the streets of Paris.

The point was, the viscount was more secretive than a

priest hearing confession. And Felicity disapproved of secrets.

Amusement flickered in the gaze that locked with hers. "Which rumors have you heard? That I was a paid assassin? That I seduced Josephine after her divorce, and Napoléon called me out for it?"

She pricked up her ears. "Not that last one." Good Lord, that would be quite a tale for the column. *If* she could coax him into confirming it, which wasn't likely.

"And I suppose you believed every rumor."

"Hardly. But in the absence of other information—like the sort you yourself might provide—what else would you have me do?"

He halted in front of her. "You might mind your own business instead of sowing rumor and gossip in your wake."

"I do *not* sow rumor and gossip!"

"Ah, yes, I forgot: You make speculations based on fact."

"I do what any good member of the press does," she said loftily.

He snorted. "The good ones write responsibly. They concern themselves with matters of national importance. I hardly think Miss Greenaway qualifies as that." When she started to retort, he held up his hand. "So you saw the woman, found out I provide her with shelter, and determined that she was my mistress, is that it?"

"It was a logical deduction."

"But wrong."

They were back to that again, were they? "If indeed I've mistaken the situation, I'll happily write a correction. So far you've told me nothing to prove me wrong."

"And *you* have failed to explain why you're so interested in my personal affairs." Strolling back to the desk where her papers were scattered willy-nilly over the scarred oak surface, the man actually had the effrontery to sort through her notes. "Tell me, what possible reason could you have for writing about me? Have I unwittingly offended you?"

She chose to ignore his obnoxious implication that revenge motivated her columns. "I write about everyone, Lord St. Clair. Your story is merely one among hundreds."

"But a mundane one." He picked up an envelope, scanned it, then set it down. "A man provides a house for a woman to whom he's not married. Surely that's boring fare for your readers. Men do it all the time."

His indifference roused her moral indignation. "That's precisely why it's offensive! Men seek out virgins to marry and want their wives to be faithful to them, yet they feel perfectly free to cavort with as many women as they can lay their hands on!"

He paused in rifling her desk to cast her a calculating glance. "You forget that I'm not married."

"No, but you're about to be."

She regretted her retort the moment he froze. It suddenly occurred to her that he'd been fishing for just such a revealing statement, and she'd foolishly taken the bait.

He ambled toward her with deceptively easy steps, like the unhooded falcon taking flight. "What do you mean?"

"N-Nothing. Only that you're a bachelor and . . . you'll marry someday and—"

Without warning, the falcon loomed over her. "You know of my offer to Miss Hastings, don't you?"

She swallowed, then nodded.

"I suppose you discovered that the same way you discover everything else—by delving into people's private business."

"No!" His insistence on seeing her as a sneak grated on her. "Lady Hastings told me. Katherine is a friend of mine." A very dear friend, sweet and loyal, though timid as a mouse. That was the trouble. Katherine didn't have the first idea how to deal with the likes of Lord St. Clair.

"I see." His jaw tightened. "So you decided to expose

my 'misbehavior' in the paper to make your 'friend' doubt me and refuse my suit."

He was very nearly right, though Felicity had really hoped to prod Katherine's *parents* into doubting him. Poor Katherine had refused to break off with the viscount if it meant making her parents—especially her mother—angry. She'd even confided wistfully to Felicity that if Lady Hastings could only be made to realize how unsuitable Lord St. Clair was, there might be some hope of refusing his suit.

Felicity had advised the young woman to oppose her mother, but Katherine didn't have it in her. Even so, Felicity mightn't have interfered if she hadn't learned that the man had both a mysterious, worrisome past and a mistress. The thought of her dear friend married to such a man chilled her blood. Felicity had met too many of Papa's "fashionable" companions not to know what miserable husbands they made.

Renewed in the rightness of her position, she met his gaze boldly. "I thought Katherine—*and* her parents—should know what she's getting herself into."

Eyes cool as black marble stared her down. "And you couldn't tell them in private because then you'd have to reveal your nasty hobby of meddling in others' affairs."

She crossed her arms over her chest. She'd had about enough of this overbearing viscount and his insults. "See here, Lord St. Clair, *I'm* not the one who's keeping a mistress while he woos a nice young gentlewo—"

"For the last time, Miss Greenaway is *not* my mistress."

"And I suppose that the baby she had with her, the son who was easily less than a year old, isn't yours either."

That stopped him cold. His expression grew shuttered, then thoughtful. "Well, well. So you know about the baby, too. And I can see what you deduced from that."

"Do you deny it?"

"Would it do me any good? You have your mind made

up that I'm a debaucher of innocent young women and a willing sire of bastards. I wouldn't want to destroy your skewed assessment of me by providing you with something so useless as the facts."

She bristled at this insult to her integrity. "If you can prove my deductions faulty, by all means do so."

"All right." Abruptly he began pacing the study from corner to corner, examining its contents as if taking inventory. He opened the silver snuff box that sat on the edge of a delicate table. "Do you take snuff, Miss Taylor?" he asked, as if it were the most natural question in the world.

"Of course not! That was Papa's."

"So this study belonged to him."

"Yes."

"I thought so. And the dress sword hanging on the wall? That was his, too?"

Where was this leading? "No, it was my grandfather's."

He peered closely at it. "Ah, yes, Colonel Ansel Taylor. The boys in the regiment often spoke of Ansel the Anvil, who had a spine of iron."

"In the regiment? What were *you* doing in a regiment?"

A little twist of a smile touched his lips. "I fought in the Peninsular Wars."

She regarded him disbelievingly. The very idea was ludicrous. Men with titles and fortune, men who were their fathers' only heirs, didn't serve in the military. If they were killed, it would mean an end to the family line and the title. No father would allow it. No heir would suggest it. Everyone knew the military was for younger sons and lower gentry. "That's what you were doing on the Continent all those years?" she asked, not bothering to hide her skepticism.

"Why? Do you wish to print my war history in your paper, too?"

His wary expression only heightened her suspicion of him. "Can you suggest some reason I should *not* print it?"

"I fear you'd claim I fought for the other side," he said with acid condescension.

She glowered at him. "I don't invent information, my lord. I merely report it."

"Or 'speculate' on it."

"When I'm relatively certain the facts support my speculation, yes."

"It helps if you have *all* the facts, and not merely the ones that interest you." He strode to the fireplace and lifted a piece of James's artwork, inspecting the crude wood carving of a sheep. Then he put it aside and faced her. "Your grandfather . . . did he have friends from his military career, men for whom he would have done anything?"

She searched her memory. "Yes. He used to dine weekly with a fellow soldier."

"Then you should understand my situation. Miss Greenaway is the sister of a man I fought with at the Battle of Vittoria. He died in my arms at that battle. And as he lay dying, he asked me to look after his sister. I promised I would. So when she was seduced by some bounder who got her with child, then abandoned her, she came to me. Of course, I agreed to help. That's why I put her up in a house in Waltham Street."

At first she felt utter guilt at her earlier supposition. How could she have been so wrong, so hasty? A poor woman found herself destitute and pregnant and—

She suddenly caught his gaze on her, a gaze that was calculating and wholly dishonest. She glanced up at Grandpapa's sword, then noticed the Army Gold Medal displayed beneath it. The one with Grandpapa's name and rank engraved on it.

The scoundrel! He'd pretended to know Grandpapa to reinforce his lies, to make her ashamed to sully his own reputation. She doubted the wretch had even *heard* of her grandfather, much less fought with men who knew him!

Probably the only time Lord St. Clair wielded a sword was in duels over married women he'd bedded.

Ooh, she would show him she was no ninny. She flashed him an insincere smile. "How noble of you to help your friend!" she gushed. "I'm so sorry I mistook you. I'll add a correction to my column at once." Hurrying to the desk, she brandished her quill over the paper, then began to write. "How's this? 'Lord St. Clair's purpose in taking the house on Waltham Street was apparently not as it seemed. Having sworn to his dying soldier friend on the battlefield that he'd look after the man's sister, his lordship was kind enough to provide her with shelter when some bounder got her with child and refused—"

"You *can't* write that!" he exploded behind her.

She pretended to reread her words. "I believe you're right." She fixed him with a hard look. "I couldn't possibly write such a blatant lie. I'd be laughed out of town."

A new admiration flickered in his gaze. "What makes you think it's a lie?"

"If Miss Greenaway's brother had been your friend and this had been a favor to him, her gratitude would immediately have compelled her to tell me of your generosity. But it didn't." She lined through the words she'd just written, then tossed her article on her desk. "Besides, rich heirs to a title rarely fight in wars. Why should they, when there are younger sons to buy commissions? No, I'm sure you were doing on the Continent exactly what you're doing here . . . gulling stupid women."

For the first time that afternoon, she seemed to have roused his anger. A muscle in his jaw worked convulsively. "I don't give a bloody damn what you think of me, but I won't have you putting your speculations about Miss Greenaway into print."

"Why not? You should thank me for enhancing your reputation among your peers. No doubt they're all congratulating you on your beautiful mistress."

"Indeed they are," he said without a trace of shame. "But it isn't my reputation that concerns me. It's Miss Greenaway's and that of her child. She doesn't deserve to have you ruin her with your gossip."

"Don't be absurd—I haven't ruined her. I didn't print her name nor the address of your house. I didn't even mention the child. I wouldn't be that cruel to one of my sex. Besides, you should have been concerned about ruining her *before* you sired her child."

"I did *not*—" He broke off with a curse that was decidedly ungentlemanly. "Very well, believe what you wish. But consider whom else you're harming—like Katherine, a woman you claim is your friend. Your article publicly humiliated her."

"That was not my intention." Indeed, she'd debated endlessly over taking such a drastic step. If it had only been Katherine's timidity standing in the way of her happiness, Felicity might have kept quiet, for a considerate husband could get past that. But this man couldn't possibly be a considerate husband, not if he kept a mistress.

There was also the person Katherine claimed to love. Lady Hastings had forced Katherine to refuse a man's suit because he was beneath her. Knowing Lady Hastings, that meant he was a younger son of a knight or a merchant or some such. Katherine hadn't revealed his name, but she still clearly adored him. Yet she wouldn't face down her harridan of a mother to accept his suit.

Not without a push. A very large, very public push that would make even her mother take notice. And that's what Felicity had given her.

"I don't regret my actions," she added forcefully. "She and her family had to be made aware of what kind of man you are."

He cast her an incredulous look. "What kind is that? A man of wealth, position, and rank—a man who possesses all a woman could require for a comfortable marriage? My

God, you have strange notions. Do you think Katherine will appreciate your meddling? Do you want her to remain a spinster all her life? To deprive her of an opportunity to have her own household, her own children?"

The question stung, reminding her painfully of her own situation. "Thank you so much for pointing out the grievous fate awaiting me and my kind."

"You're not old enough to understand the ramifications of being a spinster."

"And you're not the right sex to understand it," she snapped. "Besides, you mustn't let my size fool you, my lord. I'm already three and twenty."

"A great age indeed," he said sarcastically, one eyebrow crooking upward.

Amazing how the mere arch of his eyebrow could make her feel as much a child as the triplets. She strained to stand taller and got a cramp in her lower back for her pains. "I may not be of your *ancient* years, but associating with my father's titled friends taught me a great deal. Marriage can be every bit as unpleasant as spinsterhood when one's husband is a careless libertine with a wandering eye. Katherine may not thank me now for warning her so publicly, but she will later!"

Oh, dear, now I've gone and done it, she thought, when he strode up to her and grabbed her by the shoulders, the falcon swooping down for the kill. "You don't know what you're doing, you little fool!" he growled.

The blatant attempt to intimidate her replaced her fear with fury. Wrenching free of him, she hurried to the door. "I know exactly what I'm doing. In my own way, I write the truth. You may find this hard to understand, since subterfuge is your usual practice, but this is my charge, and I do it as faithfully as I can!" She opened the door with a dramatic flourish. "Good day, my lord. Our conversation is finished."

His eyes narrowed. "Not by half." He strode to the desk

and stabbed his finger at her article. "I'm not leaving until you write that you were mistaken about my taking a house in Waltham Street for a woman."

"Write a retraction?" The very idea appalled her. She walked over to the desk and snatched up the page, folding it and shoving it into her apron pocket. "I won't do any such thing! First of all, I stand by my conclusions. Secondly, saying you never took the house would be a lie, and regardless of what you think, I do not lie in my column."

A grim smile touched his lips. "What if I say I'll publicly reveal Lord X's identity? What then? Would your popularity be as great if your readers discovered the bluestocking female behind the witty nobleman's façade?"

That he'd actually threaten her was the last straw. Ignoring her jolt of fear, she wagged her finger at him. "Go ahead, you bully! Expose me! And I'll be after you like a magistrate after a thief! Until you convince people I'm Lord X—and that may prove difficult, mind you—I'll make you and all the rumors about you the *only* subject of my column!"

At his thunderous look, she lowered her voice to a hiss. "First I'll set up camp outside your mistress's door until she tells me every secret in your despicable life. Then I'll scour the city for information about you. One way or the other, I won't rest until I find out exactly why so many sordid rumors are linked to your name. I'll make it impossible for you to marry *anyone* in this city!"

To his credit, he didn't even blink at her threat. But she could tell she'd made her point, for if eyes were pistols, she'd be shot full of holes. "So we're at an impasse," he said icily.

She dragged in a shaky breath. Perhaps it hadn't been so wise to meet threats with threats—especially when the man she threatened had power and wealth far exceeding her own meager resources. As Papa had cautioned her whenever she wanted to rail at his patrons, "You can't taunt a cannon with a club, my child. Not if you want to keep your head."

Deliberately, she softened her tone. "I don't see it as an impasse. Things will merely continue as before. You'll forget about my article, and I'll forget we had this conversation. That seems fair."

"It 'seems fair' that you've trumped up some scandalous tale about me just to influence your friend's choice of husband? You may think it 'fair' if it pacifies your conscience, but we both know it for the nasty manipulation that it is."

"I'm sure you would recognize nasty manipulations more easily than I, given your reputation. *I* regard it as a service to womankind. And now, I have work to do. Good day, Lord St. Clair."

He straightened. "Very well, Miss Taylor. I'll leave." He walked past, pausing a few inches from where she stood. Leaning toward her, he lowered his voice until it resembled the timbre and volume of a wolf's growl. "But I warn you, I'm a dangerous man to have as an enemy. If I ever see you anywhere near my house on Waltham Street again, you'll regret the day you picked up a pen and wrote about me."

Then he turned on his heel and stalked from the room.

She said nothing, ventured no flippant remark, no hot retort. Indeed, now that he was gone, it took all her effort to tamp down the fear springing full into her breast. For despite her brave words, despite her insistence to herself that he was only bluffing, she believed him most heartily.

And the last thing she needed in her life right now was a dangerous lord.

Chapter 4

One need only note the marriages of Miss Hinton to Mr. Bartley and Lady Anne Bowes to Mr. Jessup to realize why runaways throng the road to Gretna Green lately. When haughty papas betroth their daughters to ancient lords and decent young men lack the coin to please greedy mamas, couples must follow their hearts all the way to Scotland.

LORD X, *THE EVENING GAZETTE*,
DECEMBER 8, 1820

Deep in thought, Ian descended the carpeted stairs of the Taylor town house with grim purpose. Time for a new strategy. For if Miss Taylor thought he'd simply give up, then she was not only a tart-tongued, self-righteous spinster, but a fool.

He never left loose ends, and the sanctimonious Miss Taylor was most certainly one of those. Judging from her ridiculous pronouncements about men of his rank, he doubted she'd stay out of this matter, especially if Katherine ignored her warning and married him anyway. Then what would the mad Miss Taylor do? Pester Miss Greenaway until the woman told everything? Or even delve into his past at Chesterley?

No, he must end the young woman's meddling at once.

But how to change a woman's mind for whom exposing "libertines with wandering eyes" was a holy cause? Regrettably, she was too intelligent to manipulate. She'd proven that when he'd tried out his nonsensical tale about Miss Greenaway being the sister of a dying soldier friend. And threats didn't work either. The wisp of a woman had actually tried to threaten *him*—a man who'd made mincemeat out of soldiers three times her size.

Bloody hell, he didn't need this right now. He had no time to deal with the likes of Miss Taylor. The clock was ticking. He had scarcely two years to marry and have an heir or he'd lose Chesterley to his bastard of an uncle. He refused to let that happen, no matter what "Lord X" wrote.

He reached the foyer, disappointed to see that Miss Taylor's unruly brothers had vanished. Another chat with the loose-tongued brothers might have proved useful. Ah, well, another time. That would be easy enough to arrange.

Retrieving his coat and hat, he turned just as Mrs. Box emerged in the foyer. Here was someone he could make use of. And she didn't yet know who he really was.

When she saw him, the woman could hardly suppress her mirth. Yet he couldn't blame her. His typical male arrogance had kept him from realizing sooner that Lord X was a woman, yet he should have noted the feminine writing style and the slant of the columns toward women's concerns. Well, he was paying for his blindness now.

"Did you talk to the 'master,' sir?" the housekeeper asked, eyes gleaming.

"You know the answer to that, Mrs. Box." He made his tone both teasing and reproachful. "You misled me quite effectively."

Her papery cheeks pinkened. "It was naughty of me, I know. But runnin' after the three Terrors of Taylor Hall has made me as mischievous as them in my old age."

"Old age?" he said smoothly. "You can't be more than forty."

She waggled her finger at him. "Now, Mr. Lennard, you know better than that. What a flatterer you be."

"Only with beautiful ladies. And how can I resist when the house is full of them?"

Her smile disappeared. "You didn't flatter the miss, did you? She don't like that. She used to scold that Mr. Winston somethin' awful for things he said."

"I'm sure she did," he said dryly. "Scolding men is clearly her specialty."

"With good reason, too. Men are always makin' unseemly advances t'ward her." The old woman eyed him with suspicion. "*You* didn't do nothin' like that, did you?"

He hoped his expression of outrage looked convincing. "Mrs. Box, for shame! I'm a gentleman—I would never mistreat a lady!"

But he'd wanted to. Oh, yes. Because along with the overwhelming urge to strangle Miss Taylor had been an equally overwhelming attraction. For all her annoying ideas, the woman knew how to make a man lust after her without even trying. It was that hair of hers that looked as if she'd just been tumbled. And those vibrant lips that needed kissing—

Bloody hell. This wasn't helping. Forcing himself back to the matter at hand, he donned his coat and asked, "Did Mr. Winston make advances to her?"

"The scoundrel did more than that—backed her up against a wall one day and tried to put his hands on her."

A sudden, powerful urge to throttle the absent newspaperman assailed him. He told himself he was merely reacting to the disturbing thought of any young woman being assaulted in her own home. It had nothing to do with Miss Taylor in particular. "And what did she do about it?"

"Oh, the miss can look after herself most of the time. She kneed him in the you-know-what, then told him if he ever tried it again, she'd shove him down the stairs. The man's behaved himself since then."

A smile touched his lips. He should have known Miss Taylor wouldn't act like a typical female. From the moment she'd leveled those lethal green eyes on him and given him the rough side of her tongue, he'd realized she was anything but typical.

"So Mr. Winston isn't to her liking," he mused aloud. "Does she have any suitors? Or a fiancé?" That would be ideal. He could ruin her marriage plans the same way she was trying to ruin his.

Mrs. Box shot him a knowing look. "She don't have no fiancé, and not too many suitors either. But I think the right one ain't presented himself yet, know what I mean?"

When she nudged Ian and winked, obviously misconstruing his intent, he nearly laughed aloud. This could work in his favor. He leaned toward the housekeeper with an air of confidentiality. "I'll tell you a secret, Mrs. Box. Your mistress intrigues me, even if she does hate me."

Mrs. Box's upper lip wrinkled in a moue of disbelief. "She can't hate a fellow nice as you. You just got to keep at her, do you hear? I know she seems to have a cold heart, but it's only been starved by—"

The door slamming at the top of the stairs cut off her words. He and Mrs. Box looked up to find Miss Taylor standing outside her study, a quivering pillar of rage.

"Come here, Mrs. Box, I need you at once." The glare she shot him would have fried the snow falling outside. "And Lord St. Clair, if you don't leave this house immediately and stop pestering my servants, I'll have my footman *throw* you out!"

"I told you, she hates me," he said to the gaping Mrs. Box. Then he flashed Miss Taylor a smug smile. "I can't see what harm there is in speaking to your servants after you questioned my friends."

"Joseph!" she cried, obviously making good on her silly threat.

Although he could trounce any of her footmen with both

hands tied behind his back, he'd made his point—and questioning Mrs. Box could wait for another time.

He clapped his hat on his head. "Don't trouble your footman—I'm leaving." He added, with a nod to Mrs. Box, "We'll finish our discussion later."

Miss Taylor's outraged threat to shoot him should he speak to anyone in her household again followed him out the entrance door. He grinned to himself. So Miss High-and-Mighty wasn't as impervious to threats as she pretended. Well, the little witch would soon discover what it meant to cross the Viscount St. Clair. Every woman had her weakness, and he would learn Miss Taylor's if he had to hound all her servants to do so.

He descended the outer stairs in a much better mood. Motioning to his coachman, who'd kept the carriage waiting for him in a spot down the street, he paused at the bottom of the steps to relish the chilly air after the decided stuffiness of Taylor Hall and its mistress. The snow continued to sow winter along the muddy thoroughfare. At the moment, it gilded everything with white, but it would soon turn the roads into an icy morass unnavigable by any sane man.

It reminded him of Miss Taylor herself—pure, white, and innocent at first glance. But ice was ice, whether shaved into fluffy flakes or packed solid in sheets, and it must be put to the flame to render it into harmless water. Well, he fully intended to put Miss Taylor to the flame. Before long, he'd have her scrambling to write a retraction.

But first, he had more important matters to attend to. The light was dimming and the snow thickening. He, along with Katherine and her parents, had been invited to spend a few days at the country estate of Jordan's sister, Lady Worthing. They were traveling there together in his coach this afternoon, and if they were to make it before the roads became impassable, they should leave at once. That scarcely left him time to go home, fetch his bags, and change clothes before he arrived at the Hastings town house.

The thought of two hours in a carriage with the Hastings family banished his good mood. They'd probably all read the damned column by now. He wouldn't be able to speak privately with Katherine, and even if he could, he wasn't sure what to tell her. Yet he must say something, if only to force her into a decision. He was bloody tired of looking for a wife. And two years gave him little time in which to sire an heir. Their first child might be a girl, or it might take him and Katherine months to conceive.

His coach halted in front of him, and he climbed in, ordering the coachman to drive on. As they pulled away from the front stoop he glanced up at the window to Miss Taylor's study, but there was no sign of her. Probably gone to wax her broomstick and add a few toads to her cauldron.

He could envision her bending over a steaming pot, prominently displaying that fetching derrière that made a man's mouth water and his hands itch to cup the soft—

Damn! There he went again, lusting after the woman like the cheap libertine she thought he was. He'd have to keep close rein on *those* thoughts. The woman was trouble, pure and simple, and her attractions only made her doubly so.

Better that he concentrate on his far less troublesome fiancée, the one Miss Taylor seemed determined to scare off. He needed to invent some explanation about the article that would assure Katherine of his intention to be faithful to her.

He sighed. The irony was that he intended exactly that. He'd never approved of infidelity. His father, for all his faults, had been scrupulously faithful to his mother, and Ian had admired that. Those people in the *ton* who held "sophisticated" ideas about marriage annoyed Ian, for they were shallow, concerned only with their own pleasures. But convincing Katherine would be difficult now. How could he make her believe him over the famous Lord X when she was already so shy of him?

When he arrived at the Hastings town house an hour later he was no closer to determining what to say to Katherine, which irritated him. So when the butler showed him to the drawing room, he was already in a sour mood. As the servant announced him, Ian's mood darkened even more at the sight that greeted him.

Inside the elegantly appointed room, the generally haughty Lady Hastings perched on the edge of a lavender settee like a squirrel on a branch, her head erect and her gaze darting back and forth as if to scent the approach of danger. Sir Richard, who could barely walk, had nonetheless pushed to his feet on the Aubusson carpet and was using his cane to struggle toward the sideboard and its selection of brandies.

Where was Katherine? Why wasn't she part of this strange family tableau?

"Lord St. Clair!" Lady Hastings cried as soon as he entered. "Do come join us! I'll ring for tea." She lifted a little silver bell and rang it repeatedly, until the tinkling echoed in the drawing room like a strident opera chorus.

"Agnes, that's enough!" her husband commanded. "Put the damned bell down, for God's sake! We're not having tea at a time like this!"

A frantic expression crossed her lined face as she patted the seat next to her with uncharacteristic energy. "Of course we are! Don't listen to him, Lord St. Clair. Do come sit down beside me."

Something was amiss; any fool could tell that. "What's happened?" Ian asked Sir Richard, ignoring the man's wife.

"*Nothing* has happened," Lady Hastings retorted. She shot her husband a murderous glance. "You mustn't discuss this now, Richard."

"There's no point in pretending," her husband replied as he reached the sideboard. "My man could find no trace of them. If not for these legs, I could've gone, but . . ." He trailed off, splashing a generous amount of brandy into a glass.

"You shouldn't be drinking," she said as she rose and went to his side.

The couple were trying Ian's patience. "Find no trace of whom?"

"My daughter," Sir Richard said. His wife let out a little squeak, but he forestalled any further protests. "He has a right to know, Agnes." He met Ian's gaze squarely. "You proposed marriage to my daughter, but she gave you no answer. Is that correct?"

An uneasiness settled into the pit of his stomach. "Yes." Had she run off to avoid *him*? Had she been that upset about that bloody article?

Sir Richard held the brandy glass up to his mouth, but his wife removed it before he could drink any. He scowled at her, then at Ian. "I'm afraid, Lord St. Clair, that our daughter has run off—eloped—with another man."

Eloped? Timid Katherine who had putty for a spine? His temper rapidly rose to a boil.

My God, not again. This had happened to him last year when Lord Nesfield's daughter, Sophie, had run off with a barrister. What was wrong with these young girls, always flying off to marry men without their parents' approval?

He must have the worst luck in Christendom! Despite his efforts to choose reasonable, *dull* women, he only found the ones whose quiet natures masked raging passions. Passion had never been part of his offer, but then, he'd assumed that a sensible woman didn't want that fickle emotion. Apparently, he'd been wrong. Bloody hell.

"Who did she run off with?" Ian asked.

Sir Richard snatched the glass of brandy from his wife, then downed it. He wiped his mouth with the back of his hand. "Our steward, Mr. Gerard."

Their steward. Katherine had eloped with a man she must have known for some time. He suddenly had the uncomfortable feeling he'd been duped. "Was there a prior attachment between Katherine and your steward, sir?"

"Yes," Sir Richard said at the same time his wife cried, "No!"

"Which is it?" he asked in a frigid tone.

Sir Richard scowled at his wife. "Why don't you tell him, my dear? I don't think you'd like what I have to say on the subject."

She glared at him, then faced Ian with a rustle of muslin skirts. "You see, Lord St. Clair, my daughter began fancying herself in love with Mr. Gerard years ago." She cast her husband an arch glance. "I warned my husband that he should dismiss the man, but he thought nothing would come of it. 'It's a girlish infatuation,' he used to say. 'She'll ne'er act upon it. And I shan't lose a good steward for such an idiotic reason.' "

Under other circumstances, Ian might have been amused by Lady Hastings' uncanny ability to mimic her husband. Just now, he wasn't. "Go on."

"Richard thought she'd grow out of it. She didn't. Then last year, the man had the audacity to ask for her hand. He was declined, of course. Clearly, he lacked the necessary prerequisites of birth and fortune."

"Necessary to *you*," her husband added.

She sniffed. "Don't quibble with me, Richard. You know I was right to insist on that. And you should have dismissed the man as soon as he made his feelings known."

Her husband leaned back against the sideboard. "I thought him an honorable man. Besides, I feared that dismissing him would merely tempt him to run off with the silly girl, and if I kept him on he wouldn't risk his position. They both seemed to accept the situation." He glanced apologetically at Ian. "When you came along and she acquiesced to your attentions I thought she'd forgotten her girlish fancy." His attention turned briefly to his wife. "I didn't know she wasn't pleased with your courtship."

Ian didn't have to ask what the man meant. Apparently, he'd underestimated her fear of him.

His wife waved her hand as if to erase her husband's words. "My husband doesn't know what he's talking about. Katherine was perfectly pleased with you until . . ."

She paused, and Ian felt a stab of unease. He could see where this was leading.

"Until that wretched article was printed in the newspaper," she continued, two spots of color darkening her powdered cheeks. " I know young men must have their fun, but really, Lord St. Clair, couldn't you be more discreet? The moment Mr. Gerard read that column, he rushed in here, protesting that we were marrying 'his angel' off to a profligate bounder who couldn't appreciate her."

Ian groaned. He'd known that article would bring him nothing but trouble. Damn that scribbling witch, Miss Taylor!

Lady Hastings sighed. "Of course, I told him to mind his place, and Richard—much too late, in my opinion—gave him his notice. But it was futile. My sweet, dutiful girl was impressed by his gallantry. She ran off with him the next day."

Ian stared at her agape. "That long ago? And you didn't tell me? Didn't even have the courtesy to notify me? The briefest note—'Dear Lord St. Clair, our daughter has run off with the steward, so sorry for all your trouble'—would have sufficed!"

Lady Hastings bristled and opened her mouth as if to give him a proper setdown.

Her husband hastened to intervene. "You've every right to be angry, St. Clair. I wanted to tell you at once, but Agnes hoped my man of affairs might recover Katherine before the runaways reached Scotland. I've no hope now. My man sent word that he lost them. I fear my daughter and Mr. Gerard will be married before we see them again."

A chilly silence ensued, punctuated only by the crackling

fire and the muted clopping of horses in the street outside. Ian spoke first. "Then I suppose that's that."

"Yes. Thank you for being so understanding about this."

Ian nodded. It began to dawn on him he was free of the insipid Katherine. Part of him hated having his plans destroyed, but another part rejoiced in his escape.

"I'm afraid we won't be going to the Worthings as planned," Sir Richard added. "If you'd give them our apologies—"

"Of course." He paused, then said with complete sincerity, "I wish you all the best with your new son-in-law. I'll trouble you no further concerning your daughter." That was another advantage to this disaster—he needn't endure Lady Hastings's fawning anymore.

He pivoted toward the door, but Lady Hastings cried out, "Wait! Suppose Richard is wrong, and she *is* recovered, chaste and unharmed. Perhaps then—"

"Lady Hastings," he interrupted as he faced her, "I don't want a wife who's in love with another man, no matter how chaste her body."

The two spots of color returned to her cheeks. "Yet *you* felt free to come to the marriage with the smell of your strumpet clinging to you."

"Agnes!" her husband exclaimed in shock.

Ian narrowed his gaze on the impudent woman. "If I were you, Lady Hastings, I'd beware of believing everything Lord X writes, especially under the circumstances. The Spanish have a saying—'Whoever gossips to you will gossip about you.' And Lord X is clearly no respecter of persons."

Then without another word, he left.

Chapter 5

The Earl of Worthing and his wife expect a crowd
for their first Christmas ball in Kent. It promises
to be the event of the season, if the weather does
not make roads impassable, and will allow the curious a look at the late Mr. Algernon Taylor's final
design of the scarcely year-old Worthing Manor.

LORD X, *THE EVENING GAZETTE*,
DECEMBER 9, 1820

F elicity glanced up as Mrs. Box entered the bedroom,
her hair white as a dollop of cream above her rosy
face. The housekeeper had a painting tucked under one arm
and a freshly washed petticoat draped over the other.

"Thank goodness it's dry," Felicity exclaimed, reaching
for the petticoat.

"Lord in heaven, you're not even finished packin'!" Setting down the painting, Mrs. Box cast a worried look at the
half-filled trunk at the foot of Felicity's bed. "You
should've been gone already! You should've gone last
night. It'll look bad, you arrivin' at the Worthin' estate a
day late for this visit."

"Not as bad as trudging through snow at midnight
would've looked." Felicity stuffed the petticoat into the
trunk. Could she manage with only two? Well, she must,

mustn't she? Just as she must continue to spend hard-earned
money on attractive gowns and paste jewels. The ladies of
the *ton* wouldn't invite her to their affairs if she weren't
"Algernon's charming daughter" and instead became "that
poor bankrupt Miss Taylor." Then how would she get material for her articles?

But being late to a country-house visit wouldn't enhance
her reputation either. Remembering *who* had made her late
roused her temper. "If you must blame someone, blame that
dreadful Lord St. Clair. Thanks to him, I had to sneak my
article into the *Gazette* offices last night. By the time I
arrived home, the snow was blowing so thick, I dared not
travel, especially alone in the darkness. I swear, if I ever
see that man again—"

"Be careful, luv. His lordship might be visitin' at the
Worthins, too."

Felicity gazed up at the heavens. "Please, God, don't,
under any circumstances, send that arrogant man to the
Worthings, or I can't be responsible for my actions."

Mrs. Box ignored Felicity's appeal to the Deity. "I still
can't believe it—the Viscount St. Clair himself pretendin'
to be from the *Gazette*. And you, givin' a viscount a scol-
din'! That weren't too wise, you know."

"Wisdom be damned," Felicity exclaimed. "I wouldn't
care if he were a dratted duke! That man *deserved* a scolding. Why he was the most overbearing, deceptive, son of
a—"

"And that's another thing. You ought to watch your language, luv. Picked up too many bad habits from your father,
if you ask me. Those ladies at the country house won't tell
you much if you're talkin' like a workman." The servant
cast her a considering glance. "Besides, I liked the viscount.
He cut quite a figure. Tall, and those muscles . . . Lord have
mercy on my soul, it made me wish I was young again. He
weren't at all like the gents your father was wont to bring

home. That were no pretty boy. But even with that swarthy skin, he looked appealin'."

"Appealing!" Felicity exclaimed, trying to forget that she too had found his rough looks and dark air disturbingly appealing. "If your taste runs to arrogant bullies, I suppose he's appealing. He thought he could best me because I'm a woman. Well, I set him straight. He won't bother *me* again."

"A pity that. Wouldn't hurt you none to marry a viscount."

"Stop that! You know quite well he'd never marry my kind. And even if he would, am I to latch on to any reasonably attractive gentleman who walks through the door? He keeps a mistress, for pity's sake! I could never keep silent about *that!*"

"Don't s'pose you could, bein' a forthright lass and all. Still . . . is he rich?"

"I'm sure he is, or he couldn't afford a mistress." She spotted the speculative look in her servant's eyes, and added stubbornly, "I don't care if he has a dratted fortune. His character is deficient."

Mrs. Box folded a frilly lace dressing gown and added it to the trunk. Felicity took it out. As if she'd be receiving anybody in her room at the Worthings!

Tightening her lips, Mrs. Box shoved the dressing gown back in the trunk beneath the other clothes. "A fortune can make up for a great many deficiencies in a man's character, 'specially when his face and form ain't in the least deficient. If you ask me—"

"I didn't," she snapped, though she gave up on fighting Mrs. Box over the dressing gown. The woman would simply sneak it in again once her back was turned.

"I'm merely pointin' out that we'll soon have to sell the silver, if only to keep the boys in breeches. And speakin' of that, we oughta sell this." The housekeeper held up the painting she'd brought in earlier.

"No," Felicity said, as soon as she saw what it was. "Not that one."

"It'll bring a pretty penny," Mrs. Box coaxed.

It probably would, even though the artist wasn't of any consequence. Still, she couldn't bear to part with it. The oil painting had been Papa's favorite. It depicted a sultan and his harem in rich, dark reds and golds. Papa had claimed to like it for the colors and the lines, but she suspected he'd mostly liked the scantily clad women.

Nonetheless, it was her secret favorite as well. She hated to admit to such wickedness, but she mostly liked the scantily clad *sultan*. He was so different from Englishmen, swarthy and handsome and proud . . .

Good Lord, she thought with a groan. *He's the very picture of Lord St. Clair*. No wonder she'd found the viscount so fascinating yesterday. Perhaps she *should* sell it.

"I'll think about it," she said.

"You'd better do more'n that. You scarcely have enough ready change this week to pay the vails at the Worthins."

Felicity gritted her teeth. "I'm not paying the vails." When Mrs. Box's face mirrored both horror and disapproval, Felicity added, "I'll never return there, so what do I care if the servants think ill of me when I leave without giving them a farthing?"

The woman gave an exasperated sigh. "Child, you can't go on this way. If you'd just set your cap for some young chap at the Worthin's—"

" 'Find a nice gentleman to marry'—that's your only solution. I've tried, you know. But no acceptable man marries a penniless woman with four brothers to raise, and the unacceptable ones are . . . well . . . unacceptable."

"You mean unacceptable by your grand standards," Mrs. Box said with a sniff.

"And whose standards should I use? *I'd* be the one living with the wretch and sharing his bed—not you or the boys." If she could find someone to love, perhaps . . . But no, men didn't marry women like her for love. They married blazing beauties or delicate flowers or fine-boned china dolls. Not sharp-tongued spinsters.

Not that she wanted to marry, she told herself testily. No indeed. "There are only so many things I'll sacrifice for my family, and my happiness isn't one of them. As long as Mr. Pilkington pays me regularly and doesn't quibble about what I write, I shall continue to produce my column and earn what I can from it."

"A pittance. It barely staves off your father's creditors. They're startin' to doubt me when I lie about your father leavin' you an inheritance. How long can I keep them believin' that your inheritance is slow in comin' to you legal-like?"

Mrs. Box had come up with the useful lie about the "inheritance" after they'd first discovered that she and the boys actually had an inheritance of one hundred pounds per annum, an old carriage, and a mountain of debt. Of course, James had inherited the house, which was entailed upon *his* heir, if he ever had one, and the house was mortgaged to the hilt. So far Mrs. Box's lie had kept their creditors at bay, but how much longer could that work? Yet if her choice were to marry for money . . .

"Once those nasty wretches get wind of how lackin' in funds you really are," Mrs. Box went on, "you know they'll swarm over this place like flies, forcin' you into bankruptcy. Your brother will lose the house that your poor father designed himself."

Tired of the old argument, Felicity slammed the trunk shut. "If that happens, the boys and I shall join the circus."

"Be serious, luv. You must start plannin' for the future."

What future? She had none. They both knew it, though she wasn't ready to face it yet. "I tell you what," she said lightly. "Rumor has it that Lord Worthing used to be a pirate. While I'm at his estate, I'll ask him to put in a good word for us with his fellow miscreants. The boys would make good pirates, don't you think? Swaggering about with sabers in their belts and climbing the rigging . . ."

"Lord have mercy, the navy would surely stand up and take notice of that." Mrs. Box crossed her arms over her ample chest. "What you ought to ask Lord Worthin' is if one of his friends needs a wife."

"You mean his pirate friends?" When Mrs. Box glowered at her, Felicity added impishly, "I shouldn't mind marrying a pirate, you know. As long as he bathed regularly and kept his wooden leg well polished. Or perhaps I could find one with an eye patch—"

"Enough of your nonsense," Mrs. Box grumbled. "All I'm sayin' is, if Lord Worthin' and his wife like you well enough to invite you to their estate—"

"They only invited me because Papa designed their house, and they want me to see it now that it's finished." The invitation had taken her by surprise, for she barely knew Lady Worthing and knew nothing of the woman's husband except rumor.

"I still say you ought to make the most of it."

"Oh, I will, don't worry, especially at tonight's ball. I'm sure to hear enough gossip for a scandal bouquet. Only wait until I write my *next* column—"

"You and your scandal-broths and gossip—as if that'll take care of you in your old age." Mrs. Box clucked noisily, then picked up the painting and went to the door. "Very well, don't heed the one who's looked after you since you were born. But don't come cryin' to me when the money's gone." With a sniff, she swung the door open. "I'll have Joseph fetch the trunk. The coach—the *hired* coach—is waitin' for you in front."

The housekeeper waltzed out with her nose in the air, mumbling, "Lord preserve me, I never thought to see the day when the Taylors couldn't even keep a carriage."

Felicity made a face at the doorway. Mrs. Box certainly knew how to rub it in. But at least the dear woman had stayed on, despite her dwindling salary. Only four servants remained—Mrs. Box, Joseph, one housemaid, and Cook. All of Papa's beloved paintings had been sold, as well as his architecture books and drafting instruments. Even Mama's jewels were gone, except for the paste ones Felicity used for social occasions.

And still they lacked money. The boys ate as heartily as laborers, and she had to keep up appearances. She'd made every sacrifice she could think of. They dipped their own tallow candles and made their own soap, ate chicken instead of beef, burned fires only when necessary, and rationed the tea. They had no relatives to help them, and she couldn't take a position as a governess with the boys to raise. She'd considered teaching, but it paid more abysmally than writing. Besides, most schools would require her to live on the grounds, and then what would she do with the boys?

So she spent her days writing columns, prowling the rooms for more items to sell, and praying she could keep the creditors from devouring them until the boys were old enough to help support the family. Mr. Pilkington sometimes hinted he'd publish a book of hers if she could find a subject controversial enough for her to sharpen her tongue against, but so far he'd rejected all her suggestions for such a work.

Joseph came for the trunk, and she trailed down the stairs after him. The last time she'd left for a visit of this sort, she'd gone with Papa. He'd been invited to the Duke of Dorchester's to give an opinion on restoring the west wing of the ducal mansion. She'd gone along to take notes, as she'd done since she was eleven.

During the visit to the duke's estate, however, she'd discovered a certain aptitude for speaking her mind in such a way that people listened. Sometimes they berated her for her colorful opinions, but they did listen and even found her witty. It had been an amusement then, no more. Now it was the only thing garnering her an income. Pray God she never lost her knack for it.

She repeated that prayer an hour later after a thousand admonishments to Mrs. Box about the boys and after running the gauntlet of their tearful good-byes and sloppy kisses.

She repeated it again three hours later, as the carriage crunched up the snowy drive of the Worthing estate. She wished she knew what to expect of this visit. Lady Worthing seemed nice, but who could tell with these countesses? They often made her feel like a pigeon among peacocks, even when she reminded herself she was smarter and wittier than any of them.

It wasn't her hostess who concerned her most, however. It was the host—the rumored pirate. She almost hoped the rumor *weren't* true, for a former pirate was sure to be another of those men with groping hands, like Papa's patrons. But before Papa's death, he'd said that the Worthings spent most of their time on an island or at sea, which one would expect of a pirate. Papa had considered their long absences a blessing, since it meant they didn't trouble him during his work. Indeed, they'd been away when he'd taken his fatal dunking in the Thames.

Suddenly the coach topped a rise and the house leapt into view, banishing all thoughts of her host and hostess. "Oh, Papa," she whispered, a lump catching in her throat. No wonder the Worthings had been so pleased with it. It was Papa's best, for certain. He'd always excelled with the Gothic style—the curving lines of the ogee arch, the battlemented parapets, the pointed sashes made to fit the pointed windows. The style's imposing, irregular elements reflected her imposing and entirely irregular father.

Tears stung her eyes. Drat him for letting his excesses haul him to ruin! If not for his weakness for the enjoyments only his titled and wealthy friends could afford, he might have left a legacy as great as that of the brilliant Sir Christopher Wren. Instead, he'd left only a nearly destitute family and a few beautiful buildings. Fifty was too young to die. Too, too young.

The coach arrived at the imposing entrance, and she collected herself, wiping away the tears now dampening her cheeks. It was time to be the daughter of the brilliant Algernon once more—the clever Miss Taylor, the amusing Miss Taylor.

The penniless Miss Taylor. With a sigh, she braced herself for the servants' condescension when they saw she'd traveled by hired coach. To her surprise, however, the butler supervising the unloading of her trunk was genuinely friendly. "The gentlemen are out shooting pheasant, miss, and the ladies just now went to join them for luncheon."

"In this cold?"

"They've laid a shooting luncheon at a cottage on the estate. My lady said if you arrived in time and weren't too tired, you're welcome to join them."

She wasn't tired, but she'd half hoped to wander the main house a while. But she suspected that Lady Worthing would prefer to show the house to her herself. Besides, this wasn't a holiday—it was work. And the best time to hear gossip was when one's subjects were relaxed. "I believe I *will* join them," she told the butler.

"Very good, miss. The footman will show you the way."

Despite the chilly air, the walk was pleasant, affording her a look at the grounds. Though winter had stripped leaves from the foliage and killed the grass, the number of trees and the shapes of the hills led her to think the grounds might be quite fine during summer. A copse startled her gaze in one place, a small, frozen pond glittered like a sapphire in another, and there was a long stand of overreaching oaks that Mama would have liked. Papa had always enjoyed the contrivances of mankind; Mama had preferred the contrivances of nature.

A short time later, Felicity spotted the hunting cottage

the servant had described. Had Papa built this, too? Not Papa, surely. He hated anything rustic. And a wooden cottage with a thatched roof and barkless tree trunks for a doorframe would certainly have offended his sensibilities.

The footman ushered her into a scene of warmth and energy. Three men crowded about the substantial fireplace, discussing the advantages of their weapons, while Lady Worthing and another woman chatted in a corner, and the servants bustled about laying a feast of scotch broth, game pies, venison stew, and crusty bread.

As soon as Lady Worthing spotted her, she came forward with hand extended. "You're here, after all! When you didn't come last night, I feared the heavy snow might keep you away."

Overwhelmed by the gracious greeting, Felicity hesitantly took her hostess's hand. "Some business kept me in town quite late; then I was afraid to venture out at night with the snow. Most of it had melted this morning, however, so I pressed on."

At the sound of her voice, one of the gentlemen pivoted to stare at her. The Viscount St. Clair. She froze and her pulse quickened treacherously as his gaze locked with hers. Oh, why must *he* be here? And why must the sight of him strike her with both fear and anticipation?

Within the cramped confines of the cottage, he appeared even larger and more menacing than she remembered. Although his unruly hair and the color in his cheeks enhanced his masculine appeal, the flintlock rifle he held with casual ease did nothing to assuage her fears. In doeskin breeches and a forest green frock coat, he was the very picture of a hunter ready to fire on any troublesome creature thwarting him. Judging from the bulging game bag at his feet, he could use his weapon with great accuracy.

Her muscles tightened in alarm, but she forced them to relax. She was being silly. Even the arrogant Lord St. Clair dare not *shoot* her, for pity's sake. Still, she'd feel far more comfortable if he clutched a cane instead of a gun.

Of course, his knowledge of her identity was nearly as dangerous. Would he expose her? Or had he taken her threats to heart?

"I'm delighted you went to so much trouble to get here," Lady Worthing said warmly, her gaze flitting from Felicity to Lord St. Clair. "Now our party is complete."

Felicity wrenched her gaze from the formidable Lord St. Clair. Only six of them? And so conveniently—or inconveniently—paired off? Oh, this would be disaster. "But Lady Worthing—"

"You mustn't stand on ceremony with me. You and I are nearly the same age, and if you're as nice as your father said, I'm sure we'll be friends. So please call me Sara."

Stunned by this further evidence of her hostess's graciousness, she stammered, "I-I'd be honored. And you must call me Felicity." She paused. "Have all your guests arrived then?"

"Actually, yes. We expect a hundred at tonight's ball, but no one else is staying at the manor. Mr. and Mrs. Kinsley were prevented from coming by a sudden emergency. And the Hastings were going to attend with Ian, but at the last minute, they couldn't." She cast Lord St. Clair an uncertain glance, then added, "Oh, but I'm forgetting myself. You haven't met everyone, have you?"

At Felicity's quick shake of the head, Sara turned to a man as tall as Lord St. Clair and introduced him as her husband Gideon. Felicity murmured a greeting as she studied him. This man had been a pirate? Why, his hair was short, and he bore himself like a gentleman. Perhaps the rumor had been overstated after all. She must find out while she was here, if only to assuage her own curiosity.

Sara introduced the older couple, who proved to be the Marquess and Marchioness of Dryden, Gideon's parents. What an illustrious—and unusual—group she'd stumbled into, thanks to Papa's talent. They'd make interesting companions for the next few days, but sadly wouldn't provide her with material. Their familial association made it impossible to use what they said, for they'd guess that the only stranger in the group had been the one to pass on the rumors. Besides, she could never speak badly of people who were so open and lacking in haughty airs.

Drat it all. Not only had this been an almost pointless excursion, but it had thrown her into the company of the vexing viscount.

Then she brightened. At least the ball tonight would be rife with rumors.

"Felicity's father designed Worthing Manor," Sara was explaining to her mother-in-law. "I thought she might like to see how it looked now that it was finished." The others had already begun expressing their compliments over the design when Sara added, "Oh, no, I forgot to introduce Ian."

"No need," Lord St. Clair remarked. "Miss Taylor and I have already met."

Felicity shot him a wary glance. This was the moment she'd feared. He would expose her to his friends. Well, if he did, she'd make him regret it. Just let him try.

Lord St. Clair's words seemed to intrigue Sara. "Have you indeed? I had no idea. Where did you meet, Ian?"

"Perhaps I should let the lady tell you." He taunted Felicity with a smile of such challenge it made her grit her teeth.

What did he expect? That she would expose herself? Or lie, so he could accuse her once more of "inventing" things? Well, she wouldn't do either. "Actually, we met at Taylor Hall." When the others looked shocked, she added, "Lord St. Clair came to pay his respects after Papa died." It was true. He *had* paid his respects . . . in a fashion. Still, calling on an unmarried woman to whom one hadn't been introduced was scandalous under any circumstances.

Well, she thought, she'd certainly laid down the gauntlet.

If he wanted to expose her, now was his chance. They might as well get it over with.

His smile vanished. "Miss Taylor, you'll tarnish my reputation as a gentleman. You fail to mention my companions, the ones who introduced us at your home."

Her heart skipped a beat. Apparently he wouldn't risk an open discussion of her column before his friends. That knowledge emboldened her. "Oh, yes, your companions. You and I were engaged in such lively conversation that day that I'd quite forgotten about them. Remind me again of who they were?"

He raised one eyebrow and opened his mouth to retort. She even found herself eagerly anticipating his reply.

Then Gideon broke in. "I hate to interrupt, but may we continue this discussion over luncheon? Hunting in this foul weather rouses a man's appetite something fierce."

Sara laughed. "Yes, of course, my dear."

Pleased to have had the last word in the skirmish, Felicity took the nearest seat and flashed Lord St. Clair an impudent smile. Although Gideon and his father flanked her, Lord St. Clair seated himself directly across the table from her, and his determined expression showed he had no intentions of retreating from the battle yet.

Good. She was ready for him today.

As soon as everyone was settled and the servants began serving them, Sara leaned forward a little to look over at Felicity. "You must excuse my husband's rudeness, Felicity. We spend a great part of the year on a remote island where blunt speech is more common than here in England."

"I don't mind blunt speech," Felicity replied, casting Lord St. Clair a pointed look. "It's preferable to deceptive speech."

He lifted his wineglass, a half smile playing over his lips. "Ah, then I suppose you never participate in that female diversion called 'gossip.' "

Before Felicity could reply, Sara answered him. "Like all men, you find any female talk suspect, and I'll admit it can sometimes be vicious. But even gossip has its uses. The Ladies Committee relies on rumor or the threat of it to convince recalcitrant members of Parliament that they should aid our cause." She served herself some venison stew from the plate proffered by the servant at her elbow. "And it has social uses as well, by urging unsavory men and women to avoid public censure by being more discreet in their vices. That prevents them from unduly influencing our young, don't you think?"

Felicity had never heard a more eloquent defense of her profession. She instantly added "reason" and "intelligence" to her growing list of the countess's appealing traits.

Lord St. Clair shifted his disturbing black gaze from Sara to Felicity. "And if the gossip is untrue?"

Felicity smiled smugly. "Gossip is more often true than not. Haven't you ever heard the saying, 'Where there's smoke, there's fire'?" God knows, Lord St. Clair had been smoking like a chimney.

"Yes, but who set the fire?" He drank deeply of the burgundy in his glass. "If you set a fire in my house, then report on its smoke, that only proves you can set a fire that will smoke. It proves nothing whatsoever about my tendencies to arson."

"I did not set—" She broke off when she caught the others staring at her. "We women don't set the fires, Lord St. Clair. Men build so many fires on their own that it's all we can do to keep the smoke from choking us."

"We're still discussing gossip, aren't we?" Gideon put in dryly as he cut a bite of squab pie. "You've lost me with all this talk of fires."

Sara shot her husband an exasperated look. "Only because you men think so literally. Everything is in black and white. Gossip is bad, truth is good. But sometimes gossip is good and truth is a very nasty antidote to one's vanity."

When Ian started to retort, she added, "Besides, Ian is only complaining about gossip because he was the subject of it in this week's *Gazette*."

"Really?" An urge for mischief seized Felicity. "I don't recall reading anything about his lordship in the paper. Do tell what was said."

"It's about his latest mistress." Sara's eyes twinkled. "How many is it, Ian, since you returned from the Continent? Fifteen? Twenty? And that's after Josephine and all those Spanish women. If the gossip is to be believed, you spend all your time in bed."

"That's enough of the boring and patently false rumors," Lord St. Clair clipped out. "Besides, we were discussing Mr. Taylor's work on Worthing Manor. Tell me, Sara, was that round staircase by the back parlor his idea or yours?"

With those few words he changed the subject so easily—and effectively—that he roused Felicity's grudging admiration. Trust Lord St. Clair to hit upon the one subject guaranteed to distract her.

Loath to let him win, she nonetheless couldn't resist listening when Sara began her saga of the building of the house. Soon Felicity was asking questions, scrabbling for some piece of information about those last few weeks of her father's life. Once or twice she caught Lord St. Clair watching her so closely she wondered if she'd dropped mustard on her chin or something. But she wouldn't give him the satisfaction of seeing her react. She ignored him instead.

As soon as everyone had finished their apple charlotte, the gentlemen returned to their sport. She relaxed the moment the irritating viscount disappeared out the door with his companions. Now if only she could avoid him entirely for the next few days . . .

Lady Dryden decided to walk back to the house for a nap, but Sara invited Felicity to stay in the cottage and join her for some tea. Within moments of the men's defection, the servants had whisked all the dishes into a waiting cart and tidied up. So it was with some anticipation that Felicity found herself alone with her hostess.

Sara handed her a cup of tea, then gestured to an ancient but comfortable sofa near the fireplace. As they seated themselves, Sara smiled at her. "I was astonished to discover you'd already met Ian. But I suppose I shouldn't have been. With his recent search for a wife, I'm sure he attends many of the same social gatherings as you." Sara leaned forward and added, "The two of you seem quite comfortable together. I hadn't realized you knew each other so well."

Felicity started to protest the conclusion the countess had clearly drawn, then caught herself. This might be her chance to learn more about the progress of his courtship of Katherine since Lord X's article had appeared in the *Gazette*. Katherine and her parents hadn't been "at home" to anyone recently, even her.

She dropped her gaze in seeming embarrassment. "It was my understanding that Lord St. Clair had already found a wife. Isn't he seriously courting Miss Hastings?"

Sara hesitated, as if debating what to say. Then she set down her teacup. "Yes, he was. But I have it on good authority that he isn't any longer."

Elation swept through Felicity. Her article had worked! Katherine was free of him! "Has Miss Hastings broken with him, then? I can't blame her, you know—there seemed to be no deep affection between them."

"I think you're right. His reasons for seeking a wife— the usual ones of needing an heir and perhaps some companionship—didn't require deep affection. I suppose he thought Miss Hastings would fill the position well enough."

"Not well enough if he's keeping a mistress," Felicity mumbled without thinking.

Sara shot her an interested look. "Ah, so you *did* read

that article in the *Gazette*. You pretended otherwise at lunch."

This time Felicity's embarrassment was genuine. At a loss for words to explain why she'd taunted Lord St. Clair, she hesitated.

Thankfully, Sara didn't wait for an explanation. "I understand your feelings. It did seem rather blatant of him to flaunt a mistress while he courted someone. But Ian explained the situation to all of us today." She smiled sheepishly. "We wouldn't stop teasing him about his newfound fame, so he finally told us the entire story. I suppose I shouldn't discuss it, but I hate to see Ian unfairly accused."

Felicity's ears pricked up. "Unfairly?"

"Yes. You see, the situation isn't at all as that newspaper person said. Ian was simply helping a friend of the family." She tapped her chin thoughtfully. "I believe he said the woman was the wife of a compatriot during the war. Or was it the man's sister?" She shook her head. "In any case, after Ian's friend died, the poor woman fell on hard times, and Ian stepped in to help. Ian's like that. A very generous man."

Felicity had to stifle a snort. Lord St. Clair's friends were as gullible as they were loyal if they believed the story he'd tried to pass off on her. "I would never have guessed that Lord St. Clair had served during the war. He doesn't seem the type."

"It did take us by surprise." Sara hastened to add, "Not that he would fight, he's not a coward or anything. We were merely surprised he never told us about it."

"I dare say he's modest about his accomplishments," Felicity remarked dryly. It was easy to be modest about nonexistent accomplishments.

"Ian is indeed modest. And it upset me to hear how he'd been misrepresented in the paper." She sighed. "I don't think it did him any harm, however. If anything, it might have saved him from making a terrible mistake. Apparently, his prospective fiancée had her own side interests."

"What do you mean?"

"You haven't heard? Everyone in London was talking of it this morning—or so said Emily, my sister-in-law. Emily and my brother Jordan live close by here, you see. They came in from town this morning and stopped by on their way home. Emily and I talked privately, and she told me the most astonishing news." Sara leaned forward with a conspiratorial air. "According to her . . ."

Chapter 6

Beware, my friends, the traps of romantic entanglement: vanity, unchecked urges, the arrogance of believing that the subject of your affections must needs return them. Nothing is so tragic as a woman—or a man—who mistakes a friendly smile for courtship.

LORD X, *THE EVENING GAZETTE,*
DECEMBER 9, 1820

Ian scanned the Worthings' crowded ballroom with an expert eye. How he tired of this bloody pointless endeavor. Only one thing kept him playing the wife-hunting game—the knowledge that if he didn't, he'd be handing his father's legacy to a man with the character of a snake.

He spotted an insipid woman bedecked in virginal white lace and couldn't repress a shudder. To think he'd come to this—surveying eligible women at a Christmas ball. He should never have delayed the search so long. After Father's death, when he'd first heard the terms of the will, he'd wasted precious months searching for a legal means to overturn it. The laws of entail should have protected him. But his grandfather's untimely death when his father was a child had prevented the man from carrying on the entail to Ian, leaving his father in a position to do as he liked.

And in his usual manipulative fashion, Father had done exactly that, leaving a most abominable will. Ian's realization that he couldn't break it had fallen heavily upon him.

Reluctantly, angrily, he'd sought a wife who could give him the heir he needed to fulfill the will's terms. To his surprise, he'd found he was a very ineligible bachelor, thank to all the absurd rumors. Too many people had speculated viciously about his abrupt departure from England. Too many others had whispered that he'd spied for the French.

Refuting so many long-standing rumors was impossible, especially when he had no wish to talk about what he'd actually done all those years. Besides, discussion of his activities on the Continent might provoke discussion of why he'd fled England, and that was unacceptable.

Thankfully, his unfailing attempts to behave like the perfect gentleman in the past year had softened public opinion toward him, though many people still distrusted him with their daughters. Many agreed with Miss Taylor's belief that all smoke signaled fire. Some probably saw past his façade into the howling blackness beneath.

And now two of his choices had run off with other men. Two others he'd offered for had refused him after his damned uncle paid their parents a visit.

No doubt Uncle Edgar had thought Ian wouldn't hear of his cowardly attempts to undermine Ian's search for a wife. But Uncle Edgar didn't know how much his nephew had changed in the past years. Ian was no longer the hotheaded nineteen-year-old who'd run off out of pride and stubbornness. This time he would stay and fight. He wouldn't let that bastard drag Chesterley into the ground the way he'd done his own estate. If Ian couldn't find a wife in time, he'd publicly reveal the truth about the man, even if it meant destroying himself in the process. He'd send himself to hell if that's what it took to put Edgar Lennard there, too.

Unfortunately, he now had another troublesome person to contend with. His gaze fixed on a laughing figure across the ballroom. Miss Taylor. Dressed in a modest gown more suited to a simpering virgin than a firebrand spinster, she stood with society's most accomplished rumormongers. Lady Brumley. Lord Jameson. The March sisters.

Miss Taylor was the only one among them with any sparkle or style. Given her disheveled attire at their first meeting, that surprised him. Tonight, she'd taken every care with her appearance. Her pearl-encrusted slippers were most certainly costly, her jewels tasteful and elegant, and her hair swept up by a pearl pin much more sophisticated than the two pencils she'd sported yesterday. Candlelight heightened the glow of good health on her cheeks, glancing off the creamy satin that sheathed a body even a courtesan would envy.

Bloody hell—he was thinking of her in those terms again. What dangerous idiocy. Witness the way he'd missed half his shots after luncheon today, caught up in thoughts of nonsensical things like the sudden sunrise of her smile when Sara praised her father's designs. Or the impish gleam in her eye when she'd pretended not to have read the gossip she'd written about him.

Damn the bloody woman for being so adept at invading his thoughts. And why must he feel this cursed attraction to her? It made no sense. She was a plague upon society and all good sense, a woman who traded on her father's reputation to plunder the lives of anyone so foolish as to speak to her. Even now, she conversed with Lady Brumley, sometimes dubbed the Galleon of Gossip because of her large frame and equally large mouth, not to mention her tendency to wear outrageous hats with a nautical motif. He could imagine the dirty byways their discussion wandered in.

"So you met Miss Taylor at her home, did you?" a female voice asked at his side. Without looking, he recognized the lavender scent of Jordan's wife, Emily.

Her question demonstrated why sexual attraction was dangerous. If his mind had been clear this afternoon, he wouldn't have underestimated Miss Taylor's audacity. In trying to force her into a lie, he'd instead tempted her to tell the truth, and that had caused him no small inconvenience in twisting her answer to cover up his sins.

Dragging his gaze from Miss Taylor was more difficult than he would've liked. "I see you've been talking to Sara. Yes, I met Miss Taylor at her home. I respected her father a great deal."

"Did you really? Come now, Ian, I doubt you ever even met Algernon Taylor."

Ian shrugged. "I needn't have met the man to admire him and his work."

"You must have admired him enormously to pay his daughter a condolence call. You never call on anyone without a purpose."

She knew him too well. "Be careful, my nosy friend," he said lightly. "You're dabbling in matters beyond your purview."

Emily arched one blond eyebrow, then glanced across the ballroom at Miss Taylor. "She's very pretty, isn't she?"

Pretty didn't begin to describe her. The girls who tittered and flirted with him were pretty. She was energy itself, vital, alive, like a scarlet rose among pastel lilies.

But roses had thorns, and Miss Taylor's thorns were tipped with poison.

"She doesn't interest me, I assure you." Amazing that he could speak the blatant lie with a straight face. And more amazing still that it was a lie.

"What a shame. You seem to interest *her*."

That startled him. "What do you mean?"

"According to Sara, she was full of questions about you, especially when she heard that you are once again an eligible bachelor."

He groaned. "I should've known Jordan couldn't keep a confidence from you—"

"Don't blame *him* for it. The news was circulating before I even left London this morning. Did you really think a family could keep an elopement quiet for long?"

"I suppose not." So Miss Taylor knew the entire affair now. The bloody witch probably congratulated herself over her success. So why hadn't that quelled her obsession with ruining his life? If she'd been asking about him, it clearly hadn't.

Damn. He must find a new strategy for dealing with her.

"Miss Taylor had read that beastly article about you," Emily went on, "but Sara set her straight on that matter, too."

Ian frowned. "Set her straight?"

"Sara thought you might appreciate it if an unattached female like Miss Taylor knew the truth. After you explained to us this morning about your soldier friend and his sister, we were both eager to have the truth known. You're being modest about the situation and your role, but we dislike hearing your character maligned so unfairly."

It was all Ian could do not to curse aloud. Now Miss Taylor would think him a bigger liar than before. Which, in a way, he was. "As I recall, I asked you to keep that story to yourselves to protect my friend's privacy."

Emily cast him a sidelong glance. "And we'll do so. Sara merely wanted to help. You *have* been looking for a wife, after all. It's important that eligible women know your true character."

"Women like Miss Taylor, I suppose?"

"Of course." Emily batted her fan a few times. "Surely you won't balk at marrying a respectable woman simply because she has no great claim to fortune or birth. If you're looking for a wife, Miss Taylor wouldn't be a bad choice."

He wanted to laugh. Marriage to Miss Taylor would be sheer disaster. With her loose tongue, penchant for digging up secrets, and delight in skewering men of rank, in less than a week—no, a day—after the wedding she'd be nosing into his affairs.

Besides, she'd never agree to marry him. The little he'd gleaned about her indicated that her father had left her a substantial inheritance, so money was no incentive. And since she thought him a profligate and a town rake, a man who lived to debauch women and humiliate his fiancée, the usual attractions of marriage wouldn't tempt her.

Still, marriage to Miss Taylor would be as entertaining as it would be maddening.

No, he reproached himself. *That doesn't even bear contemplation.* "You seem to have a very favorable opinion of the woman. Yet you hardly know her."

"True. But I liked her as soon as Sara introduced us. She's adorable—funny and intelligent and direct. You must admit you're far too somber these days, and certainly too secretive. You need a woman like her to bring you out of yourself. And if, like so many men, you want a wife with a spotless reputation, she has that, too."

He snorted. "Spotless? I seriously doubt it."

"Oh?" Emily looked at him with interest. "Do you know something about Miss Taylor the rest of us don't?"

A pity he couldn't tell Emily that Miss Taylor was Lord X. It would serve the loose-tongued creature right to be exposed. But he wasn't ready for open war—yet. "I merely meant that she isn't what she appears."

"Then you're the only one to think so," Emily retorted, obviously disappointed by his refusal to reveal more. "No one ever speaks ill of her."

That was precisely why Miss Taylor moved with impunity through society. She needn't be a member of Almack's. Championed by those of Lady Brumley's ilk, she need only be the daughter of the dashing Algernon Taylor to gain access to prestigious routs and balls and thus to all the gossip she required for her column.

Secure in her anonymity, she dug up old gossip, then passed judgment without ever suffering society's censure. If she'd once been the subject of speculation herself, he doubted she'd be so bloody self-righteous.

Ian stilled. What an intriguing thought—Miss Taylor, the subject of gossip. The strains of a waltz reached his ears, and he began to smile. Perhaps it was time the self-righteous Miss Taylor learned firsthand how easily a situation could be misconstrued.

Without giving himself a chance to question his motives, he excused himself to Emily, then strode purposefully across the room. Ah, yes, he knew exactly how to teach Miss Taylor a much-needed lesson in humility, especially if her reputation was as "spotless" as Emily implied.

As soon as Felicity saw Lord St. Clair heading toward her, she braced herself for trouble. Devil take Katherine! Felicity had risked discovery to prevent her friend from marrying a degenerate, and the woman had run off with her family's steward instead!

If she'd known Mr. Gerard was the object of Katherine's affections, she would never have encouraged it. But she'd naively imagined some squire's son with less fortune than Lady Hastings wished. Not a servant, for pity's sake, who was doubtless a fortune hunter! Drat it all!

Katherine was supposed to turn St. Clair down flat, then marry a man at least marginally suitable to her genteel class. The foolish girl.

Now, for all her trouble, Felicity had a hornet on her tail. No wonder Lord St. Clair had spent luncheon baiting her—he must be furious! She watched him approach with growing unease. The man had an uncanny ability to keep his true feelings buried ten feet under, and that made him more difficult to manage than a man easy to read. If she had any sense at all, she'd run.

A pity she had nowhere to go.

"Lord St. Clair is coming this way, my dear," Lady

Brumley said beside her, with a nod of her elaborately coiffured head. "Shall I introduce you?"

"Thank you, we've met." No doubt the marchioness would make much of that. Lady Brumley hadn't reached sixty without learning how to turn the sparest comments into fodder for gossip. Felicity relied on the Galleon of Gossip for half her column, and sometimes wondered if Lady Brumley had guessed who wore Lord X's pants.

God knows, she wished it were anyone but herself just now.

Then the troublesome viscount was upon them, wearing a smile so alarming she could barely manage one in answer. He nodded briefly at the marchioness, then bowed to Felicity. "Miss Taylor, would you do me the honor of dancing with me?"

The scoundrel. He wanted to get her off on the dance floor so he could rail at her, and he knew she dared not refuse with Lady Brumley drinking in every word.

Well, she had to face his wrath some time. "I'd be happy to dance with you," she lied, extending her hand. *Though I'd be happier still if I'd never met you.*

He led her to the floor with the practiced ease of a gentleman, then settled one hand on the curve of her waist as the other closed tightly around her gloved fingers.

She groaned. God preserve her, she'd agreed to a waltz, and waltzes were *not* her forte. Her dancing in general left much to be desired, but with some figures, like the quadrille, she could follow her fellows and hide her missteps in the crowd. That was impossible with a waltz.

"Lord St. Clair—" she began, meaning to warn him. But he'd already whirled her onto the floor. *One-two-three, one-two-three, one-two-three*, she chanted in her head, futilely trying to keep from stumbling or making a misstep.

"Miss Taylor—" he began.

"Shh," she muttered, casting an envious glance at the others who so deftly managed the dance's intricacies. Her fingers dug into his shoulder. "I'm counting."

"Counting?"

"The measure. I'm very bad at the waltz."

He eyed her with suspicion. "You must be joking."

She trod on his foot completely by accident. "I-I'm sorry," she stammered as she sought to find her footing again, nearly bringing them to a halt.

He half dragged her back into step, remaining silent until she found the measure again. "How could you not have mastered the waltz? You go to a different social affair every night."

"Yes, but I don't go to dance." She resumed her death grip on his shoulder. Maybe he could simply carry her about the room. He was certainly large enough, and she'd already ruined any appearance of ladylike grace by clinging to him like a drowning woman.

When he didn't answer her comment, she risked a glance up into his face.

It was shuttered, his eyes impersonal as gems. "I forgot—you go to hear gossip."

"To gather material." His condescension and obvious ease at the waltz irritated her. "You go to hunt up a brood mare. I don't see why that's any more acceptable."

"A brood mare?" he choked out. "Is that what you gleaned from your interrogation of Sara this afternoon?"

She stumbled and he caught her, whisking her back into the step only moments before she collided with another dancer. It took her a second to regain her composure. "I did *not* interrogate Sara. She offered information."

"And you made your usual 'speculations' based on hints and innuendo."

"So you're *not* looking for a wife to bear your heir?"

A long silence ensued, during which she became aware of something besides the waltz . . . like the broad masculine chest at her eye level . . . the scent of bay rum and starched linen and plain, unadulterated male . . . the muscled arms holding her a trifle close for propriety. At some point he'd moved his hand from her side to the small of her back. Although she understood why he felt the need to manacle her waist with his arm, given her abysmal ability, it was still most improper.

She eased back from him, then nearly lost the measure, prompting him to tighten his arm further. When she met his gaze, she found him watching her with amusement.

"You really can't waltz, can you?" he said.

"Did you think I'd make something like that up?"

"Why not? You make up everything else."

"Not your reasons for needing a wife, I suspect," she said, determined to make him answer her question.

He let out an exasperated breath. "Of course I need a wife to bear me an heir. That's why most men of title and fortune need a wife." He paused. "So, shall I expect to see that in the next edition of the *Gazette*?"

She was starting to feel comfortable enough that his snide remark didn't make her lose step. "Really, Lord St. Clair, you do have an exalted opinion of yourself. I have more interesting things to write about than your courtships."

"Yes, like Katherine's elopement."

So he'd finally brought it up, had he? Tilting her head down, she focused on his expertly tied cravat. "Why should I write about that? Everyone already knows of it. Besides, despite what you think, I don't go about trying to ruin people's lives. Katherine is my friend, after all."

"You've already humiliated her by writing about my supposed mistress. Why balk at discussing her elopement?"

The unfair accusation stung. "I'll concede that my article might have given her some discomfort, but clearly it didn't last. The end result was her happiness."

"Are you so sure? This steward of hers met your impeccable standards?"

Her interest in his cravat grew amazingly acute. "I didn't

know him, but I'm sure he's a very nice man and will make her happy."

"I see. Which means you're as dismayed about the elopement as I."

He was so smug, drat him, and much too adept at reading her mind. "Not at all. At least he claims to be in love with her, which is more than I can say for you."

"You have an answer for everything, don't you? But I know you, Miss Taylor, and you don't believe in love any more than I do." He tugged her closer, plastering her to him from thigh to chest in a most indelicate manner.

She tried to shove him back, but failed. "I may not waltz very well," she hissed, "but must you hold me so close? It isn't proper, you know."

"No, it isn't."

When he didn't allow her so much as an extra inch in response to her criticism, she said, "Would you kindly release me?"

"I think not."

It dawned on her that this had nothing to do with her dancing abilities. "Why?"

"Because holding you at arm's length wouldn't be nearly as enjoyable." He coupled his comment with a smile so wicked it made her heart stop.

She trod purposely on his foot, but dancing slippers were no match for a man's leather shoes. "Lord St. Clair—" she began.

"Call me Ian." An edge entered his voice. "After all that you know about me, I see no reason we should stand on ceremony."

"Now see here, I know you're angry with me about Katherine's elopement—"

"You wrote publicly of matters that weren't your concern. You asked my friends about my private affairs." She missed a step, but he jerked her back into step unceremoniously and danced on. "And you don't even have the decency to feel remorse for what you've done."

"Because I did nothing wrong!"

"Really?" They whirled into candlelight that highlighted his taunting smile. "Then you won't mind having the situation reversed."

Uneasy foreboding made her stomach lurch. "What do you mean?"

He bent his head close enough for his lips to brush her ear. "Have you ever been gossiped about, Felicity?"

She froze in his arms. Good Lord. *That's* why he'd asked her to dance. She'd been so engrossed in not stumbling all over her feet that she hadn't cared how closely he held her—until it was too late.

Glancing around, she noticed for the first time the whispers and looks of interest from the dancers closest to them. No one ever danced the waltz so closely unless they were courting . . . or worse.

"Why, you heartless, contemptuous—"

"Careful, my dear," he whispered smugly, "someone might overhear you. And what would they think?"

"That you're rude and unconscionably bad-mannered!"

"Or that you've drunk too much wine, which is why you're allowing me such liberties. Or that you're eager to take the place of my supposed mistress. Or any number of unsavory assumptions based on nothing more than my holding you too closely."

Drat him for being the most logical, devious creature in breeches! "All right," she grumbled after they'd taken another turn. "You've made your point. Now let me go!"

"Oh, I haven't even begun to make my point," he murmured in a voice as silky as it was menacing.

Her thundering heart drowned out the ebbing music. He held her trapped in his arms more effectively than any truss. To escape him, she'd have to make a scene that half the ballroom would notice, which would only prove his point.

Yes, he would enjoy watching her embarrass herself before so many important people, wouldn't he?

And what did he mean, *I haven't even begun to make my point*? With the next turn, they reached the edge of the crowd, and suddenly she knew. Panic ripped through her as she realized they danced toward the closed French doors leading onto the balcony.

"No," she whispered, vainly trying to halt their forward movement. But she might as well have been pushing against a mill wheel. Like the mighty river that powered it, he moved inexorably, taking her with him, willing or no.

Two more deft turns, and they were at the doors. He released her hand only long enough to open one.

"I won't go out there with you alone!" she hissed, but he shoved her through the door and onto the balcony as if she were no more than a rag doll.

Yanking her hand free, she whirled and headed back toward the ballroom. With alarming speed, he stepped between her and escape, shutting the glass door with a click.

Her breath came in puffs of frost, and she shivered. "You can't mean to keep me out here. It's freezing, for God's sake."

"Take my coat—" he began as he reached for the buttons.

"Don't you dare!" That was the last thing she wanted, the Viscount St. Clair disrobing in such a private setting.

His unrepentant grin reminded her of her brothers when they were up to mischief. "I'm merely trying to be a gentleman."

"And failing miserably." She tried to peer over his shoulder into the ballroom to see if anyone had noticed their retreat, but his great height blocked her view. Then she cast a furtive glance around the balcony. Thankfully they were alone. "All right, you have me out here. What do you want from me?"

"That's simple: I want you to see what it's like to have

your pristine reputation soiled by the unjust 'speculations' of gossiping females." His grin faded abruptly. "Turnabout is fair play, Felicity."

Why, of all the shameless, obnoxious—"Fair? You don't know the meaning of the word! My pristine reputation was achieved by pristine living, and I'm sure you can't say the same for yourself! If you don't like your reputation, don't blame me! I was *not* the one who made it so, you . . . you philandering oaf!"

He advanced on her, his jaw tightening dangerously. "Yes, that's me. A ne'er-do-well who doesn't deserve to marry any decent woman. A man whom no woman in her right mind would trust." He caught her around the waist, tugging her into a close embrace. Sarcasm heavily laced his voice. "So why should I behave or treat you differently than the thousands of women I've debauched!"

"Why, you cursed—"

He gave her no chance to finish the insult. His mouth came down hard on hers.

It shocked her so utterly that for a moment she did nothing. It had been ages since a man had forced a kiss on her—when one of Papa's patrons had done so.

That had been awful, however. This was not.

It commanded where the other had blustered, enticed where the other had revolted. Although he took complete charge of her person and showed no concern for propriety, she wasn't disgusted. On the contrary, his kiss stirred strange feelings in her belly . . . and lower. The intimacy curled her toes and dissolved her insides into a puddle, which had certainly never happened with any other man. And to her horror, when he released her and stepped back, she felt an instant of disappointment.

A blush heated her cheeks, angering her. She never blushed, for almost nothing embarrassed her. And to think that this dratted viscount could make her do so . . .

"I see I've rendered you speechless." His eyes smoldered

as they passed over her face to fasten on her still-burning lips. "I didn't think that possible."

She ignored the insult. "Is this how you cow all your enemies?"

"Only the pretty ones." He arched an eyebrow. "And you don't look particularly cowed. I must be slipping."

Desperate to hide her bewildering reaction to his assault, she retorted, "It would take a great deal more than a rude kiss to cow me."

"Would it really?" A devilish smile touched his lips as he once more clasped her waist. When she arched away, he caught her jaw between his thumb and forefinger to hold it still. "Then I'm certainly willing to oblige."

She stiffened, prepared to resist this time. But he took her by surprise. His mouth barely brushed hers, a gossamer touch that roused gooseflesh on her arms. Playfully, seductively, he toyed with her lips, the kiss as tempting as sweets to a starving child.

Until now, she hadn't known how starving she was. But his mouth feeding on hers made hunger knot inside her belly, hunger for the unknown, the exotic. Then he slanted his lips over hers more firmly, and her world tilted. His fingers traced the line of her jaw in a whispery stroke that left her skin heated and tingling.

Pressing his thumb down on her chin, he opened her mouth beneath his, then plunged his tongue inside. The sudden intimacy made her stiffen, but he gentled her with his hand—fondled her neck . . . the base of her throat where her pulse beat erratically . . . her bared shoulder. When she relaxed beneath his touch, he deepened the kiss, exploring her mouth as if it were a succulent peach he wished to savor. With each foray of his tongue, he tasted and caressed her so intriguingly she thought it might drive her mad.

She hadn't expected this disarming sweetness. Men of his sort didn't treat women with such consideration, did they?

Resisting its pull was beyond her. She'd never known desire could be this intense . . . this sweeping a madness. She clasped his coat lapels and hung on for dear life, crushing the superfine in her fists. She didn't know when she closed her eyes and surrendered herself to the heady richness of his mouth exploring hers, but it didn't matter. Forbidden liquor pooled in her belly, hot and luscious and irresistible.

Some instinct made her slip her tongue tentatively into *his* mouth. With a groan, he dragged her flush against him, his lips crushing hers. The tenor of his kiss altered instantly to the raw energy of possession. His wretched control had vanished—she felt it in her blood, which thrummed and sang beneath the wild passion of his kiss.

Exquisite pleasures danced from her reeling head down to the tips of her frozen toes. She felt engulfed by his heat, by the urgency of his need, by the sheer size of his large frame. Yet strangely she felt no fear—nor any desire to stop him. She would never have allowed the cold, calculating viscount to touch her like this, but this warm-blooded man with his large hands playing over her ribs, her waist, her hips . . . He swept his tongue through her mouth as if he owned her, and eagerly she handed herself over to him.

The sudden sound of voices intruded on her senses, shattering her dazed enjoyment and reminding her why she mustn't do this. Not here, at least. She tore her lips from his. "Lord St. Clair—"

"Ian," he commanded, hot need in his gaze.

"Ian, someone's coming," she warned.

"Let them." She tried to twist away, but he caught her face between his hands, kissing her again with such force she almost forgot what she'd been protesting. But when she heard a gasp behind them, she roused herself and shoved him hard.

His grip on her went slack. For a long moment, his gaze locked with hers, eyes glittering hungrily in the darkness.

Then his expression grew shuttered and his rapid breathing slowed. He glanced behind her at whoever had caught them.

And a self-satisfied smile spread over his face.

The heat of desire drained out of her at once. Oh, good Lord. She'd been wrong, horribly wrong. His kiss had only been a stratagem. Expert philanderer that he was, he'd made her believe it was more, made her believe he was as wrapped in the spell as she. And all the time, he'd been using seduction to lull her into embarrassing herself publicly!

Shame spread through her, rapidly replaced by fury. The unconscionable wretch! She slapped him, the crack of her hand on his cheek sounding loudly on the balcony. But it didn't wipe the gloating expression from his face.

To think that she'd fallen into his trap—and even enjoyed it! She braced herself and turned to meet their audience.

There stood their hostess, Sara. And with her was the Galleon of Gossip, Lady Brumley herself. Curse him to hell for this!

Trying not to look like a woman who'd wantonly been welcoming a rake's kisses, Felicity forced an expression of surprise to her face, as if she hadn't realized they'd been standing there. "Oh, I beg your pardon. Lord St. Clair and I were having a discussion."

"I see that." Lady Brumley smiled like a cat who'd fallen into the cream pot.

"And if you'll excuse us, we wish to continue it," Ian said behind her. "Privately."

His bland tone rubbed salt in the wound. She'd thought he felt passion because he'd made *her* feel something. How could she have been so stupid!

"We wish nothing of the sort," she said with vehemence. "Apparently his lordship doesn't understand the word 'no.'" Forcing herself to face him, she added, "Good night,

Lord St. Clair. I suggest you keep your hands to yourself in the future." It was an ineffectual attempt to undo the damage, and she knew it.

"I will if you will," he mocked, eyes gleaming with triumph.

Pulling together the shredded rags of her self-respect, she fled through the glass doors into the ballroom.

There were people everywhere, and it felt as if they all watched her. Oh, if only the marble floor would open up and swallow her whole! Keeping her eyes averted, she hurried through the ballroom. Her body trembled, and tears stung her eyes.

Fool! she chastised herself. *Idiot! Ninny!* How could she—who *knew* what sort of man he was—have allowed him to kiss her like that? She wished she could say he'd forced it on her, but she knew better. He'd only needed to caress her to have her swooning in his arms like a foolish schoolgirl.

Long ago, she'd resigned herself to never experiencing passion. The likelihood that she would marry was small, and she'd balked at the thought of indulging her urges any other way. But she'd still had them, those aching feelings deep in her belly, especially when she looked at the sultan painting or saw adoring couples. She'd been primed for Ian's advances long before she'd met him.

Drat him for guessing her weakness so easily!

Mortification dogged her as she threaded her way through the dancing couples. She'd played right into his hands. He'd heard Lady Brumley and Sara approaching, yet he'd deliberately continued to kiss her so he could have his revenge and "soil" her "pristine reputation." He'd no doubt reveled in her silly acquiescence, congratulating himself on making her accept his touch, nay, *welcome* it!

More tears stung her eyes, and she forced them back, drawing on her anger to keep from dissolving into weeping as she escaped the ballroom's prying eyes. The scoundrel!

So he wanted to ruin her reputation, did he? Well, he'd gone too far. Two could play that game! She would make that arrogant, unfeeling viscount pay for his presumption and his dratted tactics; make him regret he'd ever set foot inside the Taylor home.

Ooh, just wait until she wrote her next column!

Chapter 7

Last week a well-known heir to an earldom was
seen with a respectable but penniless young
woman in Lady Bellingham's orchard. The heir's
father insists that his son intends only friendship.
Judging from the son's behavior, however, the father's statement may be grounded in wishful
thinking rather than fact.

LORD X, *THE EVENING GAZETTE*,
DECEMBER 10, 1820

Thunderclouds formed ugly gray bruises across the
dawn sky when Ian strode toward the Worthing dining room the morning after the ball. He'd abandoned all
thought of sleep hours ago, and now hoped to breakfast
alone. Surely no one would be about at this hour, even on
a Sunday when the family could be expected to attend services.

But luck wasn't with him. He halted in the dining room
entrance, suppressing a groan when he saw Sara glance at
him from the far end of the amply laden table. Bloody hell,
he should have known better. Of all the people who must
be up, it *would* be her. And now she would attempt a discussion of last night's little scene on the balcony.

Last night's disturbing, inexplicable scene.

"Good morning," she said tersely. "You're quite the early riser, aren't you?"

He chose a seat far enough away to discourage intimacy, but close enough not to appear boorish. "I could say the same about you." The servant scurried to place a boiled egg before him, and Ian served himself some toast from a platter on the table.

Sara flicked her hand dismissively. "I can never sleep when guests are in the house. I'm always worried about making them comfortable."

He grunted a response.

That didn't daunt her. "You'd be surprised how many people are around at this time of the morning." She pushed a sausage about on her plate with her fork. "Miss Taylor, for example, was up quite early."

He refused to discuss Felicity with Sara. "Is there any coffee?"

"Certainly." Sara motioned to the servant, who was already rounding the table with a pitcher. Watching Ian closely, Sara added, "She was up and off over an hour ago."

"Who?" he said, feigning distraction.

"Miss Taylor, of course."

"Of course," he repeated dryly. Had he finally succeeded in driving the woman off? The thought didn't sit well with him. "I suppose she had to leave early to reach home before the weather worsened. It looks as if we're in for a devilish day."

"Home? No, she didn't go home. She merely went into Pickering for a while."

He ignored the sudden increase of his pulse. Of course Felicity hadn't run off. She never behaved like other women.

Last night, for example. He'd kissed her to make a point, fully expecting her to react in outrage, horror, even disgust, given her ideas about "philandering." Instead she'd blinked

and gaped at him, looking for all the devil like she'd never
been properly kissed.

So what the bloody hell was he supposed to do when a
lively, gorgeous creature gazed at him, her lips parted in
invitation and her breath a medley of soft, urgent gasps?
Ignore it? God Himself couldn't have stopped him from
kissing her just then. His second kiss had definitely *not*
been to make a point. Unless the point was that he wanted
her. Fiercely. Intensely.

And she'd wanted him, too, no matter what she said later.
She'd met his kiss with utter compliance: her curving body
fluid in his arms . . . her mouth sweet-scented and yielding
. . . her pert breasts crushed against his chest—

Damn it, memories like these had kept him up half the
night. He might have won their skirmish and tarnished her
reputation, but thanks to that kiss, the rest of his evening
had been one long parade of remembered images and sensations—of verdant eyes shadowed by night, lips pliant beneath his, a waist he could span with his hands, the rustle
of satin as she'd let him fold her in his arms.

And her tart comment afterward hadn't left him, either—
Apparently his lordship doesn't understand the word "no."
Impudent witch. She'd been just as impudent in his dreams
after he'd finally fallen asleep. Oh, God, yes—impudent
and eager, lying in his bed with her masses of coffee-hued
hair tumbled out over the sheets and her body stripped of
satin and lace. First she'd taunted him with that bold mouth
of hers. Then she'd put it to better use against his lips, his
chest . . . all over his randy body.

He groaned. It had seemed so real, he'd awakened as
hard as the house's stone pillars. The woman was a walking
invitation to seduction, damn her, and now all he wanted
was a chance to bare her body for his eyes and lips and
hands.

The hands he now clenched into fists. God, how he desired her. He wanted her begging for his kisses. He wanted

her lying beneath him and writhing in pleasure. He couldn't remember a time when he'd wanted a woman so much. Not even his triumph at giving her a taste of her own medicine could banish that.

"I'm worried about Miss Taylor," Sara continued, sipping her tea as if the topic of conversation were only of passing interest. "She should have returned by now. She said she was merely going into town to post a letter, but she went by horseback some time ago, and if she stays out much longer, she may find herself caught in the rain."

An image of Felicity soaked to the skin, wet muslin clinging to every curve, leapt into his mind before he squelched it. And why was she posting a letter? Whom could she be writing? Thoughtfully he cracked his egg and tore off the top half of the shell. Ah, yes, her brothers. Naturally, she was notifying them that she'd arrived safely yesterday.

When he said nothing, Sara added, "I do hope she didn't doze off in the saddle. She told me she didn't sleep well last night."

Undoubtedly Sara blamed him for Felicity's inability to sleep. Her reproving reformer expression was firmly in place, the one that had driven her pirate husband to mend his ways.

Well, his own ways needed no mending. Pretending not to understand her implication, he dug out the egg's center with a spoon, and said, "It's hard to sleep well in a strange house, no matter how comfortable the arrangements."

"I don't think it was the house that kept her from sleeping."

"Oh?" He ate some egg. "Then perhaps Miss Taylor was simply too excited after the ball to sleep. Such a reaction is common in young women."

"Particularly when they've been insulted."

He feigned an expression of innocent bewilderment.

" 'Insulted'? Who in their right mind would insult Miss Taylor?"

"You know very well who." Sara stabbed her sausage so viciously with her fork that it made him uneasy. "She was quite distraught over your treatment of her."

Guilt trickled into his consciousness. Damn her; he had no reason to feel guilt. He'd done nothing to Felicity she hadn't deserved. "She wasn't mistreated, I assure you." When Sara opened her mouth to retort, he held up one hand. "This is a personal matter that even your license to meddle doesn't cover, so stay out of it."

"If you could have seen the way—"

"*Sara*—" he warned.

"You made her cry!" Sara said bluntly. "A stalwart little thing like Miss Taylor. When we found her, she'd been weeping, though she strove very hard to cover the fact."

He couldn't imagine Felicity crying over anything, and the thought of his kisses driving her to such an extreme was too ludicrous to comprehend. Setting down his spoon, he leaned back and knit his hands over his belly. "Go on; you're clearly determined to talk about this. Out with it. And who is 'we'?"

"Lady Brumley and I. We went in search of Miss Taylor because her disappearance from the ballroom concerned us."

"Concerned *you,* perhaps. I doubt Lady Brumley felt anything more than a burning urge to root out more gossip."

The faintest tinge of color touched Sara's cheeks. "That may be true. All the same, we found Miss Taylor sitting at the writing table in her room, her cheeks damp and her eyes red from copious tears."

Ian squelched more guilt. Felicity's crying couldn't have been genuine. She must have heard Sara and Lady Brumley coming up the hall and produced crocodile tears to influence them. "The woman is easily wounded indeed if she dissolves into tears merely because a man kisses her."

Outrage shone in Sara's face. She held his gaze, then made a sharp, deliberate slice through her sausage. His thighs tightened defensively.

"It wasn't just that," she snapped, "as you well know. I heard the shameful way you implied that she'd encouraged your advances."

He refused to justify himself on that score. Sara didn't know the whole of it, nor should she.

"And you did something more than kiss her, I think."

If he had, he sure as hell would have remembered. "What the devil do you mean?"

Sara threw down her fork and knife. "You know what I mean. Taking advantage; putting your hands where they don't belong. That's why she slapped you."

Ian glowered at her. "She *told* you I did that?"

"She said you'd gone too far. And I saw the way you held her, remember? So I could easily believe you touched her in ways you shouldn't." Sara rose, working the napkin through her hands in agitation.

He was by turns incensed and impressed. Felicity certainly knew how to turn a situation to her advantage. But he had the facts on his side. "Did she actually say that I took advantage of her, that I touched her in ways I shouldn't?"

Sara wandered to the sideboard and concentrated on arranging the covers on the dishes. "Not exactly. She was shocked to see us, so at first she didn't want to talk at all. But I couldn't leave her alone when she was so distraught. Besides, as her hostess, I felt it my duty to find out what you'd done to distress her. So I asked if . . . if you'd behaved in any way you shouldn't have—other than kissing her, of course."

At his muttered curse, she added quickly, "I expected her to say *no*, you understand. But she burst out that she should have known better than to be alone with a man of your reputation, that she should have stopped you before you went too far."

Sara faced him and planted her hands on her hips. "Those were her very words—*too far*. She said that it pained her to tell me the true character of my friend, but that you were a scoundrel. She was most specific about that."

His short bark of laughter garnered him Sara's most indignant stare. "I'm sure she was, though I seriously doubt it pained her to blacken my character to you. She probably delighted in your dismay over my behavior.' "

"I'm not so disloyal to my friends as all that," Sara protested with a sniff. "It's not as if she invented a tale that I believed without question. Matters have been odd between you two from the moment she arrived. You must confess that your connection to her is curious. You admit going to her house, which we both know had nothing to do with her father's death. As Emily pointed out to me, you hardly knew her father."

He groaned. He did *not* need Emily and Sara allied with Felicity against him. "Keeping aside my connection with Miss Taylor, you know very well I'd never force myself on a woman, no matter what my previous association with her, and especially not under your roof. We've been friends long enough for you to realize that."

Her lower lip trembled, but whether with agitation or anger, he couldn't tell. "The Ian I knew when Jordan and I were children would never do such a thing, true." A hint of sadness filled her voice. "But you aren't the same as you were then. Ever since you returned from the Continent, you've been different—harder, cynical, more of a . . . a—"

"Scoundrel?" he snapped.

"I was going to say 'enigma.' " Sara's tone was quiet, thoughtful. "You left England without a word even to Jordan, estranging yourself from all of your family even though your uncle had just suffered the death of his wife. You didn't return until your father died, and then you began seeking a wife in an utterly ruthless manner."

She paused as if waiting for an explanation, but he had none to give. There were some things he couldn't discuss, even with his closest friends.

Her lips tightened into a thin line. "And now you seem to feel no qualm about destroying the reputation of a respectable young lady like Miss Taylor—"

"Enough about Miss Taylor!" He shot to his feet. "The woman can take care of herself, I assure you. And despite what she implied to you and that harpy Lady Brumley, she did *not* protest my kisses, nor was she ever in danger of being compromised by me!" Although the next time he saw her, she might well be. It was either compromise her or throttle her within an inch of her life. Both sounded equally appealing at the moment.

"Are you saying she *wanted* your attentions?"

He closed his fists on the back of the chair. "I'm saying she did not protest them."

"She slapped you, didn't she?"

With difficulty, he repressed a foul oath. "Sara, you must take my word for it that matters between Miss Taylor and me aren't as they appear to be."

"Then what—"

"I won't discuss this with you any further. It's private. So you might as well stay out of it." He stalked off toward the entrance of the dining room.

But her voice stopped him. "I can't stay out of it. This is my house, and I won't allow you to toy with a helpless young woman beneath my very nose."

He rounded on her in amazement. He'd never heard that note of steel in Sara's tone directed toward *him*. Damn, Felicity had played her role most convincingly. "What exactly are you saying, Sara?"

"I think perhaps you should stay at Jordan's for the rest of your visit."

His gaze on her narrowed.

Turning to pace the floor at the end of the table, she went on quickly, "I've already spoken to Emily, and she has agreed. The baby isn't giving them any trouble, so she said they'd be delighted to have you. Of course, you may join us here for the other activities we're planning, but at night—"

"At night, you don't want the cock sleeping in the hen-house," he bit out.

She colored. "I suppose that's one way to put it."

Under other circumstances, he might have been insulted. But Sara was merely behaving as Felicity had intended. He couldn't blame Sara for being taken in. Felicity could play righteous indignation very convincingly, and Sara was just the sort to believe in a martyred heroine.

Well, Felicity's martyrdom would come at a price, whether she knew it or not. Though he preferred to stay at Jordan's anyway, he didn't intend to let Felicity think for even one moment that she'd won.

An idea had sprung into his mind that was sure to work on the imagination-plagued Felicity. "All right, I'll move my things to Jordan's." He continued toward the door, then paused to cast Sara a cool smile. "Oh, and do pass on a message to Miss Taylor for me, will you?"

Sara regarded him warily. "What?"

"Tell her that even John Pilkington has his price."

"John Pilkington? Who is he? What on earth—"

"Just tell her. She'll know what it means." Then, whistling to himself, he sauntered from the room.

Chapter 8

*E*ven John Pilkington has his price.

With a frown, Felicity slapped *The Mysteries of Udolpho* down on her lap. Drat it, why must Ian's insidious threats about Pilkington plague her even while she read a novel? At home with the boys underfoot, she seldom got to indulge her love of reading. Now she'd been given a few hours to herself, and *he* had to intrude.

A chill hung in the air of the Worthings' card room, made all the more harsh by the lack of a fire. Felicity tugged her heavy wool shawl more closely about the simple day dress she'd kept on instead of dressing for dinner. Sara had told her no one ever used this room, which is why she'd come here while the others were dining. She'd excused herself from attending the meal by telling Sara she was too embarrassed to face Lord St. Clair. The Black-

100

mores had arrived, and Ian was with them for the first time in three days.

But the truth was, she was a coward. The prospect of eating dinner across from a man determined to ruin her life—and invade even her thoughts—was unendurable. He would surely see how his parting words to Sara worried her. And how could she keep from blurting out some revealing statement?

Worse, how in creation could she keep from remembering those kisses he'd given her? No, *stolen* from her. He'd stolen more than kisses—he'd stolen a long-ago dream of experiencing a man's passion. Now that she'd seen how easily men could feign it, she could never trust a man's kisses again. So dining with Ian tonight was unthinkable.

Besides, she had another perfectly good reason for avoiding him. The man was clearly bent on revenge. Why else make that statement to Sara? And why else accompany the Blackmores to dinner at Worthing Manor tonight? He'd been noticeably absent when the Blackmores had come for luncheon the day after his conversation with Sara. Then he'd gone off to London on business the next day, prompting her to congratulate herself on being rid of him.

But he was back, and now she was worried. Why had he gone to London in the midst of a country visit with close friends? What business could be so compelling? And why had he returned?

She could guess some of the answers. It could concern her column. She'd sent it in an express to Mr. Pilkington Monday, so it had undoubtedly appeared in the *Gazette* while Ian was in town. If so, he must have seen it.

Unless he'd prevented it from being published at all. She turned his words over again in her head. She could only assume he'd intended to bribe Mr. Pilkington into either censoring her words or refusing to publish them. The question was, what would Mr. Pilkington say to such a despicable offer?

Surely he wouldn't cut her off. Why, Mr. Pilkington always professed she was his best correspondent.

Then again . . . *even John Pilkington has his price.*

She lifted her eyes to the heavens. "Can't you give me a hint?" she muttered at God. "Ian must have some plan in mind. Lord knows—I mean, *You* know—Ian has enough money to make Mr. Pilkington salivate. I hardly think my literary prowess would sway the publisher if St. Clair bombards him with gold."

"To whom are you speaking?" asked a familiar female voice from the doorway, and she nearly jumped out of her skin.

The countess entered the room with the rest of the party behind her—Sara's husband Gideon, both of the Blackmores, and worst of all, Ian. Only the Drydens were absent, and they'd probably already retired for the evening.

Felicity sprang to her feet, her book sliding off her lap and onto the floor with a thud. "I wasn't speaking to anyone!" Heat flooded her face. Oh, to be caught acting like a ninny in front of this crowd, especially *him*! How much had they heard? How much had *he* heard? "I-I mean, I have this bad habit of talking to . . . to myself sometimes when I'm distracted."

"Are we distracting you, Miss Taylor?" Ian asked as he sauntered past Sara. With a quick motion, he picked Felicity's book up off the floor. When she reached for it, he ignored her outstretched hand and tucked the volume under his arm. "We didn't mean to do so." Amusement laced his voice. No doubt he'd guessed precisely why she'd not been at dinner.

Guessed, and was pleased about it. Indeed, he looked abominably self-assured and handsome, with his tail coat of cobalt saxony fitting those broad shoulders to perfection, his pantaloon trousers of fine kerseymere hugging thighs too muscular for a nobleman, and his cravat tied simply, as if he had more important things to do than wait for a valet to engineer a complicated knot. Next to him and his finely dressed friends, she looked like the drabbest creature in the realm in her muslin day dress and old woolen shawl.

"We're so pleased to see you up and about," Ian continued. "We thought you were ill. A headache. That's what Sara told us."

"Yes, Miss Taylor had a most monstrous headache," Sara hastened to say. "You should have seen her earlier. She nearly fainted while we were out walking." Sara's apologetic glance at Felicity held a wealth of meaning. *I'm sorry I didn't know you were here. I'm sorry I had to invent a headache to explain your absence at dinner.*

It touched Felicity, increasing her already enormous guilt over misleading the countess about what had happened the night of the ball. Felicity hadn't meant to mislead her. When Sara and Lady Brumley had caught her at the writing table in her room penning her angry column, she'd tried to get rid of them.

But it had been fruitless. Felicity should have known that the kindly countess wouldn't let her tears go unremarked. And when in a burst of angry feeling, Felicity had said that Ian had done more than kiss her, Sara's inordinate indignation had made Felicity realize how her words had been interpreted. But she hadn't dared explain, not in front of Lady Brumley.

Still, she hadn't expected Sara to banish Ian from the house for it. Apparently Felicity had underestimated the countess's fierce sense of protectiveness toward all unmarried women. After several discussions about reform and the community the Worthings were building on a remote island, Felicity knew the woman better, and now she understood precisely how Sara must have regarded Felicity's claims about Ian. Which only tripled her guilt. And her reluctance to admit the truth to the woman.

Well, at least she could support the countess's story now. "I did have a headache. But after I slept a while, it abated, so I wandered downstairs to find a book to read and discovered this lovely little card room."

Emily, the other countess present, glanced at the barren fireplace, where servants now layered cords of wood with kindling. "You shouldn't have sat here without a fire. You might catch a chill to add to that headache."

Belatedly remembering that Emily had a penchant for physic, Felicity murmured, "I didn't want to trouble the servants. And I don't take chill easily."

"All the same," Sara said firmly, "we don't wish to disturb your solitary pleasure. We'll understand if you'd like to retire with your book now—"

"Retire?" Ian interrupted in a crisp tone. "We've finally gained her company, and you're banishing her to bed? That's inhospitable of you, Sara." He didn't seem to notice Sara's look of reproach. "Besides, I'm sure your guest won't object to spending a few minutes with us. Will you, Miss Taylor?"

Felicity met his gaze, her heart thumping faster at the challenge glowing in his devil's eyes. He wanted her to stay, which should send her bolting from the room faster than a hare startled by a wolf. Because if she stayed, he would pounce.

Yet if she fled, he'd run her to ground another way. At least here she had Sara on her side. "I'd love to stay, Lord St. Clair, especially now that I'm feeling better. Besides, you've taken my book prisoner, so I can't very well leave, can I?"

"Ah, yes, your book." Ian held it at arms' length and read the spine. "*The Mysteries of Udolpho* by Ann Radcliffe. A novel—how interesting." He smiled coolly at Felicity. "I must say I'm not surprised to discover that you like *fiction*."

Felicity crossed her arms over her chest. "Of course I like fiction. What else would I read when my head pains me? Dry works of science or business?"

Ian shrugged. "At least they contain facts and the truth. These novels are some person's invention, and how can reading false tales help anyone?"

The man simply wouldn't relent. Felicity snatched the book from him, heedless of his laughing gaze. "Fiction *is* truth, no matter what you say. Where do you think novelists get their material? From real life, not from some scientist's speculations about what life might be. Novels can better prepare us for life's difficulties than ancient history. Indeed, I encourage my brothers to read them whenever possible. They often provide a truer vision of society than all the supposed facts printed in other books."

"Or in newspapers?" he asked, one eyebrow raised.

As his gaze locked with hers, full of meaning, full of threat, her fervor drained out of her. This was it—his next assault. She waited for it with her heart pounding.

He turned to where Jordan and his wife were finding seats around the card tables. "Speaking of newspapers, Jordan, I brought a number back from London for you. I have an interesting article to show you."

Felicity's knees went weak. Her column—it had to be. But if he'd seen it, why would he want his friends to read it?

Thankfully, Emily said, "I thought we were going to play cards. That *is* why you suggested we go to the card room, isn't it?"

Ian had suggested it? Oh, of course. Her heart plummeted as she noted the servants who scurried about lighting candles and making the room comfortable. The party's move to the card room had been no sudden impulse. He'd planned this "accidental" encounter, the devil. He must have discovered her whereabouts from a servant during dinner. So this truly was it: their next battle. And she wasn't ready.

"Well, isn't it, Ian?" Emily repeated. "I do so want to play whist. I seldom get the chance."

Jordan laughed. "You see what happens when you expose a country girl to some fun? She can hardly get enough of it."

With a cross look, Emily retorted, "You know that's not the only reason. There's never enough people here in the country to play, since Gideon dislikes the game so."

"Confoundedly stupid game," Gideon muttered. He sat in a wing chair near the fire warming his hands.

"Unfortunately, Emily, we now have too many people to play," Ian said. "We wouldn't want to leave Miss Taylor out of the game."

"Oh, don't trouble yourselves over *that*," Felicity hurriedly said. "I'll simply continue reading. You four go on with your game, by all means."

"Impossible," Ian remarked. "We'll be noisy, and that'll restore your headache."

Glaring at him, Felicity gritted out, "Then perhaps I *should* retire."

"No, I insist that we cancel our plans. I won't be responsible for depriving everyone of your company, especially when you're returning to London tomorrow. Besides, I think you, too, will find the newspaper interesting."

His amused gaze met Felicity's baleful one, and she wanted to strangle him. What was he planning, drat him?

The others didn't seem annoyed by his insistence on dictating their entertainment. Emily even graciously conceded it would be unfair to leave Miss Taylor out of the game. Nor did anyone protest when he sent a servant off to fetch his newspapers.

After the servant had gone, he took a seat on a spindly chair, dwarfing it with his large frame. When he leaned back, legs splayed and thumbs tucked into his waistcoat pockets, he wore the smug air of a man who always got his way. "Now we can all join you in reading, Miss Taylor. I brought copies of *Ackermann's Repository* for you females." The smile he fixed on her was as insidious as coal dust in a chimney. "And for Jordan, I brought the *Gazette*. He's a great admirer of Lord X's column."

She swallowed. This made no sense. Why would Ian want his friends to read her column about him? Was it simply his obnoxious way of leading up to exposing her?

She forced a note of contempt into her voice. "Isn't Lord X that man who writes the gossip?" She strolled nonchalantly to the opposite side of the room and perched herself on a silk-upholstered settee. "Lord St. Clair, I can't believe you criticized my preference for fiction when you read a rumormonger like Lord X."

"Ian doesn't read him; he hates the fellow," Jordan interjected. "But I admit to admiring the writer myself. His biting comments are a tonic to all the hypocrisy among our peers. Lord X is quite a wit, even if he does take a poke at Ian occasionally."

Ian's gaze was riveted on her. "Yes, he's a wit. At other people's expense."

A slow churn began in her stomach. Why the devil wouldn't he get it over with? If he wanted to expose her . . .

"That's not true," Emily remarked. "The man's judicious in his wit. He only sharpens it on the pompous, cruel, and unthinking. Only last week he defended young women who ignore their parents' greed to elope with the men they love."

The young countess's unexpected defense lifted Felicity's spirits.

Then she noted the sudden tension in the room. Jordan cast his wife a reproachful glance. "You shouldn't mention elopements around Ian, darling. He's not so fond of them as you are."

Emily colored. "Goodness gracious, I forgot . . . that is, I . . ."

The newspapers arrived at that moment, sparing Lady Blackmore any further embarrassment. Now scowling, Ian flipped quickly through them, then drew out one that looked like the *Gazette* and tossed it to Jordan. "Well, there's no mention of elopements in Lord X's latest column. But I dare say it will interest you and Emily all the same. It seems the rumormonger hasn't tired of me as a subject."

"What?" Jordan looked genuinely surprised, a reaction that seemed to be shared by everyone else in the room. Felicity prepared herself for doomsday.

Jordan shook open the paper and began turning pages. "Ian, I thought you intended to find out Lord X's true identity. Don't tell me you couldn't convince the man to keep quiet about your affairs."

Felicity sucked in a quick breath as her gaze shot to Ian.

Ian took his time about answering, obviously delighting in the power he held over her. "I had some trouble tracking down a *man* named Lord X. But I did talk to Pilkington. Though he wouldn't reveal the identity of his correspondent, he told me something very interesting."

Felicity's stomach began to rival a butter churn for activity.

"Pilkington?" Sara interjected. "But Ian, isn't he the man you mentioned when—" She broke off, her gaze flitting from Ian to Felicity.

Felicity couldn't meet her friend's gaze.

"Pilkington is the *Gazette's* publisher," Jordan explained, oblivious to the new tension in the room. He scanned through the paper for the column. "Wait, here it is."

"Read it aloud," Ian commanded, shooting each word at her like a dratted archer.

Felicity truly felt ill now. It was one thing to write the words while alone in her room, bolstered by her anger. But to hear them read by Ian's own friend . . .

Drat it, she wouldn't let Ian provoke her guilt! She'd had every right to retaliate after his nasty tactics on the balcony. If her column embarrassed him before his friends, then he shouldn't make them read it. Besides, it didn't begin to compare to the utter humiliation he'd heaped upon her that night, the way he'd made her respond to his kisses, then taunted her about her response before Sara and Lady Brumley.

She balled her fists in her lap as Jordan's amused voice rumbled across the room:

Take heed, my friends, lest you invoke Lord St. Clair's ire by reading this column. He was unhappy to be mentioned here last week. It seems the good viscount would have us believe that the woman on Waltham Street is not his mistress, but his wartime compatriot's sister to whom he's providing friendly aid during a time of difficulty.

If this be true, his behavior deserves praise, not censure. Your faithful correspondent, however, finds the possibility dubious, especially his assertion that he fought in the war. Has anyone heard of his feats or seen his bravery in battle firsthand? If so, let the *Gazette* know at once. We would be most happy to print tales from his lordship's years abroad fighting Napoleon.

Yours truly suspects, however, that the viscount's "war years" are as questionable as his "benevolence," in which case his claims insult the bravery of all those men who truly fought for our country.

Jordan tossed the newspaper down, eyes alight with anger. "I take back every compliment I've ever given the man, Ian! This is libelous! You should bring suit against him! He can't defame you like this—he must be forced to retract this insult or provide you with satisfaction on the dueling field!"

Felicity made herself continue to hold Ian's gaze. His lack of expression amply demonstrated that he awaited her reaction. No doubt he expected her to blush or flinch or show other evidence of shame.

He wouldn't get it from her, the scoundrel! She didn't regret a single word she'd written! Truly, she didn't!

Well, perhaps that last little bit was excessive. She probably shouldn't have asserted her doubts so boldly. But she'd been angry, and with good reason. He'd humiliated her as publicly as she had him. No, she didn't regret what she'd written. He deserved everything she could throw at him.

"What I don't understand," Emily put in, "is how Lord X knew what you'd told us about your friend, Ian. I swear I never said a word to anyone outside this room."

"Nor did I," Sara chimed in.

Felicity listened in disbelief. What? It couldn't be. The two countesses must have told others. Sara had told *her*. And surely Ian's reason for lying to them in the first place had been to make sure they cleared his name among the gossips.

Ian flashed Felicity the barest taunting smile. "It's all right, Sara. I know you probably told quite a few people in my defense. I don't blame you for that."

"But I didn't!" Sara protested. "You asked us not to say anything, and I upheld your wish!" Her gaze turned to Felicity, confused, upset.

The roiling in Felicity's stomach now threatened to make her faint. He'd asked them not to say anything? Good Lord. How had he known that Sara had told her and only her? What sort of devil was he, anyway?

"You or Emily must have said *something*," Ian replied in apparent innocence. "You couldn't have known it would be passed on. Pilkington himself told me that Lord X has a woman helping him gather information. No doubt she heard the truth from one of you at the ball."

What a liar! Felicity thought angrily. *Mr. Pilkington told him no such thing!*

He added slyly, "It's probably Lady Brumley, with her penchant for gossip."

"No!" Sara exclaimed. "I didn't say a word to her! The only person I told was—"

She broke off at exactly the same moment Felicity felt the trap spring upon her. Why, that manipulative, lying son of a bachelor!

He leaned back with an utterly cocksure expression, basking in the success of his machinations. This ambush had been his plan—he thought to ruin her with his friends, prevent her from discovering anything else from them. To defend herself, she'd have to admit she was Lord X. But he didn't want that—oh, no, because revealing her identity to his friends would prompt her to tell the whole truth, even the parts he hid from them!

So instead he made her out to be a sneak who passed on gossip for her own enjoyment. At least Lord X had a noble purpose; but Lord X's assistant could only be a pawn at best, a conniving witch at worst! They would all despise her now!

She glanced at Sara, wincing to see her wounded expression. They already despised her. She scrambled for a defense, pretending not to realize the conclusion Sara had clearly drawn. "You did tell *me,* Sara, so you surely told someone else."

Sara wore a heart-wrenching look of betrayal. "No. No one but you."

Felicity wanted to protest, to act insulted, anything to wipe that horrible look from Sara's face. But protest would only make her look more guilty. Never had she guessed she would care so much about what some countess thought of her. She'd had few close friends in her life, thanks to her father's odd position, and she'd foolishly thought Sara might become one. How dared Ian take that from her?

Now they would all unite against her, and it would only be worse if she revealed she was Lord X. Either way, she was the outsider. They wouldn't believe her when she said Ian's "secret" was a blatant lie. And there would be no one else to support her tale. Except for Miss Greenaway, the only other person who knew the truth, whatever it was.

Sudden hope filled her. Of course! Miss Greenaway! Striving for calmness, she said to Ian, "You know, it might not have been one of us at all who spoke to Lord X. Your friend—the one on this Waltham Street—might have gone to the newspaper herself to explain. I know if *I* had been the subject of unfair gossip, I would have done so."

There was a long pause as everyone digested this new possibility. For the first time since he'd entered the room, Ian's self-assured stance altered a fraction. "I assure you, Miss Taylor, that Miss G— That my friend would never do such a foolish thing. She would uphold my desire for privacy."

Sara seemed more than willing, however, to grasp at Felicity's hypothesis. "Yes, but would she have risked her own reputation just to please you? I doubt it. And even if she would have, perhaps she couldn't bear to see your character falsely maligned after you'd been so generous. Think how it would have weighed on her conscience."

"Sara's right," Felicity added as relief surged through her. "I'm sure the woman would have found it most distressing."

Let him wriggle out of *this* tale, she thought fiercely. He couldn't refute her hypothesis without telling the truth, and he wouldn't tell the truth to his friends after presenting them with such an outrageous lie.

Gone was his smug demeanor. Like two flints newly struck, his eyes glittered at her. He jumped to his feet and strode to where Jordan had thrown down the paper. "The lady in question did *not* go to the paper." He picked up the *Gazette*, scanned it, then stabbed one long finger at the column. "It says here, 'The good viscount would have us

believe,' et cetera. That implies that Lord X thinks *I* am
the one making false claims."

"Not necessarily," Jordan put in. "If he's determined to
skewer you on his pen, he might not want his readers to
know your lady friend is his source, for that would weigh
in your favor. Thus he couches his assertion more vaguely.
After all, he didn't come right out and *say* he got his information from you or one of your friends, did he?"

Sara threw Felicity an apologetic glance. "You see, Ian?
It probably wasn't one of us at all."

Sara's dear defense ruined Felicity's triumph. Sara didn't
deserve to be a pawn in this battle. It was Felicity's fault
that Sara had been drawn into it in the first place. Nor did
Ian's glance of scathing contempt make her feel any better.
He was right to despise her. She should never have allowed
Sara to believe he'd taken liberties with her on the balcony.
Until then, the war had remained between the two of them.
But now it seemed to be spiraling out of control.

"It doesn't matter how Lord X found out," Jordan said.
"What right does he have to assume you lied about fighting
in the war? He gives no proof. For that alone, you should
sue the paper. If I were you, I'd *make* the government set
the *Gazette* straight."

"The government wouldn't bother." Ian shifted his gaze
from Felicity to Jordan. "What I did on the Continent was
unofficial. I doubt anyone even remembers my role."

"What did you do?" Jordan asked.

"Nothing worth discussing."

Of course not, Felicity thought, renewed in the rightness
of her position. A nonexistent military career wouldn't be.
How convenient that no one remembered his role.

"Wellington remembers what you did," Gideon suddenly
remarked from his solitary position by the fire. "He told
me they couldn't have won the war without you."

All eyes turned to him, most especially Felicity's.

"The duke himself told you that?" Jordan asked his

brother-in-law. "When the devil did you meet the Duke of Wellington?"

Gideon shrugged. "Some ball or another, I don't remember. Wellington and I were arguing about the British peerage's role in the military. I'd just learned that Wellington wasn't born a peer, but made one after his efforts for his country. So I told him I thought it was stupid to have a system where the best-educated men—the peers and all the eldest sons—were discouraged from defending their country by the demands of inheritance. In the heat of the moment, he gave Ian as an example of an eldest son and a peer who'd participated bravely and effectively in the war."

Shock kept Felicity motionless. Could it be true? Ian *hadn't* lied about his war record? It was impossible! How . . . why would a viscount's heir fight in the war?

"Wellington was probably drunk," Ian muttered.

"If he was, he hid it well," Gideon said. "When his comment roused my curiosity, I asked more questions about you, and he suddenly remembered I used to be an American privateer. Got very quiet on the subject. I didn't think it wise to press him."

"It wouldn't have mattered who you'd been," Ian said tersely. "I'm surprised he said anything at all. It's a great exaggeration of my small help."

"Wellington doesn't exaggerate," Jordan put in, a note of awe in his voice. "What the devil did you do during the war? Were you a spy? Why won't anyone speak of it?"

"Because it's nothing anyone wishes to discuss. Nothing *I* want to discuss." Ian's gaze locked with Felicity's, dire with warning. "Or to have discussed in the newspaper."

Felicity had never felt so small. If Ian had been telling the truth, then she'd committed a great wrong by publicly questioning his honor.

Avoiding his gaze, she sank against the unforgivingly hard settee. She deserved worse—to be on the rack. What a fool she'd been to assume his rakish habits were the only facet to his character. She'd glimpsed the darkness in him when she'd first met him, a darkness only pain could carve into a man's soul and the kind of pain that only came from witnessing horrors. Why had she been so quick to ignore her instincts?

Because of Katherine? No, to be fair, it had been more than that. It had been her bias against men of his station. He'd been so . . . so typically arrogant and secretive about his affairs that it had blinded her to other considerations. Like the rumors about his spying and his absence from England, which corresponded with the years of the war.

And his treatment of her on the balcony had aggravated her anger against him. But she should never have aired her grievances in her column, especially without knowing the truth. It was wrong. She saw that now.

"Why has Lord X made you his enemy?" Gideon asked Ian. "Perhaps you should assess your friendships among society to determine whose throat to cut."

"Let's have no talk of throat-cutting," Jordan reproached his brother-in-law. "You're thinking like a pirate again, Gideon, and not like a civilized man."

Gideon cast his wife an amused glance that her brother couldn't see. "Sometimes the pirate way is more effective."

"Only if you want to hang," Jordan retorted hotly.

"Enough." Ian held up his hands. "Thank you for all the advice, my friends, but I'll deal with this my own way. And I assure you, Jordan, I'll take care of Lord X without cutting any throats. There will be no need for this discussion in the future."

Although he hadn't so much as glanced at her while he spoke, she knew his words were intended for her. Good Lord, she'd really done it now. After tonight, he would grind her into the dust with all the weapons and power at his disposal. Her heart dropped into her stomach. She'd been foolish to take him on, especially with her future and that of the boys at stake. She should have heeded Papa's adage about not taunting a cannon with a club if one wanted to keep one's head.

For although she desperately wished to keep her head now, she very much feared it was too late to avoid the cannon.

Chapter 9

Rumor has it that a certain duchess did not appreciate her husband's birthday gift of *je ne sais quoi* stays. Upon being presented with the corset constructed to prevent male access to the female body, she tossed it into the fire, then informed him he could better keep men away by staying at home more.

LORD X, *THE EVENING GAZETTE*,
DECEMBER 13, 1820

Felicity hurried up the wide staircase to her room, wondering how she'd survived the past hour. Ian a war hero? A liar, yes, about his Miss Greenaway, and surely a calculating scoundrel when it came to women. But still a hero.

That thought had tormented her in the awkward minutes following her and Ian's skirmish. Despite Sara's attempts to steer the conversation toward an innocuous subject, there'd been nothing but fits and starts and one uncomfortable silence after another.

She'd nearly cried with relief when Gideon had suggested that the men retire to his study to look at the blueprints of a ship he'd just acquired. One more minute in Ian's presence and she would've betrayed her flood of feelings. She'd remained in the card room long enough to be sure Emily and Sara no longer suspected her of being Lord X's accomplice, before excusing herself to go to bed.

Not that she could sleep. Her hand tightened on the banister. How could she, with Ian's condemning look branded in her mind? She'd deserved it, she knew, no matter how much she tried to rationalize it away. Her retaliation had been far too excessive—she must acknowledge it.

Stifling a sob, she tucked her book more securely under her arm and raced up the last few steps, anxious to reach the sanctuary of her bedchamber. He wouldn't let the insult pass—she knew him too well to think otherwise. Oh, how could she have let matters progress so far? How could she have let her feelings overwhelm her good sense? In her precarious situation, she should *not* have provoked a viscount.

She reached the top of the stairs, then swept along the hall past silk-shot tapestries and imposing pillars designed by Papa. If only Papa were here—he could tell her what to do. He'd always excelled at managing men of lofty position. It had never been her forte. Thankfully, after the birth of the triplets and Mama's death, Felicity had been needed to care for the babies, which had put an end to trips with her father. She'd been able to avoid further contact with Papa's patrons, except when he brought them home.

Home—thank God she'd be there tomorrow. After the tumult of these last hours, she would endure, even welcome, the worst the boys could throw at her. She couldn't wait to unburden herself to Mrs. Box. The woman would soothe her guilty conscience and understand what had prompted Felicity to behave so rashly. Yes, and Mrs. Box would help her figure out a way to prevent Lord St. Clair's revenge.

With a heavy sigh, she swung open the door to her room, grateful to see that the servants had already laid a cheery fire in the hearth, turned down the velvet coverlet on the massive tester bed, and lit enough candles to cast a faint glow about the room. Absorbed by her morose thoughts, she shut the door and strolled to the oak bureau, tossing her book atop the bed as she passed. She removed her shawl, then opened the bureau to put it away.

Her gaze fell on the frilly dressing gown Mrs. Box had packed. It had belonged to Mama, given to Felicity when she was sixteen and full of hopes for the future. At that age, she'd imagined a husband who would see her in it, his eyes shining with approval the way Papa's had shone on Mama.

But that would never happen, would it? Papa's wild living and subsequent death had ended those hopes, had thrust her into this awful position where she could only survive by writing things that locked her into combat with the likes of Lord St. Clair.

More tears crowded her eyes. She stroked the lacy wrapper as she swallowed back her sobs. She wouldn't cry over this. There was no point.

Forcing her attention to the silky confection before her, she fingered one intricate flower. Mama, whose prowess with a needle always awed her daughter, had done the delicate tracery work. Felicity lifted the gown and crushed it to her cheeks, breathing in the faintest scent of the rosewater Mama had been wont to wear.

Needing to feel a connection, any connection, to her mother, she determined to wear it tonight. Impatiently, she stripped off her day dress and dispensed with her hose, garters, and petticoat. Then she pulled the lovely wrapper over her chemise. Her hair tumbled down in the process, and she shook it out, heedless of where the pins fell.

Walking to the harewood dressing table that stood between the two pointed windows of the large bedchamber, she gazed at herself in the oval mirror that hung above it. For a moment, all she saw was a scantily dressed young woman with red-rimmed eyes and a lost look on her face.

Then a movement in the reflection made her breath halt in her throat. Behind her, a man leaned against the wall near the closed door. Ian! Good Lord, Ian had come for his revenge.

His muscular arms were crossed over his chest, and his intent gaze held such dark power that for a moment she couldn't move, couldn't blink, like the glassy-eyed victim of a mesmerizing magician. "Go on." His eyes insolently drank in every aspect of her appearance. "Don't let me stop you."

That released her from his spell. She whirled to face him, clutching the gaping ends of the wrapper tightly to her chest. "How dare you! How long have you—"

"I've been waiting for you ever since I left the card room. Gideon and Jordan think I returned to the Blackmore estate. But I couldn't leave without speaking to you."

"Not here, not like this! Go downstairs, and I'll meet you—"

"Meet me?" He laughed—a hollow, ominous sound. "You think I trust you to *meet* me? Before I could reach the stairs, you'd be screaming for Sara to throw me out."

"What makes you think I won't scream now?"

"You won't while you're dressed like that." He shot her another devouring look, exactly like the sultan in her painting determining how to punish his houri.

It shook her, yet threaded with the fear was a heat that traveled from her head to her breasts to her loins. Curse him for that.

"Besides," he added, "if you scream, and Sara rushes up here demanding an explanation, you'd have a damned sight more trouble convincing her of your innocence than you did last time."

He had an excellent point. But she hadn't expected the wretch to waylay her in her own bedchamber.

Outrage helped to banish her fear. Tossing her head back, she surveyed him for some sign of his intentions. With the sconce protruding from the wall a few inches above his head, he was illuminated most perversely, his face and body a study of shadows in the flickering candlelight that accentuated his size while playing hide-and-seek with his expression. Still, she needn't see his face to read his mood. For the first time since they'd met, his voice showed every nuance of feeling, the clipped tone blatant in its fury.

And this invasion was ample proof that she'd provoked him once too often. No man entered an unmarried woman's bedchamber at night uninvited . . . and certainly no man stood silent while that woman undressed, not unless his intentions were less than honorable. She'd expected retaliation, but not this. Good Lord, not this.

A brief flash of terror blinded her courage, for she'd experienced the unwelcome advances of too many of Papa's patrons not to know what came next. She'd always managed to fend them off before they went too far, but Ian would be impossible to fight off. He was too big, too sure of his strength. Too justified in his anger.

Her heart sank. Trying not to look obvious, she scoured the table's green surface behind her for a weapon, but spotted nothing more helpful than a hairbrush, a comb, and a tangle of ribbons. Unless she wanted to groom him to death, she was defenseless.

But she would still fight him somehow. She met his gaze once more, summoning all her resistance. "You didn't come here only to talk, or you wouldn't have watched me undress." She added with an accusing air, "Have you now advanced to assaulting women in their bedchambers? Gideon will be so disappointed—he seems to think you're a hero."

His lips tightened grimly. "We both know how deceived he is in *that* opinion, don't we? I'm merely living up to your image of me. According to your carefully researched column, I'm a liar, even a debaucher. A man with no honor."

Each crisply spoken word was like a blow of a hammer upon her conscience. "I didn't quite call you a liar," she said defensively. "I merely . . . questioned certain statements you made about your past."

"Statements I never wanted published."

"Why not? Gideon says you've nothing to be ashamed of."

"But you don't believe that, do you?" he said bitterly. "No, you're much too clever to be fooled by the claims of a man's friends."

He cocked his head, unwittingly exposing more of his rigid features to the candles. Amber light glinted off the snapping black eyes and taut chin. Oh, yes, he was angry— furious, even. The sight was awe-inspiring and terrifying at the same time.

With a hard swallow, she clutched her wrapper against her chest. "I-I believe it now. But surely you understand why I didn't before. How could you expect me to believe your assertions when you insist on hiding so much of your past? Despite all those wildly contradictory rumors, no one ever professed to have fought with you. There was no public mention of your military career."

"That's how I prefer it. If I'd wanted my war history made public, I would have sent the details to the newspapers upon my return three years ago. A pity you didn't feel the need to consult me concerning my wishes in the matter."

She bristled at his accusing tone. "It's your own fault I spoke of it. You know quite well that your story about Miss Greenaway begged to be questioned. Besides, I would never have written more about you if you hadn't assaulted me—"

"Assaulted?" He shoved away from the wall. "You call a mere kiss an *assault*?"

"It was *not* a mere kiss to me," she burst out before she could stop herself. She continued in a more muted tone. "If it had been, I wouldn't have reacted as I did."

That seemed to take him by surprise. His fathomless gaze dropped to her lips and lingered, reminding her of the last time he'd touched them with his. Her mouth tingled in response.

"It was not a mere kiss to me, either." His voice resonated in the dimly lit chamber. "Not in any way."

An unwarranted thrill shot through her at his words. He didn't mean them. She knew exactly how sincere he could seem and how easily his sincerity could turn into betrayal. Yet she wanted to believe them.

The air felt thick and close, the space too small to contain them both, though he stood several feet away. They were alone, more completely alone than they'd been before. No one knew he was here—not the lady's maid she'd dismissed earlier or Sara or any of the Worthings' other visitors and servants.

And she wore only a lace dressing gown, her chemise, and her drawers. She tried to wrap the gown more tightly about her body, but short of pinning it shut, keeping it closed was impossible.

Worse yet, her actions seemed to draw his attention to it. Midnight eyes trailed over her, hungry and eager, stripping away her defenses with the deftness of a printer's knife. He'd worn that look before, when he'd been inches away with his hands locked on her waist and his lips lowering to her mouth. . . .

With an unspoken curse, she tore her gaze from his.

He cleared his throat. "Nonetheless," he continued gruffly as if angry at her for mentioning their kiss, "what I did was insufficient provocation for your tarnishing my reputation."

"You tarnished *my* reputation first, that night on the balcony."

"Not true. Have you forgotten your first column?"

She groaned. Amazingly, she had. "Our opinions differ

as to whether that tarnished your reputation."

"It drove my fiancée to elope with another man. If it didn't tarnish my reputation, it at least dulled its shine."

"You got your revenge for it, didn't you? Subjecting me to your kisses and—"

"Subjecting you—" He approached her, his brow lowering. "Are you claiming you didn't enjoy them?"

"Of course I enjoyed them!" she blurted out. At his pleased look, she added, "How could I not? You're a rake—making women enjoy your kisses is your avocation. But that doesn't change the fact that they were forced upon me."

"I am *not* a rake." He dragged his fingers through his hair in exasperation. "If you'd actually researched your spurious columns, you'd know that. As for forcing you, believe me, if you'd slapped me after the first kiss, I wouldn't have stayed for a second." His gaze narrowed. "But you grabbed my coat to draw me back. You *welcomed* those kisses, no matter what you claimed later. You lied about our entire encounter to Sara. At least have the good grace to admit it."

"I did *not* lie to her," she protested.

"You told her I'd taken advantage of you."

"No! She merely . . . assumed that you'd done so because . . . because—"

"Because you said I went 'too far.' " Slowly he neared her, eyes glittering like onyx set in silver. "What exactly is 'too far,' Felicity?"

She shrank against the dressing table. "I'm sure you know that better than I, given your reputation."

"My reputation." He snorted. "I hardly know what it is these days, it's been so mangled by you and all the gossips. But that doesn't answer my question. If you didn't lie, then what did you mean when you told Sara I'd gone 'too far'?"

He now stood scant inches from her, and though she wanted to flee, she refused to let him see how he intimidated her. Besides, the dressing table at her back prevented it.

Trying to retain some semblance of a spinsterish air, she retorted, "You *know* what I meant. I meant you kissed me with . . . with—" Oh, how did one describe the heart-stopping plunge into passion and sheer intensity of a man's kiss without sounding like a milksop schoolgirl? "With great enthusiasm," she finished lamely.

A half smile touched his lips. "I won't deny that. I'd say we both showed 'great enthusiasm.' Yet even the most enthusiastic of kisses wouldn't have prompted Sara to evict me from her house." Without warning, he hooked his arm about her waist, tugging her so close she could see the dark smudge of whiskers along his upper lip. "So tell me, my deceptive Felicity, what did I do to make her think so ill of me? I swear I don't remember anything that would shame me."

"That's because nothing shames you!" She dug the heels of her palms into his chest and shoved, which proved utterly pointless and merely made her dressing gown gape open. "Let go, Ian, or I shall . . . shall . . ." Her heart sank as she remembered why she couldn't scream. "Shall be convinced you're a blackguard and a scoundrel!"

His quick burst of laughter echoed in the room. "You're already convinced of that. Besides, I won't leave until you demonstrate what 'too far' is. Just so I don't make the same mistake in the future, you understand."

"In the future?" she squeaked.

"Much as I hope our little skirmishes are over, I know you better than that. So I want to know what's allowed and what's not." Snagging the edge of the dressing gown with two fingers, he peeled it open, his gaze dipping brazenly to examine her chemise.

Her blood quickened, leapt, rushed through her veins. She should scream that this was definitely not allowed, yet all she could do was fight to drag breath into her lungs.

Then he bent his head to press a kiss where her collarbone lay exposed above her chemise. It was so intimate a caress she strained away, which threw her off-balance so that she fell against the edge of the dressing table, her hands catching at it for support.

He took advantage of her imbalance to catch her wrapper in his fists and push it slowly, sensuously off her shoulders. As it pooled on the dressing table behind her, he wound a lock of her hair around his finger, then kissed it.

"Don't," she whispered hoarsely. A heady pleasure already raced through her traitorous body. She fought it fiercely. The last time she'd let him kiss her, he'd trampled on her feelings afterward. "You . . . you . . . mustn't . . ."

He dropped the lock of hair, stroking it where it fell across her shoulder. Then he swept her shoulder free of it. "Is this what you meant by 'too far'?" He edged the sleeve of her chemise over to bare her shoulder. She caught her breath when he lowered his mouth to kiss the exposed skin. His breath was a feathery caress, a teasing promise.

When a soft sigh spiraled out of her, he turned his lips to the base of her throat. "Or this?" He skimmed his mouth along the smooth hollow as if seeking the pulse that jumped in a frenzy beneath his touch, and when he found it he kissed that, too, then followed it up the arch of her neck.

By the time he lifted his head, his eyes smoldered like barely banked embers in the flame that was his face. "No, I'd forgotten. Those are kisses, and 'too far' is more than a kiss or two, isn't it? 'Too far' must be enough to make my childhood friend doubt my good character. Now, what could that be?"

With his gaze still fixed on her face, he caught one sleeve of her chemise in his fist and inched it down past her shoulder. Color flooded her cheeks as she grabbed his hand at the wrist to stop him, but then he brought his mouth down on hers and she forgot why he shouldn't be here with her alone . . . why he shouldn't touch her like this, kiss her like this . . . why she didn't trust him . . . everything.

His kiss was deep and immediately possessive, his tongue entering her mouth before she even realized she'd parted her lips. The table edge dug into her palm where she gripped it in an attempt not to "draw him back" as he'd accused her of before.

But that was only a small victory, for she couldn't keep the rest of her body from responding, from straining against him, from welcoming his mouth as it urgently explored hers . . . or his hands as they worked the sleeves of her chemise over her shoulders . . . or his knee pressing in to part her thighs within the muslin prison of her scanty clothing. She even helped him by angling her head back as his lips kissed a path down her throat.

When he loosened the ties of her chemise, however, she came briefly to her senses, catching the muslin's edge before it could gape open and reveal her bare breasts. "Stop it! What do you think you're doing?"

"Determining my limits," he said in a husky voice. "How far is 'too far'?"

"*This* most certainly is!"

"Oh? But you said you didn't lie to Sara about my 'assault' that night, and I definitely don't remember doing this." His night black gaze locked on her face, but his hand cupped one muslin-covered breast in a bold caress that made her suck in a breath. "Then again, my memory *is* sometimes faulty. Perhaps I should refresh it."

"No, you . . . you . . ." Her mind went blank when his hand moved on her breast. It was exquisitely shameful and very delicious. "Oh, my word," said a throaty voice that surely belonged to someone other than her, the voice of a wanton.

"Did I touch you like this that night, Felicity?"

She closed her eyes to keep from witnessing his triumphant expression. He flattened his palm against her breast

and began a rotating motion that made her nipple tighten
into an aching kernel.

At her sharp intake of breath, he leaned close, his own
breath beating a hot tattoo against her cheek. "Tell me,
querida. Did I do this?"

The foreign word caught her off guard until she remembered that he was half-Spanish. And she was too embarrassed to ask what it meant.

"Answer me," he commanded in a harsher tone.

"No," she blurted out, heedless of her pride. "You know
you didn't."

When she forced her eyes open to face the gloating expression sure to be there, she was shocked to see he wasn't
gloating.

Raw need fractured his normally controlled features. "It's
a miracle I didn't," he confessed raggedly. "Because I
wanted to. God, how I wanted to."

His assertion salved her wounded pride. He hadn't been
merely manipulating her that night—he *had* felt what she'd
felt. And the things he did to her now—the kisses, the
caresses—were more than one of his cursed stratagems.

The realization renewed all her repressed longings, and
they gusted through her like an errant wind, blowing away
any thought of modesty or maidenly restraint. She leaned
eagerly into his hand. With a groan of pure male satisfaction, he caressed her in earnest . . . plucking at her nipple
through the muslin, gently pinching it with obvious exper-
tise, finding the other breast and submitting it to the same
torturous, glorious fondling.

To her shame, his caresses roused a most deplorable curiosity. How would it feel to have his bare fingers against
her skin? Or even his mouth? Scandalous thought!

But one he must have sensed, for he slid his hand inside
her chemise to cup her naked breast. The ensuing whirlwind of pleasure made her close her eyes and sigh aloud.
Good Lord, it was better than she'd imagined. Skin to skin,

his hand intimate with her flesh. Any lingering objections faded until the only thing remaining was an urgent need to know more, feel more, have him touch her more.

Her breathing grew labored, as if the insolent motion of his hand—no, his *hands*, for both of them were now inside her chemise—worked a magic that siphoned the very breath from her body. She'd never guessed her body possessed such an astonishing capacity for enjoyment or that a man could discover it with unerring ease.

"Ian . . ." she murmured, not even knowing what she wanted to say.

"Yes." His voice sounded hoarse and far away. "My God, you feel like heaven in my hands . . . so good . . . so sweet . . ."

He knelt on one knee and drew her chemise down so he could seize her breast with his mouth exactly as she'd imagined. Shocked as much by his uncanny ability to know her body's longings as by what he did, she clasped his head between her hands. He must stop this. She should make him stop this.

Yet she cradled his head closer, breathing in the scent of pipe smoke that clung to his hair. He made a growling noise in the back of his throat and slid his free hand around her thighs, then pulled her forward until she fell onto his bent leg, straddling it as she caught at his shoulders for balance. Her chemise bunched up her calves to accommodate the awkward position and exposed the buttoned bands of her drawers just below her knees. As he settled her more firmly astride his thigh, the slit in her drawers gaped open so that her most deeply private part pressed directly against his leg, with only a whisper of kerseymere separating his skin from hers.

Shock kept her motionless for a moment. This was a most decadent position. But when she squirmed in a vain attempt to sit more decorously, she found only more decadence. The intimate pressure was delicious. Indeed, whenever she squirmed away, the juncture between her thighs began to throb with an unseemly ache that only eased when she pressed herself against his thigh again.

She'd felt this ache before, late at night when she was half-asleep and dreaming of her sultan. The only thing that satisfied it, she was ashamed to admit, was pressure. She'd resorted to it once or twice, secretly, guiltily. And now she resorted to it again, rocking against his leg.

"That's it," he murmured against her breast. "Ride me, *querida*. Yes . . . yes . . ."

Though she didn't entirely understand what he meant, she needed no more encouragement to rub her most private place along his thigh. She clutched his head close again, leaning into him, straining to press more of her breast into his boldly sucking mouth. Thick strands of his hair spilled over her hands. The inky threads tickled her splayed fingers, sprouting up between them like wild rushes.

He made her feel wild—this rampant yearning between her legs, the delight of satisfying it by undulating on his thigh. His mouth was almost savage at her breast now, rousing such sinful responses in her that he had to be the devil.

She rocked forward on his thigh, a purring sound erupting from her when every shift of position sent glorious sensations through her lower limbs. He tore his mouth from her flesh, only to seize the other breast with equal fervor. His hand took over on the first breast, caressing the engorged, damp nipple while his mouth and tongue pleasured the plump curves of the other breast.

She was drowning, pleasure lapping over her in waves, the tobacco scent and the hard feel of him rising around her like floodwaters, threatening to engulf her, dissolve her.

A fierce urge to know more of him assailed her. She tugged restlessly at his lapels, and he shrugged his coat off, tossing it heedlessly to the floor as he returned to laving her breast with his tongue. She molded his muscles through his shirt, relishing the way they flexed beneath her fingers. He ran his large hand up her calf, then her knee and inside the leg of her drawers until the curve of her bare hip filled his fingers, his wondrous, caressing fingers . . .

Abruptly he stiffened and dragged his mouth from her breast, though his hand still cupped one naked buttock.

"Ian?" she questioned in disappointment.

"Shh," he cautioned, his head cocked as if he were listening.

Then she heard it, too, sounds of female conversation and meandering footsteps in the hall. She froze, her throat burning with raw emotion. Surely he hadn't planned for them to be caught again. And in a much more compromising position. Oh, Lord, if he'd done all this purposely to shame her—

He jerked his hand out of her drawers, his eyes an inky black as he met her gaze. The concern in them reassured her that he hadn't planned this. He gripped her upper arms. "It's Sara and Emily. Are you expecting them?"

She shook her head wordlessly, and he dug his fingers into her skin, every muscle of his face taut as he glanced back to the door.

The nursery lay across the hall from her room, and she wondered if that were their destination. The footsteps stopped outside her doorway, but the voices quickly lowered. They thought she was asleep. Little did they know.

Only when she heard the door across the hall opening and closing could she breathe again.

Ian's grip on her slackened. "Felicity." Though he merely whispered the word, it seemed to echo in the silence of her bedchamber.

"Yes?"

"*This* is 'too far.' "

She squelched her mad impulse to laugh. "I do believe you're right, my lord." She should get off his knee, thrust him away, take her fingers out of his hair. But she couldn't do any of those things.

He bent his head to tug at her nipple with his teeth, eliciting a gasp from her. Wanting him to do it again, she clasped him close. Her body wanted more from him, though she didn't know what. If he would only kiss her, suck her breast again, lay his hand upon her hip . . . His mouth did close urgently over her breast, sucking and teasing it until her yearning turned to an ache that was almost real pain.

But when she groaned and swayed against him, he went still. Laying his cheek against the nipple he'd just been devouring, he pressed a kiss to the inside curve of the opposite breast. "Make me stop this," he demanded, his tone harsh and guttural, his words an earnest plea.

It took a moment for his meaning to penetrate her dazed state. "Why?"

There was a long pause. He propped his forehead against her chest and after a second, she saw his head shaking. When he lifted his face, she realized he was laughing— mirthlessly, silently laughing.

"Trust you to be the only virgin in the realm who'd say that." Giving her breast one last tender kiss, he lifted her off his thigh and set her on her feet on the floor. Then he rose from his kneeling position.

Her wobbly legs threatened to buckle beneath her weight. When he caught her by the shoulders to steady her, then released her just as quickly, shame suffused her cheeks with scarlet.

Too late, much too late, she realized how far she'd gone. And that he'd been the one to stop it, not her. Yanking up her chemise, she fumbled awkwardly with the ties. "Good Lord in heaven, you must think me the most wanton creature—"

"No." He laid his index finger against her lips to silence her. "No, I don't. But you're the last woman on earth I should have touched like this." His thumb outlined her lips in a sensuous stroke that made her heart race.

Her fingers stilled on the ties of her chemise. She stared up into his unreadable face, hoping shamelessly that he'd kiss her again. When he dropped his hand instead, the intensity of her disappointment surprised her.

"Yet I cannot regret it," he added, almost as an afterthought.

Nor could she. She felt like a deaf-mute suddenly given the gift of hearing and speech. All those times she'd railed against men for using women to satisfy their passions, she hadn't dreamed women had passions, too, that could be as powerful, as devastating as this. It cast new light on all her assumptions.

When she dropped her gaze to where the ties of her chemise still lay half-knotted in her hands, he extricated them from her suddenly inept fingers and deftly finished tying them.

"One thing is for certain," he said in a low voice. "This time, you have every right to complain of me to Sara."

"I wouldn't do that," she whispered, hurt that he could even think it.

"Why not? Nothing has changed."

"*Everything* has changed." She didn't know why, but the entire world was different now. He was more moral than she'd expected, and she wasn't moral in the least. Indeed, she'd become a creature she didn't recognize, all in the space of a few heart-stopping kisses and caresses.

He tipped up her chin, his gaze boring into hers. "You don't think I'm a snake for trapping you in your room and taking liberties with you?"

She shook her head. "You stopped yourself, even though you could have done as you wished with me and I would have . . . would have . . ." She turned away from him with a choked sob, unable to finish the shameful statement.

When he'd kissed her on the balcony, she'd convinced herself that her dreamy capitulation had been a momentary and perfectly understandable reaction to a rake's charms. He'd kept her there by force, she'd told herself. He'd taken her off guard.

But although tonight had begun as before, it hadn't ended the same. She'd reveled in her sin, had welcomed each caress. In short, she'd behaved like a wanton. Only his presence of mind had prevented her from giving herself to him.

Lifting her head, she caught sight of her image in the mirror. She even looked the part—her lips were reddened, her hair mussed, and she wore only her chemise and her drawers. With an anguished moan, she snatched her dressing gown off the floor and shoved her arms back through the opaque sleeves.

"It's nothing to be ashamed of," he reassured her, laying his hand on her shoulder. "Everyone has desires, and women can control them no easier than men. If anything, it's harder for women. Society expects men to sate their desires at will, but respectable women are expected to suppress theirs, even with their own husbands. It doesn't make for easy relations. Or fair ones."

The observation astonished her so much that she forgot her guilty thoughts. She faced him with widened eyes. "That's a very progressive opinion, you know."

"I'm a very progressive man," he said dryly, "despite what you think of me."

Her gaze locked with his. Yes, she'd begun to realize that. Certainly he wasn't the dissolute rake she'd thought him to be. But what was he? What kind of man restrained his urges when he had both the opportunity and the motive to take advantage of a woman? Lord knows she'd been too swept up by his expert seductions to quibble over niceties like reputation, honor, and chastity.

"You *are* progressive," she acknowledged. "And you've shown me mercy when I didn't expect it. Or . . . deserve it."

"Mercy?" He gave a hollow laugh. "Is that what this is? Strange, but it feels like insanity." He cupped her cheek in his hand. "No man in his right mind would turn you away when he could bed you. I must have lost my wits."

This time she couldn't doubt his sincerity, and his fervent words made hot desire bubble up inside her once more. She forced it down firmly. "No. You simply exercised restraint, which demonstrates that you're indeed a gentleman."

With a curse, he dropped his hand and pivoted away from her. "Don't fool yourself. I didn't do it out of any gentlemanly impulse, I assure you. I merely can't afford too many more of your damned articles in the paper."

She didn't believe him. Maybe she *was* fooling herself, but she doubted he'd drawn back out of fear of her articles. The man feared nothing under the heavens, and certainly not her.

He stared across the room at the closed door, tucking his thumbs in the waistband of his glove-tight pantaloon trousers. "So are we even now? Or shall I expect more reports of my activities in the *Gazette?*" His face was rigid, expectant, as if he wouldn't be surprised to hear that she intended to continue her attacks on him.

It shamed her that he could think she'd go on writing about him after what they'd done. "Shall I expect more of your attempts to expose my identity to your friends?"

He shot her a solemn glance. "I'll keep quiet if you will."

"Then we're agreed. Lord X no longer has any quarrel with the Viscount St. Clair and vice versa." *Nor any reason to speak to him,* she thought, an inexplicable pain gripping her chest. *No connection to him now whatsoever.*

His jaw went taut. He faced her fully, trailing his gaze down over her trembling body, then back up to her face. He now wore an expression of resigned acceptance. "That's probably best. After all, it wouldn't do for the viscount to quarrel with his fiancée so publicly."

She gaped at him. "Fiancée?"

"Our encounter here this evening has brought me to a decision." He cleared his throat, his gaze sweeping over her once more. "Felicity, you and I should marry."

Chapter 10

Colonel Shelby informed his long-suffering fiancée that due to his injuries during the war, he did not think it fair of him to hold her to their engagement. But when the faithful woman said she loved him for his heart alone, he gladly relented. The wedding will take place on Candlemas at St. Martin-in-the-Fields.

LORD X, *THE EVENING GAZETTE*,
DECEMBER 13, 1820

Ian could tell from Felicity's incredulous expression that he'd surprised her. What else could he expect? He'd bloody well shocked himself.

"Wh-What did you say?" she stammered.

"I said we should marry."

He hadn't meant to be so blunt. He certainly hadn't intended to propose when he'd come up to her room an hour ago. He'd meant only to scare her a little, make her see she couldn't continue this battle between them.

Then she'd put on that damned dressing gown, the bit of lace that showed more than it concealed. He should never have watched her undress. He should have revealed his presence before then. But three days away from her had made him hungry, even after reading her inflammatory column. Three days and three nights of remembering their searing kisses had made him want a glimpse of her body, and she'd obliged him so quickly that he'd been powerless to end it by revealing his presence in the room.

Still, he didn't regret a minute of it. Nor did he regret proposing marriage. True, his decision had been hasty and his reasons complex and tangled even to him. Felicity, with her love of rumor and her unbounded curiosity, was the last person he should marry.

Yet he wanted her in his life. No other woman could match him tactic for tactic and forever surprise him. Marriage to her would be anything but boring.

He watched as she swung around and walked to the fireplace. Lambent light bathed her slender body, and her flimsy wrapper clung greedily to her very attractive derriere. Lust bolted through him anew. With a groan, he admitted the truth to himself. He didn't only want her in his life—he wanted her in his bed. That was the trouble; he wasn't thinking with his head—or at least not the one with a brain. Otherwise, he'd never be considering marriage to this clever miss with her penchant for gossip.

But he'd made up his mind. He needed a wife—why not have one he'd enjoy? God knows he would enjoy her; it had taken every ounce of his self-control to keep from stripping her naked and acting on all the carnal impulses her winsome body inspired.

Two things had prevented him. The first was her status as a respectable virgin. It went against his moral code to deflower that sort of woman. The second—and perhaps more compelling—reason was the sure knowledge that a single night with her would never satisfy him, and she'd never allow him more. He might seduce her once, but his self-righteous gossipmonger would cut her throat before she'd consent to being any man's mistress.

Besides, he didn't need a mistress. He needed a wife. And if he married her, they could have as many nights in bed as their passions allowed. The very thought made him hard again.

"Well?" he bit out impatiently when she lifted the brass poker and stoked the fire in apparent distraction. Sparks danced in the cold air about her tempting body.

"You're asking me . . . to marry you." She stumbled over the words, as if they still seemed alien to her.

"It's not such an odd idea, is it?"

"I-I don't know. I mean, yes, it is. You're a viscount."

"Now that's an astute observation," he muttered, garnering a frown from her. He made a dismissive gesture. "It has nothing to do with anything."

She set the poker aside and faced him. "Doesn't it? I'm a nobody. Why would you want to marry *me*?"

Deliberately, he trailed his gaze down her welter of rich cinnamon hair, past the delicious breasts he'd pleasured, to the part of her he wished he'd also pleasured and tasted and sampled . . . When his gaze snapped back to her face, he saw she understood. "I want to marry you for the same reason any man marries a woman he desires."

Scarlet color stained her cheeks, and it occurred to him that he seldom saw her blush. It was becoming, especially on her. He'd have to make her blush frequently once they were married.

"But men of your sort—"

"Be careful, Felicity. I tire of your generalizations about men of my 'sort.' "

She eyed him with disbelief. "You can't tell me you don't care at all that I have no family connections or great wealth or—"

"Why should I? I have enough for both of us. That's not what I want in a wife."

"Yes, I forgot." Her fingers clutched at the edges of her wrapper as she struggled to keep it closed. She looked suddenly very young, young and tormented, her eyes bleak with dismay. "You want a woman to bear your heir."

"That would be one of your duties, yes." When she went rigid, he added, "But children are the usual result of indulging one's desires, and as I recall, you find that particular activity appealing."

Her gaze shot to his, shadowed with embarrassment. "You said there was nothing wrong with feeling desire."

"I meant it," he reassured her, remembering how ashamed her eager response to his caresses had made her. "And marriage makes desire far more convenient."

He realized he'd said the wrong thing when her pretty chin quivered. "Yes, marriage would make it convenient, for *you* as well as me. After all, why rely on two separate women for all your needs—one to bear your children and the other to satisfy your . . . your manly urges?" Her voice grew bitter. "Think how convenient it would be to have only one woman serve both purposes. What a revolutionary concept."

"I've never wanted more than one woman at a time," he ground out, wondering how this discussion had gotten out of hand. "And yes, I prefer to have a wife I can desire. Although I'd previously resigned myself to a comfortable, if passionless, marriage, I now realize I can have more. Is there anything wrong with that?"

"I don't know." She stuck her chin out. "What would Miss Greenaway think?"

The air crackled between them, fraught with sudden tension. He should have seen the question coming. If he'd been this dense during the war, he would have gotten himself killed half a dozen times. That he hadn't anticipated her objections was a testimony to how much she and her adorable body had disconcerted him.

Carefully, he weighed his words. "Her opinion is of no matter."

"Oh? Then what role will she play in this marriage?"

"None at all." Sheer exasperation sharpened his tone. "I

told you before—the woman is *not* my mistress. I'm helping her and her son, nothing more."

"You still expect me to believe that fairy tale about her
brother being your soldier friend?" When he glowered at
her, she added, "I realize you told the truth about fighting
for England—I can hardly ignore the assertions of a man
like Wellington. But I know you're lying about Miss
Greenaway's connection to you. I'm not a fool, you know."

"Of course not." Sarcasm edged his words. "You're
much too intelligent to believe in my generosity or loyalty
to a friend."

A pained expression crossed her face. "I deserve that, I
suppose, but you're wrong—I can believe many good
things about you. What I can't believe is that Miss Greenaway would have refused to set me straight concerning your
kindness. Any woman in her position would have defended
you at once. Or gone to the *Gazette* after the article was
published to demand a retraction."

Why must the woman be so bloody logical? "Miss
Greenaway understands, as you do not, that I prefer to keep
certain aspects of my past *out* of the newspapers."

"And secret from your prospective fiancée?"

He groaned. "Damn it, Felicity—"

"I want to know what she is to you." Hurt dulled her
green eyes, and when she spoke again, her voice cracked.
"I-I don't think it's an unreasonable request, considering
your proposal to me."

It hit him then. My God, the woman was jealous! Though
that absurdly pleased him, it also complicated matters. He
was sorely tempted to tell her the truth and put an end to
her foolish concerns. But that would require more than a
simple explanation of how he knew Miss Greenaway. He'd
have to explain why he was helping the woman, why she
was necessary to his plans for his uncle, and why he and
his uncle were enemies. He'd have to entrust London's
most notorious scribbler with the scandalous details of his

life. And he'd have to do it without even being sure it would gain him her hand. No one in their right mind would agree to that.

Still, he wouldn't let her jealousy stand between them.

He advanced on her with grim determination. "I'll tell you what Miss Greenaway is *not*. She's *not* my mistress nor any temptation to me. Her son isn't mine, or I would have claimed him long ago. Most importantly, what she is to me has nothing to do with you. She will never have any influence over our marriage. That's all you need to know."

Anger flared in her face. "You won't even tell me how you met her?"

"No." He paused a few feet from her, deliberately softening his tone. "Trust me, there's no reason why her mere existence in a house that I own should concern you."

"And that's your final word on the subject?"

"Yes."

"Then my answer is no."

His eyes narrowed. "Your answer to what?"

"Your offer of marriage. I can't marry a man who won't be honest with me."

He couldn't believe his ears. "You're refusing me because you're jealous of some woman I'm helping?"

"I'm *not* jealous!" she protested, though her expression belied her words. "I'm . . . I'm refusing you because you don't want a real marriage. You want a business arrangement: I am to perform my duty by bearing you children without interfering in your life, and in exchange you'll give me your name and pay for my gowns."

"And make love to you," he added in a husky voice, determined to remind her of why this conversation had first come about.

She edged closer to the fireplace, the tips of her ears pinkening. "Yes. That, too. But anyone could serve that purpose for you. I merely happen to be convenient."

"Believe me, if I were choosing a wife by convenience,

you would *not* be on the list. The last thing I need is a loose-tongued newspaper writer sharing my bed!"

Her gaze shot back to him, a new comprehension shining in their depths. "So *that's* your reason for proposing! You want to marry me so I won't dig up the nasty secrets in your past and publish them in my column!"

"Oh, for God's— You already agreed to keep quiet. Why on earth should I marry you merely to gain *that*?"

"Because you don't trust me. If you did, you'd tell me the truth about Miss Greenaway."

He ground his teeth in frustration. Damn the bloody female and her ideals! Most men kept secrets from their wives—it was accepted, even expected. But she wouldn't allow it—oh, no. Not his self-righteous little troublemaker, with her unrealistic ideas about how men should behave in marriage! He should have heeded his earlier warning that she'd never agree to marry him. But no, he'd had to let his cock do his thinking.

Well, he'd proposed and made a fool of himself sufficiently. Now he should wash his hands of her, leave her to her suspicions. Could any woman be worth all this trouble?

He gazed at her angry stance, at the delicate hands planted on the choicest pair of hips this side of the Channel, at the expressive eyes flashing emerald. Even haphazardly attired with pencils stuck through her hair, she'd been enticing, but now, wearing that excuse for a wrapper, she was irresistible. He'd never seen a young woman so full of life, audacity, and a sensual promise shimmering from her in waves, especially when her temper was roused.

Yes, this woman was worth any trouble. And he began to see that convincing her to marry him would take more than one seductive interlude and some discussion.

All right, so he'd plan a more elaborate strategy. He hadn't been a spy for nothing. And he still had a little time to be patient.

"Well?" she said, interrupting his thoughts. "You do understand, don't you? I shan't marry you, Ian, and nothing you say will change my decision."

"You've made that perfectly clear," he said in a neutral tone.

She eyed him with suspicion. "So you won't pursue this any further?"

"No." *Not until I think of a suitable strategy for it.*

She seemed startled by his easy acquiescence. "And my refusal of your proposal won't affect our agreement?"

"What agreement?"

"That I won't write anything about you in my column, and you won't expose me."

He'd forgotten about that. Bloody hell, that was perfect! She was handing him his strategy on the proverbial platter! He could use her fear of exposure to his advantage.

Turning away, he clasped his hands together behind his back and strolled the room as if deep in thought. "That's a different matter entirely, isn't it? Thanks to the false insinuations in your most recent column, I now have the reputation of being a coward and a liar, which will make it difficult for me to find a wife. In essence, you've 'ruined' me, yet you refuse to do the honorable thing and marry me. So why shouldn't I expose you?"

"Don't be absurd! I haven't 'ruined' you—surely many women would marry you for your fortune and your title alone!"

Halting near the bed, he shrugged. "It's not easy to find a wife when one has my reputation. I've looked for two years." She needn't know that he'd been more particular than most, which was partly responsible for his current dilemma. "In that time, the closest I've come to an actual engagement was with your friend Katherine, and you ended that with your revelations about my private life."

"Revelations that were true! It's not my fault you have a mistress!"

"Even if Miss Greenaway *were* my mistress, which she

isn't," he said evenly, "it was you who exposed my association with her, thus destroying my engagement. In the process, you drove Katherine to elope with a man who might very well be a fortune hunter. Your meddling cost me and your friend a great deal. Surely you'll admit that."

She sniffed. "I admit only that I wrote what my conscience dictated."

Sometimes he found her bloody self-righteousness almost amusing. "And in the second column? Did your conscience also dictate that you make baseless assumptions about my war career?"

Guilt suffused her face, as he'd known it would. "All right, I'll admit that was badly done, and I regret it." She set her shoulders with stubborn determination. "But I can set the record straight in Lord X's next col—"

"How? I assure you, Wellington won't repeat his words to Gideon. No one in the government will acknowledge me. And if you present only rumor, that will make your readers doubt me more, not less. No, you've opened that Pandora's box, and you'll never be able to shut it."

"What do you *want* from me? I can't marry you, Ian!"

"Yet I still need a wife." He rubbed his chin, casting her a speculative glance. "So why don't you provide me with a replacement for yourself."

Clearly, he'd startled her. "Whatever do you mean?"

"You know many young women, and you have the ear of society even without your column. I'm sure you could find me someone to marry."

"Find you a wife?" The panic in her expression pleased him inordinately. "Don't be ridiculous! I-I wouldn't know who or how or—"

"Then you plan to leave me in this situation?"

"Yes. No! I-I mean—" She broke off, her eyes narrowing. "You act as if you must marry at once. But if you'll only wait until the gossip dies down—"

"I can't," he bit out, then cursed himself when her brow knit in confusion.

"Why not?"

After years of spying, coming up with a plausible reason for his urgency took only a second's thought, especially since it was almost true. "Searching for a wife takes me away from my estate. I've spent two fruitless years on the endeavor; I can ill afford another." A sudden inspiration hit him. "And consider this—you spend a great deal of time at social events advancing your profession, while I spend the same time looking for a wife. It would make perfect sense for us to help each other in our endeavors."

With a wary look, she folded her arms over her chest. "Each other? Exactly how would you help *me*?"

He raised an eyebrow. "By not exposing your real identity, of course."

Alarm lit her features. "You mean if I don't find you a wife, you'll expose me?"

He suppressed a smile. "Let's just say that your refusal to help me with my problem will encourage me to start a rumor or two about Lord X's true identity. You could hardly blame me for that, given the 'rumors' you've spread about *me*."

Gliding away from the fireplace, she wandered to the dressing table. She braced her hands on the greenish wood surface and stared into the mirror as if to find answers in her reflection. His gut tightened at the sight. He didn't like playing these games, but he saw no other way to secure her.

And secure her he would, no matter what stratagem he must use. He'd have that waist-length hair scattered across a pillow and those hands clutching him close. He'd have those honey-sweet lips and that lissome body, rampant with sensual secrets. And yes, that bloody sharp mind of hers would be his, too. He wanted it all. As soon as he could get it.

In the mirror, he saw her gaze shift to him, haunted, reluctant. Bitter. "To think that a few minutes ago, I called you a gentleman."

The accusation stung, but not enough to change his mind. "Everyone makes mistakes," he said softly. "And your mistake lies in underestimating me. I'm not a gentleman when it comes to getting what I want. You should have learned that by now."

Folding her arms over her breasts like a Christian maid meeting the heathens, she faced him. "What if I do as I threatened before? Find out your secrets and print them?"

"Come now, Felicity, do you really want war between us? Over the mere possibility of helping with my hunt for a wife?" He stepped toward her. "I'm not asking you to drag a woman into the church for me. I merely want you to praise me to your unattached female friends, introduce me here and there, and try to negate the effects of your most recent column. Surely you don't think me undeserving of *anyone* simply because I don't suit *you*. Am I so evil as all that?"

The starch went out of her posture. Bending her head, she fiddled with the lace ties of her wrapper. "N-No, of course not."

He pressed his advantage. "Think of the opportunity this will afford you to make my life miserable. You can choose only sharp-tongued women or ugly women or even cruel women. In my current state of desperation, I'll take nearly anyone you find me."

Meeting his gaze, she said archly, "Somehow I doubt that."

He smiled. "You know me so well. You see? You could be a great help to me."

Her consternation at his words was so transparent, he marveled that she didn't realize herself how unwilling she was to marry him off elsewhere. Stubborn woman. Her pride kept her from accepting him. *And* her jealousy, no matter what she protested.

Well, he'd use that jealousy against her. He'd make her see that watching him court someone else was much worse than enduring his protection of Miss Greenaway. And if he had to dance with ten thousand women to make her see that, so be it.

Felicity cast a quick look up to heaven as if hoping for the Deity to advise her on his proposal. Then she lowered her gaze to his. "All right. I'll do what I can."

"Thank you." When she went limp, he added, "And don't think to renege once we're back in London. I shall hold you to your promise."

"I'm sure you will," she said morosely.

Her misery delighted him. She was his already, whether she admitted it or not. "Tomorrow," he said, "I must be off early to attend to business in London, but tomorrow night, I'll be at Lord Caswell's party. You intend to go, too, don't you?"

She gave a stiff nod.

"Good. You can begin your efforts on my behalf then." He couldn't resist adding, "Of course, if you change your mind about my proposal—"

"I shan't," she retorted, though he noticed her words lacked conviction this time.

"Very well. Until tomorrow." He gave a slight bow, then headed off toward the door. He didn't want to leave. What he wanted was to toss her onto the feather bed and make love to her until morning. With any other woman, that would ensure a marriage.

But it might not with Felicity, and he wouldn't risk the possibility that compromising her might firm her resolve to resist him.

As he opened the door, she called out behind him. "Wait, Ian!"

He turned with his hand on the knob to find her coming

toward him with his coat, which he'd forgotten on the floor. As she neared him, however, her gaze shifted to a spot behind him, and the color drained from her face. He followed the direction of her gaze, already guessing what he would find.

Standing outside the nursery across the hall were several people who'd apparently been engaged in earnest conversation until he opened the door: Sara's housekeeper, a nursery maid, another servant . . . and Sara and Emily. All eyes were locked on him standing in his shirtsleeves and Felicity clutching his coat, dressed in only her chemise and wrapper.

The servants melted away at once, averting their eyes as they scurried off along the hallway, but Sara and Emily stood frozen. Then shock hardened Sara's expression, while Emily began to smile.

Ian scarcely had time to decide how to handle the awkward situation. Much as he wished he could use it to force Felicity's hand, he doubted that would work. She was much too independent to be swayed by his friends' advice and would resent him even more if he urged the marriage on the basis of her now-compromised reputation.

Yet as his gaze locked with Sara's, it occurred to him that Sara would be a good ally. The only way to gain her support, however, was to ensure she had a clear grasp of the facts and not merely what tale Felicity might spin.

"Good evening, ladies." He smiled with casual ease. "I hope there's nothing wrong in the nursery." He heard Felicity groan behind him, but ignored her, focusing instead on Sara.

The young countess glared at him. "What are you doing here, Ian?"

"Miss Taylor has agreed to help me in my search for a wife," he said truthfully. "We were consulting on strategy."

"Yes," Felicity chimed in with great eagerness. "Lord St. Clair and I were having a long discussion on the matter."

As Emily rolled her eyes, Sara glanced at Felicity. "But my dear, the way you're dressed—"

Ian shot Felicity an amused glance, wondering how she would explain *that* one away. With a little gasp of dismay, Felicity tugged her wrapper closed. Clearly, she'd forgotten she was wearing only her chemise and a scrap of lace.

"Don't blame Miss Taylor," Ian told Sara with great magnanimity. "I surprised her after she'd already prepared for bed, and we became so engrossed in our conversation that we completely forgot about the proprieties. Besides, Miss Taylor is fairly nonchalant about such matters."

"So nonchalant that you removed your coat?" Her tone was stiff as starch, as stern as any mother's. "Don't try to fool me, Ian. I know how you men work. And if you think I'll allow you to take advantage of a woman in my house—"

"Truly, Sara, nothing happened," Felicity protested. "I know it looks bad, but—"

"You needn't defend him," Sara retorted. "I know what he is about."

Ian raised one eyebrow. "Do you really? Then you must know that I proposed marriage to Miss Taylor."

With a look of shock, Sara shifted her gaze to Felicity. "Is this true?"

He fancied he could feel the heat of Felicity's anger warm his back.

"Yes." Felicity hurried to add, "But I refused him. We discussed it, and that's all that happened. I swear it."

Ian bit back a smile of triumph. Felicity might think her revelation would extricate her from this, but she didn't know Sara as well as he did. The woman loved making matches, and both she and Emily were eager to see him married. They'd be on his side from now on, especially if it looked as if he were reasonable and Felicity were simply foolish.

How else *could* it look, after all? Without revealing what

she knew about his connection to Miss Greenaway and how she knew it, Felicity could never reasonably explain why she'd refused him. Thus her refusal would seem inexplicable, and Sara would have all the more reason to work at matching them up.

In truth, there was already a dangerously familiar gleam in his friend's eye. "You refused Ian?"

"Yes." Felicity looked from Sara to Emily. When she caught sight of Emily's broad smile, her expression grew panicky. "That's why I agreed to help. Him, I mean. You know, find a wife. Because I refused him. He said if I wouldn't marry him, I ought to help, and I agreed, and we . . . we had a perfectly civil conversation. That's all that happened. Truly . . ."

As Felicity trailed off, Sara shot him a questioning look. His only answer was a smile. Her brown eyes darkened. "Ian, I'll speak to you in a moment downstairs. Just now I wish to talk to Miss Taylor. Alone."

"Of course." He glanced at Felicity, whose wide eyes and pale face showed her bewilderment. If she only knew what Sara was about to put her through . . . He didn't envy her that, having once or twice been at the mercy of Sara's matchmaking attempts.

Still, he felt a perverse need to reassure Felicity that he'd keep silent about her identity as Lord X. He laid his hand on her shoulder, trying not to react to the sheer pleasure of touching her. "You needn't worry about my discretion in this matter, nor that of my friends. I'm sure they can keep the servants quiet as well. Despite all the talk earlier this evening, no one will discuss this affair with the gossips, and especially not with Lord X. The man won't be brought into it, I assure you. Certainly not by me."

Felicity's eyes locked with his, and he saw understanding flicker briefly in them. He owed her that much . . . to protect her secret.

But though he didn't realize it, Felicity was still confused. What was he attempting with this new ploy? He could have used this opportunity to force her into marriage, but he hadn't. Why was he being so truthful with his friends, so defensive of her honor? And so willing to keep her secrets?

"If you ladies will excuse me," he added, "I'll leave you to your talk."

He strolled off down the hall, leaving Felicity to shake her head. "I'll never understand that man."

"None of us ever have," Sara remarked at her side. Gently, she took Felicity's arm. "Come, my dear, let's go into your room before more servants happen along and see you standing here in *that*. Never fear, we'll help you figure out how to deal with Ian."

The statement brought Felicity up short. What was there to figure out? She and Ian had made a simple agreement, and she'd told Sara and Emily there would be no marriage. What else was left to discuss?

Yet the two women obviously thought there was *something* to talk about. They both stared at her expectantly. Suddenly it dawned on her—they wanted to discuss why she wouldn't marry Ian. His reasonable manner and willingness to marry her had convinced them that he was behaving like a gentleman while she was either a fool or a wanton. They wanted to know which one it was.

Her heart began to thud in her chest. She couldn't even explain, not without revealing what she knew of Ian's character. That would mean revealing her identity.

Very well, she thought defiantly, she wouldn't tell them a dratted thing. Let them think what they wanted of her.

Then she saw Sara's sympathetic smile. She groaned. Sara had championed her earlier tonight. She'd taken Felicity's side for no reason other than friendship. And brazening this out would mean losing that friendship. Ian could make her out to be whatever he wished—fickle, a fool, even a wanton—and they would believe him because she'd provided no explanation of her own.

She searched her mind frantically for a plausible explanation of her refusal, but could think of nothing. Any reason would require blatantly lying about Ian, and she couldn't do that—not to Sara. Not after what had happened before.

Ian had realized that, hadn't he? The manipulative rat. He was counting on her not to lie or come up with a believable explanation. He was counting on her to brazen it out. Then Sara and Emily would remain on his side, and she'd lose them as friends.

She couldn't win. Not unless she told them the truth. Her spirits lightened suddenly. Yes, the truth—perhaps it was as simple as that. Unburden herself to them, explain everything from beginning to end, and trust to their good sense.

It was risky, yet they were both sensible women. Surely they would understand and stand by her once they knew everything.

The possibility was enticing beyond belief. Oh, to have someone who knew enough to give her good, honest advice. They *could* help her figure out how to deal with Ian— him and his secrets, him and his insistence that she help him find a wife when the very thought of it made her sick with jealousy.

"You really can trust us," Sara was saying. "Ian spoke the truth about our discretion, you know—we would never gossip about you. And as for Lord X, I can't imagine why he mentioned the man. I don't even know the columnist—"

"Yes, you do," Felicity broke in. "Lord X has been in your midst all along."

The mixture of confusion and disbelief on their faces almost struck her as humorous. Almost. After all, they might take her confession ill. They might hate her afterward.

She only hoped they didn't.

"What do you mean?" Emily asked. "Surely you don't think one of us—"

"No." Felicity hesitated, but only for a second. This was her best course of action, and she would follow it wherever it led. "Not one of you: me. *I* am Lord X."

Chapter 11

In these enlightened times, it is troublesome to see so many marital unions formed without respect to affection, disposition, or compatibility. Does it matter if financial or political success results from such a union when the individual parties cannot enjoy it?

LORD X, *THE EVENING GAZETTE*,
DECEMBER 13, 1820

Sara sat on Felicity's bed with her legs tucked up beneath her, unable to pretend nonchalance as she watched the young woman pace the dimly lit bedchamber relating her amazing tale. Sara might have questioned its veracity if everything hadn't fit so beautifully with what she herself had observed in the past few days.

Felicity Taylor was Lord X? All this time London's most notorious columnist had been visiting in her home, and Sara had never once guessed the truth. How astonishing!

She glanced over at Emily, who perched on the dressing-table stool. Emily's occasional nod and encouraging murmur indicated that she sympathized deeply with the young woman. That was understandable—Emily knew what it was like to maintain an elaborate pretense, having been forced into a masquerade last year that had nearly lost her everything. But then Emily had acted upon peril to her life, whereas Felicity . . .

Sara shook her head, returning her attention to Felicity, whose bold telling of her story contrasted with the feminine lace of her attire. Felicity was *not* like other young women of society that Sara knew. Then again, neither was Emily. Or herself.

Indeed, Sara did sympathize with Felicity's motives for her actions—the woman's concern for Miss Hastings's future and then her humiliation after Ian had embarrassed her on the balcony. While Sara could never have initiated so public a battle, she certainly would have done *something* to retaliate. For heaven's sake, Ian had toyed with Felicity's affections, then pretended *she* was the wanton. Sara ought to have done more than toss Ian out of the house; she should have boxed his ears, too. Just wait until she got him alone later—he'd get an earful from her!

One thing puzzled her, however. Why had Ian persisted in keeping Felicity's secret about Lord X? Felicity said he had something to hide, but Sara wondered if he had another reason, one more romantic. That possibility intrigued her enormously.

The young woman was staring at her now, a guilty expression on her face. "You must find all this so horrible," Felicity said, apparently misinterpreting Sara's look of concentration. "You can never know how sorry I am that I misled you about Ian. I still think of it with shame. But I didn't know you then. I couldn't believe you might understand what really happened. And I didn't know how kind you are or how different from most—" She broke off, her embarrassment more than obvious.

"Most what?" Sara prodded.

Felicity swallowed visibly. "Most women of rank. They all treat me with condescension." She glanced away, her gaze hardening. "They like me to entertain them with gossip or tales about Papa, but when I'm done, they cast me aside like any other amusement, leaving me to fend for myself with their sons and their husbands."

"As did I," Sara said softly.

"No! It wasn't the same. Despite what I let you believe that night, Ian never took advantage of me. Not really. It was my own fault that I . . . that I . . ."

"Took his actions to heart? Believed in his kisses? No, that wasn't your fault."

"But I brought it on myself with my columns," Felicity protested.

"Which you had every reason to write," Sara interjected. "I don't blame you in this. I wouldn't like having my feelings trampled on by some careless lord either."

"Still, it wasn't the same," she said in a low voice.

"The same as what?"

Felicity crossed her arms over her chest, her gaze downcast. "Those others. The ones I met because of Papa."

Sara sucked in a breath. "What did the others do to you?"

"Oh, nothing very terrible," Felicity said hastily, though her arms tightened over her chest. "An unwanted kiss here, a groping hand there, when I got older. I-I was eleven when I began to go with Papa to his patrons' houses and take notes for him."

A faint smile touched her lips. "He had awful handwriting. He couldn't even read it himself half the time. And I liked going with him to all those grand houses." Her smile faded. "That is, until I found out what the people in them were like."

"Not all of them, surely," Emily put in.

"Oh, no! Just some of the men. It was usually the eldest sons who wanted to 'entertain' me when Papa was busy with their parents, after I grew old enough to interest them. But I could handle them most of the time. And our footman showed me how to . . . um . . . hit them with my knee where it hurt."

"Good for him," Sara said, glad of protective servants.

"It was only the fathers who gave me any real trouble. I knew it wasn't wise to rebuff them as boldly as I did their sons, so I had to be more creative in my refusals."

The thought of a girl fighting off a grown man's advances roused Sara's outrage. "Where were these men's wives, for God's sake? The young men—where were their mothers? Did they not teach their sons any better than to assault young female guests?"

"Women tend to look the other way. Or worse." Felicity spoke the words dispassionately, but Sara saw the pain she tried to hide. "Pelh—One man's wife who caught her husband . . . making advances to me blamed me to Papa and advised him to give me a good thrashing."

"Surely he didn't take her advice!" Sara exclaimed in horror.

Felicity looked startled. "Oh, no, Papa never lifted a hand to any of his children. In the case of my brothers, it might have been better if he had. Papa told the woman she was a jealous old witch with an octopus for a husband, and refused to continue the project." Her tone filled with self-reproach. "It took him a year to find another that paid as well, and Mama and I worked ourselves to death taking in mending."

Sara saw bitterness flash across Felicity's face, and her tender heart softened all the more. "So you learned not to complain about the men's roving hands, didn't you? Better to put up with it than be responsible for your family's loss of fortune."

A wan smile touched Felicity's lips. "As always, Lady Worthing, you are more perceptive than most."

"Won't you call me by my given name anymore?" Sara asked gently.

"I don't deserve to." Felicity's face was wrought with remorse as she turned to pace once more. "I'm so ashamed. You've been nothing but kind to me from the day I arrived, but I abused your hospitality horribly that night on the balcony."

"Nonsense," Emily put in with a glance at Sara. "You did what was needed to survive. When men use seduction as a weapon, they leave us with only deceit as a defense. Besides, if I remember what Sara told me, Lady Brumley was also present. You could hardly have let her know what had really gone on."

"Emily's right," Sara said. "I don't blame you for misleading me." Suddenly, an image of Ian glaring at her when she'd thrown him out of the house sprang into her head, making her laugh. "And if ever a man needed his pride pricked, it's Ian. You should have seen his face when I accused him of taking advantage of you under my roof. I've never seen him look so offended."

"And with good reason." Felicity's gaze swept briefly to the dressing table. "Although he repaid me amply for that maneuver."

Sara sobered. "You haven't yet told us what he did this evening after you left the card room and came up here. I know the two of you didn't simply talk. Yet I also can't believe Ian would be so callous as to . . . I mean, he did not . . . he didn't—"

"No." But Felicity's blush belied the words. "He kissed me again. That's all."

Emily laughed. "If that's true, then Ian is more of a gentleman than my husband ever was."

"And mine," Sara added with a chuckle.

Their words seemed to shock Felicity. "But your husbands are so gentlemanly!"

"Oh, they have the trappings of civilized men, to be sure." Sara reclined against a pillow on Felicity's bed, propping herself up at the elbows. "That's only because we won't tolerate anything less in public. In private, well . . ." She couldn't prevent the smile that curved her mouth when she remembered Gideon's fierce lovemaking this morning.

"They're wicked as can be, aren't they, Emily?"

"Thank goodness," Emily retorted, her eyes shining in the firelight.

Felicity halted her pacing, looking from one to the other in complete confusion. "So this evening when I let Ian . . . when he made me feel . . . Am I not—"

"Wicked because you felt desire?" Sara shook her head, remembering all too well her self-disgust when Gideon had first stolen past her defenses and made her desire him. "There's nothing wrong in feeling desire, my dear."

"That's what Ian said, too," Felicity whispered.

"Still," Sara added hastily, "that doesn't mean he can make love to you without taking responsibility for his actions."

Felicity scowled. "Oh, he's eager to take responsibility, even though all he did was . . ." She blushed again. "Anyway, that's the trouble—he wants to marry me."

"Yes, he did say that. Which means his feelings were sincere."

"Or at least his desire was sincere," Emily added with an edge of cynicism.

Sara regarded her sister-in-law thoughtfully. Emily knew Ian's recent character better than she. Did Emily think Ian incapable of anything but desire? Sara couldn't believe that. "In any case," she went on, returning her gaze to Felicity, "you refused him. You truly have no wish to marry Ian?"

"None." Felicity's words held conviction; her expression did not. She began to pace again. "How could I marry a man whose only interest in me is as a mother to his heir? I have responsibilities—I have four brothers to care for and an entire household that depends on me. Ian wouldn't want to take all that upon himself."

"How do you know? Did you ask him?"

"I don't need to. He only wants me because I can provide him with his heir. And I'm sure he also hopes to rid himself of my troublesome interference in his affairs. He thinks to do all of it by marrying me. Ours wouldn't be a real marriage, however." Her tone grew wistful. "It wouldn't be like either of yours, and I want nothing less."

"Good for you," Emily said. "Every woman deserves a man who cares about her. But judging from the way Ian looks at no one else when you're in the room, the way only you seem to rouse his fury—and his passions—I think he *does* care for you."

"The man doesn't know the first thing about caring," Felicity said petulantly, "or he wouldn't lie to me about that . . . that *woman*!"

Sara straightened, her interest piqued. "You mean his friend on Waltham Street?"

"Yes! He won't tell me the truth about her! He admits that Miss Greenaway isn't a soldier friend's sister, but he won't say who she is to him. He wants me simply to ignore her existence."

"Miss Greenaway?" The name nagged at Sara's memory. She touched a finger to her brow, trying to think where she'd heard it before.

With great animation, Felicity hurried to the bed and sank onto the down mattress. "Do you know her? Who is she? Why won't he talk about her?"

Miss Greenaway's identity suddenly flashed into Sara's mind, and she cursed herself for not having remembered it before. "Oh, she's not anyone to concern yourself with," she said, attempting to cover up her mistake.

The look of betrayal in Felicity's eyes was unmistakable. "That's what *he* said." She sighed. "But I don't blame you for not wanting to tell me, given my profession."

"That's not why!" Sara took Felicity's hand, wondering how she'd managed not to notice the ink-stained tips of the woman's fingers before. "I simply don't want you to leap to conclusions about Miss Greenaway and Ian based on my little information."

"It doesn't matter what you tell me. I *know* she's his mistress."

"I'm not so sure." Sara debated a moment. But Felicity deserved to hear the truth, even if Ian wouldn't reveal it. "When I knew Miss Greenaway, she worked for Ian's uncle as governess to the man's children."

"Then she's an older woman?" Emily asked from her perch on the stool. "If so, she couldn't be Ian's mistress."

"She's not that old," Sara said. "She can't be more than thirty-two. Miss Greenaway went to work at the Lennard household when she was only twenty, a few years older than Ian at the time. Edgar Lennard's estate adjoined Chesterley, so I imagine Ian had many opportunities to see her. But I never heard of anything between them."

"Well, there's something between them now," Felicity said tersely. "She bore a child not long after Ian put her up on Waltham Street. She *must* be his mistress. I don't know why he doesn't just admit it."

"There's a child?"

Felicity nodded. "He says it's not his." Her voice sounded brittle and unconcerned, but Sara could tell that Felicity was anything but that.

A wave of pity for the young woman swamped her. "Then perhaps you should believe him. Ian's an honorable man, despite the impression he's given you. He would claim any child of his, bastard or no. The woman may be another man's mistress, perhaps his uncle's."

"Why didn't he say that, if it's so innocuous? And why isn't his uncle keeping her instead of Ian?" She swiped at her eyes, and only then did Sara realize she was crying. Felicity jumped to her feet, turning her back to them. "Well, I don't care what Ian does with her. I won't marry a man with a mistress. Other women accept it, but I couldn't."

"*I* don't accept it," Emily said sympathetically. "Believe me, Jordan knows if I ever found him with another woman, I'd take an ax to a certain part of his anatomy."

Sara smiled at the image, but her smile vanished when she saw Felicity's unbending posture. The poor woman wouldn't admit the reason for her distress, but Sara knew. And she wished she could put Felicity's mind at ease.

The trouble was, she no longer knew Ian at all. Over the years, he'd grown secretive. Just look at his recent behavior. He'd lied to them from the time he'd arrived—about how he knew Felicity, the woman he kept in London, and probably even his reasons for his hurried trip to town.

What's more, his manner had changed. These days he was always distant, aloof. The only time he'd behaved like his old congenial self was tonight in the hall. When he was speaking to Felicity.

Hmm. Sara surveyed the young woman thoughtfully. Perhaps Felicity was wrong about Ian's motives for proposing marriage. What if Ian was merely having the same trouble accepting that he was falling in love as Gideon and Jordan had both had?

One thing her experience had taught her—men hated falling in love. They fought it, they explained it away, they called it sex or passion or lust, anything but love. A man would rather brave hell than admit his weakness for a woman and give her power over him. So why should Ian be different? The more she thought about his behavior toward Felicity, the more that possibility made sense.

"So what do you plan to do about this mess?" she asked Felicity.

The young woman faced them. "I don't know. Ian says he wants me to help him find a wife."

"The two of you didn't invent that tale to mislead us earlier?"

A mournful look crossed Felicity's face. "I'm afraid not. He says I owe it to him, since my columns have ruined his chances and I refuse to marry him. He has a point, you know. So he wants me to introduce him to other women, advise him on who to marry . . . that sort of thing."

The sly dog, Sara thought. She understood his purpose now, and he was shrewder than she would ever have guessed. "And you intend to do so?"

"I suppose. But I know so few women who might suit him that it seems pointless for me to try." Her voice grew sullen. "Yet he insists that I do so. It's very annoying."

"Perhaps you dislike the thought of matching him with another woman."

"Not at all!" Felicity sounded as if she were trying to convince herself. "I don't *want* to marry him! And I don't care who else he marries, as long as it isn't me!"

The devil you say, Sara thought. The prospect of watching Ian court other women was killing Felicity, and Ian undoubtedly counted on that to help him win his suit. What a clever maneuver. And guaranteed to work, judging from Felicity's misery.

Maybe Felicity was right, after all, and Ian was simply the most calculating male in England. He'd certainly been moving them all around like chess pieces. Such attention to strategy didn't bode well for his feeling any strong emotion for the woman.

Then again, something had glittered in his eyes when he looked at Felicity—

There was only one way to discover his true intentions. "You know, I could help you with your endeavor if you want," Sara said in an offhand manner.

Felicity seemed more than eager to pounce on her offer. "Could you? How?"

Sara shrugged. "I know as many young women as you. I can make introductions and help dispel the rumors about him myself."

"Yes, that would be wonderful! I wouldn't have to be around hi—" Felicity broke off quickly. "That is, it would free me to attend to my own business."

"What business?" Emily asked.

"My work, of course. I must be free at social occasions

to gather gossip for my column, and I can't do that if I'm busy helping Ian find a wife."

"Ah, yes," Sara remarked, watching Felicity with new interest. How odd that a young woman with such intelligence and sensitivity could be so eager to write scandalous material for a common newspaper. "I forgot you're Lord X. But surely your Mr. Pilkington could do without Lord X's column for a short time."

"He could, but—" The woman broke off, her gaze flitting from Sara to Emily. "I-I wouldn't want to stop writing it. I like it, and I worked hard to gain my readers. I don't want to lose them. Besides, after all the holiday parties in the next few weeks, there will be nothing until the Season begins. I must be free to move about *now*."

A lame explanation if Sara had ever heard one. Felicity clearly had some other reason for continuing her writing. But what? Judging from the woman's apparel and rumors about her father's inheritance, Felicity had no financial difficulties. "Will my help free you to write?"

"Oh, yes!" Felicity said earnestly.

"Very well, then I shall help you. Gideon and I planned to spend Christmas in town this year anyway. We'll take you home tomorrow, and then accompany you to those social events Ian expects you to attend." She watched Felicity closely. "I'm sure I can find him a wife without you if need be."

"Yes, of course you could," Felicity said in an oddly deflated tone.

Her look of desolation told Sara all she needed to know about Felicity's feelings. Whether Ian was in love or not, Felicity was halfway to being there already.

"But will Ian mind if it's you and not me who helps him?" Felicity asked. "He seemed to think he needed my help."

Sara caught Emily's eye, and a look of understanding passed between them. Not surprisingly, Emily had guessed

Ian's purpose as well. Their husbands had trained them well to recognize the machinations of devious men.

"I'm sure Ian would welcome anyone's help," Emily told Felicity cheerily, her mischievous expression showing that she thought no such thing.

"I'll speak to him this evening on the matter," Sara added. "No doubt he'll be delighted at my involvement."

The devil he would. If he was, it meant that Ian possessed as little real interest in Felicity as he'd had in Lady Sophie and the Hastings girl. In such a case, it would be best for Felicity to discover that now.

But Sara doubted that Ian wanted anyone's interference in this matter. Sara had never seen the man so agitated by a woman, so reckless in his pursuit. God knows he'd never cornered Lady Sophie in *her* bedchamber.

If Sara's instincts proved as correct as they usually did, he wouldn't like what she told him tonight. Not one little bit.

Barely controlling his anger, Ian glared at Sara from his stance beside the fireplace in the card room. "What the hell do you mean—you plan to help me find a wife? I don't want your help, Sara!"

"But Miss Taylor said you were adamant about needing hers." Sara swept about the room, picking up a newspaper here, straightening a cushion there. "I don't see why my help would be any less welcome."

"Because I bloody well don't want to marry *you*, that's why!"

She cocked her head to stare thoughtfully at him. "I'm afraid I don't understand."

Her voice was entirely too smug. He searched her face with narrowed eyes. "Yes, you do. You're too intelligent for your own good. And you know quite well that the best way for me to secure Felicity's affections is to make her realize how badly she wants to marry me."

"Is that so?"

"Yes, it is, my meddling friend. She wants to marry me, and I'll force her to admit it if I have to dance attendance on half of London's eligible women in front of her!"

A sudden urge to smash one of Sara's china figurines against the wall possessed him. The last thing he wanted was Sara mucking things up, especially if it put more distance between him and Felicity. He lowered his voice, striving for control. "I appreciate your attempt to help, but I have this well in hand. I've already set my sights on the wife I want, and I don't need you destroying all my plans!"

"Good heavens, Ian, if she doesn't want to marry you, why waste your time over it? Surely you don't wish to have a wife who cares nothing for you."

"She *does* care for me, no matter what she said. And she'd make me the perfect wife. She's merely being stubborn about—" He broke off, suddenly conscious of Sara's intent interest.

"About what?"

He narrowed his eyes on Sara. "How much did she tell you of our discussion?"

Sara looked as if she debated something, then shrugged. "Merely that she refused to marry you."

"Did she say why?"

"She claimed you wouldn't suit. Apparently, while she agrees that she'd make you the perfect wife, she's not so sure you'd make her the perfect husband."

He scowled. "That's only because she doesn't know me."

"Or because she knows you too well."

Her barb hit more deeply than he would have thought. "Thanks for all your confidence in me."

She ignored his sharp tone. "Tell me, Ian, why do you think she'd make you the perfect wife? She's not the sort of woman you always claim to prefer. She's not quiet or docile. And she has a huge family that she'd expect you to support."

"I can afford it."

Sara inexplicably smiled. "Yes, I suppose you can. Then there is her very troublesome profession—"

"She told you about that?" he asked incredulously.

"Her identity as Lord X?" With an air of complete nonchalance, she sank into a plush chair. "Of course. She told me all about your little war."

That stunned him into silence. He hadn't expected Felicity to reveal so much to Sara. What did it mean? And how would this affect his plans?

"I must say," Sara went on, "that although her tale explained the events of the past few days, it shed no light on why the two of you should marry. Given your apparent disagreement on many matters, I would think you rather unsuitable for each other."

"Would you?" He glowered at her. "I suppose that means you're on *her* side. You think she's right to refuse me."

She smoothed her skirts with sudden concentration. "Perhaps I'm on both sides."

Striding up to where she sat, he bent down and braced his hands on the arms of her chair. "Don't play games with me, Sara. I'm not in the mood. You can't be on both sides. I want her to marry me, and she wishes to remain unencumbered. So you must choose: either help me or help her. Or stay out of the matter entirely."

The infuriating woman merely smiled up at him. "I need more information before I make a decision."

"What kind of information?"

"Do you love her?"

The words exploded in his brain. *Love her?* The subject hadn't come up in his previous courtships. That it should do so with Felicity was very disconcerting.

He shoved back from Sara's chair. "Not all men marry for that reason. Just because you and your brother fancy yourselves in love with your spouses doesn't mean it's the same for everyone else."

"Then why do you wish to marry her?"

"You know why," he evaded. "For the same reason every man of my situation wishes to marry. Because I require a wife to run my household and bear my children."

"Of course. But why her? She's beneath you in station, after all."

"That didn't matter to your stepfather, your husband, or your brother, so I don't know why you think it would matter to me."

"All right, so you don't care about that. What *do* you care about that makes you think you should marry her?"

"She has four brothers," he retorted, seizing upon a fact he'd scarcely considered until now. "Need I point out what that says about the likelihood she can bear me a son?"

"So can many women. You still haven't told me what I wish to know. Why should I help you snag my friend as a wife when any woman will suit your purpose?"

Dragging his fingers through his hair, he glared at her. "You know she's better off married to me than in her father's old house tending four scamps and dabbling in gossip."

"Are you so sure? She seems to enjoy her odd life. To my knowledge she has no financial difficulties, so she doesn't need to marry you for money. But you haven't answered my question. Why her?"

"Because I *want* her!" he burst out. "She's the only one I want!"

He regretted his admission the moment he saw Sara's delighted expression. With a groan, he shifted his gaze past her. Damn the woman for pressing him into saying more than he'd intended.

But it was the truth. Felicity had stirred something primitive in him, something he thought he'd suppressed long ago. Excitement. Passion. The sheer enjoyment of kissing a woman he truly desired. Just when he'd resigned himself to doing his duty no matter the cost, she'd burst into his life like fireworks against a midnight sky.

Now he was addicted to the brightness she showered around her whenever she swept through a room. He ached to possess that brightness, to make it his own. He needed to possess her in every possible way. And he could only do that by marrying her.

His gaze shot back to Sara. "Well? Have I given you enough information? Will you help me win her? Or do you still think Felicity and I won't suit?"

"Oh, I begin to think you'll suit each other nicely." She cast him a blazing but enigmatic smile. "Yes, I'll help you. Sit down, Ian. It's time we made some plans."

Chapter 12

Lord Hartley has strict requirements for his heir's prospective wife, particularly that she have "a striking appearance and a presentable wit." One only hopes that the heir apparent recognizes what his father does not—that a woman with a presentable appearance and a striking wit is far more interesting.

LORD X, *THE EVENING GAZETTE*,
DECEMBER 21, 1820

Felicity scowled fiercely at the pale-cheeked face in the huge square mirror over her dressing table. *Fool!* she told herself. *Ninny! Ridiculous dreamer!*

She had no reason to be so somber, and certainly no reason to let her listlessness show in her face! In the week since her return from the country, she'd gone to four Christmas balls, three parties, and a private concert. She'd provided Mr. Pilkington with six good columns for which he'd paid her decently. Tonight she was attending Lady Brumley's annual St. Thomas's Day party, the most prestigious ball of the season, with London's most interesting characters, who would provide her with ample material for even more columns. So why did her malaise persist?

Because of *him*, of course. That false-hearted viscount with the roving eye.

He would attend tonight as well, dancing with one woman after another, seeking a wife with blithe nonchalance. It was what she wanted, wasn't it? She'd refused him, so what did she expect him to do—pine for her?

That's precisely what she'd expected, fool that she was. But she should have known better. She'd done nothing but torment the man since the day she met him. Not that he didn't deserve it, because he did. Still . . .

Glancing back into the mirror, she scowled again. No wonder he'd given up on her so easily. Look at her colorless face and dull expression! She looked exactly like the common-born woman she was!

Furiously, she dabbed rouge onto her cheeks, then just as furiously, scoured it off. No respectable woman wore rouge these days. Mama had done so in her day, but it was acceptable then.

Why did she care what he thought of her anyway? They were quits now.

"Lissy, what's that red stuff you're playing with?" a boy's voice asked behind her.

It was Ansel who'd spoken, but all her little tin soldiers were ranged at her back, having invaded her chamber en masse this evening. James sat cross-legged on her closed trunk, keeping his posture meticulously erect as he'd been taught at Islington Academy. Devoid of such training, William and Ansel sprawled on their bellies across her bed with their heads resting on their elbows and their bare feet kicking idly in the air. And George, true to form, wandered the room in search of mischief.

"I'm not playing with it." She set her mother's old rouge pot firmly aside. She would *not* give Ian the satisfaction of seeing her appear all rouged and plucked like some tart. Then he'd know how she regretted refusing his proposal.

Regretted? Hah! She did *not* regret refusing to marry a

man for whom women were merely an amusement and a wife was a manufacturer of dutiful children. Marry a man with a mistress? A man who within a day of her refusal was courting every eligible female thrown his way? Never!

"Do you *have* to go to a ball tonight?" Ansel asked, his golden head cocked to one side as he watched her latch Mama's paste ruby necklace about her neck.

"Yes, Lissy, do you have to?" Georgie put in. "You've been going to parties all week. Don't see why you can't stay here with us tonight."

James supplied an answer for her. "Lissy's got to have something to write about, lads, so she has to go to parties. You know that. If she doesn't, then we shan't have enough money for Christmas goose. You wouldn't want that, would you?"

The triplets shook their heads in unison, and Felicity bit back a smile. "Tomorrow I promise to spend the entire day with you. Mr. Pilkington sent over tickets to Madame Tussaud's Waxworks Exhibition. It's in the Strand again. Would you like to go see it?"

Even James perked up. "Can we, Lissy, truly? You'll take us?"

"I most certainly will." She'd seen the exhibition often as a girl and looked forward to discovering what Madame Tussaud had added to the collection.

"Can we go into the Separate Room?" Georgie asked in a hushed whisper.

Felicity frowned at his mention of the notorious collection of death masks from the French Revolution that had started Madame Tussaud on the path of such a strange profession. "Indeed, you may not! It'll give you nightmares."

"No, it won't!" Georgie protested. "Nothin' scares *me*, Lissy!"

She cast an irritated look into the heavens, questioning God for his wisdom in making little boys so fearless in theory and craven in practice. The triplets were generally all bluster and bombast . . . until nighttime brought the standard childhood nightmares.

"We'll see," she said noncommittally.

The door to her bedroom swung open, and Mrs. Box hurried in. "The Worthin's has arrived. You don't want to keep 'em waitin', luv."

Snatching up her fan, she rose from the dressing table and faced her brothers. "Well? How do I look?"

"You look like a peacock!" William said, giving his highest compliment.

"She don't look like no peacock, Will." Georgie sneered at his brother. "There ain't a single feather on that dress."

Felicity opened her mouth, then shut it, realizing it was pointless to correct so many grammatical errors at once. George really must stop spending time with Mrs. Box and Joseph, neither of whom had adequate grammar.

"You look very beautiful," James said artlessly, ignoring his brothers, who now argued over William's words. He left the trunk and approached with arm extended. "May I escort you downstairs, lovely lady?"

Stifling a laugh, she nodded and took his arm. "I'd be honored, kind sir."

With a haughty expression, James waved his brothers closer. "You may carry the train, lads, if you like."

"I don't have a train," Felicity protested, but it was too late. Three pairs of grimy hands now struggled for purchase on the back edge of her peach skirt. She winced, but didn't stop them. Her skirts would be soiled the moment she walked into the muddy street anyway. And though the boys held her skirt high enough to reveal a full foot of her petticoat, she knew she must give them *some* chance to participate in her evening, or they'd be little terrors for Mrs. Box the rest of the night.

The top of the stairs was her limit, however. The possibility of tumbling to the bottom with her three enthusiastic helpers tangled in her gown was too real to risk. With a gentle word, she shook them free like so many clinging kittens. "Now, boys, you might as well stay here—"

"But we want to talk to Lord Worthing," Georgie protested. "He hasn't come with Lady Worthing before. Ain't he the pirate?"

With a quick glance down to where the Worthings conversed with Mrs. Box, she hissed under her breath, "Who told you that?"

"*You* did," Ansel put in. "The day you got back from your trip."

She'd forgotten. And of course they were interested in his adventures on the high seas. That was precisely what she did *not* need—the triplets cornering an earl with earnest questions about how to run a man through.

"Can we talk to him, huh, Lissy?" William asked.

She forced a smile. "Not tonight. Another time, all right?" At their crestfallen expressions, she bent down to buss each one on the cheek. "You'll see plenty of pirates at Madame Tussaud's Exhibition tomorrow."

That wiped the disappointment from their faces.

"Be sure to mind Mrs. Box," she added, ruffling Georgie's hair with affection. "And don't stay up waiting for me. I'll be late."

She felt their eyes on her as James, looking quite the adult, led her downstairs. The boys were growing up much too quickly. Although some days she couldn't wait until they could help with the family's financial burden, most days she regretted the circumstances that would thrust them into adulthood far too soon.

Mrs. Box looked up, caught sight of her and James, and smiled broadly. "There she is, milady. And the young master with her."

James drew himself up straighter, and a lump lodged in Felicity's throat. He wouldn't be master of anything soon. Today three different creditors had assailed her—the butcher, a shopkeeper from Cheapside, and some gambling companion of her father's. The last man, a knight, had threatened to bring the magistrate after her if she didn't pay off her father's debt. Thankfully, she'd had the coal money to give him, or there was no telling what he would have done. But the other two she'd sent away empty-handed.

Good Lord, did she need money—bushels and bushels of it. She'd never pay off all the debts at the rate she was going.

Tonight she'd have to gather more material than usual. Perhaps if she could find enough, she might secretly approach a rival newspaper about writing a second column under a second name. If she could only pay a large sum on the worst of the bills . . .

"You're looking well this evening," Sara commented as Felicity reached the bottom of the stairs. With a warm smile, the countess turned to James. "And what a handsome man you have at your side."

James fairly beamed at the countess's praise. He'd been half in love with the woman from the day the Worthings had brought Felicity home from the country.

"I suppose the triplets are already in bed." Sara's face showed disappointment. "I do so enjoy the darlings, and I'd hoped to introduce Gideon to them. They were asleep when we arrived from the country last week."

"Actually—" James began.

"Actually," Felicity repeated, glowering at her brother before he could say more, "I promised them an outing tomorrow, so I had to send them to bed early."

"Lissy's taking us to see Madame Tussaud's Waxworks Exhibition," James put in. "The lads are very excited about it."

"I imagine they are." Sara laughed, then eyed Felicity speculatively. "I've never been. It's usually in the Strand, isn't it?'

"Yes." Felicity glanced up the stairs to where her brothers stood peeking around the banister, then swiftly added, "I suppose we should be off."

After a quick good-bye to James, they left.

The ride to Lady Brumley's was sheer torture. Sara and Gideon shared so many secretive smiles and fond looks it made her envy their happiness. It also reminded her of Ian . . . his kissing her, touching her intimately, whispering endearments . . .

She sat up straight. Gideon might know the answer to a question that had plagued her for days. "Gideon, do you speak Spanish?"

"A little."

"What does *querida* mean?"

His gaze narrowed on her. "It means 'darling.' "

Her heart gave a little twist. Ian had called her "darling" that night at the Worthings? What did it signify? Nothing, judging from his behavior this week.

"Who called you 'darling' in Spanish?" Sara asked with a smile.

Felicity laughed weakly. "Oh, no one. I read it in a book."

Sara and Gideon exchanged knowing glances.

The clamor outside the carriage thankfully drew their attention from the subject. As usual, Lady Brumley's affair was a great crush. Coaches crammed the narrow street like dogs trampling each other to reach a bone. One thing was certain—Ian would have plenty of eligible women to choose from tonight.

The thought depressed her. Firmly, she thrust it aside. Who cared about that philandering lord and his roving eye? Not *her*, to be sure. Just because he called her "darling" and knew exactly how to use his hands on a woman's body—

"Drat it," she muttered under her breath.

"I agree," Sara said, mistaking the source of her distress.

"It's chaos out there. But don't worry, we'll get through. Wait until you see Gideon handle a crowd."

A few moments later, Felicity got to see exactly that. Once Gideon stepped from the carriage, every eye was on him, and not only because of his imposing frame. His reputation had apparently preceded him, for everyone gawked at the dark-haired American rumored to have been the Pirate Lord. With his purposeful stride, which Sara and Felicity had to hurry to match, Gideon knifed through the crowd like a hot blade through ice. Thank God. She was eager to be out of the winter wind that slapped them like icy metal paddles. In moments, the three of them were inside the cramped villa and at the top of the stairs to the ballroom, being announced.

"There's Ian," Sara whispered to Felicity as they strolled down into the swirling scent of crushed bay branches, sweat-dampened wool, and smoking beeswax. Felicity followed Sara's gaze to where Ian danced a quadrille. Superbly. With a pretty woman only half his age, or so Felicity told herself in a burst of temper.

"Ah," Sara continued, "he's standing up with Miss Trent. Excellent. I suggested her to him, you know. She's a bit of a flirt, but her bloodlines are impeccable and she has three brothers. If he can snag her, she's sure to give him an heir."

I have four *brothers, remember?* Felicity wanted to retort. Of course, her own bloodlines were less than impeccable, especially when one considered a father whose liking for drink had sent him tumbling into the Thames.

It didn't matter, she told herself with a scowl. There would be no marriage between Ian and her, and she didn't want one anyway.

She caught Sara watching her and smoothed her features. "Has Ian offered for anyone yet? Considering how he complained of his difficulty in finding a wife, he seems to have done quite well under your tutelage."

"Yes." Sara trained her gaze on Ian. "And I've ensured

that you're free to pursue your own concerns."

"I do appreciate it," Felicity said hollowly. Sara hadn't answered her question. Had Ian set his sights on someone in particular?

The lowering thought dogged her for the rest of the evening. Though she gathered information for her column and agreed to several dances, more often than not she found herself drawn to watching Ian dance.

Some of his partners she dismissed as inconsequential. He stood up with Lady Brumley and Sara out of duty, of course. Then he danced with Lady Jane, who was surely too frivolous for him to consider as a wife, and Miss Childs, whose well-known affection for champagne would tax both his finances and his patience.

It was his second dance with Miss Trent that alarmed her. Miss Trent had intelligence, wit, an even temper, and worst of all, gorgeous blond hair and sweet blue eyes. Miss Trent would certainly meet all of Ian's requirements for an uncomplicated wife, drat her. Not to mention the woman's "impeccable bloodlines."

"I see Ian is standing up with Miss Trent again," Sara remarked to Felicity after returning from a galop with her husband. "She'd be a good choice for him."

"If he could ignore her poor taste in accessories," Felicity said peevishly, seizing upon Miss Trent's only apparent flaw. "Look at that dreadful reticule she carries."

"Somehow I don't think it's Miss Trent's reticule that concerns Ian." There was a hint of laughter in Sara's voice, but when Felicity shot her a chilly look, Sara masked her amusement.

"Speaking of men and their partners, the Earl of Masefield is headed toward you," Sara added in an undertone. "I do believe he's aiming for a second dance himself."

Felicity checked her dance card. "Oh, yes, I forgot. I promised him a waltz." Thank goodness she'd been practicing with James. She'd begun under the pretense of preparing James for adult life, but in truth, her lack of ability in that area galled her. It was one of many inadequacies in her character, skills, and appearance that tormented her of late. Ever since she'd met a certain viscount, to be honest.

"Lord Masefield seems enamored of you," Sara commented. "He rarely dances twice with anyone."

Felicity waved a hand dismissively, her gaze still on her dance card. "He likes to talk, that's all, and I'm a good listener. It's my profession, you know."

In a strained tone, Sara said, "Ian seems to be coming this way as well."

Felicity's head shot up. Only a few paces behind Lord Masefield, he barreled toward them looking inexplicably grim. For a second, she hoped Miss Trent had said something to annoy him. Then she chastised herself for the thought. She *wanted* Ian to marry, so she could put him from her mind once and for all.

Lord Masefield reached them moments later. With a courtly bow, the handsome earl offered his hand to Felicity. "I believe this dance is ours, is it not, Miss Taylor?"

She cast him a smile that broadened as she saw Ian approach. "Indeed it is, my lord," she said sweetly.

Taking his hand, she stepped forward, but Ian moved to block their path. "I'd like to claim the dance after this one, Miss Taylor, if you're free."

Drat the man! Not since their one waltz had he requested a dance, yet he expected her to fall down at his feet because he asked her now. Well, he could forget it. "I'm sorry, but my card is full. Now, if you'll excuse us, Lord Masefield has this dance."

Though Ian's eyes blazed, he stepped aside with utmost politeness to let them pass. "I beg your pardon," he said in a perfectly even tone, but she felt his gaze boring into her back as they moved away.

Indeed, Ian wanted to strangle her as he watched young Masefield and Felicity face each other for the waltz. A bloody idiot, that Masefield, a veritable copy of his idiot father. Masefield didn't deserve to dance with her, and certainly not twice.

Sara approached to stand beside him. "Was that wise?" she asked in an undertone. "Asking her to dance when you've done so well to date?"

"Have I? I've stood up with more women than I can count, and I've yet to see her show any sign of caring."

Sara arched an eyebrow. "I thought you were so sure of her."

"I was. I am." He speared his long fingers through his hair. "Bloody hell, I don't know anymore. All I know is I couldn't bear not touching her another minute, especially when that fool Masefield headed toward her. What is she doing with a full dance card anyway? I thought she was here to gather material for her damned columns?"

"You men always assume that only women gossip, but nothing is further from the truth."

Masefield drew Felicity closer in the turn, and Ian scowled blackly. "Well, Masefield isn't gossiping, is he? He's got his hands all over her. You should warn her away from him—he's only toying with her. His father wants him to marry an heiress, and he has the title to do so. Besides, he's fresh from the schoolroom, barely more than a boy. He wouldn't even know what to say to her if he got her alone."

"Are you so sure?" Sara asked in a deceptively innocent voice.

He glared at her. She was laughing at him, the brazen chit, enjoying his fit of temper. The woman probably thought it meant something. What it meant was that he needed to bed Felicity Taylor before he exploded with need.

A need that had grown to mammoth proportions the minute he'd seen her enter tonight, wearing a most enticing scrap of fashion. With that gauzy material, it would take only a few tugs in the right places to render her naked. The sleeves clung to her shoulders for dear life, and the seductively draped bodice slipped down whenever she bowed to reveal a generous amount of golden bosom. It was a miracle the bloody thing stayed up. Every man in the place probably waited to see when it would fall. "Why don't you caution her against wearing those flimsy gowns? She's making a fool of herself."

"I've seen no one laughing at her. And her gown is no more flimsy than mine." Sara hid her face with her fan, but he knew she was smiling behind it.

"You're a married woman—you can get away with it. But she's unattached, and it isn't the same. You should speak to her about that gown. It shows entirely too much of her figure. She'll ruin her reputation."

"As I recall, the only thing ruining her reputation so far is her association with *you*."

Her tart words didn't sit any easier on him for being true. "Well, I intend to remedy that by making her my very respectable wife. I'm tired of this game, Sara. It's not working. I need a new strategy."

Sara's expression softened. "Ah, but it is working. She hides it, but she's as jealous as you are. You should have heard her criticism of the incomparable Miss Trent."

Her words mollified his temper only a little. "I can't go on this way, paying court to women I don't wish to marry. I long ago rejected half of them as possibilities, and the other half have fathers who'd never countenance my suit, even if I wanted the daughters. Which I don't. *She's* the one I want."

"You must be patient—"

"I can't." He had no time for patience. He must have a wife, and soon. And it must, it *would* be Felicity. "Surely there's another way to secure her. I need time alone with her. A moment on the balcony in this crush will do me no good, even if I could get her out there. No, I need more time, enough to convince her she's wrong about me."

"Or enough to seduce her?"

He met Sara's questioning gaze and considered lying.
But Sara could detect that sort of lie from twenty paces.
"If necessary." He should have seduced Felicity the last
time he'd had her alone instead of taking a more subtle
approach. Subtlety didn't work on her any better than
threats. Or jealousy.

Sara looked indecisive, then sighed. "Well, I shan't help
you seduce her, but I do know how you could spend time
with her and her brothers. She's taking them to the
waxworks exhibition tomorrow."

A slow smile spread over his lips. He began exploring
possibilities, tactics, maneuvers. "You mean the one in the
Strand?"

Sara nodded. "But make it look as if you met up with
them accidentally or she'll never trust me again."

"I can do that." Ah, yes. And afterward, he'd accompany
them home and wrangle an invitation to dinner. From there
. . . His smile broadened.

"I know how your devious brain works," Sara remarked,
"but I should caution you that seduction might not succeed
in changing Felicity's mind. She has a strong will."

"It'll succeed," he vowed, although he hadn't been sure
of that himself a week ago.

Still, he had no choice. What had begun as an impractical
desire to possess her had become an obsession. He couldn't
lie down without imagining her in his bed, couldn't eat
without tasting her on his lips. For God's sake, he even
heard her laugh in his sleep sometimes. But that wasn't as
bad as hearing her sighs of pleasure, which he also did in
his sleep, in his dreams.

She wanted him, too. He knew it. And she needed him,
whether she acknowledged it or not.

Very well—he *would* seduce her and it *would* succeed.

Because if the first seduction failed to convince Felicity she should marry him, he'd seduce her as many times as it took to either change her mind or get her with child. But one way or the other, he would have her as his wife.

Chapter 13

Lady Brumley's annual St. Thomas's Day ball is sure to be grander than any previous one. As Lord Jameson says, "No one hosts a ball like Lady Brumley. The city could not prevent a crush at her affairs even if they put her house under quarantine."

LORD X, *THE EVENING GAZETTE*,
DECEMBER 21, 1820

Thank God I'm rid of him, Felicity thought as she escaped Lord Masefield with the excuse of going to the necessary. The man's idea of scintillating discussion was a chat about the Ascot. She couldn't imagine Ian—

No! Must she keep thinking of that dratted viscount? The man had actually glowered at her during her waltz with Lord Masefield, like a wolf brooding over escaped prey. How dare he, after dancing with half the women in London!

She dearly wished the man would sift through society's eligible women without sifting through her affections as well. She sighed. She had only herself to blame. She could have accepted his proposal, after all.

As she walked down the long hall leading to the necessary, she heard footsteps behind her and a voice call out, "Miss Taylor, wait!"

Halting, she peered back down the dim corridor. A tall man in his late forties approached. She didn't recognize him, yet something familiar about his features made her pause until he reached her.

"We haven't been introduced," he said, "but I know you. You're Algernon Taylor's daughter, are you not?"

"Yes. And who are you?"

"The name is Edgar Lennard." He bowed stiffly. "I believe you're acquainted with my nephew, Lord St. Clair. The son of my brother."

Her interest was instantly engaged. So this was Ian's uncle and Miss Greenaway's employer. Yes, she could see the resemblance between Ian and him in the shape of the forehead and the great height. But there the resemblance ended. Where Ian was dark, this man was fair. Where Ian's features held a certain roughness, this man's were classically handsome, despite his age. She could easily imagine a beauty like Miss Greenaway being this man's mistress. So that theory at least might be true.

Or not. Felicity squared her shoulders. Either way, the man might tell her what she desperately wished to hear—what Miss Greenaway's relationship was to Ian. "I do know your nephew, as a matter of fact. I know him quite well."

The man pursed his lips disapprovingly. "Then I'd like to speak to you for a moment, if you don't mind."

"I don't mind at all." *Tell me everything*, she added to herself.

Noting the nearby open door of a parlor, he gestured to it. "This way, if you please. What I wish to say requires privacy."

"Very well." She walked inside. But when he closed the parlor door behind her, she gave him her frostiest smile and opened it again. It wouldn't do to be found alone with this man, even if he was old enough to be her father. Besides, something in his manner put her on her guard, and she'd learned never to ignore such instincts.

He acquiesced, though he maneuvered matters so that they sat as far from the door as possible. "I won't waste your time," he began as soon as they were seated. "I've heard your name linked to my nephew's of late."

"Have you?" Lady Brumley had certainly wasted no time in spreading her news.

"As you probably know, he's looking for a wife."

She played dumb. "Really?"

"Speculation has it that he's about to offer for you. Is this true?"

Good Lord, the gossip had been more accurate than she'd expected. And it seemed to have agitated Mr. Lennard. She shouldn't be surprised that Ian's relatives might be concerned about Ian marrying a woman so far beneath him in wealth, station, and connections, but it annoyed her all the same.

She lifted her chin haughtily. "You can't expect me to know what your nephew is 'about to' do, sir. I don't read minds."

The man regarded her gravely. "That's a pity, Miss Taylor, for if you could, you'd know he isn't the sort of man a respectable young woman should marry."

She gaped at him. She'd had it all wrong. The man wanted to warn her away from Ian, not protect Ian from her. But why? "He seems perfectly acceptable to me." Well, if he didn't keep a mistress and have more secrets than a mummy's tomb.

"That's because you don't know him. My nephew is a bounder and a scoundrel. He's led many women to ruin, including the one recently mentioned in the *Gazette*."

"You mean your former governess, Miss Greenaway?" Felicity asked, to see his reaction.

That startled him indeed. "You know her identity?"

"Of course."

Anger shone in his beautiful features before he smothered it with a false smile. "I suppose my nephew said she was my mistress or some such lie."

How curious that Ian's uncle would jump to defend himself without knowing what he'd been accused of or even if he'd been accused at all. "Your nephew told me nothing about her. I have my . . . own sources."

"I hope they gave you the entire story without slanting it toward my nephew."

There it was again—that assumption. She kept silent, raising an eyebrow as if to imply she knew more than she did. The ploy often worked in her investigations, especially when the person she questioned was guilty of something.

And it worked very well with Mr. Lennard. He leaned toward her as if to impart something of great import. "Did your sources also tell you the real reason my nephew took Miss Greenaway under his protection?"

"To irritate you perhaps?" she guessed.

He looked affronted. "No. To make sure she kept quiet about his real character."

She was rapidly coming to dislike this man. "Don't keep me in suspense, Mr. Lennard. I can see you're eager to inform me of what Miss Greenaway is hiding."

Apparently her sarcastic tone wasn't enough to dissuade him from further confidences. "You must understand, I tell you this only because I can't bear to see my family honor besmirched by my nephew's activities."

"Go on." Two weeks ago, she would have been ready to believe anything he said. But two weeks ago, she hadn't witnessed Ian's honorable streak firsthand. She found it difficult to reconcile Ian's concern for her feelings and reputation the last night at Worthing Manor with this man's veiled implications.

"I presume you know that my nephew fled England at nineteen," he said.

She nodded.

"He fled because his father threw him out for what he did to my wife."

He paused for effect, and she struggled to keep her face expressionless. But it was a good thing he couldn't see her insides, for they were twisting into knots of terrible foreboding. Perhaps it hadn't been such a good idea to encourage his confidences.

At her silence, he continued. "You see, my wife Cynthia was younger than I, and she and Ian were much thrown together." His tone harshened. "One can never truly know what tempts a young man to folly, but it seems he mistook her kindness to him. One day when he caught her alone, he— Well, he took advantage of her. In a carnal way, you understand."

The accusation slithered into the air, as sudden, ugly, and impossible to ignore as a viper dropping from a tree. "You don't mean—"

"Yes, he—" He broke off, his lips drawing into a tight line. "I'm sorry. Though many years have passed, it's still difficult to speak of it. But for your sake, I must." Gathering himself up, he said baldly, "My nephew, Ian, forced himself on my wife."

With every word, an awful weight pounded Felicity's chest, like the thousand descents of a printing press onto paper. Could it be true? Could Ian have raped his own aunt? At nineteen?

Ian's secretiveness did lend the man's words some credibility, and the mere possibility of its being true sickened Felicity. She thought of all the young heirs apparent she'd known, the ones who'd cornered her in bay windows or pressed against her "accidentally." Such lords were brought up to believe they were invincible, that they were entitled to everything. And their arrogant behavior toward women was nurtured so young that she'd once had to fend off a slobbering fourteen-year-old.

But Ian wasn't like the lords she'd known, young or old.

In many respects, he was honorable, and his behavior toward women circumspect . . . well, except for the mysterious Miss Greenaway. She couldn't believe Ian would violate any woman, especially not a relation. The man had an iron control. Yes, he'd forced one kiss on her, but he'd had a reason and had gone no further. In her other encounters with him, he'd shown more restraint than she.

Now that the initial shock of Mr. Lennard's accusation was past, she wondered at his impropriety in telling her this. If it was so difficult for him to speak of it, why had he done so to a complete stranger? For the noble reasons he claimed, of wanting to protect her? Or something less noble?

"If what you say is true," she finally said, "then Ian is clearly despicable. But are you sure he forced your wife? She told you of it?"

"Yes. She came to me at once, full of shame and tears."

"And what did you do about this outrage?"

"Do?" He frowned.

"Surely you called him out, at the very least, for the insult to your wife."

"My *nephew*? I couldn't call him out! His father would never have forgiven me!"

Yet you can make accusations behind his back without giving him the chance to defend himself, she thought. *How very noble of you.*

"So that's when Lord St. Clair fled to the Continent?" she persisted.

He tugged nervously at his cravat. "Yes. I confronted him and demanded that he make reparations. And like the coward he was, he slunk off to the Continent in the dead of night with his tail between his legs."

How strange. The Duke of Wellington praised Ian's bravery, yet his uncle called him a coward. If she had to wager which one lied, her money would be on Mr. Lennard.

"That must have been difficult for your wife, to see her tormentor go unpunished."

With a long sigh, he stared down at his hands. "The shame of Ian's violation tortured her, so she took her own life, leaving me and our two children to grieve. And all because I couldn't keep my nephew from ravishing her."

"That's a very inventive story, Edgar," came a feminine voice from the doorway, "and so convincingly presented, too. You rival even me in your ability to tell a tale."

As Felicity swung her head toward the door, Edgar Lennard leapt from his chair. Standing in the doorway was the Galleon of Gossip herself, Lady Brumley. Felicity had ignored the woman all evening, knowing that the marchioness would pelt her with questions about the Worthings' ball. But now she felt insanely glad to see her. Listening to Edgar Lennard's sordid accusations made her skin crawl.

Mr. Lennard didn't appear happy to see the woman, however. "This is none of your affair, Margaret. Miss Taylor and I were having a private conversation."

"Yes, but in *my* house." Lady Brumley moved into the room, the glittering embellishments of her headdress catching the candlelight. A gold satin turban with embroidered ship's anchors circled her head like a crown, and from it dangled an enormous gold brooch of a ship that bobbed as if actually at sea when she walked.

"You weren't invited to my ball, Edgar. So imagine my surprise when I saw you dart out of the ballroom after Miss Taylor. I only wish the crush hadn't prevented me from joining you sooner."

The marchioness's tinpot-colored eyes revealed such malignance that a chill scrambled down Felicity's spine. At some time in the past, the Honorable Edgar Lennard had foolishly made the marchioness his enemy.

He crossed his arms over his chest. "I heard the rumors you've been spreading about my nephew—how he might offer for Miss Taylor. When I learned that he and Miss

Taylor would be here, I wished to see for myself if they were true."

"And what did you decide?" Lady Brumley asked, her features stony.

"Judging from his noticeable jealousy toward Lord Masefield and the way he couldn't tear his eyes from Miss Taylor half the night, I'd say you were right."

The impropriety of this conversation began to grate on Felicity, especially when both parties seemed oblivious not only to her but to the facts of Ian's friendship with her. She opened her mouth to tell them so, but was prevented by Lady Brumley's next words.

"So you've decided to scuttle this courtship the way you scuttled two of his others, have you? Is that why you're telling lies to the poor girl?"

"They aren't lies," he protested.

Two liveried footmen appeared in the doorway behind the marchioness. Without even turning, Lady Brumley pointed to Mr. Lennard. "That's the man. Throw him out." As the footmen hurried into the room, the flickering tapers lent a hellish glow to Lady Brumley's smile. "One thing I learned from you twenty-five years ago, Edgar, is not to allow riffraff into one's house. I'm afraid you'll have to leave."

"You have no call to interfere in this," Mr. Lennard protested as the footmen flanked him.

"No, but my interference irritates you, which is what I live for, as you well know."

The footmen led him to the door, but before leaving he glanced back at Felicity. "Don't listen to this harpy's tales. Remember what I said—my nephew isn't what he seems."

"Get him out of here!" Lady Brumley snapped, and Lennard was dragged off.

Felicity stood motionless, her mind and emotions in a turmoil. She couldn't believe Edgar Lennard's strange accusations, yet the very fact that Lady Brumley didn't want them heard made her wonder at them. What was going on?

Lady Brumley waited until no sound came from the hall, then closed the door and walked to a sideboard that held a carafe and some glasses. Hands shaking, she poured herself a generous amount of purple fluid, then took a gulp. "Do you want some port?" she asked as she lowered the glass.

"No." What she wanted was answers.

Lady Brumley faced her, the glass clutched tightly in both hands. "You didn't believe all that balderdash Edgar fed you."

"I don't know what to believe."

"He's only trying to dissuade you from marrying Lord St. Clair, you know."

Felicity sighed. "You and Mr. Lennard labor under a false assumption. Lord St. Clair has no intention of marrying me. In case you hadn't noticed, he stood up with half a dozen ladies tonight and didn't stand up with me once."

Lady Brumley chuckled. "I'll be hanged if that's not jealousy I hear in your voice. And I haven't seen St. Clair kissing any of those ladies passionately on the balcony, my dear Miss Taylor. Or taking advantage of them as you implied he did."

Felicity groaned. Her deception had returned to haunt her. "He didn't— What happened at the Worthings was a mere flirtation. He and I have both forgotten it."

"I see." Lady Brumley set down her glass. Walking to the door, she opened it. "Well, if you're not considering marriage to the man, you don't care about Edgar's tale, and certainly you needn't hear *my* opinions. So we might as well return to the ballroom."

She waited expectantly, and Felicity scowled. The woman was a Machiavelli of the first order! If Felicity admitted wanting to know more, it would confirm her interest in Ian. Yet not admitting it meant letting this opportunity go by. How could she? Mr. Lennard's nasty assertions tormented her, and she needed to find out if there was any

truth to them. The Galleon of Gossip would be more likely
to know than anyone.

Felicity sighed. "I didn't say I wasn't interested. I'm still
a friend to Ian—I mean, Lord St. Clair. So of course any
gossip that might hurt his reputation interests me."

With only the twitch of her upper lip acknowledging that
she'd won, the marchioness closed the door once more. "A
friend. Hmm. I suppose that will do for now. Sit down,
Miss Taylor, and I'll tell you what I know."

Trying not to look as anxious as she felt, Felicity perched
on the edge of a settee and folded her clammy hands in her
lap.

Lady Brumley took another large swallow of port before
settling her stalwart frame in an overstuffed chair by the
fire. "I assume Edgar told you the same ridiculous tale he's
related to the other women St. Clair courted—that St. Clair
raped Cynthia and she killed herself out of shame, prompting him to flee to the Continent."

Put so bluntly, it sounded ridiculously melodramatic.
"Yes. Mr. Lennard said that the woman linked to Lord St.
Clair in the paper knows the truth, which is why the viscount took her under his protection. He says Lord St. Clair
ruined her."

Lady Brumley waved her hand dismissively. "Poppycock. If anyone ruined her, it was Edgar. The woman you
refer to—whose name is Penelope Greenaway—was not
only the governess to Edgar's children, but was also Edgar's mistress after his wife died. He cast her out when he
discovered she was pregnant with his bastard."

"How do you know this?"

"Let's just say I make it my business to know all about
Edgar Lennard and his affairs. Which is easy enough, since
he pays his servants so ill that they don't mind making an
extra guinea simply for giving me information." Lady
Brumley's low chuckle held a certain bitterness. "In any
case, when Edgar threw Miss Greenaway out I would have

aided her simply to annoy him, but Lord St. Clair got to her first. Since he has as much contempt for his uncle as I, he saw the advantage to helping the one woman who might bring his uncle down. Besides, he has a soft heart, and her child is his cousin, after all, bastard or no."

"You think that's the only reason he helped her?"

"Of course. No matter what Edgar claims and a certain gossip columnist has written—" She paused to shoot Felicity a knowing look. "Miss Greenaway is *not* Lord St. Clair's mistress."

Then why hadn't Ian simply said that? "Just because she was Mr. Lennard's mistress doesn't necessarily mean she's not Lord St. Clair's now," Felicity remarked, disappointed that Lady Brumley hadn't given her more certain proof. "If Lord St. Clair hates his uncle, it would be a fitting revenge to make her his mistress, don't you think?"

"And take his uncle's leavings? He'd be too proud to do so."

That was a good point, she thought, feeling a bit more easy.

"Besides, St. Clair wouldn't keep a mistress while he's courting. Men keep mistresses regularly, to be sure, but the occasional mama does frown on it. So why risk it, especially when Edgar seems so bent on preventing him from marrying?"

"Yes, and why is Mr. Lennard determined to prevent him? I don't understand."

Lady Brumley tapped her fingers impatiently on the arm of her chair. "I suppose he has the usual motives—if Ian dies childless, Edgar or his son will inherit eventually. That's as good a reason as any for Edgar to scare off St. Clair's young women. But I shan't let him scare off anyone else with his sordid lies."

"You're certain they're lies?" Felicity asked hopefully.

"As certain as anyone who knows the two men can be.

It's not in St. Clair's character to force a woman. You know it as well as I."

She felt numb. "But you have no proof," she said dully.

The older woman hesitated, as if debating something. Then she sighed. "I should have known you wouldn't simply take my word for it. Very well. I have some information I gleaned from Edgar's servants. It's not much, but I believe it's closer to the truth."

Lady Brumley adjusted her turban, making the little ship brooch bob. "It's true that Cynthia Lennard died shortly after St. Clair left for the Continent. But the Lennard servants heard nary a hint that she killed herself over a rape. No, they believe her death resulted from a mutual love affair."

Her heart sank. "You mean, between Lord St. Clair and Mrs. Lennard?"

"Yes. It's plausible, even understandable. Cynthia was twenty-five to St. Clair's nineteen. She was pretty and quite naive. Edgar swept her off her feet, but I believe she later regretted it. His age exceeded hers by some seventeen years. So it's understandable why she'd fall in love with her young nephew, Ian, and take him into her bed."

This version didn't please Felicity any more than the other one. Although it exonerated Ian of rape, it meant he'd had an adulterous affair with his aunt. The thought twisted her insides.

The marchioness didn't seem to notice Felicity's distress. "The servants think that Ian's guilt over the illicit affair led him to flee to the Continent. And Cynthia died pining away for him. No one knows for certain, however. All the servants who worked there ten years ago were paid or pensioned off to keep quiet about the scandal."

Felicity's blood thudded dully in her veins. This was almost as treacherous a tale as the other. In the eyes of the law, it was incest, and certainly it made Ian indirectly responsible for his aunt's death. It was also a terrible betrayal of his father's brother and even his father. It was hard to imagine Ian betraying his family's trust.

But if he'd been in love? Her heart wrenched to think of it.

She hated to admit it, but Lady Brumley's tale explained a great deal—why Ian had gone to the Continent without telling his friends, why he'd been adamant about her staying out of his affairs, and why he hadn't wanted her talking to Miss Greenaway.

It might even explain why he'd been so careful with her that night in her bedchamber. Perhaps he'd stopped short of seducing her because he remembered what had happened the last time he'd made love to a respectable woman.

"In any case," Lady Brumley went on, "none of it may even be true. And if it is, it's all in the past. It occurred when St. Clair was a green lad. But his six years on the Continent made him into a man, a very good man if I am any judge. That man deserves a wife, no matter what Edgar thinks or tries to do about it."

Felicity hardly heard her. She rose in a daze, her mind awhirl. "I must return to the ball. My companions will be looking for me."

"But Miss Taylor—"

"Please, Lady Brumley, let me go. I need to think on all this."

"All right. Just be sensible about it. You know as well as I do that St. Clair is no violator of women. Edgar is lying—surely you can see that."

"Yes." The trouble was that the idea of an adulterous affair with his aunt, of him lying with his own aunt and then running off, leaving the woman to grieve herself to death, sickened her.

Of course, as Lady Brumley said, it might all be lies. Considering the sources, how could she know? Especially when he wouldn't confide in her?

She started for the door.

Lady Brumley called out, "If he *should* offer for you—"

"He won't," she whispered, then fled the room.

Even if he did offer again, she couldn't accept. This dark secret in his past still tormented him—anyone could see that. And as long as he refused to unburden himself, it would stand between them, an ugly beast rearing up whenever she tried to come close. She would always wonder if Miss Greenaway were his mistress or if he still loved Cynthia Lennard. She couldn't be one of those ladies who pretended not to notice their husband's infidelities.

Yet despite the rumors and speculations and probable lies, despite his secretiveness, her heart still leapt and her blood quickened whenever he turned those sin black eyes in her direction.

Damn the seductive devil to hell. He'd certainly had a fine revenge. She'd just been handed the juiciest bit of gossip ever, and not only did she not want to write about it, she didn't even want to think about it. How he would laugh if he knew. With a few kisses and caresses, he'd taken the gossip out of the gossip writer. And she would never be the same.

Chapter 14

Madame Tussaud's exhibit is in the Strand. Tales abound of fair ladies fainting in the Separate Room, but how could that be? Some of those ladies have husbands whose looks would shame a donkey. If the ladies don't faint at the sight of their husbands in the bedchamber, I don't see why a death mask or two should make them do so.

LORD X, *THE EVENING GAZETTE.*
DECEMBER 22, 1820

Even a blind man couldn't miss the four scamps alighting from a carriage, Ian thought. Their racket actually overcame the noise in the Strand—the coaches trundling by with badly oiled springs, the workmen knocking about as they renovated a great house across the way, the vendors caterwauling. He spotted the Taylor Terrors out the window at once, a familial gaggle that Felicity attempted to keep in order while arguing with the hack driver, who'd climbed down from his perch to point at something on his coach.

With a knock on the ceiling, Ian sent his coachman driving past the hack as prearranged. Ian's second knock brought the St. Clair carriage to a halt just ahead of the hack. Disembarking quickly, Ian clapped his hat on and strode toward his prey.

He could hear Felicity's protesting voice as he approached. "I shan't pay a single shilling for damages, I tell you!" Enveloped in a black woolen cloak that looked as if it had seen better days, she shook her finger to punctuate every phrase.

The grimy driver shut the door, which didn't latch until he lifted the flimsy panel an inch and forced it into place. Then he opened it again, letting it list down as he faced Felicity triumphantly. "You see that it's broke, don't you, miss?"

"I see only that you're trying to cheat me. I don't dispute that it's broken; it's *who* broke it that I question. It was like that before we got in!"

"No, it weren't!" The burly man crossed his arms over his barrel chest. "I take good care of me coach, I do, and that door were closing right proper when I stopped for you and yer brood. It's those lads of yours what broke it."

"That's a lie! You probably broke the dratted thing yourself!"

"I'm warnin' you, miss—"

Ian stepped in quickly. "How much will it cost to repair the damage?"

The driver swung around, his eyes lighting up as he assessed Ian's worth by the cut of his coat and the fineness of his linen. "Well, now, sir, that depends—"

"What are *you* doing here?" Felicity's wary gaze flew to his coach not ten feet away, then back to him.

Ian tipped his hat. "Good morning, Miss Taylor. I was on my way to consult with my man of affairs when I saw the commotion. I thought I'd stop and offer my services."

"There's no need," she said primly. "I have the situation well in hand."

"Yes, but you and your brothers are obviously on an

outing, and I'd hate to see it spoiled. I'll be happy to pay for the damages myself if you'll allow it."

"Don't you dare pay this scoundrel! I won't have thievery rewarded, and he—" She pointed an accusing finger at the driver. "He is trying to cheat us!"

"Now see here, Miss Skinflint, you ain't gonna be lyin' to the gentleman about me!" the driver said belligerently.

Ian drew Felicity aside. Keeping an eye on the irate coachman, he murmured, "My God, don't quarrel with him over a few shillings. It isn't worth it."

"But that door was broken before we—"

"I'm sure it was. What do you care?"

"It's the principle of the thing!"

He gritted his teeth. "The principle of the thing will shortly have you and your brothers embroiled in a fight." Jerking his head, he indicated two men descending from hacks across the street and hailing their compatriot. One scowled; the other swaggered. Both looked troublesome.

When Felicity paled, he went on in an undertone. "It's your word against his, and you're a woman with four energetic boys in tow. This isn't the time or place for your bloody self-righteousness. I can trounce them for you if you like, but that's not the lesson you want to provide your little charges, is it?"

She glanced over at the triplets, who stood mute for once, looking warily from the driver to her and Ian. She winced. "No, I suppose not."

"Then let me pay the damages. Unless you insist on paying them yourself."

She flushed. "The driver wants two shillings, and I only brought enough money with me to cover the expense of the ride here and back. So if you wouldn't mind . . ."

"I don't mind in the least."

"But it's a loan," she hastened to add. "I'll repay you later."

"Fine."

The point would be moot anyway once she agreed to marry him. Still, her lack of money struck him as odd. She'd brought less than two extra shillings with her on an outing with four boys? Was she worried about pickpockets?

They returned to where the driver conferred with his sneering reinforcements. The man faced him with a more aggressive stance, not even sparing Felicity a glance. "Well, sir? Does the miss agree to pay?"

"Yes. Two shillings, isn't it?"

"Two guineas."

He raised an eyebrow at the man's blatant greed. "The lady must have misunderstood." Approaching the hackney, he bent to examine the broken door and noted the pattern of rust on the twisted hinge. He glanced up. "Two guineas, eh?"

The driver scratched one rank armpit, a hint of uncertainty in his expression. His burlier friend nudged him. "Aye, sir. That's wot it cost to fix a hinge these days."

Ian straightened. "Then whoever repairs your carriage is cheating you. Let me do you a favor. Take your coach to Wallace's on Chandler Street, and tell him I want the entire door replaced at my expense. For two guineas, you should at least get something decent." He drew out his calling card and presented it to the driver.

The man took it reluctantly, then blanched when he saw the name on the card. With a nervous glance at his friends, he muttered, "I only want the hinge repaired."

"Whatever you wish. Wallace will take care of you. Fair enough?"

"Fair enough, milord." He scowled at Felicity. "But I ain't comin' back for her and her lot like I said I would."

Ian felt Felicity bridle beside him and laid a hand on her arm. "There's no need. I'll take the lady and her family home."

Her muscles tensed beneath his hand and didn't relax until the hack pulled away. Then she faced him with typical

Felicity impertinence. "Well, well. It seems you understand the 'principle of the thing' after all—at least when it's *your* money."

A smile tugged at his mouth. "I admit it—I couldn't countenance paying off a rascal. Especially one who enjoys fleecing young women."

Awareness of him flickered in her gaze. It sizzled the icy winter air, making him instantly glad he'd come. "Thank you for your help," she said softly.

Then a whirling dervish of arms and legs and eager young males stampeded up to them with all the delicacy of bull elephants. Cries of " 'Ods fish!" and "Aren't you the man from the paper?" and "Why did he call you *milord*?" tumbled from the triplets' mouths as they circled him. Ian suddenly felt like the bear at a baiting, surrounded by creatures a third his size.

Creatures with worn coats and tattered hose. How strange that their sister would dress them so poorly. His gaze shot to her. Come to think of it, where was the elegant, fashionable attire she'd worn at the Worthings'? Her clothing today was serviceable, but he couldn't miss the fraying edges of the woolen cloak and the faded color of her simple black bonnet, which had clearly spent too many days in the sun.

"Stop that, boys," Felicity said sternly. "It's rude for all of you to speak at once."

He tore himself from musings about her attire. "They aren't bothering me, Miss Taylor, but it might be better if we were properly introduced." Ian smiled at the nearest urchin. "What is your name, young man?"

"I'm William."

The boy had barely gotten the words out before the one next to him piped up, "This here's my brother Ansel, and I'm George. But everybody calls me Georgie. And that's James over there. He's the eldest."

"I see." He used his observational skills to catalog identifying marks for the triplets, quickly registering Ansel's mole, the scar on Georgie's chin, and William's missing tooth. "I'm pleased to meet you all. I'm—"

"—the Viscount St. Clair," James broke in testily. When Ian cast him a quizzical look, the older boy shrugged his bony shoulders. "I asked Mrs. Box about you that day you came to our house." He looked defiant. "The day Lissy shouted at you. I thought maybe you'd . . . that is—"

"I understand," Ian interrupted. "It's good you're looking out for your sister." He shot Felicity a meaningful glance. "She needs someone to do so."

Felicity rolled her eyes. "We've kept his lordship long enough, boys. I'm sure he has more important matters to attend to."

Before he could protest, Georgie cut in. "Can't he come with us to the exhibit?"

Nervously straightening Georgie's collar, Felicity said, "Lord St. Clair has a meeting and no time to waste with us."

"My meeting isn't urgent," he said. When her gaze shot to his, he added, "And I've never seen a waxworks exhibit. Besides, I promised to take you home in my coach."

"He did. I heard him." James assessed Ian with eyes as green and sharp as his sister's. "And it'll save us half a shilling."

Ian began to wonder if the Taylor finances were as secure as he'd been told.

Felicity's anxious laughter only heightened his suspicions. "Don't be silly, James. Who cares about half a shilling?" She faced Ian. "Truly, Lord St. Clair, there's no need for you to bother. I'm sure a day with us would bore you terribly."

"Not as much as a day with my man of affairs, who considers tallying figures great entertainment. Take pity on me, and don't sentence me to a morning of arithmetic." When she still hesitated he added, "I tell you what. Let me come along, and I'll buy tea and mutton pies for everyone's supper afterward."

The shameless bribery worked perfectly, making the boys clamor for him until Felicity sighed. "Very well, but you'll regret it. These four can be very wearying."

"I'm sure I'll survive." Oh, yes. He planned to ingratiate himself so well with the Taylor boys that their sister would be forced to reconsider his proposal of marriage.

As the six of them headed for the entrance of the exhibit hall, Felicity pulled James aside and whispered in his ear. He nodded, then hurried ahead to catch his brothers and whisper in *their* ears.

It was all very mysterious and made him struggle to keep from laughing. So they had secrets, did they? Felicity was a fool to think a few words of admonishment could prevent him from prying a secret out of her brothers. Even the Terrors of Taylor Hall were no match for a man who'd once loosened the tongue of Napoléon's senior advisor.

By the end of the day, he'd know everything. Then he'd use it to make her marry him. Most assuredly.

It took three hours and the realization that they neared the end of the rented hall for Felicity to finally relax. But it had gone well. The boys had let nothing else slip concerning their finances. They'd behaved themselves like gentlemen's sons . . . most of the time, anyway. It had even been pleasant, despite Ian's intrusion.

She surveyed her companions. Georgie, Ansel, and William knelt before a wax sculpture of a Scot, peering under the kilt to determine if the conventional wisdom was true. Ian and James stood in front of her, reading the placard that went with an impressive wax version of Bonaparte.

Look at those two, she thought with a smile, *standing so much alike*. Both Ian and James stood with their hands clasped behind their backs, and both rested their weight on one foot, keeping the other knee slightly bent. They even looked a bit alike. James's straight brown locks resembled Ian's thick black hair, and both of them tended to dishevel it by running their fingers through it when agitated. They could almost be father and son.

She swallowed, a sudden longing curling down into her belly. Ian and a son. Her son. The idea intrigued her, warmed her. What would Ian be like as a father? Judging from his behavior today, he'd be wonderful. He'd halted Georgie's impetuous impulses with a word, humored William's fancies, and squelched Ansel's deplorable tattling.

But it was her sober brother James whom Ian had captivated despite the boy's initial suspicions. From the moment Ian described in riveting detail the events of the French Revolution while standing before the sculpture of Robespierre, he'd held the bookish, history-minded James in the palm of his hand.

She watched as Ian read a line aloud in French, and then translated it for James. His French was expert, far better than her smattering learned from a long-forgotten French tutor. But then Ian had lived on the Continent, spying for the British or something, for many years. The thought sobered her. She didn't know what he'd done there, because he wouldn't talk about it. Or anything else, the secretive wretch.

Last night's conversations burned through her brain. She'd tossed all night, wondering how much was true. Ian couldn't have committed rape, but seduction was believable. Was he capable of such selfishness? Perhaps not now. But at nineteen? She wanted to know. She *needed* to know. Maybe if she simply asked—

"How do you know French so well?" James asked Ian suddenly.

Ian gazed up at the sculpture with the wooden, aloof expression she'd grown to recognize. "I spent six years on the Continent."

James cocked his head. "Why?"

Gazing down at the boy, Ian shrugged. "I fought in the war."

She was still reeling from the fact that Ian had actually admitted his war activities to her brother when James retorted, "But Lissy said you lied about that."

"James!" She caught him by the shoulder and spun him around to face her. "I did *not* say any such thing!"

"You wrote it in the paper!" James's eyes widened with hurt. "I remember it."

She sighed. "Oh, *that*. I didn't realize you read my column."

"We all do," James said. "Well, not the triplets, but me and Mrs. Box and Joseph and Cook. We read it every morning, while you and the lads are still asleep."

The revelation startled her. She'd never imagined her audience might include her family. She knew Mrs. Box read the thing; that was to be expected. But her brother? She didn't know whether to be proud or mortified.

In either case, she must set him straight. "What I wrote about Ian was a mistake. I was misinformed. Ian did serve his country."

"Ian?" James asked with all the innocence of a child.

She groaned. "Lord St. Clair. He didn't lie. I was wrong."

James looked confused. "But you're never wrong. Everyone always says that. 'Lord X has the way of it,' they say. 'He knows the truth.' "

She sighed. What had she started, for pity's sake? When she'd irresponsibly written that last column, she hadn't thought of how far-reaching the consequences could be.

"I know what everyone says," she told her brother, "and I do try to write the truth. But I make mistakes. No one is perfect. You mustn't always believe what you read or hear. Sometimes it's exaggerated or even untrue."

She should listen to her own advice and treat Lady Brumley's claims cautiously, and Mr. Lennard's more so.

She glanced at Ian to find him regarding her with a guarded expression. Until she had all the facts, she would make no assumptions. Not this time.

She returned her attention to her brother. "Now apologize to Lord St. Clair. No matter what you thought, it was impolite to mention the gossip."

James faced Ian, suitably chastened. "I'm sorry, my lord. I spoke out of turn."

"It's all right." Ian laid his hand on James's shoulder, but his gaze locked with hers. "I don't mind when people ask questions, only when they jump to conclusions."

That annoyed her. "Perhaps they jump to conclusions because you don't answer their questions."

"Perhaps their questions concern private matters," he countered.

She raised an eyebrow. "James, why don't you fetch your brothers before they topple that sculpture?" As soon as he'd scurried off, she smiled sweetly at Ian. "The trouble with you is that you consider *everything* a private matter. I suppose you even enjoin your housekeeper not to discuss the contents of your closets with strangers."

"Don't you? No, I suppose not, considering your housekeeper. Mrs. Box loves to talk about you. Shall I have a long conversation with her when I take you home? See if she'll tell me the contents of your closets?" His low voice hummed through her. "I wonder if one of them contains that fetching scrap of lace you wore at Worthing Manor."

Slowly his gaze drifted down her body. Her breath caught in her throat. *Good Lord, not again*, she thought as a tumult of feelings roared through her—feminine delight, anticipation, desire . . . To her shock, his eyes seemed to mirror her feelings.

He bent his head to whisper warmly, "Or better yet, you could show me later, when we're alone."

A delicious shiver tripped along her spine. He still

wanted her. Despite all the women he'd courted this week, he still wanted *her*.

She stiffened. Yes, what *about* all those women? With an arch look, she edged away from him. "We shan't be alone later. You forget that you have several women to court tonight."

His smile—dark, sweet, and dangerous—sent a frisson of excitement clear to her toes. "Ah, but I've given up on that. I've discovered that all the women I've met and courted in the last week lack something necessary to me in a wife."

"And what is that?"

"They aren't you."

Her heart leapt in her chest, like a bird trapped inside a glass box. His tender words resounded through her body and sent hot need flooding her veins.

Georgie skidded up to them, followed closely by her other brothers. "Lissy, Lissy, the Separate Room is next door! Can we go in? Please?"

Thank God for her rascal of a brother, who drew her thoughts from the darkly handsome man at her back with his tempting hints about *later* and *alone*. "Now, Georgie, I told you last night that you couldn't. The Separate Room isn't for boys your age."

"But Lissy, I'm almost twelve," James said. "That's practically a man."

James had a point, but there'd be hell to pay if she let him enter without the triplets. "I'm sorry, James. I think it best we end our tour here."

"Aw, Lissy," Georgie cried in abject disappointment. "Why can't we go?"

Ian spoke up. "Yes, Miss Taylor, why not? I don't mind taking the lads through if you have no desire yourself to enter."

Frustration over his flirtations made her temper flare at his intrusion on her authority. "It's not myself I'm concerned about," she said firmly. "It's the boys. Such things give them nightmares. Everyone says the Separate Room is gory."

With mischief glinting in his eyes, Ian laid his hands on Georgie's shoulders. "But boys have an abiding need to steep themselves in gore. I certainly did."

"At six years old? They're too young, I tell you."

"Perhaps you should let *them* be the judge of that," Ian said.

He thought this a grand joke! Let six-year-olds decide what they could handle, indeed! Six-year-old boys thought they could fly, for God's sake. Only last month Georgie had planned to spring from the balcony armed with wings he'd fashioned from tin. Thank God for Ansel's tattling.

"May I speak to you in private, Lord St. Clair?" she said coolly.

"Certainly." He followed her to a spot a few paces away from her brothers.

She fought to keep her tone reasonable. "I know we've had our differences, but you mustn't let that influence your judgment. James is old enough, but the triplets are only babies. They have wild imaginations and frighten easily."

He looked at her askance. "The Terrors of Taylor Hall, as your housekeeper calls them? Trust me, boys are more resilient than you think. They enjoy a good scare."

Her gaze narrowed. "Tell me, would your mother have let you see such things?"

"No, but then she wouldn't have let me go to a waxworks exhibition at all. Father wouldn't have approved."

"I can see why, if you wanted to study sculptures of bloody bodies at the tender age of six."

A muscle worked in his jaw. "Whether I'd been six or sixteen, they wouldn't have let me go. I wasn't allowed to attend fairs or play games or—" He broke off. "Father considered such entertainments unproductive. He was . . . a rigid sort."

The admission stunned her. It was the first time he'd spoken of his past or even mentioned his parents. She rejoiced in this evidence that he could do so. She even sympathized with his feelings. But he was wrong about the boys.

"I agree that children need entertainment, but—"

"I tell you what. Go in with us, and if you consider it unsuitable, we'll come right back out. I swear it. You, of all people, know how newspapers exaggerate to sell tickets. It probably only contains old dog bones and an ax or two."

He had a point. She glanced from Ian to her expectant brothers. "Very well; we'll take a quick look. But if I see so much as a smashed finger displayed in that exhibit, I'll—"

They were already racing off to the opposite end of the hall where a doorway covered in a black curtain awaited them. Next to it a big sign read WARNING in bold letters, followed by smaller script, no doubt extolling the faint-inducing properties of the room's contents.

Uneasiness gripped her. If Ian were wrong . . .

She only prayed he wasn't.

Chapter 15

Though overindulging a child is unwise, what con-
stitutes overindulging? One parent considers an
extra apple tart a mere concession to hunger,
while the other believes it leads down the road to
perdition. Is it any wonder that children grow up
confused?

LORD X, *THE EVENING GAZETTE,*
DECEMBER 22, 1820

"**S**he's mad at us, ain't she?" Georgie whispered
to Ian across the carriage, so loudly that even
passersby outside could probably hear him, Ian thought.
Certainly everyone inside did, including the motionless
woman who sat beside the young scamp.

He couldn't see her reaction in the meager glow of the
scarce streetlamps. Then a trickle of light crept across her
face to dapple her cheeks with silver and highlight her fixed
gaze. His breath caught in his throat. He'd never seen her
look so forlorn.

He shifted on the seat he shared with James and William.
His normally roomy carriage was cramped and hot with six
bodies squeezed into it. "She's not mad at you." Ian didn't
bother to lower his voice. "She's mad at me."

Felicity ignored him.

"Why?" Georgie asked.

"She thinks I was wrong to take all of you into the Separate Room."

The boys began reassuring him that he wasn't, that they'd had a fine time.

Then Felicity spoke. "I'm not angry at any of you, unless it's for speaking of me as if I'm not here." Her gaze scoured them all. "I'm angry at myself. I allowed you children to enter that dreadful place when I should have stood firm."

Ian stifled an oath. Yes, stood firm against *him*. And if she wasn't angry, why did the smoke of her disapproval clog the air in his carriage?

Damn it, how could he have known the rascals would scatter as soon as their wriggling bodies entered the Separate Room? How could he have known what lay inside? All right, so they'd been met by three severed wax heads impaled on tall poles. Wax figures of criminals had lined the walls bearing bloody axes, bloody swords, bloody everything. Wax blood stained the hacked-off limbs of their victims, and wax blood dripped off the guillotine blade at one end of the hall.

Was it his fault Madame Tussaud possessed a seemingly endless vat of red wax? And a flare for the dramatic?

Apparently so, judging from the way Felicity had glared at him, then stormed about the room catching each boy by the scruff of the neck and herding them toward the entrance. By then it had been too late. By the time she'd caught Georgie, the boys had been exposed a good fifteen minutes to the horrors of the Separate Room.

Thus had begun Ian's exile from Felicity's affections. She'd spoken to him only in one-word utterances. She'd barely touched the supper of mutton pies, apple tarts, and tea at a popular cookshop, though the boys attacked theirs with gusto. Now she sat like one of Madame's cursed statues, as far from him as possible.

Everything had gone so well until then. He couldn't believe he'd ruined his plans for the evening with so heedless an act.

James spoke up from beside Ian. "Well, you shouldn't be angry about me, Lissy. I'm old enough to go in the Separate Room if I like. I'm not a child anymore."

Ian stifled a groan when Felicity flinched. Wonderful. Why must James choose this inopportune moment to assert his independence from his sister?

James continued in the unevenly pitched voice that amply illustrated his youth. "It's not as if you're our mother or anything. If I hadn't been forced to leave Islington Academy, I could have gone on my own to the exhibit, you know. And then no one would have prevented me from seeing the Separate Room."

At the mention of Islington Academy, a silence as heavy as this year's winter snow fell on the carriage. Even the triplets stopped fidgeting. Ian glanced at Felicity, whose eyes had gone wide with clear alarm.

He turned to stare at James. "Why were you forced to leave Islington Academy? You're a bright lad and well-mannered. Surely they'd have no reason to throw you out."

Panic made the boy jerk upright in his seat. "Well, I . . . I—"

"You misunderstood him, Ian," Felicity interrupted. "He didn't leave. He's merely home on holiday."

"Yes, th-that's it," James added, stumbling over the words. "For Christmas."

The brother lied as badly as his sister. Ian stared down at the beardless lad whose defense of his family was so transparent. "You know it isn't right to tell tales, James. I want the truth—did you leave the academy because your sister needs money?"

James shot his sister a helpless glance. "Lissy—"

"It's all right, James." The lamplight caught Felicity's shuttered expression. "Really, Lord St. Clair, there's no need to badger the poor boy. If you want to know something, ask me."

"All right. Do you need money?" He crossed his arms over his chest. "If you don't tell me, I'll find out the truth anyway."

She glanced out the window, her fingers clutching her reticule as if to protect it from a thief. "We don't need . . . that is . . . at the moment we're short of funds, because we're waiting for Papa's estate to be settled. But as soon as the money comes to us—"

"Settled? But he's been dead over a year!"

"Yes, it's some legal mess. The lawyers will sort it out. In the meantime, my columns support us."

He snorted. As if that could support a household as large as theirs. "Perhaps you need someone to intervene on your behalf and hasten the process. I could speak to your father's trustee—"

"No! You've no right to interfere. We're fine, I assure you."

"But Lissy—" James began.

"We're *fine*," she gritted out, casting her brother a warning glance. "I'm sure the money will come through any day, and James will be back at Islington Academy."

"Very well. Do as you see fit." He dropped the subject. No point in annoying her further when a few words with Mrs. Box would tell him what he needed to know.

Though the boys seemed to relax, Felicity began to fidget. She fiddled with the clasp to her reticule. She fussed with Georgie's clothing, plucking a leaf from his hose and finger-combing his hair until he grumbled. The one thing she didn't do was look at Ian. There was more to this than she'd admitted. He intended to get to the bottom of it tonight, but how could he wrangle an invitation inside when she was so uneasy?

Minutes later, he got his answer when something dropped onto his legs. He looked down to find William fallen over in sleep, his head nestled comfortably in Ian's lap. The poor lad; it must be nearly his bedtime. An idea struck Ian suddenly.

"Is William asleep?" Felicity asked, leaning forward. "Do you wish me to take him from you?"

"No, he's fine where he is." Ian kept his voice low, not wanting to awaken his little ticket into the Taylor house. "I suppose it was a long and tiring day for him."

"I told you it would be."

"You also told me it would be boring, and it was anything but that."

A thin blade of a smile cracked her reserve. "I doubt anyone could find the Separate Room boring. Appalling perhaps, but not boring."

"What's 'appalling' mean?" Georgie asked.

"It means that all the blood horrified your sister," Ian answered before she could.

"It wasn't *real* blood, Lissy." Georgie patted his sister's knee reassuringly. " 'Twere only wax. You mustn't be frightened by it."

Ian couldn't help it—he laughed, though softly to keep from awakening William. Soon she joined him. The sound of her muted chuckles warmed him clear to the heart, and made him yearn to reestablish their earlier closeness.

When the laughter died off, he cleared his throat. "I'm sorry about the exhibit. Even if I didn't agree with your reasons for refusing to take them in the Separate Room, I shouldn't have pressed you."

She acknowledged his apology with a wry smile. "It's all right. You couldn't have known what it would be like." She looked down at Georgie. "And I daresay this little rascal would have found some way in there anyway, permission or no."

"Probably," Ian said, feeling a little better about the afternoon.

The companionable silence that ensued was strangely

soothing. Who would have thought that rumbling along in a carriage with three little hellions, a scholar-in-the-making, and their prim sister could be so pleasant? He hadn't been around children in years, not since his youth, when he'd spent time with his young cousins. To his surprise, he realized he missed it.

The carriage shuddered to a halt and he glanced out to see bright lamps illuminating the Gothic entrance to Taylor Hall. The carriage door opened, and the boys climbed out, uncharacteristically drooping. With the help of the coachman, Felicity disembarked, then turned to reach for William. Ian stayed her with his hand. "I'll carry him in."

"I hate to inconvenience you," she protested. "The nursery's two flights up."

"I don't mind, and besides, you have to look after the others."

From her grateful smile, he guessed she hadn't been looking forward to hauling a child of four stone or more upstairs. She stepped aside as the coachman took William, allowing Ian to climb down. When the child was once more in Ian's arms he uttered a little sigh, then snuggled against Ian's chest with a sleepy expression of trust.

Ian gazed down in awe at the small fist balled against his cravat and the smooth cheeks smeared with remnants of apple tart. A surge of tenderness made him clutch the boy close. One day, it would be his son he held in his arms. His and Felicity's.

The thought hit him like a whirlwind. After today, he had no doubt she would be a good mother. But could he be a good father? He wanted the chance to find out.

Striding up the outer steps, he entered the hall. "Where to?" he asked Felicity, who was handing her cloak to the footman, a spindly creature woefully inadequate to handle the physical demands of his position. Was this the man Felicity had threatened to have throw him out the last time Ian was here? The thought made him smile.

"Follow me," she said, lifting a candelabra and heading for the main staircase.

I've breached the fortress, he thought with satisfaction as the massive oak doors closed behind them. Shifting William from arm to arm, he shrugged out of his greatcoat so the footman could take it. *Now all I have to do is stay inside long enough to make headway with Felicity.*

Mrs. Box hastened into the hall. "Well, good evening, milord." The last time he'd seen the woman, Felicity had been railing at him. Yet the housekeeper showed no surprise at his carrying one of her charges into the house bold as brass.

He greeted her, and she smiled broadly at him. He had just enough time to register that she still liked him before she went right to work shooing the boys up the stairs. "It's long past your bedtime, lads. Come along, and don't give me no fuss now."

As they climbed, James related to Mrs. Box the day's events. When the boy spoke of how Ian had bought them supper and taken them home in his carriage, Mrs. Box said, "Now ain't that gentlemanly of his lordship." On impulse, he winked at her. When she winked back, he smiled.

Well, well, he had an ally. Good—he needed all the help he could get in arranging time alone with Felicity without the children. Especially when Felicity seemed overly eager to be rid of him. Staying well ahead of him, she raced up the steps.

As he studied the slim, erect back encased in a woolen gown and guarded by a long row of pearl buttons, his mind indulged pleasant thoughts. He would undo all those little buttons and peel back the well-worn dress to find the thin chemise. She wore no corset, he was fairly certain. The chemise he would dispense with at once, so he could see her fine shoulders and kiss down the ridge of her spine to her adorable derriere.

He went hard at the thought.

Oh, yes, he'd do all that and more, perhaps even tonight. Once her brothers were settled, she'd either accept his proposal or he'd seduce her into accepting it. But one way or the other, he'd end this farce before he left Taylor Hall.

It shouldn't be too difficult to convince her to marry him this time. Ample support for his suit lay all around him. The banister creaked beneath her hand, showing itself badly in need of repair. On the first floor, one of the paintings that had hung on the wall near her study on his last visit was now missing, with only a darker square of wallpaper to mark its passing. They'd decorated the house with holly and ivy cuttings for the season, but even those couldn't hide the threadbare condition of the drapes or the paint peeling off the moldings.

He'd wager his estate that the downturn in the Taylor finances had begun long before her father's death. Indeed, he questioned the size of their inheritance. And if they needed money, they needed him. That wasn't his first choice for a weapon—he'd rather use seduction—but he'd rely on it if necessary. First, however, he must get her alone.

James obliged him by going off to his own bedchamber as they left the first floor. Now there were only the triplets to squire away, an easy task with one of them already asleep, and the other two trundling along drowsily.

As soon as they reached the top floor, Felicity ushered him into a nursery with three identical beds. She hurried to turn down the covers on one. "Lay him here, please."

After he set his warm bundle down, she faced him, looking suddenly awkward. "Thank you, Lord St. Clair. I appreciated the help. And thank you for the supper and the ride home. We all enjoyed it."

She shot Georgie and Ansel a quick glance. "Tell his lordship thank you and good night."

They obeyed at once, with Georgie giving broad hints concerning future outings. A word from his sister, however, silenced him.

"Well then," she said, "I must put the boys to bed now, so Mrs. Box will show you out. It was a lovely day, but I'm sure you're eager to be off."

"Not at all. I'll wait for you downstairs."

A look of panic crossed her face. "There's no need. It will take some time for me to settle the boys in. They must have their faces washed, and—"

"I'll tend to all that." Mrs. Box bustled toward the other beds with great efficiency. "You go on downstairs with his lordship. After all he done for you and the boys today, the least you can offer him is a bit of that good claret before he goes out in the cold." She winked at him again. "Now wouldn't that be nice, Lord St. Clair?"

He smiled. "Oh, yes. Claret would be perfect." Claret and Felicity. Not as good a combination as brandy and Felicity, but it would do for a start. Later, they could have brandy . . . and in the morning, breakfast. He doubted that Mrs. Box intended *that* outcome, but he found it more appealing by the minute.

"I'll see if we have any claret," Felicity said noncommittally, avoiding his gaze.

When they reached the hall and she'd closed the door to the nursery, he launched into a conversation meant to forestall any attempts to rush him out the door. "This is a beautiful house. Did your father design it?"

"Yes." She offered nothing else, hurrying to the stairs.

He followed her. "I thought as much. That same griffin design is on the knocker at Worthing Manor. Your father must have liked griffins."

"Yes." Again, she said nothing more, but lifted her skirts and descended the steps at an astonishing pace.

Catching up to her, he clasped her arm to halt her. "Felicity, we need to talk."

"No, you must go. You must—"

Whatever protest she was about to make was cut off when a child's high-pitched scream rent the night.

Chapter 16

Lord Byron's latest poetic endeavor is said to concern Don Juan, the legendary lover. Such a work will surely brighten Byron's fame, since everyone knows Spanish lovers are the most fiery.

Lord X, The Evening Gazette,
December 22, 1820

"Th-the monster h-had three heads," William was sobbing into Mrs. Box's shoulder when Felicity and Ian hurried into the room, "and a b-big red arm. It was ch-chopping like an ax and . . . and . . ." His face crumpled as he broke into a low wail.

The mournful sound pierced Felicity to the heart. "Oh, my sweet darling," she cried, rushing to his bed. She waved Mrs. Box away and in seconds was cradling the boy against her breast. "It's all right—Lissy's here now to take care of you. The monster can't hurt you."

"Poor dear," Mrs. Box clucked. "Had a nightmare, he did."

"Yes." Harsh, accusing words rose to Felicity's lips as she sought Ian in the dim room, but they remained unsaid when she saw him standing woodenly inside the door, his hands shoved in his pockets. Every line of his dusky features bore the marks of guilt. He met her gaze with eyes so remorseful, she couldn't be angry.

Besides, she was as much to blame as he, for allowing him to influence her decision. At least he hadn't known what could happen. She had no such excuse.

"I-It was gonna ch-chop me up," William whispered. "It was comin' to—"

"Shh, sweet boy, you must forget all about it. It was only a dream." Felicity rocked the child in her arms as she crooned in his ear. "It's all right. I'll protect you."

She felt Ian's eyes on her, reminding her that he'd wanted to speak to her privately. Not tonight, she thought, not when her emotions were so easily affected. She cast Mrs. Box a wan smile. "I've got William now. I know you have much to do, so you may go on and show Lord St. Clair out."

Mrs. Box nodded and headed for the door.

"No-o-o!" William wailed, pushing away from Felicity to waggle an arm at the door.

"You want Mrs. Box to stay?" Felicity asked.

"I-I want L-Lord St. Clair," William stammered.

Felicity groaned. The man had captivated her fatherless brothers as easily as he'd captivated her. "Come here, Ian," she said resignedly, no longer worrying if anyone heard her use his Christian name.

Looking obviously perturbed, Ian glanced over to where the other boys were settling down beneath covers tucked up to their tiny chins. Then he walked toward her. "I don't know what to do," he admitted as he reached the bed.

"Sit down." Felicity nodded to indicate the other side of the feather mattress. "Just hold his hand."

"I'll be leavin' now—" Mrs. Box began, and before Felicity could protest, had deserted her.

With an odd quiver in her belly, Felicity watched the door close behind the housekeeper. The dim lighting and confined space lent an intimacy to the nursery she'd never noticed. Having Ian help her with William was cozy and oddly satisfying.

Ian, however, seemed uncomfortable. Clasping William's pale hand in his own dark one, he stared at it as if it were a padlock to which he'd lost the key. "I'm here, William," he said, surprising her with the gentleness of his voice.

A shudder went through William's small frame. He lifted his tear-streaked face to Ian. "It was a monster."

"I know, but it's gone now."

"It wasn't real," Felicity added, annoyed that Ian spoke as if the creature existed.

"It *was* real!" William protested with a pout. He fixed his gaze on Ian. "And . . . and it'll come back to h-hurt me."

Shooting her a warning glance, Ian said, "No, it won't. We scared it off for good, Mrs. Box and your sister and I."

"Yes, but it'll come back," the boy persisted. "It wants to ch-chop me up. Like it chopped up all those people in the Separate Room."

Amber candlelight caught Ian's stricken expression. He ruffled William's hair. "I tell you what. I'll stay here for a while, and if the monster comes back, I'll tell it not to bother you anymore. I'll be very firm."

The boy's face brightened. "You . . . you mean, like you told that nasty driver not to bother Lissy? And he listened and went away?"

"Yes," Ian said solemnly. "Exactly like that."

"You promise to stay until he comes? You promise?"

"I swear it," Ian said with a fierceness that warmed Felicity's heart.

She held her breath while William screwed up his little face in thought. Then, tugging Ian's hand into his arms, he clutched it against his chest and sank back against the pillow. "All right. The monster'll listen to you. You're big, and you can beat him up."

She watched in bewilderment, then envy as William closed his eyes, Ian's hand held tightly to his heart like a precious toy. Within moments, she could hear the blessed sound of even breathing and see his features relax into sleep.

Tears stung her eyes. How many times had she assured him it was only a dream, yet been unable to calm his fears, having to wait until he exhausted himself with crying before leaving him? But Ian came in here with his commanding presence and calm assurances, and William felt safe.

She'd known the boys missed Papa, known that they often ran to Joseph for attention because the footman was the only man in the household. Until now she hadn't realized the full extent of their longing for a man's special strength. Her poor, fatherless tin soldiers. She wiped away tears, but more filled her eyes, coursing down her cheeks to drip off her chin and onto the wrinkled sheets.

"I'm sorry," rumbled a voice from the other side of the bed. "I am so sorry, Felicity. You were right, and I was wrong. I should never have taken them into that damned room." Her throat tightened when she saw him brush the hair back from William's forehead in a paternal gesture.

"It's not that. This probably sounds foolish, but you made him feel better when I couldn't. I guess I'm a bit . . . jealous."

"You've no reason. It's my fault he suffered in the first place. I ought to be shot."

Strong words indeed, coming from a man who generally hid his emotions. Her heart twisted when she saw the pain harshening his already rough features.

She tried to tease him out of his somber mood. "Shot? Oh, no, much too tame." She glanced at the other boys, who were thankfully already asleep, then added, "The punishment should fit the crime. Beheading, that's what you need. Then we could add your head to those stakes in Madame Tussaud's exhibit."

His gaze shot to hers, mirthless and even more wounded.

"I'm joking, Ian. You mustn't blame yourself. You couldn't know how he'd react."

"But you did."

"I've lived with him all his life." She kept her tone light. "Besides, you probably never had nightmares yourself and had no idea what could bring them on. I imagine you were like Georgie, able to sleep easily after the most frightening adventures. William has an active imagination, I'm afraid." She gave a shaky laugh. "He tries to be as tough as Georgie, but never quite succeeds."

Ian said nothing for several moments, fixing his gaze on William's chest, which now rose and fell in perfectly contented sleep. Then a world-weary look flitted across Ian's face. "I never had childhood adventures, frightening or not. So I never had nightmares."

Felicity caught her breath. Eager to seize the rare moment, she exclaimed, "No adventures! Every boy has adventures. Surely you must have run wild in the woods, or sneaked away to a bear-baiting, or *something*."

"No." He took a great, shuddering breath. "I was a very . . . dutiful son. I was never allowed to be anything else. Father believed that heirs should be prepared for their responsibilities at a young age, which meant not indulging them in frivolities. So there were no wild escapades in the forest. My mornings and evenings were spent with a tutor and my afternoons with my father, who took me over the estate and made me memorize all the tenants' names and how everything worked."

What a dreadful way to spend one's childhood. She'd never considered that aspect of being a great lord, but with extensive property probably came extensive duties. "Is that why all the lords run so wild when they come to London? Because their fathers are such hard taskmasters?"

"Not from what Jordan has told me. My father was unique. I suppose I should be grateful for it, since his 'preparation' has been useful in my management of Chesterley. But once in a while . . ." He trailed off.

"Once in a while, you would have enjoyed an outing or two."

He managed a smile. "I sound like a spoiled child."

"Or a man who never got to be any kind of child at all."

His gaze shot to hers and held. For that brief moment, she read so much yearning in him that she marveled she hadn't seen it before. Then he flattened his expression and glanced away. "It proved advantageous. It enabled me to endure . . . later happenings more easily."

"What about your mother?" Felicity asked softly. "Did she agree with your father's philosophy?"

He was silent so long she began to think he might not answer. Then he sighed. "Who knows? She never said. She feared crossing him. They married because Father needed her fortune to pay off my grandfather's debts. It was arranged between him and her family in Spain. She was terrified of Father and let him rule her life—and mine—until the day she died."

A lump formed in her throat at the thought of Ian as a child, being fed the gruel of duty with little love to sweeten it. "When did she die? How did she die?"

"Why so many questions?" he countered with an arched eyebrow. "More grist for your mill?"

She ignored the barb. "No, indeed. I'm very particular about my grist these days. I've sworn off the St. Clair family entirely. You see, the head of the family is an arrogant wretch who causes trouble for me whenever I write about him."

"See that you remember that," he warned, but he was smiling now.

"So? Will you tell me about your mother's death?"

He shrugged. "It's no great secret. An epidemic of smallpox hit a neighboring town when I was seventeen. Father didn't believe in inoculations—he thought they would cause the disease rather than prevent it—but I'd heard of Jenner's vaccine at school, so I consulted our local physician. On his advice, I went behind Father's back to have everyone on the estate inoculated."

She couldn't think of a single one of the seventeen-year-old lords she'd known who might take such an initiative. How amazing that Ian had. No doubt he'd saved hundreds of lives with his action.

"Unfortunately, Mother refused to go against Father's wishes as usual. She died of the disease." He looked up from the bed, his eyes glittering like shattered onyx in the dim candlelight. "And he blamed me, the stubborn old goat. He said I'd brought smallpox to the estate with the inoculations."

"How unfair!" Her heart lurched at the thought of a young Ian forced to shoulder the blame for his mother's death.

He shrugged. "Father had firm ideas about right and wrong, and I'd committed one of his cardinal sins by acting without his consent. He never forgave me for it."

"Is that why you fled to the Continent?" she whispered unthinkingly. "To escape your father and his unfairness?"

It was as if a curtain dropped over his face. "Something like that." Before she could comment, he glanced down at her brother, and said curtly, "Do you think it's safe to leave William now?"

Her breath grew leaden in her chest. She should have known Ian wouldn't answer *that* question. Even after all the time they'd spent together, he didn't trust her.

"Felicity?" he prodded. "Will the boy be all right alone?"

She straightened her shoulders with a sigh. "Yes, I think so. He never has more than one nightmare."

He released William's hand and stood. "Then we might as well have that claret."

Claret? She could hardly think about claret right now. All she could think of was the poor boy Ian had been and the tormented man he'd become, the one who wouldn't speak of his past even to his friends. Now she could see why he might have turned to his aunt in his loneliness. Why he might have been driven to do the unthinkable.

No, she mustn't think of that, or plague herself again with questions. Yet as she rose and followed Ian to the door, uneasiness built in her chest. He still wanted to talk to her alone.

Yesterday, she might have been foolish enough to believe she could resist his advances. After today she knew better—where Ian was concerned, she had the fortitude of a hare. And his revelations had softened her toward him most dangerously.

When they moved into the hall barely lit by its one candle, she realized she needed the candelabra that she'd forgotten in the nursery. "Wait," she began, turning back toward the door.

He caught her around the waist and drew her into his arms. "I've been wanting to do this all day." Then his mouth took hers in a searing kiss that stole her breath and severely battered her will.

She wound her arms about his neck. If she hadn't secretly awaited this all day herself, she might be able to resist him. But it was impossible now. She'd lain awake too many nights remembering their caresses. Too many times she'd watched him dance with another and dreamed it was her instead.

Their kiss was everything she'd remembered and more. Warm breaths melting into one . . . the rasp of his whiskers against her cheeks . . . the familiar but faint scent of tobacco clinging to his hair.

After he had her limp in the knees—and everywhere else—he drew back to smile down at her. "This is better than claret, don't you think?"

Better than any liquor she could imagine. Which was why she absolutely mustn't let him do it again. Taking him by surprise, she wrenched free and raced toward the staircase. When she heard him curse behind her, she quickened her steps, but she could hardly do more than feel her way along in the faint light from the single candle at the top of the stairs. "You must leave, Ian," she cried. "It's late."

"I'm not leaving," he growled as he hurried down the steps after her.

She'd hoped to outstrip him, but that was impossible. Apparently the man possessed the eyes of a cat, for he caught up with her just as she reached the next floor.

He swung her around to face him, his eyes reflecting the darkest desires. "There's no reason for me to leave, and you know it. I'm tired of this farce. I'm tired of going to bed wanting you and waking up wanting you more. I'm tired of pretending to court other women merely to make you jealous."

Her eyes widened in shock.

"Yes, that's why I courted them," he said, correctly interpreting her reaction. "You're the only one I've wanted since that night at the Worthings."

She swallowed hard. She should have known it was a ploy all along. She tried to summon up fury, but all she felt was a treacherous thrill that he'd gone to so much trouble to gain her.

"If you despised me, it would be one thing," he went on in a low voice. "But you don't. You want me, too. And the perfect solution to all this bloody wanting is for us to marry. So you and I shall come to an agreement. Tonight."

The thought of marrying him tempted her fiercely, not only because of "this bloody wanting," as he called it. The boys liked him. And he would give her a future—security and a home of her own, free of financial worry.

A home of her own where her husband didn't trust her with the truth about his life. Though he'd revealed a little about himself this evening, the important things he still kept secret. How could she live with a man whose past was so

dark even he wouldn't hold it up to the light? Could she
entrust her future and the boys' to such a man? More importantly, could she gift her heart to someone who didn't
love her, who only wanted her because he needed an heir?

She could not. "I told you before, I won't marry you."
Drat it, why must she sound so hesitant, as if she didn't
even believe her own words? Perhaps she too was tired of
struggling against the feelings he roused, of being wise
about the future.

"Then I must convince you otherwise." His shadowed
face hovered near hers, overwhelming, tempting. "It's time
you see what you're denying yourself."

Her heart beat faster. "What do you mean?"

"I'll show you." He kissed her again, this time so thoroughly she felt dizzy. Angling his head, he found a virgin
patch of skin under her ear and kissed it, then nipped her
earlobe. "Where's your bedchamber, *querida*? Where can
we be private?"

She blinked at him in dazed confusion. "Wh-what?" She
felt as if someone had filled her mind with cotton.

"Never mind," he growled. "I'll find it. Or someplace
equally acceptable." Scooping her up in his arms, he strode
down the darkened hall.

She would have fought him—really, she would have—
if he hadn't kissed her again. It wasn't much of a kiss, a
mere brush of his mouth against hers, but it left her aching
for more. As he continued down the hall, past the open
doors of her study, her parents' old bedchamber, and
Mama's sewing room, she marveled at her reluctance to
stop him.

What mad spell had he spun about her? Everything
seemed unreal, as if in a dream, a dream where he belonged
to her in every sense of the word. He paused outside her
bedchamber, then entered it. After setting her down, he shut
the door behind them, turning the key with the twist of one
hand.

The click of the lock jerked her out of his spell. "We shouldn't be here . . . we should—" She broke off, eyes narrowing. "How did you know this was my room, Ian? Have you been spying on me?"

He laughed and shrugged out of his frock coat. "This is the only room on this floor with a fire going and the bed turned down. It wasn't difficult to deduce."

Then she realized what he'd meant by saying he would show her what she was denying herself. Not a few kisses and caresses like before. Seduction. What a dunce she'd been not to realize it sooner! "Ian, this is wrong!"

"Not in the least. As I recall, this all started because you were determined to make sure Katherine went into marriage with her eyes open. Well, I'm offering you a similar opportunity. If you're determined to be a spinster, you should go into spinsterhood with your eyes open." He stripped off his waistcoat and went to work on his cravat. "I intend to open your eyes, to show you what you'll be missing if you deny me, *querida*."

A weakness seized her limbs. She wished he'd stop calling her "darling" in that husky voice. Spanish or no, it did naughty things to her. "My eyes are completely open. You opened them the last time you touched me, if you'll recall."

He chuckled. "Oh, I recall very well. I recall the way you kissed me back, the way you rode my thigh, the way you groaned when I touched your breasts."

The frank words shocked and titillated her at the same time, sending wild and indecent images surging through her memory. Her skin heated under his knowing look, and she had to glance away before he could see the effect of his words on her.

"But I didn't open your eyes completely," he went on. "That's the only reason you refused my proposal of marriage. I wonder what your answer would have been if I'd taken you to bed instead." Approaching her, he lifted his hand to cup her burning cheek. His thumb dipped down to stroke her throat, then outline her chin before caressing her bottom lip silkily. "Shall we find out?"

Why couldn't she say no? Why did the word stick in her throat, damn him? "I-I don't think . . . that's wise." But she said it on a breathy little gasp, and her head reeled from the intimacy of his fingers against her face, not to mention the jumble of images his words had provoked.

He clasped her waist, bringing her back into his embrace. "Yes, but since when did you ever do what was wise, *querida?*"

He had a point, she thought. Then he was kissing her again, and she was lost. Her reason shut down, along with her will and her common sense. All of them fell subject to the beating of her heart and the sheer wanton desires trampling through her unruly body.

It didn't matter what her mind screamed at her—that he'd primed her for this since that night at the Worthings, that it was a mistake, that she'd regret it later. Right now she didn't regret it. She couldn't. And she couldn't even hate him for using her weakness, her secret and shameful urges, against her.

She opened her mouth to his bold tongue as eagerly as the wanton she evidently was. His hands unfastened the buttons at the back of her gown with amazing deftness, and all she could do was twine her arms about his neck. She matched his every wicked impulse with one of her own, abandoning herself to his greater experience in a fever of need. When his hand slid inside her gown to stroke her thinly clad back, a luxurious sigh escaped her lips.

"I like to touch you," he whispered as he dropped his hand lower inside her gown to squeeze her bottom. "And you like having me touch you, don't you?"

She buried her flaming face in his shoulder, unable to admit aloud the painful truth—that she craved his hands, that she wanted them all over her body. Good Lord, how shameless of her! A sensible, respectable woman would evict him this minute!

Obviously, she was neither. But how could she resist the glittering temptation he presented? It was like having her sultan step out of her dreams and into her bedchamber. He transformed the dreary room with its simple oak furnishings and ragged curtains into a magical oasis where any sensual act was acceptable, even expected.

Dark eyes blazing with promises, he stepped back and tore impatiently at the buttons of his shirt. She waited with indrawn breath to see what lay beneath the civilized veneer.

She shivered at the sight. Skin the color of coffee with milk, skin that attested to his mixed heritage, his wild Spanish blood. A patch of rich, springy hair arrowed downward—as black as that on his head, but curly where the other was straight. As he opened the shirt, her gaze followed the trail down to where the hair thinned into a line, then disappeared beneath his waistband.

"Do you like what you see?" he asked, the sound deep and rumbling.

A mortified gasp escaped her lips as she jerked her gaze back to his finely molded chest. Had she no decency? She'd been staring at him down there and wondering . . .

His knowing smile only made it worse. "I don't suppose you've ever seen a man undress before." He stripped off his linen shirt and dropped it.

She shook her head. Although she'd seen men naked to the waist—the pugilists at Bartholomew fair always went shirtless—she'd never seen one so close, not even Papa. And what she saw made her throat go dry. Ian wasn't as brawny as those pugilists, but she'd always found their bulging muscles repulsive. His muscles were whipcord lean, but sharply defined. There was no mistaking the power in them that had enabled him to carry William up three flights of stairs without a murmur.

"Here." Catching her hand, he pressed it against his

chest. "Why don't you do more than look?" The stark need in his face called to her. "Touch me, Felicity, the way I touched you that night. I've dreamed of having your hands on me."

She needed no further invitation to mold her fingers over his muscles, feeling the steel under the hair-rough skin as he tensed at her touch. She wanted to feel it all—the wide expanse of his chest, the ridges of his ribs, the taut sinews at his waist. And touching him provoked the shameful stirrings she'd felt before . . . in her breasts, in her loins. A familiar moistness formed between her thighs, certain evidence of her loose character. She squeezed her legs shut, but that didn't assuage the ache between them.

As if he sensed her agitation, he began using his hands on her as well, though not where she wanted them. He threaded his fingers through her loosely pinned hair, shaking it free of its pins, then smoothing it out over her shoulders. Next, he stripped her down to her chemise and drawers.

He ran his hot, eager gaze over her body. "I'm glad you don't wear those abominable corsets," he growled as his hands swept lightly over her ribs. "When we're married, you must wear nothing but your chemise when we're alone."

The outrageous thought excited her, then alarmed her, for it was too much like the painting of her sultan and his scantily clad paramours. "We shan't marry," she said stubbornly. "I won't let you add me to your harem."

"Harem?" He chuckled. "I have no harem, *querida*. You'll be my wife, my *only* wife. You might as well get used to the idea."

She yanked her hands from his chest, but he caught one and pressed it to the center seam of his pantaloon trousers. "Here," he rasped. "Touch me here."

Something hard moved beneath her fingers, and she gasped, struggling to pull her hand away, but he wouldn't let her. "You have only to walk past me," he said tightly, "to make me feel this. I've never wanted any woman as much as I want you. Never."

"Not even—" She started to say "Cynthia Lennard," then caught herself, loath to mention her in such an intimate moment. "Not even Miss Greenaway?" she finished lamely, though she now doubted the woman was his mistress.

"Definitely not— I never give her a moment's thought." A warning flickered in his eyes as he bent his head toward her. "But you? You I've thought of constantly since the day we met."

He took her mouth with an almost angry need this time, his tongue stabbing deeply, his lips hard on hers. The bulge in his trousers thickened, and he ground it against her fingers. When his hand left hers to roam her breast, she found herself willingly squeezing the hot, hard length, reveling in the way it pulsed beneath her touch.

Tearing his lips from hers, he muttered, "My God, you're torturing me." He hauled her up in his arms and stalked to the bed with her. When he set her down on the edge, she scrambled to her knees, suddenly all too aware of where he'd placed her and why.

But before she could scoot away, he caught a fistful of her chemise to halt her. With a rakish smile, he dragged the flimsy muslin up her legs to bare her thighs. "Oh, no, *querida*. It's my turn to torture *you*."

Alarm coursed through her, for his foreign endearment reminded her that beneath the manners and dress of an English lord lay a half-Spanish and even half-civilized spy, with secrets so deep even the keenest gossips couldn't root them out. And this was the man she wanted to bed her! Had she lost her wits?

Then he slipped his hand inside the slit in her drawers to cover the dark triangle between her legs, and she froze. Half-civilized? He was completely *un*civilized!

"Ian, you shouldn't . . ." she whispered as she clutched

at his wrist in a futile attempt to prevent him.

"Let me touch you the way you touched me." Black eyes glittering, he cradled the secret place in the juncture of her thighs, then began fondling it, rotating his palm in slow, tempting ways she'd never dared to touch herself.

Excitement and shame burned up through her body together, and she closed her eyes, wishing she could hide from him. Any minute, he'd feel the embarrassing dampness between her legs and despise her for it.

"My God, you're so warm and wet, so ready for me," he said roughly, but without a hint of disdain.

Ready for him? What could he mean? Then he slid his finger inside the passage made slick from that indecent wetness, and she knew.

Her eyes flew open. "Wh-what are you . . ." She trailed off as another of his fingers joined the first, driving in and out of her in heated strokes that made her squirm. "Oh, Ian . . . heavens . . . *Ian* . . ."

Only the fickle firelight illuminated his features, which shone triumphant and mysterious, and lent an unearthly quality to what he did with his fingers. . . .

His wicked fingers . . . tempting and plucking at her, coaxing her to sway forward on knees gone weak.

He caught her with his other arm, his breathing as ragged now as her own. "Felicity, you do know . . . how a man makes love to a woman, don't you?"

"Like . . . like this," she whispered.

"Not quite like this."

Taking her hand, he flattened it against the bulge in his tight trousers, which seemed larger than before. "*This* is what I want to put inside you, the way my fingers are inside you now."

"I-I know," she choked out, absurdly pleased he would take the time to explain it.

"You mean you've done this before?" he rasped, a note of incredulity in his voice. His fingers delved even deeper inside her with a silken stroke so delicious she arched against his palm.

"Wh-what?" She couldn't think, could barely register the question. The wild fluttering between her legs now pulsed like the beating of her heart, and his fingers only increased the tempo. "Oh . . . no . . . I-I haven't . . . Lord Faringdon's son described it . . . told me once . . . what he wanted to do . . . to me. But I didn't . . . let him . . ."

His jaw tightened. "Lord Faringdon's son is a dead man."

At the sight of his thunderous expression, she couldn't prevent the giggle that bubbled up through her throat. "Y-You're jealous."

"Not at all. You see, I have you and he doesn't." Still, he gave her a possessive kiss that nearly shattered her. It matched the possessive thrusts of his fingers, heightening the throbbing between her legs into an unbearable ache.

Which is why the sudden withdrawal of his fingers made her whimper in disappointment beneath his mouth. He ended the kiss with a chuckle. "Don't worry, *querida,* your cravings will be satisfied. And so will mine, thank God."

He sat down on the bed to drag off his boots, then stood and peeled off his trousers and his stockings as she watched with disgraceful interest. How did he know that she craved something? How did he know what it was, when she didn't even know herself?

Then he jerked off his smallclothes, and she uttered a distinctly unladylike oath. The instrument that sprang proudly from between his muscled thighs was thick and rigid. *That* was what she'd been fondling? Oh, my Lord.

"Take off your chemise," he ordered. When she stiffened at the command, he added in a softer tone, "Please? I want to see you. All of you."

When she still hesitated, transfixed by the sight of his naked member, he stepped close and caught her chemise in his hands, pulling it over her head in one swift motion.

With sudden shyness, she sank back on her heels and crossed her hands over her chest.

"Don't, *querida*. You've nothing to be ashamed of." He drew her arms away from her breasts, and his eyes turned molten as they feasted on her body. "Nothing at all. Your body would make Venus cry with envy."

Such poetic words from a man who hid his thoughts so well—yet he wasn't hiding them now. Admiration shone in his face, sparking a most improper pride in her. As a young woman, she'd cursed the female attributes that drew unwanted attention to her when she'd accompanied her father. But now she relished them, because they made Ian want her.

God preserve her, she'd fallen far.

And he clearly meant for her to fall farther still. His mouth caught hers in a heart-stopping kiss, and his hands were all over her, fondling her waist and breasts and thighs with such expert care that she cooperated eagerly when he shifted her back to lie prone on the bed. Then he knelt between her legs, looming over her like some brooding creature of the dark, every inch of his body taut with his need.

She felt open, exposed fully beneath him, but the sensation vanished when he bent his head to suck first one breast and then the other. The fluttering between her legs began again, more urgent and piercing this time. He read her body only too well, reaching down to soothe where she ached with clever, pleasing strokes of his fingers. Only when she writhed and groaned beneath him did he part her secret lips with his hand and guide his member inside her.

The intrusion shattered her exquisite pleasure. "Good Lord, Ian!" The part of him pressing into her was larger and harder than she'd imagined. "You can't . . . it's not . . ." She started to say "right," but realized that wasn't true. It felt right, having him inside her like this. Invasive and unfamiliar . . . but *right*.

"It will only hurt a moment," he promised, inching farther inside. A shock of hair dropped over his brow to shield his eyes from her, but the fierce set to his mouth made her worry that he might be having a bit of trouble himself.

"Is it supposed to . . . I mean—"

"Yes." He flashed her a pained smile. "You're a virgin, Felicity. And the first time a man enters a virgin, it's like . . . breaching a wall."

The battle metaphor didn't exactly comfort her. "You ought to know."

"Actually . . ." He paused in his movements, a spasm of both torment and pleasure crossing his face. "I've never had a virgin."

"Well, you have one now." She wriggled back and forth, futilely trying to find a comfortable position beneath him.

"Not for long, with you doing that," he growled, then thrust boldly forward.

A pinch of pain made her gasp, then was gone. But now he was planted so deeply inside her she dared not breathe, much less move. It wasn't an entirely unpleasant sensation. Still, she would have thought there was more to lovemaking than this. "Ian . . . is this . . . are we . . . done?"

"Done?" His shoulder muscles were strained taut from the effort of holding himself off of her, but he managed a smile. "Oh, no, *querida*. Though I think we can . . . safely say the wall has been breached."

He drew out, then pushed in again, and the motion was so intimate, so intriguing that her eyes went wide in surprise. God preserve her, there *was* more. His slow, careful movements enchanted her, though they seemed to cost him some effort. Indeed, when his head swooped down and his lips seized her breast, his mouth plundered and drew hard on her while his lower body still only coaxed.

But his patience soon had the desired effect as her body began to adjust to his size, and then even relish it. The exotic yearnings he'd roused earlier returned with a vengeance, making her writhe beneath him and clutch at his waist to get more, feel more, have him deeper inside her.

He needed no more encouragement than that. Increasing the pace, his body thundered rampantly above her, inside her. The bed shook with the force of his thrusts, yet she urged him on with low, wanton moans.

He dragged his lips from her throbbing breast to whisper, "*Querida,* you're mine. Mine only." The leaping firelight made his midnight eyes and urgent expression seem almost demonic as he rocked wildly against her. "I won't let you go now. Not ever."

She shook her head from side to side, wanting to deny his claim even as she embraced it. Like a sultan possessing and never being possessed, he held her in thrall with silken chains.

But oh, how sweet the chains. The more she struggled, the more she grew entangled in them until she couldn't think except to think of him, couldn't breathe without breathing him in. He'd invaded her and now would conquer her, too. And she welcomed the conquest, damn him. Welcomed him inside her, as he'd known she would.

The ache rose again in her loins, pounding in her heart, driving her to buck beneath him. "Good . . . Lord . . . Ian . . . yes . . . yes!"

"Let it come . . ." he ground out. "Let it come, Felicity."

The unexpected explosion wracked her, ripping a cry from her lips as her body pulsed around him. Seconds later, he drove himself to the hilt inside her and cried out in Spanish, words she didn't understand but comprehended all too well, for they mirrored her own exhilaration.

For a moment, he hovered over her with eyes closed, his head thrown back and his lips still parted on their cry. Then the unholy glimmering of the fire revealed an intense satisfaction that crept over his features, softening them . . . erasing the tension that had kept his brow rigid until now.

"Ah, *querida,*" was all he whispered before he withdrew,

then rolled off to sink beside her on the bed. Tugging her on top of his spent body, he curved his arms around her to plaster her to him from chest to loins.

She settled against him with a long sigh and laid her cheek upon his sweat-dampened chest. A lovely contentment spread through her exhausted limbs. She could hear his heart thunder in her ear, feel his slowing breaths riffle her hair.

No wonder he'd been so confident he could seduce her into doing his bidding. Seduction was a potent weapon indeed. It certainly explained the vast number of fallen women running around London.

If only she could stay here like this . . . with him . . . could delude herself that a marriage between them might work . . .

She groaned. *If only* was for children who played pretend, not for young ladies who wanted more from their husbands than financial security and babes sired in lust. Ian hadn't once spoken of love. How could he? He didn't even know what it was, having never known it himself.

A draft chilled her naked skin, and she shivered. Ian stretched out a hand to grab the coverlet, then pulled it over them and tucked it around her shoulders with such tenderness, it made her want to throw all caution to the winds.

Yet nothing had changed.

No, that wasn't true. Everything had changed. Now she had the most pressing reason of all not to marry him. If he made love like this to her every night, he would reduce her to a drooling, lovesick slave in a matter of weeks, while he continued to hold his heart—and his soul—in reserve. That possibility was too horrible to contemplate.

Pushing up off his chest, she stared down into the relaxed face of the most maddening—and tempting—man she knew. "Ian," she began.

"Shh," he murmured, pressing a finger to her lips. "We can talk later."

Beneath her she felt him stir again, and her heart fluttered like a flirtatious coquette in response. Drat the man, it wouldn't be a matter of weeks. Days, more like.

Oh, who was she fooling? She wanted to be his lovesick slave this very minute.

With a self-satisfied smile, he drew her head down to capture her lips, and as he began to kiss her with lazy enjoyment, she melted all over him like butter spread on toast. Very well, she thought with a sigh when heat shot from his mouth through her body and straight down to her loins. She might as well seize one more chance at doing this with him tonight. There'd be plenty of time tomorrow for breaking the chains of slavery.

Chapter 17

The city is always rife with rumor, but it takes a perceptive individual to sort the truth from the merely titillating. Lord X is just such an individual.

LADY BRUMLEY, QUOTED IN AN ADVERTISEMENT
FOR *THE EVENING GAZETTE*,
DECEMBER 23, 1820

Lying in Felicity's bed wide-awake, Ian heard a distant clock chime the hour. Two o'clock in the morning already. With a sigh, he nuzzled the scented hair of the woman who slumbered in his arms. It was time to wake her, but not so he could make love to her. He shouldn't even have done it twice, with her newly deflowered.

But if he'd hurt her the second time, she'd certainly hidden it well. He would never have dreamed that a woman with such firm ideas about morality could take to bedding so enthusiastically. Lusty wench.

His own quenchless fever stirred him erect once more, and he groaned. There'd be no more satisfaction this evening even if she *could* endure it. Tonight he must preserve the proprieties, to spare her embarrassment at the hands of her neighbors. If he stayed, they'd be sure to notice his carriage in the street come morning.

Yet he couldn't bear to disturb her peaceful sleep. With

waking would undoubtedly come remorse—Felicity wasn't the sort of woman to happily embrace her ruin. No matter how much he told her it was inevitable, she would blame herself.

And then him.

He grimaced. Well, he'd have years to make it up to her, years of long winter nights in the master bed at Chesterley and lazy summers making love in the gazebo while the scent of roses sweetened the air. . . .

Damn it, he was hard again. Would he ever be able to think of her without having his cock shoot to attention? Bedding a woman was supposed to take the edge off desire, not sharpen the need to a fine point. Yet he wanted her now, and he would want her a hundred times more before they even reached the altar.

Footsteps sounded in the hall, and he froze. Who prowled about at this hour? One of the boys? Bloody hell, Felicity would be mortified if her brothers discovered her like this. When the steps halted outside the bedchamber door, he groaned. Touching his mouth to Felicity's ear, he murmured, "Wake up, *querida*. You must wake up."

"Hmm?" she grumbled as a soft tapping sounded on the door.

That was followed by a muffled voice he recognized as the housekeeper's. "Miss Taylor, are you in there?" The doorknob rattled, and he thanked his good fortune that he'd thought to lock the door earlier.

"Miss Taylor!" the voice said more loudly. There was no mistaking the urgency behind the three sharp raps that followed.

Felicity shot up on top of him, her expression impossible to read in the darkness. First she glanced down at him sprawled beneath her, then at the door, then back at him. He could imagine what she was thinking, especially when she jerked a sheet up to cover herself. She started to speak to him, but he gave her a quick shake of his head.

"Come on now, luv," the voice outside the door pleaded. "I know you're in there. Wake up. It's important!" There was the sound of keys clinking, and he groaned.

Felicity nearly vaulted out of the bed. "I'm coming, Mrs. Box!" She motioned for him to stay put, then scooped up her chemise and jerked it on over her head. "What is it? What's wrong? Is it one of the boys?"

"It's that nasty Mr. Hodges again," Mrs. Box said through the door. "He's drunk. Says he met up with your father's trustee in a tavern and found out the truth about—"

"Wait, I'm coming out," Felicity said, cutting Mrs. Box off. In a flash, she'd yanked on a voluminous dressing gown and tied it around her waist, then was sliding out into the hall, taking care not to let Mrs. Box see into the room.

"What's this about the butcher?" he heard her say before the door shut behind her, muffling the voices.

Quickly he climbed out of bed and lit a candle. While donning his shirt and trousers, he strained to hear the conversation that trailed off as the women apparently descended the stairs. Cursing, he searched for his Hessians until he found them lying half under the bed. As soon as he had the boots on, he eased out into the hall without bothering to put on his frock coat or waistcoat.

Voices wafted up from downstairs. The first was a man's, querulous and slurred, with the accents of a lower tradesman. "Now lookie here, Miss Taylor . . . I gots to have me money . . ."

"Keep your voice down," Felicity urged. "Do you want to wake the entire household?"

"If that's wot it takes to get me money, I will. I don't care 'bout wakin' them brothers of yours nohow . . . a lot of devils, them boys . . ."

Ian strode to the stairs and looked over the banister. The man named Hodges, a scrawny creature in disheveled frock coat and breeches, swayed unsteadily in the midst of the ill-lit foyer below. Mrs. Box stood between Hodges and the stairs with her back to Ian, plump hands planted on plumper hips.

A few paces away, Felicity, looking distinctly agitated, clutched her dressing gown closed at the throat. "You'll get your money as soon as Papa's estate is settled."

"Ha! Ain't no settlement an' you damn well know it! That fancy trustee of yers were in the tavern tonight, and I asked 'im 'bout it. Tole me the truth, 'e did, 'cause 'e was drunk. The only thing yer papa left you were a pile o' debts and them four boys to feed. An' I'm plannin' to get wot's comin' to me before everybody else finds out you ain't got a penny to yer name."

Ian had heard enough. With grim purpose, he started down the stairs.

"We can discuss this tomorrow at your shop, Mr. Hodges—" Felicity began, then squealed when the man lunged for her.

Ian vaulted down the stairs in a blind rage.

Below him, the tradesman caught hold of Felicity's shoulders. "You c'n pay me in coin or you c'n pay me in pleasure," the man was saying as Ian neared the bottom step, "but one way or t'other you'll pay me tonight, little missy—"

Before Ian even reached the bottom, however, Felicity brought her knee up into the man's crotch, then shoved the bastard backward over the leg Mrs. Box held conveniently out behind the man's knees. The man toppled over and dropped on the marble floor bent double, his hands clutching his groin.

Mrs. Box laughed as she hovered over the moaning creature. "That's the only 'pleasure' you'll be gettin' tonight, you damned—" She broke off as Ian rounded her and jerked the tradesman up in both fists.

Ian held the small man dangling off the ground. "You want money?" He shook the groaning man furiously. "You want money, you miserable bastard?"

"No, Ian!" Felicity cried as she ran up to him.

Insensible of anything but the insult to her, Ian shook the man again, heedless of the eyes going wide with terror and the head flopping back and forth. "You'll have your money, Hodges. But if you ever lay a hand on my fiancée again, I'll—"

"Fiancée?" Mrs. Box said, having apparently recovered her tongue.

"Ian, put the man down, damn you!" Felicity ordered. "Now!"

Ian hesitated. Then he ground out, "Fine," and released the wretch.

Hodges's body thudded to the floor like a sack of barley, but he scrambled to his feet, half-sober and all outrage. "I dunno who you think you are, guv'nor, but—"

"He's the Viscount St. Clair, that's who he is," Mrs. Box put in with a haughty sniff. "Y'd best not cross *him*, you fool."

The man gulped, then dropped his gaze to examine his rumpled suit. "Viscount or no, he had no cause to grab me like that," he mumbled. "It's a sad day when a man can't collect on his debts."

"You weren't collecting on debts, you bloody—" Ian began.

"I'd hold my tongue if'n I were you, Mr. Hodges," Mrs. Box said. "Now go on with you. The miss and I'll be round in the mornin' to discuss the bill."

"To *pay* the bill," Ian corrected her. "And the 'miss' will not be there. My man will attend to it." He stepped menacingly toward the butcher. "But see that you never come within a mile of Miss Taylor again, you understand? Or I swear I'll—"

"I got yer message, milord," the man said quickly, holding up a hand. "I'm leavin' now, and I won't be back. All I wanted was me money, and if yer seein' to that—"

"I'm seeing to it," Ian bit out.

Hodges fled.

As soon as the door shut behind him, Felicity turned on Ian, eyes blazing. "There was no call to come barging down here. I had the situation well under control—"

"Yes, I saw how 'well under control' you had the situation! You were stirring up a hornets' nest, damn it! What the bloody hell would you have done *after* he recovered from the blow to his groin?"

Felicity's chin came up a notch. "I would have called Joseph to throw him out."

"He couldn't throw out a mangy dog on his best day! But never fear, once we're married—"

"We are *not* going to be married! I told you before, Ian, I won't marry you, not even after . . ." She trailed off with an embarrassed glance at the housekeeper.

"What d'ye mean, you told him before?" Mrs. Box broke in. She regarded Ian with new interest. "Have you proposed to my mistress before tonight, milord?"

Ian started to say it was none of her concern, then thought better of it. If Felicity still intended to be stubborn about this—he might need Mrs. Box on his side. "My first proposal was a week ago, at the Worthings. Apparently your mistress needs more persuasion than most to do what's in her best interests."

"Beg pardon, milord," the housekeeper said tartly, her gaze taking in his scanty attire, "but I ain't sure I approve of your methods of persuasion."

"If I'd known Felicity was destitute," he snapped, "I wouldn't have needed such methods."

"I am *not* destitute!" Felicity protested.

Ian fixed his gaze on Mrs. Box. "Well? Is she?"

"Mrs. Box," Felicity threatened, "if you tell that man one word, I swear I'll dismiss you at once!"

"Never fear," Ian assured the housekeeper, "I'll find you a place at my estate no matter what happens. Now tell me, does your mistress have an inheritance or not?"

Mrs. Box shot him a considering glance, then shook her head. "Nearly penniless she is. Her papa left them a hundred pounds per annum and a mountain of debt. James inherited the house, and it's mostly mortgaged."

"Thank you," Ian said tersely, returning his gaze to Felicity.

"Mrs. Box, how could you?" Felicity cried. "I thought you were my friend!"

"I was, and I am. Somebody had to do somethin', luv, and you know it. Besides, if you like the man well enough to let him bed you, you like him well enough to marry."

The shame that spread over Felicity's reddening cheeks made Ian grimace. "That'll be all now, Mrs. Box. Felicity and I have important matters to discuss."

Accepting his right to command her as if he'd always been her master, the housekeeper nodded and headed toward the hall. Then she paused to fix him with a warning look. "One of them matters you're discussin' best be an early weddin' date, milord. Hodges ain't likely to keep his mouth shut for long, and since he saw you here, he'll guess that you and the girl were . . . well . . ."

"Will eleven A.M. on Christmas Eve suit you?" he asked dryly, wondering how he'd ever sunk to the point of accepting a servant's opinions on the date of his own wedding. "I'd marry her in the morning if I could, but I need time to procure a special license. As it is, that's earlier than even *I* had planned, and gives us only today and tomorrow morning to prepare—but you do have a point."

A brilliant smile brightened the woman's work-worn face. "Then Christmas Eve it is. That would be lovely."

As the woman walked off down the hall, Ian held his hand out to Felicity. "Come, let's return to your bedchamber. I can dress while we discuss this."

"No, indeed. I'm not such a fool as to give you another chance to seduce me." Though she spoke the words coldly, a bright blush accompanied them. He'd seen her blush more in the past day than in the entire time he'd known her. He found it vastly encouraging. A woman didn't blush before a man she hated.

With a disdainful bearing more fitting of the viscountess she was soon to become than the architect's daughter she presently was, she marched past him to a door halfway down the corridor. "We can talk in the drawing room." She turned the knob and thrust open the door. "Not that it will do you any good."

He grabbed a candle from a nearby sconce and followed her. "You know full well that marriage is our only recourse now." He entered the room and closed the door.

"Recourse for what?"

"In case you hadn't noticed," he bit out, "I've compromised you, and that generally means a wedding."

"Generally. But not necessarily."

Headstrong witch. "Damn it, I've ruined you for any other man!"

Though she flinched at his words, she stood her ground. "I never expected to marry anyway."

Sara's words leapt into his mind. *I should caution you that seduction might not succeed in changing Felicity's mind. She has a strong will.*

Bloody hell, he hadn't believed her, but obviously she'd understood Felicity better than he. What must he do to make Felicity listen? He set the candle carefully down on the closest table, fearful he might actually throw it in a fit of temper. He hadn't suffered from fits of temper in years. He'd striven hard to rid himself of that fault, and he had succeeded—until he met Miss Felicity Taylor.

Ruthlessly, he forced down his anger. Felicity was a rational woman and must be treated as such. "You know this is the best solution to your money troubles and my need for a wife."

She merely stared at him, her mouth drawn up into a

tight line. Engulfed by her oversize dressing gown, she looked fragile and pale.

"Such a union will be very much to your advantage," he went on. "You'll be a viscountess with a healthy allowance at your disposal. Your brothers won't want for anything, I'll continue the upkeep on this house, and I'll make sure your servants are provided for. I'll be a most generous husband, I assure you."

"That's probably all true. Unlike you, however, I believe a woman needs more than a comfortable home and a generous allowance to make a successful marriage."

"If it's your bloody column you're worried about, I don't care if you continue—"

"It's *not* my column," she said wearily.

What then? He thought a moment, then stiffened. "You enjoyed our lovemaking—I know you did."

"Yes." She bent her head, her lashes fluttering down to shield her eyes. "Of course I enjoyed it. I'm not a block of ice, after all."

Only when relief surged through him did he acknowledge that she'd actually made him doubt his prowess in bed. The woman was turning him into a nitwit, and he'd had enough. "Well? What is it you want from me?"

If she'd been a chit fresh from the schoolroom or a dewy-eyed lover of poetry, he might have thought she desired vows of undying love. But she was neither—she regarded all members of his sex with cynicism. And she'd never once mentioned love when refusing his last proposal.

"Felicity," he said impatiently when she lifted her gaze to his, confusion and uncertainty on her face. "Don't make this more complicated than it needs to be. Name your concessions and be done with it. I'll give you whatever you wish within reason."

"Even the truth about Miss Greenaway?" she blurted out.

Damn. He should've known. Once Felicity got an idea in her head, she worried it as a kitten worries a string. "I told you before, Miss Greenaway has nothing to do with us. You're a fool if you balk at this marriage because of her."

She pivoted away from him then, padding over to the window on slippered feet. Her slender frame looked small and delicate next to the lofty Gothic design, all the more as she shivered from the draft. He had a sudden fierce urge to enfold her in his arms and shield her from the cold, from her fears, from everything that could harm her.

With shaky hands, she tried to close the drapes at the window more tightly against the draft. "And what if . . ." She paused, as if to gather her courage. "What if I'm balking because of someone else? What if I'm balking at . . . Cynthia Lennard?"

Coming on the heels of his tender thoughts, her question hit him like a pistol shot to the chest. God, no. Not this. Not now. He strove to conceal his reaction, but his words still came out harsh. "What do you know of Cynthia Lennard?"

She bent her head against the drapes. "She was your aunt, wasn't she? I've heard . . . that you and she had a love affair. That she pined away for you after you fled England for the Continent."

She'd "heard" this? Where? How? A weight of guilt crushed his chest, making it nearly impossible for him to breathe. Bloody hell, no matter how he tried he couldn't escape Aunt Cynthia's legacy. Poor beautiful and doomed Aunt Cynthia. He didn't know which was worse—the story Felicity had heard or the truth. Neither did him credit.

He needed more information. "You've truly outdone yourself this time. Where did you get such a tale? I doubt even Lady Brumley could rival it for sheer imagination."

"Lady Brumley was the one who told me." Felicity came away from the window and began to pace, her words tumbling forth in a higher pitch that showed her nervousness. "She heard about it from your uncle's servants. She seems to detest your uncle, and so she tries to find out all she can about him. I don't know why."

"Why? Because he jilted her twenty-five years ago. He left her at the altar when he discovered her father's wealth was a sham. After that, her only choice was to marry old Brumley. She's never forgiven my uncle for that."

She seemed shaken. "I don't blame her."

"Nor do I, but surely you can see this tale is nothing but her attempt to strike back at him. It makes him appear a fool and a cuckold. That's her only reason for spreading it." Yes, perhaps it could work in his favor that Lady Brumley, of all people, had hit so near the truth.

"Actually, she told me her story because . . ." She swallowed. "Because your uncle had told me a worse one."

The blood drained from his face. "My uncle?"

"He accosted me in private at her ball, and . . . and told me that you had . . . forced his wife and she'd killed herself for shame."

He sank into a nearby chair and stared off sightlessly. Damn Uncle Edgar and his lies! Rage swam up through his senses to tear at him like a hungry shark. "I suppose you believed him!" he snapped.

"No! Of course not!" She stepped toward him and laid her hand on his shoulder, a blush tinting her cheeks a rosy color. "I know from experience that you don't force women. I found the entire tale suspect even before Lady Brumley confirmed that he was lying. But as you can see, she didn't tell me her story to strike back at your uncle. She was trying to help you. She'd guessed at your interest in me and wanted to reassure me of your character."

"I see." Shaking off her hand, he rose from his chair. "She wanted to reassure you I was merely an adulterer." My God, this was a nightmare. Both tales were horrible. Yet the truth was so awful he couldn't even speak of it, especially to her.

"Then that's a lie, too?" she asked in a whisper.

Yes, he thought, but couldn't say it, for then she'd want to know the truth. Damn them all for putting these doubts in her mind. And damn her for even thinking them partly true. "Obviously, you've decided the answer to that already. You believe I bedded my aunt—the wife of my own father's brother—and then abandoned her." An awful realization stole over him. Staring down at her, he growled, "And you let me make love to you last night even though you thought—"

"I let you make love to me, because I didn't want to believe it. I still don't." Her voice wavered, and he suddenly glimpsed the hurt she'd striven mightily to hide. "But I don't know what to believe. Everyone speculates about your life, bombarding me daily with new tales about the dangerous Lord St. Clair. And you expect me—a woman who's known you less than a month—to discern the truth amidst the lies while you act the tragic hero and keep silent about it all?"

Her logic only made it worse. "You have a history of writing lies about me, yet you wonder why I keep silent? Oh, that's rich!"

Her eyes flashed. "That's just an excuse, and you know it. Have I mentioned you once in my column in the past week? While you slobbered over every eligible woman in sight, did I write one word about you or the women you courted?"

"Slobbered over— Damn you, Felicity, I see why you insist on knowing my past." His anger at himself twisted into anger at her. "You're jealous of women I didn't even bed! It's a wonder I had time for fighting a war or for running Chesterley, considering all the women you think I lusted over."

He paced the room furiously. "There's my aunt, whom I apparently seduced at the precocious age of nineteen. Then I ran off to the Continent and into the arms of a score of Spanish women, depending on which source you credit.

Oh, and let's not forget Josephine, who apparently came to my bed despite the troublesome fact that I'm English and her sworn enemy. Not to mention all the women I've courted or supposedly bedded in the past three years in England."

Stopping short, he glared at her. "And poor Miss Greenaway—I suppose you still believe her to be my mistress." He crossed his arms over his chest. "Is that all of them, or have I missed a woman or two whose association with me you wish to question?"

"Yes, you missed *me*—the woman you want to marry. But apparently you don't want her badly enough to entrust her with the truth."

The accusation fell between them like a gauntlet. Her pain was so palpable, her green eyes so bleak. Bloody hell, he hadn't meant to hurt her. It was just that the thought of her knowing so much and yet so little roused his temper as nothing ever had.

Frustrated, he stabbed his fingers through his disheveled hair. How he wished he could unfold the entire ugly story. It would almost be a relief.

Except that once she knew, she'd never marry him—not his self-righteous Felicity.

And besotted fool that he was, he couldn't walk away from her.

"This isn't a matter of trust," he said in an attempt to placate her. "Surely the very fact that I wish to marry you shows I trust you. I trust you not to shame my family name, and I trust you to be a good wife to me. I even trust you with the management of my home and the bearing and rearing of my children. Isn't that enough for you?"

She squared her shoulders. "Ian, I'm not insensible to the amazing compliment you pay me with this offer of marriage. I'll even admit I'd like nothing better than to marry you. But I don't want a marriage full of secrets. Why can't you understand that?"

"And why can't you understand that none of my secrets has anything to do with *us*? You're torturing yourself needlessly with all these questions about other women in my life. You're jealous of a woman who died ten years ago, another woman whom I consider merely a friend, and a former empress whom I never even met, for God's sake, much less bedded. You're jealous of ghosts when all I want is *you*."

She sighed. "You insist on seeing this as mere jealousy. You can be such a vain, arrogant ass sometimes."

How much more insulting the words sounded on a woman's soft lips. "That's why you should marry me," he said in a weak attempt at humor. "It'll give you ample opportunity to prick my vanity and subdue my arrogance."

She raised one eyebrow. "That is indeed a temptation." Then she added, "But not enough of one. As long as you won't be honest with me, I can't marry you, Ian. I'll always know you don't trust me, and the thought will eat at me until I grow to hate you. I care about you too much to have that happen. I'm sorry."

He'd seen it coming, yet he couldn't believe it. How could she be so bloody stubborn? Well, she wouldn't deny him this marriage simply because of old gossip and wounded pride, not when it was the means to her salvation as well. He wouldn't let her!

"You have no choice in the matter," he told her grimly. "You *will* marry me."

She stiffened. "I told you, I don't care if you've compromised me—"

"But you do care about starving, don't you? Have you forgotten your financial situation? I haven't. If you don't marry me, I'll seek out all your father's creditors and tell them you have no real inheritance. You know too well what'll happen then. They'll swarm over this place like rats."

Shock filled her face. "You wouldn't! No gentleman would do such a cruel—"

"No gentleman would leave you penniless and compromised. I'll do what I must to ensure that you marry me, and if that means throwing you to the wolves until you see your folly, so be it. Don't be foolish, Felicity. How long do you think you'll last once those money-grubbers divide this house between them? How will you live when it's gone? In a garret, supporting four growing brothers on the proceeds from a newspaper column? I think not!"

"I have prospects! Mr. Pilkington says he'll print my book—"

"Mr. Pilkington will say anything to keep you writing that column he pays you a pittance for. Do you truly believe he cares about your book? Even if he did, it wouldn't bring you enough money to support a household of this size." He neared her and lowered his voice. "You'd turn down a secure future for your family simply because of your damned principles? No. I won't allow it. You'll marry me tomorrow, and that's the end of it."

He stalked toward the door, but she caught him by the arm before he reached it. "You don't want to do this! What kind of marriage can we have if I hate you?"

Though that was her best thrust yet, he forced himself not to heed her plea. "You won't hate me. You're too sensible for that. Eventually you'll thank me."

"Oh, you really *are* an arrogant ass! And a foolish one, too, if you think I'll *ever* thank you for forcing me to act against my will!"

"I'm only doing what's in your best interests," he bit out.
"And yours."

"Yes, and mine. But our interests mesh very well together."

"Do they? Well then, Lord St. Clair," she said, his title sounding like a curse on her lips, "I have a surprise for you. I want a real marriage, and we can only have that if

you're honest with me. So until you are, you'd best pray
our encounter tonight produced your heir. Because that will
be the last time I take you into my bed willingly. If you
force this upon me, you'll have to force the other upon me
as well, do you hear?"

The thought that she might actually mean it momentarily
paralyzed him. Then he shook it off. She was already relenting on the subject of marriage; the other would come.
"I hear you, but this petty threat won't deter me. I've
reached the end of my patience. We'll be married Christmas
Eve if I must drag you into the church myself."

She visibly recoiled at his words. "I mean what I say."

"I don't doubt it." He caught her chin and ran his thumb
deliberately over her trembling lower lip. "But I know how
easily your passions are roused. Mark my words, *querida*,
I'll have my heir by Martinmas next, and I won't need force
to get him, either."

He waited until he saw the doubt flicker in her eyes before he released her. "So no matter what you threaten, we
will be married. Is that understood?"

She stared at him white-faced, but he could see the look
of defeat in her eyes.

"Felicity?" he prodded sternly.

With a sigh of exasperation, she nodded.

His triumph tasted like the bitterest wormwood; he
wished he could have gained her some other way. On impulse, he drew off his signet ring to press it into her cold
palm, closing the fragile, ink-stained fingers around it with
a twinge of guilt. "Present this if any more of your creditors
come to call. I'll notify you of the arrangements for the
wedding once I've procured the special license."

When she merely stood there woodenly, he released her
hand. But as he left her behind him in the drawing room,
her words stayed with him.

*If you force this upon me, you'll have to force the other
upon me as well.* Damn the obstinate witch to hell—he'd
do whatever was necessary to prove her wrong.

Chapter 18

My sources tell me that Lady Marshall was seen in the Strand with her husband's paramour. If this is true, it sets a dangerous precedent, for the moment two women consult together about one man, he is likely to lose both of them.

LORD X, *THE EVENING GAZETTE,*
DECEMBER 24, 1820

It was Christmas Eve morning, and Felicity and Mrs. Box had been up since dawn. With two hours left before the wedding, they were in Felicity's bedchamber. She stood stiffly on a stool with arms outstretched as Mrs. Box altered her mother's bridal gown for her.

" 'Tis well that gowns were less fitted in your mother's day," Mrs. Box commented, "or you'd have to wear a corset with this. I know how you dislike corsets."

I'm glad you don't wear those abominable corsets, Ian had said. *When we're married, you must wear nothing but your chemise when we're alone.*

Married. They were going to be married. Heat spread through her breasts and loins at the thought. "Damn his hide," she muttered under her breath.

"Come now, luv, don't be like that. It ain't the end of the world." Pinching up a fingerful of satin bodice, Mrs.

Box stitched through the fold. "You're marrying a viscount, for heaven's sake! He'll be takin' the boys under his wing—"

"Hah! He won't even let me celebrate Christmas with them tomorrow!"

"Can you blame him? Who'd want four boys underfoot during his honeymoon? He could send 'em all off somewhere, but he ain't. He only wants a week with you to himself, so's he can show you 'round his estate. 'Tis a pity the week crosses Christmas, but you should've thought of that before you let the man bed you yesterday morn."

She glared at Mrs. Box. "And he's closing the house up—my home!"

Shoving Felicity's arm up higher, Mrs. Box made a gather beneath her arm and tacked it quickly in place. "It ain't your home no more, thank the good Lord. What was you plannin' to do after you married? Live here? Separate from your husband?"

"It's a thought," Felicity grumbled.

The housekeeper laughed. "Don't you lie to me, luv. You don't want to live separate from that great strappin' stallion, and you know it."

Tears welled up in her eyes. "Oh, damn," she whispered, fingering the heavy signet ring that hung from a slender chain around her throat. It was true. Despite Ian's dreadful missive stating his "plans"—really a list of commands—for the wedding, and although she'd done nothing but complain about it for the past day and a half, she was secretly giddy at the thought of marrying him. She couldn't wait for him to be hers. To belong only to her and to care for her.

She sniffed. Care for her, indeed! The man didn't know the meaning of the word! Him, with all his wretched talk about advantages and generous allowances. And yes, his heir. He was willing to pay a high price for his dratted heir. Well, he'd soon discover that her performance as a brood mare was contingent upon his willingness to trust her.

Unfortunately, that meant keeping him at arm's length until he came around. A bitter tear escaped her eye. As if she could manage that. Ian need only hint at seduction, and she turned into a blithering idiot. Another tear rolled down her cheek to fall headlong from her chin and onto the gown, darkening a tiny spot of shimmering blue satin.

"Here now, don't you be weepin' all over your mother's pretty wedding dress!" Mrs. Box produced a handkerchief and dabbed at Felicity's eyes. " 'Tis a miracle that the gown survived until this, and now you're like to ruin it before the wedding!"

"Good! Then I can wear what I really want—sackcloth and ashes!"

"The sackcloth I can arrange," Mrs. Box said tartly. "But I won't be puttin' no ashes in your hair after I had to go halfway across London to find orange blossoms."

"I don't know why you bothered. It would serve him right if I had no flowers and an ugly gown because he couldn't be bothered to consult me on the date of the wedding."

"He *did* consult you, and you told him you wouldn't marry him. So what else was the man to do?"

"Accept my refusal like any decent man would have."

"No decent man would let a woman go on as you have. Not if he cared for her."

"Care for me! He doesn't care for me! He just wants any woman who'll agree to be his wife, and I happen to be handy."

"Poppycock. Men don't know what they want, luv, and they sure don't know how to ask for it. They put their brains away when a woman's around. So you got to regard their actions, not their words. Take your viscount: you spoke badly of the man in your writin', and you near tossed him out of the house, yet he came back for more and here he is payin' off all your debts and sendin' James back to that school the boy loves. What more proof do you need that he cares for you?"

She needed honesty. Trust. But she couldn't tell Mrs. Box that. The housekeeper wouldn't understand. "None of that counts because it's mere money. Money means nothing to him. He's only opening his purse because he has a substantial one to open."

"Maybe. Or maybe he's opening his purse 'cause he don't know how to open his heart. Let him do the first, luv, and one day he'll feel easier about doin' the second."

If only she could believe that. But she doubted he'd ever open his heart—he kept it buried so deeply beneath his past. If she could only learn what tormented him, she might see how to reach him. But no one knew the truth except him. And perhaps Miss—

She straightened. Yes! Miss Greenaway!

"I forgot," she told Mrs. Box in a rush, "I've got to go. I've something to attend to before the wedding."

"What? His lordship's carriage is callin' for us in less than two hours! There's a hundred things to do before then!"

"I know, but this is important. I must go *now*, before Ian whisks me out of London." Felicity reached back for the top buttons of the gown. "Help me get this off!"

"You've lost your mind, that's what it is." Mrs. Box shook her head, but did begin unbuttoning the gown. "Runnin' off two hours before your weddin'! The very idea! If you don't make it to the church in time, his lordship'll have my head!"

"It won't take long, I swear." Felicity leapt from the stool and swiftly dressed herself in an old gown. "I'll return before you even know it. But if I'm not here when it's time to leave, go on without me and bring the gown. I'll meet you at the church."

Less than a minute later, she raced out of the town house and flagged down a passing hackney. *Oh, God, please help me,* she prayed as she climbed inside. She gave the man the address in Waltham Street, then sat back, lifting her gaze heavenward. She hadn't entreated the Deity since He'd deserted her at the Worthings, but she needed him now. *Let the woman be home, God. Make her agree to talk to me. And don't let me be late for the wedding. Please, I beg you, do this for me.*

He must have been listening, for twenty minutes later when she knocked on Miss Greenaway's door, the woman herself opened it, her baby cradled in her arms. "You!" she exclaimed, then tried to slam the door in Felicity's face.

Felicity thrust her foot through the opening to block the door, wincing when it crashed against her boot. Lady's footwear obviously wasn't designed to serve as a doorstop.

"Go away!" a voice called through the aperture. "I've nothing to say to you!"

"Please, Miss Greenaway, let me in, just for a moment!" When the woman only kicked at her foot, Felicity called out, "I'm Ian's fiancée!"

A sudden silence came from the other side of the door. Then Miss Greenaway leaned around the edge, clutching her baby to her chest. "You? His fiancée?"

"I'm afraid so." Unclasping the chain holding the signet ring, Felicity held both out to the woman. "I really am."

With a wary expression, the woman shifted her baby to her shoulder and took the ring. But as she studied the object, confusion replaced wariness. "I don't understand. Master Ian—I mean, Lord St. Clair—did tell me yesterday that he was marrying a Miss Felicity Taylor, but he didn't say you were also—I mean, I never imagined—"

"He'd be marrying Lord X? No, I wouldn't have thought it myself a few weeks ago." So Ian had already been here to tell Miss Greenaway of the marriage. That would increase her jealousy if not for one thing—the woman seemed surprisingly undisturbed by the idea. And would a mistress call a man by his childhood appellation? "But I *am* Felicity Taylor and I *am* engaged to be married to him. In fact, the wedding is at eleven, so I don't have much time. Would you please let me in? I truly must talk with you."

The woman hesitated only briefly before opening the door. "His lordship will be furious if he learns of this."

"Then let's not tell him," Felicity said as she stepped over the threshold.

Miss Greenaway surveyed her curiously. "All right. Let's not." She gestured to a coat stand. "You can put your cloak there, then come with me into the parlor, if you please. I have Walter's crib in there while the maid is at market, and I was about to put him down for his nap." She glanced at her son's little head, with its golden baby fuzz. "Though I think he's started on it already."

The glow of love on the woman's face heightened the flawlessness of her china-doll features. How could any one woman have such perfect beauty? Felicity thought, unable to squelch her envy. Only the faintest brush of tiny lines at the corners of Miss Greenaway's eyes revealed her to be older than Felicity. And though the woman dressed in a practical wool gown that hid every inch of skin, it did nothing to hide her matchless figure. A quick stab of jealousy went right to Felicity's heart.

As they walked down the corridor, Felicity said, "I'm sure you're wondering what I'm doing here—"

"Not at all." The woman cast her a sidelong glance. "You're here to learn whether I'm really Lord St. Clair's mistress as you postulated in your column."

Heat climbed up Felicity's neck to her cheeks. "No, I . . . That is . . . well, I—"

"Trust me, I'd do the same thing if I were in your place. But let me set your mind at ease. I am not—nor ever wished to be—his mistress or anything else."

An enormous sigh whooshed out of Felicity before she could prevent it. Ian had proclaimed a hundred times that

Miss Greenaway wasn't his mistress. Sara had been nearly certain of it, and Lady Brumley even more so. But until Felicity had heard the words from Miss Greenaway's own mouth, she hadn't quite believed it. And though she supposed the woman could be lying, she could see no reason for that.

"Thank you," Felicity whispered as they entered a small parlor.

"You're welcome." With a little cooing noise, the woman laid her son in a wooden crib that sat near a large chair. "It would be churlish of me indeed to repay his lordship's kindness by misleading his future wife." She gestured to a pretty white sofa. "Please sit down, Miss Taylor."

Felicity complied, feeling awkward. The woman was being very gracious, considering the situation. "Before I go any further, I must apologize for my article. I shouldn't have speculated so publicly about your association with Ian. He's made me see it was wrong to do so, especially when it might . . . harm your reputation."

Miss Greenaway chuckled. "My reputation?" With a grace and posture only a governess could manage, she lowered her posterior in a vertical line onto the chair beside her son. Felicity had never seen a woman's spine remain quite so elegantly straight. She certainly had never managed it herself.

"I thank you for your concern," the woman went on, "but it's unnecessary, I assure you. You didn't mention my name or Walter's, and my reputation was damaged long ago. Besides, your assumption was logical, given the circumstances. And as you well know, Lord St. Clair rouses speculation wherever he goes."

"That's true." Felicity swallowed. "It's the real reason I'm here. You see . . . I hear a great many rumors in my profession. And . . . well, I've heard some particularly nasty ones about Ian. I was hoping you might tell me what is truth and what is lies."

"I see. What have you heard?"

Under different circumstances, Felicity might have been more delicate about presenting her situation, trying to assess how best to elicit the truth from her companion. But she had no time for such subtleties today; she was forced to be blunt. Fortunately, Miss Greenaway's earlier frankness made it easier.

As briefly as possible, Felicity related the two conversations she'd had at the Brumley ball. Though Miss Greenaway's expression altered somewhat at the mention of Ian's uncle, she kept silent throughout Felicity's tale.

"So you see," Felicity finished, "I don't know what to believe, or if either of these tales is true at all. I hoped you might tell me why Ian left England. And why he and his uncle are in conflict over his marrying."

"What does his lordship say?"

Sarcasm laced her voice. "That I'm merely jealous. That it's nothing to worry my pretty little head about." She tilted up her chin. "He won't tell me anything. And as his future wife, I think I have the right to know."

"I agree," she said gently. "I will say this—his lordship's uncle can't be trusted. But beyond that, I can't tell you anything else. Lord St. Clair swore me to secrecy the day he brought me here, and I owe him too much to betray his trust."

No! Felicity thought as despair knotted in her belly. This was like one of those garden mazes she hated, where each turning only led to more turnings. Sheer frustration drove her to her feet. "Then how am I to know I'm not making the biggest mistake in my life by marrying him?"

The woman's forehead knotted into a perplexed frown. "Tell me something, Miss Taylor. Two weeks ago, Lord St. Clair instructed me never to speak to you, yet now he's marrying you. How did that come about?"

"I've wondered the same thing myself," she said glumly. "Apparently, somewhere among our many battles over my column, he came to the conclusion that I'd make him a suitable wife. I can't imagine how, since we have nothing in common."

"No indeed." The woman's lips twitched with amusement. "Except perhaps for an incredible ability to find out other people's secrets. And a tendency to act forcefully to get what you want. And let's not forget a fondness for children—he did say his fiancée had four brothers he'd be supporting, and he's always been kind to my son." She broke out in a smile. "But nothing else, certainly. Whatever do you see in each other?"

Felicity didn't like being mocked. She glared at the governess. "You're laboring under a misconception if you think this is a love match. Ian didn't choose to marry me for any such commonalities, I assure you. He wants a brood mare, that's all."

"A-A brood mare?" Miss Greenaway choked out.

"A woman to give him an heir. And in exchange for my marrying him, he's paying off my debts and providing for my brothers and me."

"Ah. So your marriage is nothing but a business arrangement?"

"Precisely."

"And the fact that you're a beautiful, intelligent young woman has nothing to do with it, just as his attractions have nothing to do with *your* decision."

She colored. "Certainly not."

"Then why, pray tell, are you so intent on uncovering his past? If this marriage is merely a business arrangement and he's keeping his end of the bargain, why do you care what he did ten years ago?"

"Because," Felicity said through gritted teeth, "in a short time, I'll be putting my life and future in his hands, and the man is so bloody secretive I don't even know if I can trust him!" That wasn't entirely true, but she had no time for shilly-shallying.

"You needn't worry about that. Lord St. Clair is quite trustworthy. He'll treat you well." Miss Greenaway rose and approached to where Felicity stood trembling. "But I think you know that. So what really torments you so much?"

Felicity ducked her head to hide the sudden tears swimming in her eyes. "What torments me is that we aren't even married and I'm already in love with the scoundrel."

She sniffled. Oh, damn—it was true. Why else did she feel sick at the thought of being his wife and not having his heart? And she'd fought so hard against it! She should've known fighting was pointless from the first time he'd sauntered into her study and informed her that she would regret tangling with him.

Oh, yes, she regretted it. She regretted that tangling with him hadn't made him love her in return. The tears straggled down her cheeks, first singly, then in solid rivulets, forlorn pilgrims streaming to the shrine of unrequited love.

Miss Greenaway drew out a sensible cotton handkerchief and handed it to Felicity. "There, there, my dear. Surely it's not so terrible to be in love with a man like Lord St. Clair."

"It is when he doesn't love me," she whispered.

"Are you sure of that?"

She nodded. "Ian has a thorn buried deep inside his heart that prevents him from loving me in return. It needs plucking out. How can I do that when I don't know what it is?" She lifted a pleading glance to Miss Greenaway. "Can't you help me?"

"Oh, Miss Taylor," the woman said sympathetically. "I'd tell you in a moment if not for my promise. You're right about the thorn in his heart. It lies so deep, he won't even speak of it to me, and I know all that happened. Yet he needs to speak of it."

"If you tell me what happened, I can *make* him speak of it."

"No. It must work its way to the surface before he can be rid of it."

Despair crept over her again. "Is there no way I can help him?"

With a smile, the older woman chucked her under the chin. "I think you've already begun. When he came yesterday to tell me of the wedding, there was a light in his eyes I haven't seen since he was a young man. In the past, his descriptions of women he courted were always unemotional recitations of their qualities. But he called *you* 'the most vexing creature in London—headstrong, brazen, and badly in need of a man's guiding hand.' It was quite clear to me he couldn't wait to provide that 'guiding hand.'"

"That proves nothing," she grumbled. "He's a bully, you know."

She chuckled. "Only with you apparently, and that's because his emotions are engaged. Besides, I find very curious his reluctance to reveal that his fiancée was Lord X. Either he wanted to protect you, or he didn't want me to think ill of you. Both show that he cares."

Felicity twisted the handkerchief. "Or that your opinion matters a lot to him."

"We're friends, yes."

Unwarranted though it was, jealousy seized her again. "So why didn't he marry *you*? I-I mean, before I met him. Your station in life is no lower than mine. Some of the women he courted were extremely ill suited to him. At least with you he would have been comfortable and needn't have feared you wouldn't accept him."

"My dear Miss Taylor, he would never have asked me. You see, I know too much about his 'thorn,' as you call it, and though I consider it only a tragic incident in his past, to him it is so deep and black, he can't imagine any woman wanting him who knows of it. That's why he won't tell you: because he fears scaring you off."

She laid her hand kindly on Felicity's. "Besides, even if he'd asked, I wouldn't have accepted."

That surprised her. "Because you were in love with his uncle?"

"Hardly." Her tone grew chilly. "I wasn't Edgar Lennard's mistress by choice. He made it quite clear after his wife died that I could either be his mistress and continue as his children's governess or be accused of a crime and transported. At twenty-two, I was terrified of him. As an orphan with no family, I lacked anyone to champion my cause, and it would have been his word against mine. So I stayed on as his mistress. I was only too happy when he discharged me, even if it meant poverty or something equally low."

She smiled. "But much as I appreciated Lord St. Clair's coming to my rescue at that moment, I had no desire to marry him. It would've been awkward, considering his ties to Edgar and my son. I'm sure he would have been perfectly kind about it, but I didn't want such kindness. I'm much like you: despite my ruined reputation, I should like to marry for love."

She drew back with a sigh. "But that's unlikely to happen. Still, I should like to see it happen for Lord St. Clair. And I think it will, if you're there to heal the wound when the festering sore around his thorn finally breaks open. You *will* be there, won't you? I've set your mind at ease concerning him?"

Oddly enough she had. There was something comforting in the knowledge that Miss Greenaway knew all the facts about Ian's past and wasn't appalled. Whatever troubled Ian, it wasn't insurmountable.

There was the sound of a door opening, and then a young woman popped her head in the parlor doorway. "I'm back, Miss Greenaway. Shall I take Walter for you?"

"No, Agnes, thank you. He's napping."

"Shall I tell the man to return the gig to the livery then?" Agnes asked.

Miss Greenaway turned to Felicity. "What time did you say was your wedding?"

Felicity froze. Damn, she'd forgotten all about the time. She scanned the room for a clock, groaning aloud when she spotted one. "Good Lord, I'm supposed to be at the church in ten minutes! I'll never make it!"

"Yes, you shall. We'll go in the gig." Miss Greenaway started for the parlor door. "I can let you out at the entrance to the church, and no one need ever know I was there. Agnes can watch Walter, and if we move quickly, we might make it in time."

"I still have to dress and everything!" Felicity wailed as she hurried after Miss Greenaway. "The gown is at the church, but we'll be so dreadfully late . . . oh, Ian is going to *kill* me!"

"No, he's not. I daresay the man is probably running a bit late himself. We'll get you there on time, never fear." Casting an anxious look at the clock, Miss Greenaway grabbed Felicity's hand and tugged her toward the parlor door. "Come on, Miss Taylor!"

Chapter 19

How wearisome are these fashionable December weddings—Lord Mortimer to Lady Henrietta, Mr. Trumble to Miss Bateson, and Sir James to Miss Fairfield. Why do brides drag their friends out into the frigid weather when a nice summer wedding is so much more comfortable?

LORD X, *THE EVENING GAZETTE*,
DECEMBER 24, 1820

Ian strode to the window of the vestibule in St. Augustine's Chapel for the tenth time in as many minutes. But the street half a floor below showed only the same spectacle: advertising wagons touting Vauxhall Gardens and Dr. Bentley's Benign Balm, mistletoe and holly sellers, and the occasional fashionable carriage bobbing among carts and gigs.

No sign of his recalcitrant bride. His carriage had disgorged its passengers half an hour ago without producing her. A dull thudding had begun in his head like that of an incompetent drummer. He wanted to be sick, but he wouldn't allow it. Not on his wedding day.

Not in front of Mrs. Box and especially not in front of Jordan, who leaned stiffly against the plastered wall a few feet away. The two of them felt sorry for him, damn them.

Though Mrs. Box peeked often into the church proper to see if her charges still sat quietly beside their idol Gideon, she spent the rest of her time blatantly watching Ian as he paced and cursed. Jordan pretended not to notice anything or anybody, but he, too, sneaked glances at Ian every few minutes.

Ian planted his fists on the windowsill and leaned out, knuckles scraping against stone as he surveyed the street as far as he could see. Nothing. No hacks with beautiful passengers, no discreetly curtained carriages. Where the hell was she?

He whirled toward Mrs. Box. "Are you sure Felicity said to meet her here?"

"Yes. If she weren't back in time. Which she weren't."

"And she said nothing of where she was going?"

"Not a word, milord, but she promised she'd be here on time."

He took out his pocket watch, snapped it open, noted the time, and snapped it closed. "She's already broken that promise by twenty-three minutes," he growled, pivoting back to the window. "If she doesn't arrive soon, I'll have to go look for her. You know Felicity. She may have gotten into another argument with a hack driver, or the coach might be stuck or . . ."

He trailed off with a groan. He sounded like one of those bloody besotted grooms who slaver over their brides.

"She'll be here, milord," Mrs. Box ventured. "She probably met with a bit more traffic than expected. A mighty lot of carriages are on the road today, its bein' Christmas Eve an' all. But she ain't the kind of girl to—"

"Leave a man at the altar?" Damn. He hadn't meant to say that. It made it seem possible. But it wasn't. Felicity would never act impulsively when her brothers' futures were at stake.

Then again, she always surprised him. What if this was a particularly nasty surprise? God knows it was what he deserved for his overbearing behavior. He rubbed his temples with unsteady hands. The drummer in his head had been joined by a cymbal player and a very enthusiastic trumpeter.

Jordan came to his side. "I suspect that if you asked, the vicar could produce a flask of spirits. Shall I fetch him? You look as if you could use liquid reinforcement."

He shouldn't have invited his friends. In truth, he hadn't expected them to hurry to London on such short notice for his wedding, especially since Sara and Gideon had just left the city. But they'd come, and now they would bear witness to his humiliation.

"No, it's just a headache," he lied, unable to meet his friend's gaze. "It's plagued me for two days." Ever since he'd made the idiotic mistake of trying to force a certain stubborn female into marriage.

"You shan't improve it by stickin' your head out in that nasty cold air," Mrs. Box put in. "Why don't you come away from the window before you catch an ague?"

Ian shot her a dire glance. "Mrs. Box, if this wedding actually takes place and you come to work for me, you and I must have a lengthy discussion concerning your bad habit of lecturing your master."

"I'm only tryin' to be useful," she said with a sniff.

" 'Useful' and 'annoying' are two distinctly different things. At the moment, you're—"

"Ian," Jordan interrupted, leaning out the window, "isn't that her?"

Already half-resigned that she wasn't coming, Ian pivoted to brace his hands on the sill and look out once more. A gig pulled up below with two women in it. The passenger was Felicity, to be sure. He let out a long breath. Then he sucked in another as he recognized the driver, whose serviceable wool gown he'd paid for himself.

Bloody hell, he was in trouble now. Why in God's name had Felicity brought *her* to the wedding?

"Who's the woman with Miss Taylor?" Jordan asked.

Ian grimaced. "My 'friend' from Waltham Street."

Jordan's silence amply demonstrated that he could guess the significance of that. So could Ian. Felicity could have only one reason for bringing Miss Greenaway to the church. His jealous fiancée probably intended to throw his "mistress" up in his face, though it astonished him that Miss Greenaway had agreed to the scheme. She must not have realized what Felicity intended.

The icy air swirling into the chilly vestibule matched the ice caking his heart as he watched Felicity leap from the gig. She paused to speak to Miss Greenaway. Then to his astonishment, she turned and ran to the steps as Miss Greenaway drove off in the gig.

What the— He headed for the door at once. His soon-to-be wife would explain this to him or by God, he'd take her over his knee.

Mrs. Box hurried after him. "Wait, milord!" she said as she caught his arm. " 'Tis bad luck for the groom to see the bride before the wedding!"

"There won't be a wedding if I don't talk to her now." Shaking off the woman's hand, he opened the door to the vestibule as Felicity reached the top step. "You're late."

Her head shot up and she halted so abruptly she nearly lost her balance. Reaching out, he caught her by the arm to steady her.

"Ian! Yes, I am . . . I didn't mean to be, but . . . Good Lord, have you been standing there long?"

"Half an hour. And yes, I saw you drive up with Miss Greenaway."

In the ethereal paleness of her face, her eyes shone dark and mysterious as the sea. "It's not what you think—"

"You don't want to know what I think, I assure you." He hauled her inside the vestibule, then turned to find Jordan and Mrs. Box regarding him uneasily, like edgy members of a Greek tragedy chorus. He leveled a black look on both of them. "Jordan, go tell the vicar the wedding will begin shortly, and fetch James, since he's giving Felicity away. Mrs. Box, join Sara and Emily in the choir room. Tell them Felicity will be there in a moment to dress."

When the housekeeper hesitated, shooting Felicity an anxious glance, Felicity said, "It's all right. Go on. I need to speak to Ian alone."

Her calm tone only further agitated his temper. As soon as the others disappeared, he faced her with a scowl. "Well? What explanation can you possibly have for this?"

"I'm truly sorry I'm late, but we were talking, and the time slipped away—"

"You know very well I'm not referring to your lateness," he interrupted. "Why in God's name did you go see Miss Greenaway? And what do you mean, you were talking? What about?"

"You, of course. What else?"

The orchestra from hell now howled in his head. "What did she say about me?"

"Nothing important." With an air of distraction, she turned away to survey the vestibule. "This is a very nice church, Ian. Is it the one you attend?"

"Damn it, Felicity!" He grabbed her shoulders and spun her around to face him. "What the bloody hell did she tell you?"

Her gaze met his, cool, composed. "What if she told me the truth?"

He didn't have to ask what truth. My God, no. Surely not. Surely if Miss Greenaway had told her the truth, Felicity wouldn't be standing here. She'd be running away from him as far as her meager funds would carry her. Wouldn't she?

Only when she reached up to pry his fingers from her shoulders did he realize he'd been digging them into her flesh.

She didn't release them, however, but clasped them in

hers. "She told me nothing, Ian, that you hadn't already told me. She said you swore her to secrecy. And that you would have to tell me yourself."

The furious pounding in his head eased, but only a little. "So she didn't satisfy your foolish curiosity about things that don't matter?"

"No."

"Yet you came here anyway."

Her brief smile reassured him. "Yes. One thing she did tell me was that your secret isn't likely to hurt me."

"I told you that myself." It was far more likely to hurt *him* by turning her against him, which was why he wouldn't speak of it until he had her wedded, bedded, and pregnant. And why he ignored her expectant look now. "What else did she tell you?"

She sighed. "She also said you'd be a good husband and treat me well."

A faint hope sprouted inside him. "And you believed her?"

"I believe you have the *potential* to be a good husband." Her tone grew frosty. "But not if you continue to treat me the way you did the other night. Your secrecy is bad enough, but to threaten to hasten my financial ruin in such a despicable manner—" She lifted her chin a notch. "I do not like being bullied, Ian."

The extent of that dislike was apparent in every rigid line of her slender body. He ground his teeth together. He'd already planned to apologize, but now that the moment was come the words seemed stuck in his throat. "I did what I thought was right."

"You thought it was right to force me?"

He dragged his hands from hers. "It was the only way to make you realize the wisdom of marrying me."

"Oh, you think so, do you?" She crossed her arms over her faded wool bodice.

With a groan, he glanced away. "No." He sighed. "I'm

sorry. I wasn't thinking. I shouldn't have forced you."

"Do you mean that?"

"Yes."

"So if I don't marry you, you'll do nothing to stop me?"

His gaze shot to hers, a cold sweat breaking out on his forehead. My God, would she refuse him now? With everyone waiting in the church? He scanned her face for some sign of what she intended.

And saw none. Yet he knew that only one answer would show his sincerity, however much it pricked his pride to give it. "No. Yes. I mean I'll do nothing to stop you."

The blood thundered in his ears as he waited for her response, but she wasn't finished with him yet. "I have one more question. If you answer it to my satisfaction, I'll marry you, Ian."

That put him on his guard. "If you mean those tales of Lady Brumley's—"

"No. It's something that . . . has been troubling me since you made love to me. Why did you choose *me* to marry? Why not any of those other women you courted?"

Sara had asked him the same thing, and his answer hadn't changed. "Because I want you more than any of them."

For the first time since they'd begun this ludicrous discussion, she looked agitated. "If by wanting me, you mean desire, I should warn you I still intend not to share your bed until we work out our differences."

"Fine." That particular threat didn't worry him. No woman with Felicity's passions abstained from pleasure after she'd had a taste of it. Not when the man with her was bent on seduction. "But that wasn't what I meant. I want *you,* the person Felicity. No other woman will suffice. You . . . intrigue me." At her slow smile, he grew inexplicably nettled. "And I don't know why, so don't ask me to elaborate further or to spout a lot of nonsense about your virtues."

"I wouldn't dream of it. If you begin cataloging my virtues, you're certain to add my flaws as well, and I'm sure the latter outweigh the former in your mind." Her smile broadened. "But I suppose that answer will do. For now, at least."

The extent of his relief staggered and alarmed him, so much so that he couldn't keep the harshness out of his voice. "Then may we please have a wedding?"

"Oh, very well. I mean, you've gone to so much trouble, after all. I wouldn't want to disappoint you. Or humiliate you publicly."

He snorted. "Yes, you're always so careful on that score."

A grin was her only response. But as she drew her hands from his and hurried to the stairs that led up to the choir room, he felt the casing of ice around his chest start to melt. He didn't care what she threatened about not bedding him. Let her have her bit of fun and think she was in control. As long as the wedding went on and she became his wife once and for all, she could threaten whatever she wished.

Because in the end, he would win.

This is a most peculiar wedding, Felicity thought. The bride given away by her twelve-year-old brother. Only two attendants, and they were sister and brother—Sara standing up for her and Jordan standing up for Ian. And a former pirate captain flanking the bride's squirming triplet brothers on the left while a housekeeper sat on the right. The only other guest was Emily, so it was both a motley assortment and small.

Yet they made up for it by being merry beyond their size, more merry than the bride and groom, to be sure. As the vicar read the service, Jordan smirked and Sara smiled indulgently. Mrs. Box cried tears of joy from the beginning, while the boys wiggled and grinned in the pew, only too delighted to add a viscount to the family. And the generally stern-faced Gideon actually looked pleased at the whole affair, even while darting out a hand to subdue the antics of one triplet or another.

As the vicar read the vows, Felicity stole a glance at her husband-to-be, looking so tall and strong in his white velvet waistcoat and his tail coat of dark blue saxony with gilt buttons. One would have thought from his unruffled countenance that this wedding was as easy for him as a ride in the country.

But she knew better. There'd been that moment in the vestibule when she'd glimpsed the depth of his uncertainty, the sheer intensity of his desire to marry her and his equally intense fear that she might not. That glimpse had prodded her forward when every thought in her head had told her this was madness.

Somewhere inside his cool façade lay a heart so bruised that he couldn't love until it was healed. And she wanted to heal it. She had to. For she'd already lost her heart to him, and she wasn't giving up until he'd done the same.

Ian began to repeat the vows, and the steadiness of his deep voice soothed her worries. *It will be all right. Somehow I'll make it all right.*

When it was her turn, she spoke slowly, the words weighing down her tongue, for they were most solemn vows. If she were wrong about Ian, they might one day rise up to haunt her. But his stalwart presence at her side gave her the strength to finish them.

She and Ian exchanged rings. She gave him her father's old wedding ring—it was all she could afford—but the one Ian slid on her finger was obviously new and costly. He'd certainly meant it when he'd promised to be a generous husband.

"You may kiss the bride," the vicar intoned.

Her blood clamored foolishly as Ian faced her and lifted her veil. She'd forgotten about this part of the ceremony, and it had been two days since he'd last kissed her. His kiss was swift and circumspect, a mere press of his lips to hers, but flames scorched her lips where he'd touched them, and fire rose up in her loins. Nor could she mistake the possessive glint in his midnight eyes as he drew back from her. It found an answer in the smile she couldn't keep from springing to her lips.

Oh, but she was a hopeless case. His every motion called to her senses, which in turn clamored for his attentions. A glance here, a touch there . . . any and all sparked flames in naughty places.

And she thought to resist *this*? She hardly even noticed the wedding guests' broad smiles as she and Ian walked down the aisle. His gloved hand covered hers where it was tucked in the crook of his elbow, but even the chaste contact proved too much for her wild imagination, which kept seeing his naked hands on her breasts and belly and thighs.

She swallowed. Thank God they both wore gloves, or their hands would surely meld together from the heat of her thoughts. In a sensual haze, she let him lead her into the vestibule. In the same sensual haze, she went with him and the vicar into the chamber where they signed all the necessary papers.

Though it was only a few minutes, it seemed like hours before they walked out of the church to the carriage that would take them to the wedding breakfast Sara had insisted upon giving them. By the time they reached his carriage her body was awash with accursed need, and all from just the mildest of husbandly contacts.

If she could only escape him for a moment, only catch her breath before Ian had her to himself. But that was impossible. Now they would be alone in the carriage all the way to Sara's breakfast. Well, he would surely not attempt anything in so short a distance. Maybe that would give her time to clamp down on her wicked urges before they set off on the two-hour journey to his estate.

Unfortunately, once they were in his carriage, he took

the seat next to her. The curtains were closed, and the coach was as intimate as any bedchamber. She groaned aloud at the thought, and he shot her a concerned glance.

"Was the wedding not acceptable?" he asked as the coach set off.

"The wedding was fine," was all she could manage. His carriage was roomy, but she couldn't avoid touching him when he shared her seat, and the press of his thigh to hers offered new temptations. Having shared a bed with the man should have quelled all her body's eager stammerings and starts, but if anything, it made them worse.

"I'm glad it met with your approval," he said. "I meant to tell you, your choice of a gown is excellent. How did you manage it on such short notice?"

"It was Mama's wedding gown. Mrs. Box altered it for me."

"With admirable success. It fits you well."

Good Lord, must he say it in that rumbling male voice that made the most innocuous of comments seem seductive? "I'll tell her you said so."

Catching her hand, he laced his fingers with hers. "You look lovely in it."

Now *that* he'd intended to be seductive. She mustn't let the conversation wander in that direction. "If I'd had time," she said, trying to sound irritated, "I could have had one made that was more fashionable. But you were in such a dratted hurry to have your bargain sealed."

She'd hoped to annoy him enough to drop her hand, but his grip merely shifted so that his thumb could stroke across her wrist. She could feel the sensuous touch even through her gloves.

"I compromised you, remember? We had to move swiftly to preserve your reputation."

"Yes, and to gain possession of any heir you may have sired. You paid quite dearly for that heir of yours."

That didn't work either. As if he knew why she goaded

him, he chuckled, then released her hand, but only to draw off his gloves with slow movements that turned her insides to mush.

She swallowed and added, "Well, you may find you got the worst of the bargain."

He tossed the gloves aside. "How so?"

"Papa's debts are rather substantial; my brothers are likely to eat you into the poorhouse; and I myself may decide it's time to indulge my taste for luxuries heretofore inaccessible to me."

With a laugh, he settled back against the padded seat and took her gloved hands in his. He turned one over and lifted it to press a kiss into her curving palm. "You may indulge yourself to your heart's content, *querida*. When you and your father's trustee discussed the terms of the marriage settlement yesterday, I'm sure he told you of the allowance I'm providing you and your brothers."

"Yes." In truth, she had more "pin money" per annum than she could spend in a lifetime. Lifting her face to his, she grumbled, "I don't see how you can possibly get your money's worth out of me."

She cursed her unthinking tongue when desire flared in his gaze. "It would have been a bargain at thrice the price," he said, his voice thick with need.

Oh, no. She knew what that look meant, knew what it signaled. Yet like a fool she stared transfixed as he bent his head with infinite slowness toward her. By the time his mouth covered hers, warm, firm, and scented with wine, she ached for it. The knowledge that he was her husband now, that this was not only accepted, but expected, further eroded her will, softening her, making her relent so gradually she didn't recognize it as relenting until too late.

He took his time, leisurely partaking of her mouth, first with softly caressing lips and then with tender strokes of his tongue. When she lifted her hands to cup his cheeks, he hauled her onto his lap so he could plunder her mouth in earnest. The kiss was no longer tender or gentle. It was the explosion of all his hunger and hers, mouths seeking pleasure with unashamed enthusiasm.

One of his hands slid her gown and petticoats up her legs until they cleared the tops of her garters. Then he was finding the aching place between her legs and sliding his thumb inside the slit in her drawers to tease the soft flesh into a hard little kernel. She shifted half-consciously to allow him better access, and he took full advantage of it, slipping a finger deep inside her slick passage. He stroked her with such boldness, it wrung a shocked gasp from her that he swallowed with his kiss.

It felt so wanton to indulge in these caresses when only a curtain and a sheet of glass separated them from the rest of London. The thought excited her beyond reason. And she wasn't the only one excited. His arousal swelled beneath her bottom as surely as her own arousal throbbed between her thighs.

She wouldn't even have noticed the carriage halting if he hadn't abruptly stopped kissing and caressing her. Even after he drew back, her head still spun giddily.

Then he gazed down at her, and his mouth—his teasing, wicked mouth—curved into a smile. "I'll have my heir by Martinmas next," he reminded her in a whisper. "Or sooner."

As the reminder sank in and his eyes gleamed with triumph, all her pleasure vanished. Drat him, drat him, *drat* him! He already had her sitting on his lap like some tart with his hand up her skirts! How could she have let him win so easily?

"Let go of me," she whispered, unable to think of any witty rejoinder to hide her mortification.

"Are you sure that's what you want?" He had the audacity to thumb her tight little nodule of flesh again.

She yanked his hand out from beneath her skirts. "Yes. We're here. It's time to go inside."

"We could head straight on to Chesterley—it's a good two-hour drive; plenty of time for . . . private enjoyments. I'm perfectly willing to forego Sara's breakfast—"

"Well, I'm not," she snapped, wriggling from his lap. "I've had nothing to eat since dawn, and I must have sustenance, my lord."

"I can give you sustenance, *querida*," he whispered as she reached for the door.

Frantic to be free of him, she shoved it open. "Man doth not live by bed alone," she quipped before stepping nimbly from the carriage without waiting for him to hand her out. "Nor doth woman."

He grinned as he followed her out. "Very well. I can wait until later."

"There will be no 'later,' " she murmured as much to him as to herself. "Next time, I'll be better prepared."

Refusing the arm he offered, she hurried up the entrance steps, her anger increasing when she glanced back to see him tugging on his gloves. The gloves he'd deliberately removed so he could fondle her. He'd done that on purpose, drat him, to prove he could seduce her whenever he liked. Ooh, she should have expected that from him. He saw her refusal to bed him as a challenge, and Ian never backed down from a challenge.

Well, he was in for a surprise. This time he'd made her angry enough to resist him. Let him try that little seduction again later. He would *not* like the result.

Ian congratulated himself as he regarded his new bride's stiff back from behind. It had been ridiculously easy to prove she couldn't resist her own passions. He probably shouldn't have taunted her there at the end, but how could he not gloat when she'd turned to pure butter in his hands a mere hour after forbidding him her bed?

His little hypocrite, that's what she was. And he would enjoy peeling away her hypocrisy when he peeled the gown from her later.

She paused at the top of the stairs to wait for him, eyes flashing. Perversely, he slowed his steps and let his gaze drink her in. He liked looking at her in that gown—her mother's. That bespoke a sentimental attachment for him, did it not?

Surely once they settled into married life, she'd forget all about his secrets. It would be easy sailing, provided he sired an heir soon. And there was no reason to think he wouldn't, now that he was sure she couldn't resist his seductions. His father had been one of two sons, and she was the only girl out of five children. Yes, he'd have his heir. Maybe even before Martinmas. Maybe by Michaelmas.

He took her arm when he reached the top. "How long must we stay to satisfy your need for sustenance? I doubt the Worthings can offer me anything to satisfy mine."

"That's because your appetite is jaded," she said tartly.

"Not jaded . . . carnal. And satisfying those appetites here would shock my friends." He leaned close to whisper, "Though I believe it would please my wife."

"You overestimate your powers of seduction," she hissed under her breath as the door opened before them.

"And you, your powers of resistance."

As the servants descended to take her cloak and his coat, her heightened color told him she knew his will and wasn't as certain of her own. It was enough to make him inordinately pleased with himself.

As soon as they reached the dining room, his friends surrounded them, but even that didn't dent his good humor. The women carried Felicity off, clamoring for details about the sudden wedding. He wondered what she was telling them. The truth? He doubted it.

Whatever it was, she'd barely started before she was cut off as the double doors opened at one end of the room and the Taylor Terrors raced toward her at a full gallop. She knelt to gather the triplets to her, and her hips strained against the blue silk. In a flash of memory he saw himself kissing the shapely globes, then turning her over to part her thighs and . . .

His recalcitrant member came to instant attention inside his tight-fitting breeches. Damn, he would never make it until tonight.

Jordan came up and handed him a glass of champagne. Since Ian couldn't tear his eyes from Felicity and the damned thing in his breeches was fixed on her like a compass pointing north, Ian moved so that a chair blocked the view of his lower body.

Clearly noting Ian's none-too-subtle maneuver, Jordan grinned. "Congratulations, my friend. You've got yourself quite a wife—though it looks as if she came with a great deal of baggage. You're the only man I know who'd take on such a large and boisterous family for a woman."

"She's worth it," he heard himself saying, realizing he meant it.

"I daresay she is." Jordan sipped his own champagne. "You know, Emily told me something odd. She claims your wife is the famous Lord X."

Felicity's laughter floated on the air, making Ian's gut tighten instantly. He gulped some champagne. "She is. So watch what you say around her. I doubt she has any intention of retiring from her profession simply because she married me."

"And all her columns about you—"

"Were a peculiar form of courtship, you could say." Ian watched as she stood and began speaking to the boys with an earnest expression. "Other people send gifts—Felicity and I proffer rumors about each other."

A sudden outcry came from one of the triplets. The boy hurtled across the room toward Ian and grabbed him around the legs, sobbing into one of Ian's knees.

Startled, Ian tousled the boy's hair and said soothingly, "There now, what's wrong?"

When the boy lifted a tear-streaked face to him, he recognized William by his missing tooth. "Lissy says that y-you're taking her away to l-live with you!" William stammered between sobs. "A-And we're to st-stay here without her!"

Felicity approached, her gaze on Ian. "I'm sorry . . . I didn't tell them until now. I knew they'd be so disappointed."

"Please don't take away our s-sister—we need Lissy!"

Kneeling on one knee, Ian cupped William's damp cheeks. "I need her, too. And you've got Mrs. Box to take care of you. But who have I got? No one. Besides, it will only be a week. On New Year's Day, we'll be back to fetch you all. Then you'll come out to my estate to live with me and your sister. You'd like that, wouldn't you?"

"But Christmas will be over by then!" William wailed. "We can't have Christmas without Lissy!"

The cry tortured him. Christmas. Of course. It had been years since he'd celebrated Christmas in more than a cursory fashion, so although he'd vaguely noted that Lissy and the boys would be separated for the holiday, he hadn't worried about it. He'd sent a selection of playthings to Taylor Hall sufficient to please any child and had considered himself done with the problem.

He was a bloody idiot. The woman was the nearest thing to their mother, and now he was whisking her away at Christmas. What was wrong with him these days? The Ian Lennard who'd spied for His Majesty would have recognized the importance of the boys having Felicity around for Christmas. The Ian besotted by his wife, however, had thought only of getting her off to himself as soon as possible.

His gaze flew to Felicity, who was watching William with misty eyes. Damn. He stood and touched her arm. "Why didn't you say anything?"

Glancing away, she stammered, "A-About what?"

"You want to be here for Christmas, too, don't you? I'm sorry, I didn't—" He broke off with a groan. "I'm not so callous as to wrench you from your family during their holiday."

He looked down at William's red nose and heaving chest. Slighting her siblings wouldn't endear him to his new wife. Yet the only solution didn't appeal to him.

So it took him completely by surprise when he heard himself say, "How about if Lissy and I stay at Taylor Hall tonight, William? We'll celebrate Christmas with you in the morning and leave tomorrow after Christmas dinner. Will that please you?"

William's eyes lit up. "Oh, yes! Do you hear, Lissy? We'll have Christmas all together!" He ran off to tell his brothers.

"But it's just for tonight!" Ian called out after the boy. Then he sighed. Another night sharing Felicity with her brothers. Bloody hell.

Felicity slipped her hand in the crook of his elbow, then kissed him on the cheek. "Thank you." She beamed at him. "But you may regret your generous gesture later when my brothers are plaguing you unmercifully."

"I regret it now," he grumbled, laying his hand over hers. "Perhaps I can persuade them that Father Christmas will be more likely to come early if they retire early."

"Good luck." Her smile turned mischievous. "They're always so excited about Christmas, we'll be fortunate if they sleep at all tonight."

"Why should they? *We* certainly won't."

She looked blank, then colored and tried to remove her hand from his. "I beg your pardon. *I* shall sleep well. I always do when I'm in my own bed—alone."

"Alone?" He tightened his grip on her hand. "Absolutely not. You're my wife now, and I won't have your servants gossiping around London about why the Viscount St. Clair didn't share a bed with his wife on their wedding night."

Her dagger of a glance showed she understood his position and knew she couldn't hope to alter it. "Very well. We'll sleep together. But sleep is *all* we'll do, Ian."

"If you say so," he mocked. He'd let her keep her hypocrisy for the moment. After all, he had all evening to strip it from her, one piece at a time.

Chapter 20

The deplorable tendency of some to overimbibe during the Christmas season will wreak havoc on our society if we don't check it.

LORD X, *THE EVENING GAZETTE*,
DECEMBER 25, 1820

Felicity came awake slowly, morning light glowing through her closed eyelids. Opening her eyes, she saw the familiar moldings on the ceiling. It was her own bed, and she was dressed in her chemise. But how did she get here? The last thing she remembered was telling Georgie a story in the nursery. And the strange dream afterward ... arms lifting her ... a low voice muttering ... a sensation of floating—

Ian! She shot up in bed, then spotted him slumped in a chair not far away. Shirtless and barefoot, he wore only his smallclothes. His hairy legs were splayed in front of him, and his arms were crossed over his bare chest. And his eyes were open, fixed on her with a dark intensity that made her shiver.

He'd never looked more threatening. Or tempting.

"At last Sleeping Beauty awakes," he growled, faintly slurring the words. He straightened in the chair and pain spasmed over his unusually pale face.

"Are you unwell?" she asked in instant concern.

Bending down, he picked up something and brandished it before her. A brandy bottle. And nearly empty by the look of it.

"For pity's sake, you're foxed!" she exclaimed.

He lifted the bottle, inspecting its meager contents sullenly. "Not foxed enough. It was half-empty when I found it."

How strange for Ian to drink excessively. Being drunk meant losing control of a situation, and Ian never lost control. What could have made him drink? "Did something happen last night that I don't remember?"

"*Nothing* happened." He settled back against the chair to glower at her, the bottle bumping against his leg. "That's the problem. Between your celebration of Christmas, all that time spent hanging stockings and singing carols with your brothers, and your insistence on taking the boys up to bed, not a damned thing happened. You wouldn't let me go up with you—gave me some nonsense about its being your last night alone with them for a while. So like a fool I came down here to wait for you."

Tilting up the bottle, he swigged the rest of the brandy, the muscles in his throat working convulsively as he swallowed it. He wiped his mouth with the back of his hand. "When you didn't come, I went looking for you and found you asleep on Georgie's bed."

He sounded so put out she smiled. "Oh. It must have been the champagne. It always puts me right to sleep. And I did rise very early yesterday morn—"

"I tried to wake you. *That* was pointless, so I finally gave up and carried you to bed." His gaze drifted down her body, then halted at her breasts.

The sudden alteration in his expression from anger to desire made her look down at her chemise. Good Lord. It gaped open where the ties were undone. Swiftly, she retied them, careful not to meet his hungry gaze. "Did you . . . undress me?"

"Certainly. I couldn't very well let you sleep in your gown, could I?"

Heat swam over her at the thought of his unbuttoning her dress and sliding it slowly off her body. Had he touched her? Perhaps. But he hadn't bedded her—she was fairly certain of that. She would remember if he had. Besides, if he'd bedded her, he probably wouldn't be drunk now.

He held the bottle up, regarded it with a scowl, then tossed it aside like a surly child displeased with a toy. "Empty, damn it. Is there any more in this place?"

"If there was, I wouldn't give it to you," she said matter-of-factly. "You shouldn't be drinking at this hour, for pity's sake."

"I daresay any man who spent his wedding night watching his wife coddle a lot of thankless scamps and then fall into a dead sleep would be drinking at this hour."

He sounded so forlorn, the poor dear. It almost made up for the fact that *he* had spent last night trying to wear down her resistance to him. A caress when her brothers weren't looking . . . an arm around the waist . . . handholding. Not to mention two stolen kisses in the hall and one blatant one under the mistletoe. Oh, yes, he deserved a wedding night alone after what he'd put her through.

She didn't realize she'd smiled until he grumbled, "You find this vastly amusing, don't you? You're very proud of yourself for all your delaying tactics."

"Well, I didn't exactly plan it that way, so I can hardly be proud of it. But it did work in my favor." She slipped from the bed and donned her dressing gown, then went to the door and unlocked it.

"Where do you think you're going?" He rose from the chair, his movements surprisingly steady.

She faced him, and her mouth went dry. His worsted smallclothes left nothing to the imagination, outlining his arousal in loving detail. When combined with his half-naked and quite glorious physique, the sight sent her heart racing. Drat the man. Even slightly drunk, he was tempting.

But she wouldn't let him distract her from her purpose this time. Thinking quickly, she palmed the key so he couldn't lock the door again. "I thought I'd fetch you something for your aching head. The boys will be up any minute, and—"

"Lock the door," he ordered as he stalked toward her. "We may have missed our wedding night, wife, but there's nothing that says we can't have a wedding morning."

Heart pounding, she opened the door, but in two steps he was at her side, slamming it closed before she could get through. He sandwiched her body between his and the door. Every inch of hard, determined male flexed against her.

"Give me the key," he commanded, eyes glittering down at her.

Defiantly, she tossed it across the room. "Get it yourself."

He hesitated, apparently debating how to get the key without leaving her long enough for her to escape. Then he smiled and his hand cupped her hip. "Never mind."

But as he bent his head to kiss her, she wriggled from between him and the door. "You're in no condition to be doing this," she said, backing away from him.

"No man has ever been in a better condition to do this, *querida*." He stalked her with leisurely intent. "You're my wife now. And we *will* consummate this marriage."

The uneven series of raps and knocks on her bedchamber door startled them both. Ian halted, turning to glare at the door.

"Lissy!" came a child's loud whisper beyond it. "Lissy, are you awake?"

"Say nothing, and the little imps will leave," he growled under his breath.

She laughed, partly from the ludicrousness of his statement and partly out of relief at being spared once more.

"It's Christmas morning, Ian. They won't leave. Just be happy they didn't burst in here without knocking. That's what they usually do."

That sent him back against the door in a flash. "Go away, lads!" he called through it. "Your sister isn't ready to get up yet. She'll come out in a while."

She smirked at him. "Nor will anything you say put them off. Not on Christmas morn."

As if to support her claims, the door handle rattled and a child's voice cried, "Are you in there, Lissy? We want to see if Father Christmas filled our stockings!"

"So go look at them!" Ian shouted at the door.

"We can't! Lissy locked them in the parlor!"

His gaze shot to her. "You didn't."

"I always do. Otherwise, they'd be in there at midnight."

He glowered at her. "Tell them to wait until we come out."

"Not on your life." With a grin, she called out, "I'll only be a moment, boys! I just have to dress!"

"Hurry up! It's Christmas!" Georgie cried through the door.

A curse erupted from Ian's lips. He glanced from her to the door handle and back to her as she headed for her dresser at the other end of the room. She could guess his thoughts. Open the door and order the boys to leave? No, they might dash in, putting an end to anything. Leave the door and search for the key? Then she would run out.

She chuckled to herself. This ought to repay him amply for his little maneuvers in the carriage yesterday and his taunts and caresses last night. She drew out a fresh chemise, drawers, and hose, then chose a front-closing gown she could put on easily, since she didn't want his help. She started for the privacy screen, but stopped as a wicked thought entered her head.

She had an even better way of repaying him.

Feeling daring, she faced him and removed her dressing

gown as casually as if he weren't watching her with hooded eyes from his position at the door. She hesitated a moment, unsure of the wisdom of her plan. But he had one shoulder braced against the door and couldn't move. She would be safe.

Besides, it was time to remind him what he'd be missing as long as he considered her a brood mare and not a wife. Slowly, she untied her chemise and shrugged off one sleeve, then the other.

His eyes widened. "What the bloody hell are you doing?"

"I'm changing clothes, of course. I have to dress." With a teasing smile, she dropped the chemise to the floor, baring her breasts.

His gaze raked her hungrily. "Come here, and I'll help you," he said in that thrumming voice that scrambled her insides.

Oh, she was tempted. Sorely tempted. But she wouldn't cave in, especially after he'd been so sure of himself yesterday. "I don't need any help. Besides, you have to keep the door closed. You never know when the boys might try to come in."

She reached for the ties of her drawers, and he growled, "Don't you dare!"

Enjoying the feeling of power over him, she untied them very slowly, remembering his bold caresses yesterday and the taunt that had followed them.

His eyes blazed at her. "This is not amusing, Felicity."

"No? Are you worried that you might not have your heir 'by Martinmas' after all?" she said saucily. Then she shimmied out of her drawers.

With an oath, he shoved away from the door.

"Boys?" she called out loudly.

They tried the handle outside and Ian slammed back against the door. "Go away!" he hissed at the door, but his eyes ate her up.

She reveled in the wicked thrill that shot through her as

his gaze raked every inch of her naked body. This was reckless, audacious in the extreme. She ought to be ashamed of herself, but she wasn't. Not at all. It served him right to suffer a little of the torture he'd put her through yesterday.

"At least have the decency to use the screen," he bit out.

"All you have to do is close your eyes."

"I can't," he said hoarsely.

In truth, he seemed frozen, the very picture of a frustrated male as he leaned against the door and drank up her every move, the rest of his body as rigid as the thing inside his smallclothes. Raising an eyebrow, she held up one stocking, then lifted her foot and propped it on the bed so she could put the stocking on. From his vantage point, he had to have an excellent view of a certain area of her anatomy.

A strangled noise, a cross between a groan and a curse, erupted from him. She tied the stocking with a garter, then put down her foot and reached for the other stocking.

"Enough!" he roared. When she lifted an eyebrow at him, he straightened. "Two can play this game, you know. Continue displaying your assets, *querida*, and I will describe exactly what I wish to do with you. Loudly. We might as well give your brothers an education as long as they're listening in on the other side of the door."

She hesitated. Indeed, it had become very quiet out in the hall, and she knew her brothers too well to think they'd left. "You wouldn't."

His eyes narrowed. "That little patch of skin above your garter? I want to take my tongue and run it up—"

"All right, all right!" Scooping up her clothes, she darted behind the privacy screen.

His sigh of relief echoed in the room. She dressed quickly, and when she came out from behind the screen, it was to find him donning his shirt and pantaloon trousers with a scowl. He'd propped a chair under the doorknob but had clearly relinquished any further plans to bed her this morning, since the boys were making such a clatter outside the door that it was clear neither of them would get any peace until it was opened.

As she hurried past him, however, he caught her by the arm and pulled her close enough to whisper, "Tonight, my teasing wife, there won't be any boys pounding on our door."

A shiver skittered along her spine. Perhaps her method of revenge hadn't been such a good idea after all. "Tonight, I'll have my own bedchamber."

"For sleeping only." His roguish smile made her skin come alive. "In fact, I want you to repeat this morning's stunning performance in the privacy of my bedchamber at Chesterley."

She lifted an earnest face to him. "Gladly. As soon as you tell me what I wish to know, Ian, I'll be happy to join you in your bedchamber."

His smile vanished. "Do you never quit?"

"No. I'd rather forego the many pleasures of your embraces than spend one moment in your bed knowing it's nothing to you but a mating."

For a moment he looked as if he might say something. Then his jaw tightened and he glanced at the door. "You'd best open it before the little hellions break it down."

No doubt about it, he'd married a wanton, Ian thought sullenly as he sat in the parlor where the Taylor Terrors eviscerated a score of wrapped boxes and packages. His gaze was fixed on his new wife—in truth, he'd been unable to turn it anywhere else since her little stunt in the bedroom. Her hair mantled her shoulders like a rumpled velvet cape, and a fresh, sweet smile curved her mouth every time her brothers opened one of his many presents. Seated on the floor with her body hidden behind mounds of shredded paper and tangled ribbons, she might have been mistaken for another of the children.

But not by him. My God, this morning when she'd slipped out of her drawers . . .

He groaned. She was a piece of work. The image of her naked body, drenched in sunlight that kissed the high, small breasts and the tempting curls between her legs, was still emblazoned on his memory. As were all her come-hither-but-not-now smiles. If he hadn't taken her virginity himself he'd doubt her virtue, but apparently her provocative instincts were as natural to her as writing gossip. She'd be the death of him yet.

A self-mocking smile touched his lips. And yesterday, he'd had the arrogance to think this would be easy! If he didn't take care, she'd have him blurting out not only all the secrets about his past, but a thousand others, anything to regain the privilege of spreading those supple white thighs and—

Bloody hell. Time for a new strategy. But what? Overt attempts to seduce her merely roused her determination to resist, and covert attempts made her respond in kind, only to stop short of the act.

William bounded toward him, dragging behind him the hobbyhorse he'd received from "Father Christmas," an elaborate affair with real horse's hair that Ian had picked out with the boy especially in mind. George and Ansel had already darted out the door to try theirs on the stairs, and James sat beside his sister beaming at a set of woodcarving tools.

But William approached Ian with a shy smile. "Look, Lord St. Clair, it has leather reins and everything!"

The boy's excitement banished any lingering resentment he'd felt toward the lads for ruining his plans for his honeymoon. "You know, William, now that I've married your sister, you and I are brothers. So why don't you call me Ian?"

William beamed. "Truly?"

"Truly." Ian lifted the boy to sit on his knee, surprised

at the flood of familial affection that possessed him. "And when your sister and I return to town next week to bring you and your brothers to Chesterley, we'll see about buying all of you real ponies."

" 'Ods fish!" William threw his arms about Ian's neck. "You're the best brother ever!"

"Or at least the richest," Felicity quipped. When Ian grinned at her undaunted over William's head, she added, "You'll spoil them if you keep that up."

"I'm merely looking for ways to keep them occupied in the early-morning hours, so they don't go about knocking on people's bedroom doors."

She raised an eyebrow. "Well, you overshot your mark." She swept her hand around the room. "Father Christmas has been far too extravagant."

"I should hope so. He seems to have bypassed the Taylors lately, so he owed them more than usual, don't you think?" He jiggled William on his knee. "Do you mind Father Christmas giving you so many presents at once, my boy?"

The answer was predictably a loud "no."

"You see?" Ian continued laughingly. "The males of this family have no trouble agreeing on anything. You're the only naysayer."

She sniffed. "Because I'm the only sensible one."

"Does that mean you don't want the gift I bought for you?"

Her cheeks flushed with pleasure. "You bought me a gift?"

"Of course. You're my wife."

Averting her face from his, she stammered, "Y-Yes, but I haven't got one for you . . . that is . . . there was no time—"

"And no money. It's all right."

He set William aside, and the boy dashed from the room

to join the other two triplets, shouting, "Guess what, Georgie! Ian's gonna get us real ponies!"

Ian stood, then walked to the window and retrieved a stack of presents from behind the curtain. Returning to where she sat, he handed them to her. "I don't need anything. You do."

Her eyes shone with delight as she took the packages from him. "I don't know what to say."

"Open them before you say anything. You might not like them."

He found himself tensing as she reached for the small rectangular box on top. He hadn't given many gifts to women, but somehow he'd assumed she wouldn't be like his few paramours and wish for baubles and frills and lace. Now he reconsidered. He might have been wrong; she might hate it. But it was too late to do anything about it.

Opening the box, she withdrew a silver-plated cylindrical object. She turned it over in her hand in perplexed concentration.

James had come to sit cross-legged beside her on the floor, and now he peered over her shoulder at the object. "What is it?"

"It's a fountain pen," Ian explained. "A man named John Scheffer obtained the patent on it last year. It makes the inkpot unnecessary." He took it from her and demonstrated how it worked, pushing a little button that triggered the release of ink to the nib. "I've invested in Scheffer's company. I think it'll be a great success. I asked him to make this one specially for you after we returned from the Worthings last week. See here? It's engraved with your initials."

After using a scrap of wrapping paper to wipe off the little bit of ink that had collected on the nib, he handed it back to her. She clasped it so silently, his throat went raw. She hated it. Damn. He should have bought her more of the fripperies in the other boxes, instead of risking such a foolish gift.

A pen was too commonplace, not passionate enough for her wild nature. But what did he know about buying gifts for a wife, especially one as unusual as Felicity?

At her continued silence, Ian said offhandedly, "Go on and open the others. The pen is more an experiment than a gift anyway. I thought you could use it and tell me if it works right."

Then she lifted her head, tears shining in her eyes. "It's the most wonderful thing anyone has ever given me."

The look on her face made his heart leap, an unfamiliar sensation. "You like it."

"Oh, Ian, I love it! I hate those messy inkpots. This will be so useful." Rubbing tears from her eyes with one hand, she carefully replaced the pen in its box with the other. "I'll treasure it always."

He cleared his throat, unused to such effusive thanks. "Here," he said, thrusting the second gift at her again. "Open this."

"You shouldn't have bought so much. I feel awful that I have nothing for you."

Yet she opened them all with enthusiasm. The rest of his gifts were more typical—a lace fan, silk hose, and a pair of exquisite ruby earrings that he'd paid a king's ransom for. Although she exclaimed loudly over each one, when she was finished it was the pen she took out to examine again. As she stroked it, pleasure shining in her face, he thought of her hands on him that night. My God, what he wouldn't give to have them on him again.

Suddenly she glanced up at him, her pretty face brightening even further. "Wait!" Turning to James, she whispered instructions, and he ran off.

"What are you up to now?" Ian asked, raising an eyebrow.

Her smile was secretive. "You'll see."

James returned moments later with a framed canvas. He handed it to his sister, who held it out to Ian. "This was

Papa's favorite painting," she explained. "I couldn't bear to sell it. But now that we're married . . . well, I see no reason *you* can't enjoy it."

He took the canvas from her and stared at it in surprise. He could easily see why her reckless father had liked it. It was a harem painting, probably meant for someone's collection of erotic art, though not badly done. A dusky-skinned sultan stood upon a dais with chest bared and arms crossed. Below him a bevy of scantily clad young women posed in various positions about a pool painted in lush colors.

"You're giving me an erotic painting?" he asked.

Her quick blush and furtive glance at James, who was listening avidly, told him she hadn't thought of it like that. "It's not . . . Well, it is, but . . . It's by a Spaniard. That's why I thought of you. Though the artist isn't anyone of consequence."

"No, he wouldn't be." He examined the painting more closely, unable to keep the smile off his face. Only Felicity could give her husband something so patently scandalous for a seemingly innocent reason.

"Papa bought it because he admired the colors and the lines," she persisted.

"I'm sure he admired them a great deal." He chuckled. "Especially the flesh colors and curving lines."

"Ian!" she exclaimed with a worried glance at James, who'd lost interest in the conversation and now examined her new pen. "The sultan is also well-done, don't you think?"

The sultan? He looked at the figure again. Then it dawned on him why she'd thought to give him the painting. The realization lightened his mood considerably. His eyes met hers over the top of the canvas. "Very well done indeed."

"You can tell the artist was a Spaniard," she babbled on.

"He made the sultan look Spanish. His features are Castilian, not Turkish."

"Yes, Castilian." He lowered his voice. "Like mine."

Ducking her head, she swallowed, the motion of her throat doing something wicked to his insides. "Anyway, I thought you might like it. And now I'd best go help Mrs. Box oversee the preparations for dinner. If you'd keep an eye on the boys for me—"

"Certainly." She thought to run off after dropping this surprise in his lap, did she? "You and I can discuss the painting later."

Her gaze shot to him. "What do you mean, 'discuss it'?"

"I'm curious to know what attracts *you* to the painting."

"Me? Nothing at all." But her high color confirmed his suspicions, as did her mumbled, "I-I'd better go."

He watched, trying not to laugh as she fled the parlor. At last he'd figured out his strategy for winning her. He hadn't gained a bit of ground by advancing on her with all the subtlety of a battalion. She wanted him as badly as he did her, but whenever he blustered at her and backed her against a wall, her pride rose against him.

No, he must use her own needs against her. He must provoke her, tempt her. Her pleasure at his gifts, her shy offering of a most erotic painting, demonstrated that she felt enough ambivalence about him to be vulnerable to courtship. Now that he thought of it, she'd succumbed to his seduction after his week of heightening her jealousy and his day of squiring her about town with her brothers.

So although he was impatient to have her in his bed again, he would progress slowly, wooing her without any overt advance until he had her on her knees begging him to take her.

He had a week alone with her. If by the end of that time he hadn't brought her willingly to his bed, he was no kind of tactician at all.

Chapter 21

The marriage of the Viscount St. Clair to Miss Felicity Taylor, daughter of the late architect Algernon Taylor, took society by surprise. Though rumors had circulated about the two, no one expected such a hasty wedding.

LORD X, *THE EVENING GAZETTE.*
DECEMBER 27, 1820

On the third night after her wedding, Felicity sat writing with her new pen at the table in her spacious bedchamber at Chesterley. But her mind soon wandered from her column to her enigmatic husband.

What was she to make of Ian's behavior? After their Christmas morning confrontation, she'd expected a long and bitter battle. One she would win, of course, but still a battle. She'd been determined to make him see the advantages of a true marriage, where the partners shared everything with each other. Abstinence from marital relations had seemed the only thing that might make an impression on him.

Now she wasn't so sure. After she'd spent all of Christmas morning and afternoon girding herself to resist his too-tempting kisses and caresses, there'd been none. He'd given a reason for it the day he'd brought her here—some non-

sense about allowing her time to adjust to the marriage—
but she didn't believe *that* for a moment. Ian had never
allowed her time to adjust to anything before. Why be so
considerate now? Besides, Ian never acted without a purpose. He was up to something.

Very well. Ian might be a master at stratagems, but she'd
spent an inordinate amount of time studying the workings
of the men and women who populated London society.
Surely she could figure out his intentions.

But not tonight, she thought wearily. This wasn't the
time to brood on such matters, not when her courses had
just come, with all the attendant discomfort and moodiness.
She should dwell on happy things, on how much she liked
Chesterley and its staff, who'd surprised her with their welcome. When her courses were upon her, she couldn't think
rationally. She made mountains out of molehills and cried
for no reason, which was *not* an advantage when dealing
with her husband's cool tactical mind.

My husband. The thought gave her a little thrill. Oh, why
must the thought of his being her husband soften her resolve?

Perhaps because as Lord St. Clair, he'd been the enemy
and as Ian, he'd been an irritation, even a temptation, but
not someone capable of altering her life substantially. As
her husband, however, he was the most dangerous creature
on earth, an incubus rising up from hell and demanding her
soul in exchange for satisfaction of her wicked desires . . .
her hot, abandoned dreams . . . her flagrant fantasies . . .

She sighed and took up her pen again. These days she
dearly wanted to strip naked and throw herself at the man's
feet. Which was exactly what he hoped for.

A knock at the door between their bedchambers made
her jump. "Who is it?" she snapped without thinking.

"Your husband, who else? May I come in?"

"Of course." Good Lord, how did he do that? Appear
like that whenever she thought of him? And even know to

use the one word calculated to reduce her to mush? The man truly was the devil.

Especially now, when he entered the room wearing only a half-buttoned shirt that scarcely disguised the breadth of his dark-skinned chest and a pair of pantaloon trousers that fit snugly over strong thighs. Give him Persian garb and he would be her sultan in the flesh, all rough features and exquisite muscles and splendid economy of motion.

Not that his state of undress should surprise her at this time of the evening. Still, he seemed to only enter her bedchamber when he could reasonably do so half-dressed, as if to use the casualness of his attire to reinforce the intimacy of their being husband and wife. Then he roamed the room with familiarity, or worse yet, sprawled on the bed to discuss the day's events or plans for the morrow.

The man didn't miss a single opportunity to disturb her equilibrium. Thankfully, she had good reason to rebuff him this evening if he should try, for surely he would not wish to bed her during this time of the month.

Besides, tonight he didn't look like a man bent on seduction. He had a newspaper tucked under one arm, and although she was scantily clad, his eyes flicked only briefly over her attire. "I missed you at dinner. Your maid informed me you were unwell."

She blushed. "Yes." She said nothing else. He might be her husband, but discussing her monthly courses with him seemed too intimate.

"I brought you the latest edition of *The Evening Gazette*. I thought it might cheer you." His expression was unreadable. "I see Lord X announced our marriage."

"It would've seemed odd if Lord X had ignored such a topic." She swallowed. Had he read the entire article? And what did he think? Two days ago, she'd thought that a little prodding in her usual manner might have some impact on him. Now she wasn't at all sure that had been wise. "You don't mind, do you?" she ventured.

"That everyone knows I married you? Why should I?"
He ambled toward her. "But as you know, that wasn't all
you discussed." He lifted the newspaper and read:

> Some may question how a marriage between Lord
> St. Clair and any respectable woman can succeed
> when the man's past is so mysterious, but despite
> what your faithful correspondent has previously
> written concerning the viscount, I wager that the
> man's honor will compel him to be forthcoming
> with his wife, if not with anyone else.

"Yes," she responded nervously, "I inserted my usual
commentary."

"You mean, your usual reprimand." He folded the paper
with a smile. "Tell me, *querida*, do you intend to lecture
me in *every* edition of your column?"

Drat it, he wasn't even angry. "It's a thought," she said
peevishly. "It got your attention in the past, didn't it?"

With a roguish smile, he dropped the newspaper in her
lap. "Yes, but if you mention our marriage in every column,
even the most dim-witted reader will eventually guess your
identity."

His continued good humor made her feel defeated. She
returned to writing. "Rest assured, I've no intention of doing such a ninny thing." Especially when her one mention
had nettled him so little.

"That's a relief." Leaning over her, he snatched up the
article she was working on. Quickly he scanned the lines,
and his smile abruptly vanished. "How very interesting, my
dear. Apparently you don't need to mention our marriage
to make your point. You simply choose those pieces of
gossip that are material to our situation."

His amused tone had hardened to sarcasm. "Merrington's
mysterious quarrel with his uncle? Pelham's latest mistress
and his pathetic wife's ignorance of his unsavory character?

How clever of you to lecture me in a manner no one would understand but you and me." He tossed the foolscap on her writing table with a look of disgust.

She'd certainly gotten a reaction now, only this wasn't one she'd sought. "I didn't lecture you in this column. I simply wrote gossip as I always do. You're reading more into it than I wrote."

"Oh, yes, it's mere coincidence that you mention Merrington and his uncle."

"That tale has been all the talk of London, and you know it!'

A wealth of contempt laced his tone. "And what about Pelham? You can't tell me that the 'unfeeling brute who enjoys mocking his silly wife by taking mistresses before her very eyes' isn't meant to be me. I know you too well."

The unfair accusation stung. She would never liken Ian to Pelham, of all people! "Apparently not as well as you think. It isn't about you, Ian."

"But you do enjoy taunting me in your column. And an 'unfeeling brute who enjoys mocking his wife'—"

"Everything is not always about *you*." She rose from the chair, emotions roiling as she crossed the room to put herself as far away from his nasty temper as possible. "How clearly must I say it? I didn't even consider our situation when I wrote it!"

Bracing his hip on the writing table, he glared at her. "You forget that I'm an expert on your column. You never poke fun at the helpless or the weak as you do here with Pelham's pathetic wife."

"Perhaps that's because she isn't pathetic, nor do I refer to her as such."

He ignored the remark. "Besides, there's too much passion in your words for them not to have some personal meaning. 'Unfeeling brute'? 'Mocking his wife'? As a spy, I excelled at interpreting coded messages. But then you know that, don't you? That's why you write such things—

so that I'll understand your meaning even when no one else will."

"Sometimes you can be such an arrogant ass!" The foolish man refused to listen to her, and she was in no mood for this. Resolutely, she headed for the door. "Think whatever you like. Clearly I'm not the only person in this marriage who jumps to conclusions."

In a few strides, he was beside her, catching her arm to halt her. "You can't mean you pilloried Pelham and his wife for their own sakes? He's a vain idiot, to be sure, and has an eye for young women, but . . ." His words trailed off, and she felt his hard stare on her. "Wait a minute. Your father designed one of Pelham's houses, didn't he? I heard the duke mention it once."

Old memories rose to choke her, and she nodded, unable to speak.

Ian's fingers tightened on her arm. "At Lady Brumley's ball, Pelham made remarks about your person that I shrugged off because he speaks of all young women that way, but—" He turned her to face him, his expression stark in its remorse. "My God, he did something to you, didn't he? That's why you wrote about him! He hurt you!"

"It was nothing . . . a silly nothing."

She bent her head to hide her tears, but he wouldn't let her, tipping up her chin so he could look at her. When he saw the tears in her eyes, he swore under his breath. "Obviously not a silly nothing."

That was all it took for the tears to escape and flow freely down her cheeks.

Looking stricken, he gathered her up in his arms and moved to sit on the bed where he could cradle her on his lap. "There, there, *querida*." He stroked her back, her hair, her arms. "You mustn't cry. He can't hurt you again."

"I know." She rubbed away the tears and cursed the melancholy that made her so weepy at this time of the month. "I'm not afraid of him."

Ian pressed soft, penitent kisses into her hair. "What did he do? And where was your father? Why wasn't he protecting you?"

"You mustn't think it was Papa's fault. He was always so engrossed in his work that he never noticed the men's advances."

Ian stared at her, a mixture of horror and disbelief on his face. "*Men's*? Pelham wasn't the only one? What did they do? How did it happen—"

"Truly, it's not as bad as it sounds." She lifted her face to his. "Papa took me along when he visited his employers, and occasionally . . . one of them or their sons were a bit forward, that's all."

"That's all?" His jaw tautened and his eyes sparked fire. "Tell me who hurt you, and I swear I'll—"

"No one did anything more than steal a kiss or two," she lied, alarmed by his sudden fury. "You know yourself I was a virgin when we made love."

"Yes, but there are more ways to hurt a woman than to take her virginity. Pelham must have been cruel indeed if you feel compelled to write like this about him. You don't show your claws heedlessly."

She shrugged and bent her head, but he grasped her by the shoulders. "Tell me, Felicity. What did Pelham do to you?"

She'd wanted for so long to tell someone everything, and Ian had caught her in a weak moment. The words poured out of her. "He cornered me in the library at his estate. Papa didn't need me at the moment, so I'd gone there to read."

The image shot instantly into her mind . . . Pelham entering the room, the nasty smile that had spread over his face, the way he'd trapped her in the armchair with his thick body. She went on, almost in a trance, "His kiss so took me by surprise that I didn't at first react, but when he . . . he put his hands inside my bodice, I slapped him." Which had done nothing, of course, except make him laugh and squeeze her breasts cruelly. But she couldn't tell Ian that. "That was the end of it."

"Put his hands— Damn him, I'll put my hands inside his *breeches* and tear off his balls! Better yet, I'll put my hands around his throat!"

"No! It was long ago, Ian. It doesn't matter anymore."

"Clearly, it does." He gazed into her face. "And I know Pelham. A slap wouldn't deter him."

She glanced away, unable to lie again.

"Tell me the rest, *querida*," he coaxed.

"There's not much else to tell. He grabbed my hand and forced it against his breeches. So I . . . I squeezed him as hard as I could and he yelped. Thankfully, that brought his wife. She burst in just as he drew back his hand to hit me."

"My God," he said hoarsely. "You made a narrow escape."

She hadn't thought of that before, but it was true. Everything could have been worse. Pelham hadn't taken her virtue; he hadn't even gotten the chance to really hurt her. Yet she'd nursed her grievance against him and his wife for years, letting it—and other incidents—color her perception to the point that she'd regarded every man of rank with suspicion. How foolish.

"I wish I'd been there to see his wife reprimand him," Ian added.

"The only person she reprimanded was me." Strangely enough, however, she spoke the words with no rancor. It was as if telling Ian about it vanquished its power to hurt her. "Lady Pelham marched me right off to Papa, announcing that I was a wanton and a flirt and that he ought to cane me soundly."

"That bitch!"

She laughed. "You don't mince words, do you?"

"I don't have to." He clutched her to him. "I don't write for the public. If I'd written your column, I'd have been far more ungenerous to the woman than you were."

Her column. She'd forgotten all about it. "I shouldn't have put that in tonight, not when I'm feeling . . . unwell. You're right about its being personal. I'm usually less overtly antagonistic, even when I write about Papa's old patrons, but tonight I was testy."

"And I'm sure I didn't help by being an 'arrogant ass.' "

She groaned. "I shouldn't have called you that."

"It was true. I've been as bad as Pelham."

"No!"

"Yes. I kissed you against your will, and I attacked you at the Worthings—"

"You did *not* attack me!" She gazed into his remorseful eyes. "It was entirely different with you. I liked what you did. Pelham made me feel dirty and cheap. You made me feel desirable. And when you withdrew, as an honorable man should, you convinced me that not all men of rank are like Pelham."

His eyes glittered. "But I seduced you a week later. I—"

She placed her finger against his lips to silence him. "I won't let you speak of yourself in the same breath with him. You're nothing like Pelham—nothing, I tell you! You never forced me to give my body to you. I chose that myself. And I don't regret it."

Her fervent tone must have convinced him. But it did something more, something she hadn't counted on. She felt the change in him even before he lowered his head.

And to her shame, she welcomed his kiss, welcomed his easy intimacy. He was her husband. She was his wife. There was nothing wrong in it. His kiss was full of delights, tender and thorough at the same time. It blotted out everything but thoughts of their last joining.

He shoved her wrapper off her shoulders, and she shifted to twine her arms about his neck. She was heedless of how that crushed one of her breasts against him until he slipped his hand inside her chemise to cup the soft weight.

"My sweet *querida*," he muttered against her lips, teasing her nipple into a hard button with little tweaks of his thumb and forefinger that made her blood race hot and silky through her veins.

My love, she thought in answer. *My sweet love.*

Dragging her chemise down to bare one breast, he covered it with his mouth and drew hard, the rasps of his tongue sending exotic pleasures shooting through her. She clutched his head to her and rained tender kisses in his hair, which seemed to make him only more ravenous.

Then everything moved too quickly. He was laying her back on the bed, half-covering her body, his hands stroking up her inner thighs beneath her chemise. A sudden panic hit her. She was on her courses . . . he could not . . . he mustn't . . .

She caught his wrist frantically. "No, Ian, you mustn't . . ."

"Don't do this to me again, *querida*," he growled as he lifted his head to stare at her with bleak, haunted eyes. "You can't mean to stop me this time!"

"I don't want to, truly I don't! Not anymore. But . . ." Here a violent blush stained her cheeks. "But I . . . my . . . oh, dear heavens, this is so embarrassing." She swallowed. "My courses came today. That's why I didn't feel well enough to come down for dinner."

Ian hovered over her, looking blank. Then as what she'd said sank in, he groaned and dropped his head onto her shoulder. "Damn it, was ever a man so cursed?"

She lay still beneath him, stricken by remorse. "I-I'm sorry. I should have said something sooner . . . I truly did want to . . . you know . . ."

"There will be other nights." He pressed a perfunctory kiss to her cheek as if anything more might test his endurance. Then he drew back and raised an eyebrow. "There *will* be other nights, won't there?"

She knew what he was asking, and now she knew her

answer. It was time to make their marriage what it should be. Her attempts to force his hand weren't working, because deep down he distrusted her motives. She'd realized that when he'd grown so angry over her column.

So she must show him that her motives were pure, that she loved him so much it didn't matter what he told her. *That* was the way to make their marriage a true one.

"Yes," she said softly. "And my courses are generally of short duration. In a few days we can—"

"Enough, *querida*." He smiled wryly. "Unless you want to torment me further, do not tell me what we can do in a few days, I beg you. A few days seems like an eternity."

"For me, too," she said shyly.

He sighed and sank back on the bed beside her, staring up at the canopy. He was quiet a long time, so long she wondered what else she could say to reassure him. Then he spoke in clipped tones. "I suppose this means you aren't with child."

"No. For that, too, I'm sorry."

Rolling to his side, he propped his head up on his elbow. "It's nothing to be sorry about. That's one of those matters only nature can control. But we have plenty of time."

So why did he look so disappointed? Why did he seem compelled to sire an heir with all due haste?

He shoved himself up to sit beside her on the bed. "I'd best leave you now. You need your rest."

Not ready to lose his company yet, she sat up and took his hand. "You could sleep here tonight." She traced the long lean fingers, the broad palm with the tiny scars probably gained when he was a soldier.

"Sleep and not touch you?" he said softly. "Impossible. Forgive me, *querida*, but the last time we shared a bed without making love, I got drunk to endure it. And I fear I'd have to do the same tonight. So I'd best return to my room."

He rose to leave, and she said, "Ian?"

"Yes?"

"I meant what I told you. I'm done fighting you. I'm your wife, and I mean to be your wife in every way from now on."

He cupped her cheek. "Sleep well." He paused, then added, "If you feel up to it in the morning, we'll visit my tenants so I can introduce you to them."

She smiled. "I'd like that."

"It's all I can think of to take our minds off other things," he admitted ruefully.

Then he was gone. Feeling bereft, she rose and went to the desk. Her article still lay where Ian had tossed it. She sat down at the desk and read it over again. The lines now seemed silly, like a child sticking its tongue out at her tormentors.

For the first time in years, Felicity's bitterness toward Pelham was gone. In its place was the most profound pity. For Pelham, because he could never have a woman care for him without browbeating her into it. And for his wife, because she must live with the wretch. Nothing Lord X could say would alter that situation one whit.

She deliberated a moment longer. Then she took up her pen and crossed through the lines about Pelham and his wife.

Chapter 22

As Ian left Felicity's bedchamber, her parting words echoed sweetly in his mind. *I'm done fighting you . . . I mean to be your wife in every way from now on.* At last he'd won her, and without relinquishing his secrets.

But later, as he lay in his cold bed alone, he examined her words more closely, and they struck him with foreboding. She hadn't said, *I'm done fighting you because I want you,* though he knew she desired him. She hadn't spoken of *wanting* to be his wife in every way. She'd spoken of her will—*I mean to be* . . . As if acknowledging her duty. Or her weariness of fighting him.

That wasn't what he wanted—a wife by default. He wanted her to care for him freely, to be his wife because she desired it, not because she felt trapped into it. He'd gained her acquiescence at a great price to his own conscience.

The following morning, he sent a servant with his excuses for canceling their visit with his tenants. He could no longer bear to face her. She'd said too much last night,

317

revealed just enough of her past to make him see his behavior in a new light.

And examining his own behavior—or rather, contemplating his many sins—was all he did for the next three days. He certainly didn't go anywhere near his long-suffering wife. For God's sake, what could he say to her that would excuse his earlier arrogance? The very thought of her tortured his conscience. So what would the sight of her do to it?

Now it was late afternoon on the day before New Year's Eve, and he was in a quandary. The day after tomorrow, they'd return to London. What was he to do about Felicity?

Pacing his study restlessly, he paused to glance out the window, then started when he saw the object of his thoughts standing in the garden below and jotting down notes in a tablet. What was she planning? To improve the garden? Or level it and put in a pond? Hard to know with his darling wife.

Regardless, it was such a domestic action it briefly salved his conscience. Too briefly.

He turned from the window to stare blindly about the impressive study, a veritable bastion of masculinity, thanks to Father's decorating preferences and Ian's own lack of time to oversee its redecoration. Mahogany furniture and velvet hangings and ancient bronze lent it a dark, almost gloomy air. He hated it.

But not only for its appearance. My God, that massive, ugly desk—how often he'd hunched over it while Father laid into his backside with a cane. Not that the canings had hurt his ass any more than those he'd routinely suffered at Eton, but they'd tortured his pride. He'd hated having them administered by the man he wanted most to please. He'd despised being forced to submit against his will. Most of all, he'd been humiliated the few times his father had wrung tears from him.

Ian had always regarded it a matter of pride not to cry,

and Father had always regarded it a matter of pride to make him do so. No one understood their private duel. His mother had wanted Ian to shed fake tears to end the caning. Jordan had said he was insane to hold back the real ones. But every time Ian had outlasted his father's whipping arm without crying, he'd considered it a triumph over the whole degrading process.

From that he'd learned that physical force didn't work, that manipulation and strategy were the keys to getting what you want, because his father's canings had never done anything but stiffen his resistance.

Now Felicity had taught him something else—there were more kinds of force than physical, and they were just as destructive. Unwittingly, she'd taught him that in countless ways. Her tears in front of Sara, which had apparently been genuine. Her horror at his threats to make her marry him. Most of all, the way she'd refused him her bed after the wedding. *If you force this upon me, you'll have to force the other upon me as well,* she'd said, and he'd been so arrogant he'd ignored her legitimate complaint.

Instead, he'd acted exactly like the long string of so-called gentlemen before him, the Pelhams and the Faringdons and all the other bastards. He'd browbeaten her. Taken advantage of her. Seduced her. The list of his offenses was so long, he choked on them.

He'd still succeeded in making her willing, or as willing as a woman can be whose pride has been trampled on, whose energies have been exhausted by the fight. He'd won without giving in one whit to her simple request for the truth about his past.

How hollow was his triumph.

Because eventually she would learn the truth—if not from him, then from another. Someone would make a random comment or Uncle Edgar would tell her just to spite him. Then she'd have reason enough to leave him, since the truth would surely break any bonds of duty he'd managed to make her feel for him.

He gazed out the window again. She looked so fetching, so perfectly at home in his garden. He could grow used to having her always in his sight. Which made the thought of her leaving him all the more terrifying. What good was winning the fight against his uncle if she weren't here? Or worse yet, if she stayed, despising him with every breath? The very thought made him ill.

No, he must heed the call of his conscience. He'd made a mistake by forcing her into this marriage—he saw that now. But Fate had kept her from bearing his child just yet, thus handing him the chance to undo his mistake.

So he must seize that chance and offer her back what he'd taken from her—her pride, her independence, and yes, her freedom. After all the indignities she'd suffered at the hands of men of his kind, she deserved that much from him.

Even if he had to cut out his heart to do so.

"Good evening, milady," Ian's butler, Spencer, greeted Felicity as she entered the dining room and took her usual place.

Milady. She always wanted to look around for the stately and elegant personage to whom they surely referred.

Spencer bent over her place to pour her a glass of burgundy. "His lordship sent word that he will not be dining this evening, milady."

A keen disappointment seized her. She'd dressed with such care, looking forward to telling Ian that her courses had ended. "Oh."

The elderly butler hesitated. When she glanced at him, he said, "If you should need the master, however, he's in his rooms."

She brightened. "He told you to say that?"

"No, milady. I merely thought you might find the information of interest."

Her spirits fell once more. "I do. Thank you."

He motioned to the footman to serve her the first course—a consommé. She stared into the bowl, but her mind was elsewhere. Ian's absence at dinner for the past three nights had garnered even the servants' attention. No doubt they'd also noticed his avoidance of her. The promised visit to the tenants hadn't materialized. He'd sent word that he would be too busy with other affairs to carry her round and introduce her.

She detested that phrase—"sent word." Ian forever "sent word" to her. That he couldn't accompany her into the village. That he would be out all day inspecting his properties. That he wouldn't be at dinner. She only wished the wretch would "send word" about why her behavior the other night had made him avoid her.

"Milady?" Spencer asked.

She looked up to find him at her elbow. "Yes?"

"Is there . . . something wrong with the soup?"

She'd been staring into it for several minutes. "No." She shoved back her chair. "I'm not hungry, I'm afraid. I believe I'll do without dinner tonight."

"Yes, milady," he murmured, bowing.

She stood abruptly, took a fortifying gulp of wine, and then set the glass down and headed for the door. She'd had enough of this nonsense. She'd seen less of Ian in the past three days of married life at Chesterley than she had in one day of unmarried life in London. It wasn't like Ian to sulk simply because her courses had prevented him from bedding her. But why else could he be avoiding her?

Well, she would find out. They were married, for pity's sake, and if he thought being married meant ignoring his wife when he couldn't bed her, he was very much mistaken. It was time she informed him of that fact.

When she arrived at Ian's bedchamber, she was relieved

to find the door open and Ian clearly visible inside. He must have just come from his bath, for his hair was still damp and he wore a dressing gown of figured silk tied at the waist with a sash. He stood at the foot of the bed, directing his valet who was . . .

Packing an open trunk.

"Where are you going?" she asked sharply from the doorway.

His valet looked up in surprise, but a quick nod from Ian toward the door was all it took for the servant to slip past Felicity and off down the hall.

"To London," he answered.

Her heart skipped a beat. She entered the room with unsteady steps, closing the door behind her. "I thought we weren't returning to London until the day after tomorrow."

He continued where his valet had left off by tossing a pair of drawers into the trunk. "There's been a change of plan. You'll want to attend Lord Stratton's New Year's Eve ball, won't you, so you can write about it in your column? That means leaving tomorrow. I'd planned to tell you this evening."

"Oh." She wished he'd asked her about it first. The ball wasn't nearly as important to her as consummating their marriage, and now there would only be tonight before her brothers were with them again.

Still, she only needed one night. Feeling a bit nervous, she strolled to the bed and sat down on the edge. "I . . . I came to tell you that my courses are finished."

He obviously didn't miss the significance of that. His hands paused in the act of reaching for something in his bureau. "I see."

She waited for him to say more . . . to look at her or kiss her . . . anything at all. When he returned to packing, she couldn't believe it. What had happened to him? Three days ago, he wouldn't have left her alone on his bed for more than a second after such a pronouncement. "Ian, that means there's no reason for us not to—"

"I know what it means." His profile was to her, the taut muscles more unyielding than marble. "It means we should have left for London today."

She stared at him in utter bewilderment. "Whyever for?"

"Felicity." His voice cracked a little on her name. He straightened as if steeling himself for an unpleasant task. When he faced her, his expression was grim. "We're going to London early for another reason as well."

This didn't sound good, not good at all. "Oh?"

"I sent a message off today to a solicitor, requesting an appointment for tomorrow. I think he'll oblige me." He paused. "This particular solicitor specializes in annulments."

She jumped up, her heart lurching sickeningly in her chest. "What do you mean?"

His gaze locked with hers. "It's time we acknowledged this was a mistake."

A mistake? He was seeking an annulment? How dare he! "Why? Because I took so long to let you bed me again?"

"Of course not! But thanks to our abstinence, you aren't yet pregnant. Under the law, the marriage hasn't even been consummated. We should take advantage of that and obtain an annulment while we still can."

"I don't want an annulment!"

He sighed. "If it's the money you're worried about, be assured that I'll settle on you an allowance that will provide handsomely for you and your brothers."

"Damn you, Ian, it's not the money! I don't care about money—I never did! I care about *you*! I don't want an annulment, and you don't either!"

"What I want is of no importance." Eyes of deepest obsidian stared earnestly into hers. "I once thought it was—that my need for a wife superseded any claims of morality or conscience or even simple courtesy. I wanted a wife, so

I set out to get one. And I fixed upon you. When you refused me, I seduced you. When you balked at marrying me to save your reputation, I made it so you couldn't refuse. And all because I wanted you."

She opened her mouth to protest that she'd wanted him as well, but he held up a hand to forestall her. "Now I find that my conscience plagues me. The only solution is to annul this farce of a marriage."

And she'd expected to seduce him tonight. "Drat it, Ian, why must you choose *now* to repent your sins?" *Now that I love you so dearly.*

"Better late than never, don't you think?"

"No, I do not! I don't want you heeding your conscience if it means ending our marriage. I didn't marry you for your conscience!"

"You didn't marry me for anything at all—I forced you to marry me!"

"The devil you did! Remember that conversation we had in the church vestibule? If I'd wanted to be rid of you, I'd have turned you away then. But I didn't!" Should she tell him why? Would he withdraw into himself if she did? She must take that chance. "It was love that kept me from turning you away, damn it. I knew it even before I arrived at the church. I married you because I love you, Ian!"

The words visibly shook him. Although he didn't offer the same, she gained encouragement from his expression, which showed uncertainty, not disgust. Surely that was a good start.

Averting his gaze from hers, he raked his fingers through his hair. "I can't imagine why," he said finally.

"Can't you?" She strode up to stand in front of him, wanting him to look at her. "You're generous and patient with my brothers. You listen to me when I talk, unlike other men who think that anything a woman says must necessarily be stupid. You're considerate to your servants as well as to me."

"That's only one side of me. You've already seen a little of the other side—the one that manipulated you into marriage. But I assure you, if you really knew the blackness in my soul, you wouldn't be speaking of—" His voice grew choked. "You'd be begging to leave this marriage."

Ah. So that was his real reason for wanting an annulment. The thorn in his heart. She'd finally brought it to the surface, and he not only refused to let her pluck it out, but insisted on driving her away from him before she saw it.

Well, it wouldn't work. She'd fought too hard for him and loved him too much. Maybe he couldn't speak of it yet, but he would eventually—and when he did she'd be *here*, not off in London living separate from him. "I know you better than you think."

"Do you?" His gaze shot to hers, black eyes snapping. "Did you know I'd lied to you all along about my reasons for marriage?"

She willed herself not to react. He wanted to drive her away, and she wouldn't let him. "How so?"

"I need an heir because if I don't sire one within two years, I'll lose Chesterley and most of my income. I'll be a viscount, but very little more."

She gaped at him. "How can that be? Surely your estate is entailed—"

"No. My grandfather died when my father was but a boy. So although the estate was entailed upon my father, he had no one to force him into continuing the entail to me. And since Father had peculiar ideas about inheritance, he chose to hold the estate over my head until I came of age and married. Thus there was no legal document protecting my right to it when I left home for the Continent."

His lips thinned into a line. "That's when Father apparently decided I should only inherit under certain conditions. His will states that I must have an heir by the end of my thirtieth year, or my uncle will inherit it all."

"Your uncle!" she said in horror.

"Yes. And having seen evidence of his character, you realize what would happen then. He would crush this estate under his heel until it was no more than a stain upon the shire." He turned away from her, bracing one hand against a bedpost. "So you see, Felicity, when you accused me of seeking a 'brood mare,' you were very close to the truth. I reached twenty-nine last month, so I have this year and the next to sire an heir. That's why I forced you to marry me."

"I see. What you're telling me is that you had even more compelling reasons to force a marriage than I realized. You weren't simply being your usual autocratic self; you were desperate. And I should blame you for that, despise you for that?"

"You should blame me for lying to you about it! I could have told you the truth—laid the entire story before you. But I couldn't risk your refusing to be my 'brood mare,' so I did as I always did with you—seduced and manipulated and deceived you."

She chose her words with care. "I forgave you for that long ago, just as you forgave me all my misjudgments of you. I don't care anymore that you lied to me about your reasons for marriage. It wasn't much of a lie. You'd already made it clear you were marrying me for practical considerations. Learning that those considerations were more urgent than I'd guessed makes little difference, and it certainly is no reason to seek an annulment. Nor does it change my feelings for you one bit."

A muscle twitched in his jaw. "It should."

"It doesn't. I'm not foolish enough to believe that one small mistake defines a man's character."

He rounded on her, eyes glittering darkly. "You don't know my character, damn it! Those years on the Continent—what do you think I was doing? I was a spy, Felicity, and that means I lived a life of constant deception and betrayal. Because I wasn't just a spy, I was a *good* spy. Do you know what it takes to be a good spy?"

The vehemence behind the question caught her off guard. All she could do was shake her head mutely.

"It takes not giving a bloody damn what happens to you or what you do. Morality has no place in your actions— you do whatever your government deems necessary. Back then I felt that the world had turned its back on me, so I did the same. I turned my back on my family, on Chester- ley, on everything I held dear. I taught myself not to feel, not to let my emotions get the better of me. I relied on intellect instead, and it carried me far. My superiors soon discovered I would take on any task as long as it was dan- gerous enough to make me forget—"

He broke off, his face tortured. "No matter what Wel- lington said, the things I did were nothing to be proud of. Yes, I found out information no one could. Yes, thanks to my coloring and my talent for languages, I insinuated my- self deeply into the ranks of Napoléon's army in Spain. Do you know how many French and Spanish 'friends' I be- trayed to do that? How many lies I told?"

"But they were the enemy—"

"That was my excuse, too. But they weren't all the en- emy. There were Spanish camp followers and civilians and— Spying is a nasty business. It spills over very quickly into all of life. You can't possibly know how many things I did that I now regret." He spoke the words with such sharp self-contempt it wrenched her heart.

"The fact that you regret them only proves your good character. It's one of the many reasons I love you, Ian."

"Stop saying that! You couldn't possibly love a man like me!"

Talking would clearly not convince him. So she moved closer and said, "Then I see I must *prove* that I love you."

And before he could stop her, she looped her arms about his neck and dragged his head down for her kiss.

Chapter 23

New Year's Eve promises many enticing amuse-
ments, among them the fireworks display at Vauxhall, Mr. and Mrs. Locksley's entertainment, Lord
Stratton's annual ball, and His Majesty's lavish
dinner at Frogmore-lodge. There will be something
for every level of society, so the night is sure to be
enjoyed all round.

LORD X, *THE EVENING GAZETTE*,
DECEMBER 30, 1820

Ian stood frozen with his wife's mouth on his. Damn
her, he couldn't let this happen! Bedding her would
make it impossible for him to annul the marriage. Why
hadn't he considered his wife's passionate temperament in
all his earlier strategizing?

Because he hadn't known she fancied herself in love with
him. That's why she was trying this damned maneuver. She
thought that because they'd made love she was *in* love,
which wasn't the same thing. The things he'd told her had
made no difference, because they were only a fraction of
the real horror. Once she learned the truth about that, her
feelings of love would dissipate rapidly enough. So he
ought to tell her everything. Then she would despise him,
and the battle would be over.

328

He reached up to pry her arms from around his neck, but she held on tight, and with his fingers around her wrists, he could feel her wildly beating pulse. But it was worse when she moved her lips on his. Damn it, they were sweet. Literally. Sweet with burgundy, making him think of ripe, luscious fruit . . . as ripe and luscious as the breasts crushed against his chest by her tiptoed stance.

My God, those breasts. He itched to touch them. Ignoring her lips was manageable. Possibly. If he kept his mouth closed and didn't breathe in her scent.

But ignoring her body, the full length of it so soft against him, was impossible. Not when he'd mangled his sheets for a week trying not to think of having her again. He wasn't a bloody stone, for God's sake. He wrapped his fingers around her wrists, trying frantically to unlock the hands manacled about his neck.

She drew back and frowned up at him. "Have you forgotten how to kiss me, Ian?"

"No," he said hoarsely, fire eating him up inside. "I don't *want* to kiss you."

A smile curled up her temptress's lips. "Yes, you do. You're just being stubborn, and I won't have it. I want you to make love to me again."

Erotic images danced in his vision—of throwing her back on that bed and having his way with her. "No. We should talk. I have more to tell you—"

"Later. I want to do this first."

Do it! Yes, yes! his body cried. Thankfully, his mind still functioned, and it said *no,* though the *no* grew feebler by the second.

Then she flattened her lower body against his already burgeoning erection, and he had to struggle to remember why he would say *no* at all.

"I want you, Ian. Now." She released his neck suddenly, and he released her wrists even more quickly, but she only moved her hands to her hair, where she proceeded to re-move the pins.

He scowled at her. "Don't do that."

"You give me no choice. If you won't make love to me, you force me to resort to the same tactics I used on the morning after our wedding."

Bloody hell, what fevered images those words sent run-ning through his head! And every image was of her sliding out of a pair of silk drawers and lifting one leg—

He grabbed her hands and forced them to her sides. "I won't let you do this."

"You can't stop me, and you know it." She ground her pelvis against his loins again, and he went a little mad. "If you don't let me undress, I'll resort to *your* tactics that morning—I'll tell you exactly what I want to do to every part of your body."

A truly wicked look entered her eyes as she let her gaze trail slowly down his chin and neck. "You know that line of hair just there on your chest, the one that starts below your throat? I want to run my finger all the way down that line, very, very slowly."

Her sultry gaze mirrored the actions she described, skim-ming down his chest to the sash. His shaft strained to es-cape his stockinette smallclothes. If she didn't shut up—

"I want to follow that intriguing line of hair to your belly and once around your navel. I might even plant a kiss or two there. Yes, I believe I'll continue on with kisses. I'll scatter a few warm, wet kisses down your belly until my mouth reaches your hard—"

He never let her finish. He crushed her mouth beneath his, devouring it, invading it with his tongue the second she parted her lips. Thoughts of annulments and plans and salv-ing his conscience vanished. His wife was in his arms, and he wanted her.

God, how he wanted her. Only Felicity could combine the most sensuous impulses of a courtesan and the wondering enjoyment of an innocent—a combination no man could resist. Certainly not he.

He still held her hands at her sides, but didn't resist when she dragged them free, then slid them inside his dressing gown to skim his ribs. When he felt her fumbling with the ties of his smallclothes, he aided her in unfastening them, then shimmied out of them and his dressing gown with astonishing speed.

Her eagerness to undress him gave him license to undress her next, tearing at buttons, ripping at tangled tapes and ties, shoving and peeling and discarding layers of lacy feminine fluff until she wore only her chemise and stockings. Apparently she wore no drawers, and that realization stiffened him to a rigidity unsurpassed in his lifetime.

Pulling back from her, he yanked at the ties of her chemise, knotting them so badly he swore under his breath. She made a little sound that prompted him to glance up, and her expression checked his haste at once. She looked alarmed.

Of course. For all her teasing, she was still nearly an innocent. She'd completed the act only twice, and his violent haste in undressing her had shocked her.

He forced himself to pause and take a breath instead of tossing her on the bed as he wanted to. She deserved better. She deserved none of this, but he couldn't stop himself now, so he must make it good for her instead.

If he could keep from going insane in the meantime.

He needed a little distance. Releasing her chemise, he said hoarsely, "Take this off for me." *Then I won't be tempted to rip it off and ravish you too quickly.*

Her cheeks grew rosy, but she nodded. Stepping back from him, she bent her head and concentrated on unknotting the ties of her chemise, which gave him a second to breathe. And to feast his eyes on the sight of her in her chemise. He'd never seen this one on her before. It was something a wife would wear on her honeymoon—made of a silky gauze thin enough to reveal more than it should and less than he wanted.

It showed clearly the dark peach buds of her nipples where they pressed against the fabric, but the rest of her breasts remained cloaked. The feminine swell of her belly was hidden, but the hair of the luscious vee between her legs showed darkly beneath the opaque cloth. He had to will his hands to be still, will them not to rip the damned thing in half so he could feast on her naked body.

She reached for the hem as if to draw it up over her head.

"No," he commanded. "Do it the way you did it the morning after our wedding. Lower it. Slowly."

Her gaze met his. Her alarm was gone, replaced with a wide-eyed excitement. She did as he asked, and as she revealed inch after inch of female flesh, his mouth went dry. Candlelight shimmered on her smooth skin. Her breasts were as lovely as he remembered, pert and firm and the shape he liked—not too large, for he'd never been fond of blowsy women.

Then came her belly, with its fine dimple of a navel, and then . . .

"You can drop the chemise," he rasped.

She did, and he groaned. Tendrils of hair curled sweetly about the spot he wanted to kiss and caress and lick.

She started to undo one garter, and he said, "Wait. Leave it on." Leaning forward, he tugged her into his arms for a long, probing kiss. Then he lifted her bodily, and turned to set her on her feet on the bed so that she stood a few feet above him.

"Ian, what are you—"

"Shh," he murmured as he skimmed his hands over her hips and thighs. Had a woman ever been so perfectly made? Or was it that his need for her made him see perfection everywhere? "Hold on to the bedpost, *querida*."

When she did as he bade, he took her other hand and

placed it on his shoulder. Then he lifted the opposite leg and hooked it over his other shoulder, spreading her open for his gaze. And his mouth.

"Ian?" she said, her skin pinkening everywhere.

"Remember what I said I wanted to do to you that morning?" He planted a kiss on the band of thigh above her garter. "What I wanted to do with my tongue?"

She gave a little gasp of surprise when he did precisely what he'd threatened, running his tongue slowly up the inside of her thigh to the outer edges of her curly hair.

"Good Lord," she whispered as his mouth found the place he craved kissing, "you can't mean to . . . It's . . . it's . . . Ohhhhh, *Ian* . . ."

She didn't protest after that. He kissed her there in earnest, enjoying the taste of her, relishing her approving murmurs as he laved the petals of her skin with his tongue. She'd abandoned the bedpost, so both of her hands clutched his head to force it closer. He liked that, liked the way his wanton little wife threw herself into the most intimate of marital acts.

Now if only he could keep from losing control. Her musky scent and eager undulations were building the tension in him, too, and he wasn't sure how much longer he could go without embarrassing himself.

"Yes, yes . . . Ian," she moaned, "yes . . . like that . . . oh, that's even better . . . my God . . . my sweet God . . ."

Her explosion came so quickly he had to anchor her hips against him to keep her from falling as the shudders swept her body and she cried out his name. She swayed there a moment as if suspended, her leg slipping off his shoulder.

Then slowly she sank to her knees on the bed. She stared into his eyes, the dazed light of pleasure still shining in her face. "I never realized . . ."

"Neither did I." He'd never realized that giving pleasure to a woman could be so sublime. Or that he could want a woman urgently, yet want to please her even more. Or that he could find himself so enamored of her he never wanted to let her out of his sight.

She glanced down at his erection, and her eyes went round. "What about . . ."

He froze. He could end this now, and they could still have an annulment. She'd found her pleasure, so she wouldn't quibble much if he didn't find his.

But she must have guessed his thoughts, for she murmured, "Oh, no, you don't," and pulled his head down to hers.

After that, he was scarcely conscious of how she ended up laid out on the bed with her thighs parted and him kneeling between them. His cock was leading him, that's all. Next thing he knew, he was sliding into her slick, welcoming passage.

"My God, *querida,* you're so warm." Warm and tight and incredible. Was it possible to die of pleasure? Because if anybody could prompt it, it was his darling wife.

Like a natural wanton, she clamped her legs instinctively about his hips, drawing him in, sucking him down into her. He couldn't go slowly. Not a chance. She felt too good with her legs locked around him and her body straining up to meet his thrusts. He drove deep and hard . . . he couldn't help himself.

He wanted to be inside her so fully she could never forget him, never want to leave him. He wanted to imprint himself on her like a key pressed into the locksmith's wax, so that only they two fit together.

"You've lost . . . your chance . . . for an annulment," he warned as he pounded into her.

"Good." She kissed him full on the mouth to seal the agreement. Her tongue darted inside to tease him, and he sucked hard on it, wanting . . . needing as much of her as he could get.

She was his. Forever. The thought made him so glad, he

drove to the hilt inside her and spilled his seed almost in the same instant.

"I love you," she cried against his mouth as she found her own release again. "I love you . . . I love you . . . I love you . . ."

I love you, too, he thought in that instant. *God help me, I love you, too.*

Which meant he had to tell her everything. He couldn't let her go on imagining herself in love with him when she didn't truly know him. She deserved to know what she'd just gotten herself into.

But not now. In the morning. Let him have this one sweet night with her.

Something tickled Felicity's ear, dragging her up through the fog of sleep. A whisper. Someone was whispering her name in her ear. She snuggled deeper into the covers, which were tucked up under her chin. "Go away," she grumbled.

A male voice chuckled. "You can't sleep all day, *querida.*"

She opened one eye to glare at Ian, then shut it. "Why not?"

"We're leaving for London today, remember?"

It took a second for that to sink in, but when it did, her eyes flew open. Ian sat on the edge of the bed beside her, his hand resting on her well-draped hip. He was already dressed, for pity's sake. Of course, the room was flooded with light, which might have something to do with that.

"What time is it?" she asked.

"Noon."

"Noon? Good Lord, I slept late!"

"That's understandable. You didn't get much sleep last night."

No, I didn't, she thought, flushing. They'd had quite an evening. If he hadn't sired an heir *last* night, it wasn't for want of trying.

A hot flood of pleasant memories made her smile coyly at him. "You didn't get much sleep, either. Perhaps you should come back to bed."

He laughed. "In the words of the immortal Lord X, 'Man doth not live by bed alone.' You must get up, *querida*. I hope to be off by one o'clock."

She gazed up at him, her heart beating triple time. "Why so early?"

"Don't you want to spend a few hours with your brothers before the ball? And you'll need time to dress."

A relieved sigh escaped her lips. "So you're not . . . still going to visit that solicitor about the annulment."

He glanced away. "I'm afraid that's no longer possible. Now that we've consummated the marriage, we can't pursue the matter until we make sure you're not pregnant. By then no judge with eyes will believe we haven't had conjugal relations, even if you don't prove to be pregnant."

The tinge of regret in his tone made her tip up her chin and say stoutly, "Good."

His gaze swung back to her. "We'll see if you feel the same later."

"What do you mean?"

"We need to talk. We should have talked about this last night before it was too late, but we were—"

"I don't regret last night."

The brief flicker of satisfaction in his eyes told her he didn't either, no matter what he said. "I only hope you can say the same after we talk. But we can do that in the carriage on the way to London." He grabbed the edge of the covers tucked up under her chin. "Now get out of bed and get dressed, lazybones. Or I'll dress you myself."

With a taunting smile, he whisked back the covers, then froze. Apparently he'd forgotten she hadn't donned a nightgown last night. His gaze trailed hungrily over her naked body.

"Dress me?" she teased. "You'd never manage it." She

reached up and grabbed his cravat, then tugged him toward her.

He went willingly. "I suppose we *could* leave a little later," he conceded as he lowered his head to nibble on her ear. "An hour will do no harm."

"Or two. Or three." She unbuttoned his waistcoat. "In the words of the immortal Lord X, passion must never be hurried."

"He never said that."

"He just did." Then she muffled his laughter with her kiss.

Four hours later, they entered the St. Clair carriage. All plans for stopping by the Taylor home had been abandoned now that they were so late, since she didn't wish to excite her brothers by showing up for only an hour or so, then flitting off to a ball. They weren't expecting her until tomorrow anyway, so she and Ian would go to the St. Clair town house and dress.

Felicity sank back onto her seat, feeling warm, sated, and yes, loved. Ian had yet to say the words, but she felt his love in every caress, every look. She was sure he loved her. And one day she'd make him say the words. Just see if she didn't.

This wouldn't be the day, however. Judging from the grim set to his face as he took the seat across from her, he was intent upon his "talk," and it didn't look as if it would be pleasant for either of them.

The carriage set off, and they traveled a mile or so in silence with her watching out the window and dreading the coming discussion. Nor did the day look promising for it. The sunlight that had shone so brightly while they made love had vanished behind a blanket of sullen clouds that threatened snow. A bleak, dreary day, to be sure.

Suddenly, Ian cleared his throat. "It's time I told you everything."

Her heart pounded as she turned her gaze to his. "About

what?" But she knew and braced herself for the worst.

"My past. All that 'truth' you were so intent upon getting at a week ago."

"Why now?" It dawned on her that she feared knowing the truth almost as much as she wanted it. His telling her might change them both irrevocably.

"You deserve to know. We can't annul the marriage, but we could still dissolve it some other way. Divorce, separation, whatever you wish. I want you to know what kind of man you've married before you continue in this . . . illusion that you love me."

There was such pain in his countenance, it banished her reluctance to hear him. He needed to reveal the thorn in his heart, and she could endure it. "My love for you isn't an illusion," she said softly. "Nothing you can say will change it."

He glanced out the window, a muscle working in his jaw. "What if I . . . tell you I did something so awful it left several people's lives in ruin?"

"If you mean that story about your seduction of your aunt—"

"The truth is worse than that—ten times worse."

Did he imply that his uncle's darker accusation was the truth? No, she couldn't believe it. "I know in my heart that you're decent and good, no matter what you tell me."

"You think so?" He paused. "Very well. We'll see what you think after you hear everything. You see, I didn't seduce my aunt as Lady Brumley claimed, or even force myself on her as my uncle claimed."

His gaze swung back to hers, wrought with grief and guilt and self-hatred. "The truth is—I killed her."

Chapter 24

On New Year's Eve, we do well not to look ahead, but back. The man who cannot learn from past mistakes has faint hope of avoiding future ones.

LORD X, *THE EVENING GAZETTE*,
DECEMBER 31, 1820

Felicity sat frozen, uncertain how to understand him. "You mean, because she killed herself for love of you—"

"No. She never loved me, and she didn't kill herself, not for love or anything else. *I* killed her."

Her hands began to shake so much she clasped them tightly together in her lap. "I-I don't believe you. How could that be?"

He sighed heavily. "I should start at the beginning. The year I reached nineteen, I spent a long holiday at Chesterley with my father. We fought about everything. My aunt and uncle were often around during those battles. Uncle Edgar always took Father's side, which aggravated matters. But my aunt . . ."

His voice softened. "My aunt tried to smooth things over. She listened to my complaints with understanding, having endured my uncle's formidable temper for three years. Although she wasn't much older than I, she was a sensible woman who offered sound advice, so I turned to her a great deal. We spent so much time in each other's company and she was so kind that I came to care for her very much."

The carriage hit a rut, jolting them, but Ian hardly seemed to notice. "And yes, I suppose I was infatuated with her and even desired her, although at that age young men desire anything in a petticoat. I doubt she realized my feelings. Despite the tales you've heard, Aunt Cynthia was always conscious of her duty to my uncle and never behaved toward me with anything but the most circumspect propriety."

Though he looked at her, she could tell he didn't see her. He saw his own past, and his despairing expression tore at Felicity's heart. She wished he would come sit by her while he told his sad tale, but he wasn't the sort of man to want a woman's coddling at such a time. And she feared stopping the flow of words.

"One afternoon," he went on, "I was walking past a cottage on my uncle's estate when I heard noises coming from within. The unmistakable sound of flesh hitting flesh. A woman weeping. A man shouting. I recognized my uncle's voice."

His large hands tightened into cannonball fists where they lay on his thighs. "I'd noticed bruises on my aunt before without realizing that her plausible explanations for them were lies. But I couldn't mistake what I was hearing. So I stopped outside the door."

It was so like her dear husband to leap to the defense of a woman. She could imagine how painful it must have been for him to hear his aunt being mistreated.

He uttered a low curse. "If I'd taken even a moment to think, I would have realized that any direct interference on my part would only further enrage my uncle. I could have either found my father and begged him to come, or knocked on the door with some lie about needing my uncle's assistance." He paused, as if unable to continue.

She willed him silently to go on. He turned his gaze out the window. "But I *didn't* take a moment to think. I acted in exactly the thoughtless manner my father always criticized. I burst through the door."

He was silent so long that she finally whispered, "And was he . . . Had he—"

"Hit her? Oh, yes. She already had red marks on her cheeks and a black eye. She was huddled in a corner, sobbing as he stood over her with his hands still fisted—*fisted*, mind you!" His voice grew hoarse and thick. "My God, she was half his size, a little wisp of a thing. And the bastard had been using his *fists* on her!"

Horror filled her, deepening even more as she thought of how the sight must have tortured her beloved husband. "Oh, Ian," she murmured sympathetically.

But he seemed not to hear her. "I went a little insane. I launched myself at his back. We . . . fought, but he was no match for a hotheaded lad of nineteen, nearly twenty years younger than he. I soon had him on the floor and was pummeling his face over and over . . . My fury was so feverish it blotted out everything but a lust for his blood."

He dragged in a long breath. "And when my aunt came up behind me and grabbed my arm to stop me before I killed him, I shook her off with such strength that she . . . she . . ." He broke off, nearly losing his voice. Then he squared his shoulders, his tortured gaze returning to her. "She lost her balance and fell back against the stone mantel. She . . . hit her head. The doctor said she died instantly."

"Good Lord," she whispered, "your poor aunt." But it wasn't his poor aunt her heart broke for. It was him, her sweet husband. Who'd held all this blackness inside him for so long in silence. She wished she'd known sooner.

"Yes, my poor aunt." The words were heavy with self-reproach. "Caught between two violent creatures like me and my uncle, she had no chance for life or happiness."

He buried his face in his hands. Desperate to comfort

him, she leaned forward and laid her hand on his back. For a long moment, there was no sound inside the carriage save its creaking, the pounding hooves of the horses, and Ian's tortured breathing. When she could bear it no longer, she said, "I understand your suffering, my love, but it wasn't your fault—"

"Not my fault?" he cried as his head snapped up. "How was it not my fault? I stepped in where I had no business being! I let my temper so possess me that I shoved a tiny woman hard enough to make her fall and kill herself!"

Frantically, she searched for words that would assuage his guilt. "She could have fallen on a cushion instead. That she didn't was tragic, I agree, yet you can't blame yourself for bad circumstances. Besides, your uncle might have killed her anyway if you hadn't stepped in."

His eyes blazed into hers. "But he didn't, don't you understand? *I* did!"

"You were trying to protect her! No one could reasonably fault you for that!"

"My family did!"

A chill struck her heart. "Your uncle—"

"Not my uncle." His expression hardened into stone. "I mean, he blamed me—he still blames me—but there's not much he can do about it. He's no fool. He knew even then that if he accused me outright of murder, I'd accuse him outright of wife-beating. He had no desire to drag the truth out before the world. Nor did he wish to reveal his true character to my father."

"So the two of you didn't tell your father what really happened?"

He sat up, away from the reach of her hand. Shifting restlessly, he tightened and untightened his fists. "By the time Father was summoned and found me holding her body and raging at myself, Uncle Edgar had regained his composure enough to present his own version of what happened. It didn't include any mention of wife-beating, I assure you. He told Father he'd . . . caught me seducing Aunt Cynthia, and in the struggle between us she'd tried to stop us from fighting and had fallen."

"The bastard!" she said, even more furious at Ian's uncle than before. How dare the man blacken Ian before his father when the old viscount had already been so distrustful of his son? "Well, at least your damned uncle is consistent in his lies. That's a variation on the tale he told me." She added dryly, "He didn't mention wife-beating to me either. Though I'm surprised he didn't just accuse you of killing his wife."

"I think he's always feared that if he did, I would simply lie and accuse *him* of murder. It would be more plausible to most hearers. I was nineteen and fairly young; he was a grown man. The woman was his wife. I have evidence of his wife-beating—Miss Greenaway would be only too happy to testify to it, for she witnessed it once herself."

Which explained Ian's continued interest in the woman. As usual, he'd been strategizing, keeping Miss Greenaway on his side until he might need her. And Felicity had assumed the worst. No wonder he'd been so angry at her.

"No," he went on, "I'm sure my uncle thought that telling you I'd seduced, even raped, his wife was far less risky. It fed into the tales circulating about me and made me look like the evil seducer while he played the betrayed husband, a role more to his liking. Even so, he never circulated his story about me generally. He must have known that if I realized what he'd told the women I courted, I might take stronger measures against him. And I would have, if I hadn't married in time to produce an heir."

"What I don't understand is why your father wrote such an abominable will. You did tell him what really happened that day, didn't you?"

"I told him," he said hollowly. "He simply chose not to believe me."

"His own son?" The enormity of it cut her to the heart.

"He believed his brother over *you*? What kind of father would do that?" Oh, her poor love, enduring so much torment and guilt at the hands of his own family! She squeezed his leg, wondering how much more it must hurt him, if it made her hurt so badly for him.

Ian shrugged, as if it hardly mattered, but she knew it mattered a great deal. "Father already blamed me for Mother's death. He thought me a rash and intemperate young man, which I suppose I was. It took little to convince him I'd seduced my aunt. I'd been fairly obvious in my adoration of her."

She sat there speechless. What possible comfort could one offer to remedy the pain of such a terrible betrayal? It was a good thing Ian's father was dead. Otherwise, she'd be tempted to kill him herself.

"I left that night for the Continent," Ian continued, "left them to deal with the questions and the rumors and the mess. If I'd known then what I learned later—that Miss Greenaway and most of Uncle Edgar's staff knew of his frequent beatings of my aunt—I would have stayed and tried to convince my father. But I didn't know, and I couldn't go on living there, seeing my uncle every day, enduring my father's disapproval, hiding the nasty secret." His voice broke. "And I *had* killed her. All I wanted was escape."

Moving to sit beside him, she took his hand in hers. He squeezed it so tightly she was sure she'd bear the imprint of his fingers later.

"Of course, Father took my flight as ample demonstration of my guilt," he went on. "It was a stupid thing to do, but then I was only nineteen. I hadn't yet learned to think before acting. If I had, she'd still be alive today."

She couldn't stand it any longer. "You must stop blaming yourself for it, my love. Your actions were perfectly understandable."

His bleakly staring eyes told her that her words had

changed nothing for him. "Understandable or not, I deprived two children of their mother. I daresay my poor cousins don't much care how it happened." He released her hand and stared out the opposite window. "As far as they're concerned, I murdered her as surely as if I'd put a gun to her head."

She started to protest, then realized that wasn't how to reach him. "You're saying that an accidental death is the same as a murder."

"The result is the same, isn't it?" he ground out.

"Well then, you have even more crimes on your conscience."

"What do you mean?"

"You raped me, didn't you?"

"What!" He swung his head around to glare at her. "You said yourself you wanted—"

"It doesn't matter if I wanted it or not. 'The result is the same.' Isn't that what you said? I'm no longer a virgin, so it follows that you raped me, because rape and seduction and mutual lovemaking all have the same results, do they not?"

He was silent a long moment, the muscles of his face so taut that she feared they might snap. "I see what you're trying to do, but it won't work. You can't banish my guilt with rhetoric."

"I'm not trying to banish it. Soften it perhaps, but not banish it. If I could banish it with only a few words, your character would be faulty indeed." She laid her hand on his knee again. "I'm only asking that you let me share it, help you learn to live with it."

A shudder passed through him. "I have no right to expect that of you," he said hoarsely. "When you married me, you didn't know what darkness lay inside me. By not telling you about it, I gave you no chance to refuse it. No one would fault you for leaving me now that you know the truth."

"Why would I wish to leave the man I love?"

"Damn it, the man you said you loved isn't the man you're married to!" He shoved her hand off his knee. "I may not be the philanderer you thought, but I *am* unprincipled and unscrupulous. I don't deserve you or any decent woman!"

He stared blindly out of the carriage. "I should never have married. If I hadn't been so certain that Uncle Edgar would destroy Chesterley, I would never have sought a wife. That's why I tried to choose a woman who'd marry me for other considerations, so she wouldn't be devastated when she learned of my true character." An anguished sound escaped him. "Then you came along, and I was so tempted by you . . . I justified my actions by telling myself that you had no future—"

"Which was the truth!" she broke in.

"No. I could have helped you without marrying you. And there was that damned Masefield—"

"He would never have married me, and you know it. I certainly didn't want to marry *him*. Not when I could have you." She tucked her hand beneath his bent arm. "And can't you see how all your care in choosing a wife proves your goodness? An unscrupulous man would have taken any wife who served his purpose. But you did your duty while also trying to protect the women you courted."

"The way I protected you? My God, look at how I've treated you. I manipulated you, lied to you, forced you to marry me—"

"If we compare mistreatments, my darling, I fear I'll fare as poorly as you." A lump caught in her throat. "You had this terrible secret inside, and I did everything to bring it to light. My actions were motivated by emotions as reckless and thoughtless as yours, except that I don't have the excuse of youth or attenuating circumstances to soothe my guilt. Yet I can still ask for your forgiveness and go on. Why can't you?"

He swung his head around to gaze at her uncertainly. "What I did is so much worse. You say it doesn't matter, but after you've considered all its implications—"

"I will still love you. Once my heart has decided something, it doesn't alter, and my heart is quite certain what it feels about you."

Picking up her hand, he stared down at it. "You're forgetting that this isn't over yet. If for some reason, we don't have a son in the prescribed time, we lose Chesterley."

She took heart from the fact that he said "we." "When I met you I had less than nothing. So how could I complain about having only nothing?"

A ghost of a smile touched his lips. "You have the strangest way of looking at things."

"Which is why you love me." The second she said the words, she wished them unsaid. He hadn't said he loved her, after all.

But he lifted his head, eyes clear and steady. "I do love you, you know. More than anyone in my life. I shouldn't say it and bind you further to me, but it's true. And the thought of losing you tortures me."

"Oh, Ian," she said, so happy she could hardly contain it, "you'll never lose me!"

His fingers gripped hers tightly. "Listen to me, Felicity. There are other ramifications of the fight with my uncle. If we don't fulfill the terms of the will, I intend to fight it. He's already sucked his own estate dry; I won't let him do the same to Chesterley. But that would mean contesting the will in court, and with a public forum, there's always a risk that this story may come out."

"We'll cross that bridge when we come to it."

"There's more. If we do fulfill the terms, my uncle may retaliate. Until you told me what he said to you, I hadn't realized how far he'd go to stop me from inheriting. He's a coward as all bullies are, which is why he has confined himself to telling tales to women I've courted. But if he finds he has nothing to lose, there's no predicting what he'll say. You may discover yourself cut off from society, your husband vilified, and your brothers and children pitied. I love you too much to want that for you."

"And I love you too much to let you face it alone." She squeezed his hands.

His eyes searched hers a long moment. "You seem determined on this course. Very well, here's what I propose. At tonight's ball there will be speculation—some of it distasteful—about why we married so quickly. The old rumors about me will circulate again, thanks to our wedding. If you find you can endure the most vicious gossip—though I know it's only a fraction of what could occur later in our marriage—I'll speak to you no more of separation or divorce."

She bristled. "I don't need this test to know I want to remain married to you."

"Don't look at it as a test." He smiled wanly. "It's your last chance to escape. Though it will tear my heart out to watch you leave, I can endure it if it means your happiness." His solemn gaze bore into hers. "But if you decide after tonight to remain with me, I'll never let you go, do you hear? You'll be stuck with me for all our lives no matter what my uncle tries. So make your decision carefully."

"I will. And now you listen to me, Lord St. Clair. When I give you my decision after tonight, you must abide by it. No more of this 'I know what's best for you' and 'you might regret it.' We'll start afresh, two people who love each other and who married for that reason alone."

He hesitated a moment, then sighed. "As always, you drive a hard bargain."

"Then you agree?"

Bending his head, he pressed a fervent kiss to their clasped hands. "Yes, my love. I agree."

Chapter 25

Rumors seem to abound on New Year's Eve, when the prospect of another year tempts the gossips to be daring.

LORD X, *THE EVENING GAZETTE*, DECEMBER 31, 1820

Felicity glanced over at Ian as the carriage approached Lord Stratton's town house. He'd been quiet ever since their talk, all through dressing for the ball and the ride here. Now he looked positively somber. She wished he didn't feel compelled to make this test of her love, but she understood it. He couldn't accept her love until he forgave himself, and she would help him do that in time.

Despite his concerns, they were truly married now. She couldn't wait to see Mrs. Box to tell her how content she was with her situation. *More* than content. A lifetime with Ian, free of secrets and uncertainties—what woman wouldn't be ecstatic over the thought?

"What are you smiling about?" he grumbled.

She couldn't resist teasing him. "It's my first ball as the Viscountess St. Clair. If Miss Taylor could gain the confidences of so many people, only think how much material the Viscountess St. Clair can gather for Lord X!"

"Then thank God it's Lord X's name on your bloody

349

column, that's all I have to say," he muttered, though a ghost of a smile touched his lips. "Otherwise, I'll be fighting duels every week over it."

Delighted that his words implied a future for them, she quipped, "Oh, but I'm thinking of using my real name now. When I went to tell Mr. Pilkington I was marrying, he suggested calling it, 'Her Ladyship's Secrets, by the Viscountess St. Clair.' Doesn't that have a nice ring?"

He raised one eyebrow. "Are you trying to send me to an early grave?"

"Hmm. If you die, I'd be the *Dowager* Viscountess St. Clair. That has a nice ring, too." When he scowled, she added, "It's a joke, Ian. Must I always explain my jokes to you?"

"When they're not funny, yes."

He didn't smile, and she regretted teasing him. It would be some time before he felt secure of her, she could see. But she could wait. As long as he loved her.

"Don't worry," she said softly, "I've no intention of using my real name. I told Pilkington you would never approve. He was disappointed, but when I pointed out that the other choice was having me stop writing for him, he saw it my way."

That finally brought a smile. "I'm sure he did. Pilkington is no fool. He knows better than to cross swords with you, my love."

My love. Now that has an even nicer ring to it, she thought.

The carriage stopped, and they disembarked. He offered her his arm, and she took it with a burst of possessive gladness. They began to climb the stairs, but had scarcely moved halfway up before Jordan came running out to greet them.

"Ian," he said without preamble, "I've been watching for you."

The muscles in Ian's arm stiffened beneath her fingers. "What's wrong?"

"Your uncle is here."

A quick shudder went through Felicity.

Jordan hurried on. "He's heard about your marriage and is . . . telling tales. About you and Felicity."

"What kind of tales?" Felicity asked.

Jordan shot her a glance. "Well, for one thing, he found out you're Lord X. He's spread the news of that quite broadly."

"It appears your new pen name will become necessary after all," Ian said coolly.

Felicity groaned. "No doubt Mr. Pilkington decided I needed a little push in that direction, and your uncle was handy for his purpose."

"Yes, but Lennard has twisted it to suit his own purposes, whatever they are," Jordan said. "He's told everyone that you discovered Ian's darkest secrets as Lord X, so Ian forced you to marry him to keep you quiet. That's why the wedding was so hasty, and why you wrote those comments about Ian's being honest with his wife."

Felicity winced. Must all her columns return to haunt her? She glanced up at Ian's rigid face. He hated this and blamed himself for it. She could tell.

"There's more, my friend," Jordan went on. "Your uncle is saying other things as well—about you in particular."

Ian's arm was like a band of iron under her fingers. "Not the usual gossip, I take it. What's he saying?"

Jordan shrugged. "Lies . . . rumors . . . idiocy. I thought you should know."

"What 'lies'?" Ian asked firmly.

Jordan's gaze shot to Felicity. "Perhaps we should speak privately, Ian."

"I have no secrets from her," Ian retorted. "Tell me."

"As you wish. He's claiming you forced yourself on his wife, then left England to avoid the scandal of her suicide.

He says you took advantage of both Felicity and your friend Miss Greenaway. He paints you as the worst debaucher who ever lived."

As Ian jerked away from her to go stand with his fists braced against the stone rails, anger slammed into Felicity. Ian's wretched uncle hadn't even had the decency to wait until he was sure Ian had sired an heir before he attacked. What a sniveling coward—to air his grievances in this despicable manner!

"Is that all?" she snapped at Jordan. "Why doesn't he just accuse Ian of drinking the blood of virgins and torturing women in his dungeon?"

"I warned you this might happen," Ian said in a low voice meant only for her. "I just didn't expect it so soon."

"He won't get away with it," she vowed. "I won't let him."

"If you try to deny his tales," Jordan put in, "it'll only make matters worse. They'll think Ian is forcing you to defend him. Ian's always been so mysterious about his past they'll believe anything his uncle says. And the sudden wedding surprised everyone. The best thing for both of you is to brazen it out, say nothing about it. Emily and I will be at your side, as well as Sara and Gideon—"

"No!" Ian whirled around to face them. "My uncle's quarrel is with me. I don't want the rest of you involved. You and Emily and the others should disassociate yourselves from me until this is over. And Felicity, you're going home."

"The devil I am! Run from that weasel's accusations? Never!"

"I agree, Lady St. Clair." Jordan crossed his arms over his chest, daring Ian to contradict him. "I'm not 'disassociating' myself from anyone."

Ian shot his friend a dark look. "We'll discuss that in a moment. But first I need a word in private with my wife."

"Of course." Jordan retreated up the stairs a short distance, still looking affronted.

Ian turned his glittering gaze on her. "I won't have you harmed by this. I won't let my uncle hurt you."

"And I won't let him hurt *you*. These rumors involve both of us, so I have as much right to fight this battle as you. Besides, I know precisely how to deal with his sort of vermin." When Ian started to protest, she added softly, "You promised me a chance to prove myself this evening. Well, this is my chance, and I'm taking it."

"Damn it, *querida*, you've never been the subject of vicious rumor. I have, and I tell you, I won't put you through that. You don't know how cruel people can be!"

"*I* don't know? Have you forgotten to whom you're talking? The best way to fight gossip is with gossip, and as you know, that's my forte. Give me a chance to thwart him, Ian. I can do it. I know I can." Well, she *thought* she could, anyway. She'd had all afternoon to think about what to do if some of Ian's fears came to pass, and she'd formed a plan. It was risky and might not work, but she had to try.

"You needn't sacrifice your reputation to prove you love me."

"I don't care about my reputation. Besides, I'm not trying to prove I love you. I'm trying to prove you can trust me. Always. Have faith in me, Ian. I won't betray your darkest secrets."

"I know that, damn it! But I don't want you involved. I should never have dragged you into this marriage in the first place—"

"Stop it! You've lived so long with this guilt that you think you deserve punishment, and you plan to exact it by denying yourself the pleasures of our love. Well, I'm in this marriage, too. If you punish yourself, you punish me, remember? I won't let you salve your conscience by forcing me from this marriage to live in misery without you. I intend to be very firm on this subject."

That brought him up short. He regarded her thoughtfully. "I wouldn't want you to live in misery, my love." He brushed his thumb over her chin, then sighed. "Very well. When you put it that way, I have little choice in the matter."

Her heart soaring, she grabbed his palm and kissed it, then glanced up to where Jordan paced the top of the stairs, shooting them long, exasperated glances. "That goes for your friends, too, Ian. They believe in you as I do, and they don't want to lose your friendship. They want to help. You need their help, whether you admit it or not. It's one thing for Edgar Lennard to libel his nephew. It's quite another for him to libel the Viscount St. Clair, the Earl and Countess of Blackmore, and the Earl and Countess of Worthing. If you let them stand beside you, it will only help your case."

He groaned. "You're asking me to let them suffer on my account. At least you have a full knowledge of why this is happening; they don't. I have no right to ask for their help when they don't know the truth."

"Then tell them the truth. You can trust them, you know. They're good people. They'll only think more of you for your honesty. I promise they won't disappoint you." Clasping his lapels, she gave him a reassuring smile. "Nor will I."

The light of the gas lamps flickered over his torn expression. Slowly he swept his hand along her cheek in a gentle caress. "You couldn't disappoint me if you walked into that ballroom, stripped yourself naked, and stuck your tongue out at everyone."

Some of the tension left her. Maybe there was hope for her husband after all. "I suppose that might work," she quipped, "but it's much too cold this evening. I think I'll try my plan first, if you don't mind."

"My God," he said hoarsely, "what did I do to deserve you?"

"The same thing I did to deserve you—nothing. You were yourself. And that's enough."

She smiled at him, and without warning, he dragged her against him and kissed her long and deep. When he released her, she stared up at him dazed. "What was that for?"

"For luck."

"Luck?" she said loftily. "I don't *need* luck. I'll have you know I'm the Viscountess St. Clair, soon to be the most notorious female writer of gossip in London. If *I* can't turn rumor to my advantage, who can?"

The corners of his mouth twitched. "I beg your pardon. I didn't mean to question your capabilities." He offered her his arm. "Shall we go in and face the snakes, my lady?"

She tilted her chin up proudly as she hooked her hand in his elbow. "By all means, my lord."

Jordan awaited them at the top of the stairs. The three of them entered Lord Stratton's town house together and were shown to the ballroom by a footman. When she and Ian were announced, there was a general stir in the room.

She swallowed. This wasn't like the time she'd fled through a ballroom after Ian's kiss. This time, the gossip could ruin her. And Ian. Indeed, if her plan failed, she might leave her husband worse off than before. She glanced up at Ian, then took strength from his arrogant expression. If he could face down this crowd with defiance, then so could she.

As they walked inside, Emily and Sara joined them, looking anxious. But before she could say anything to allay their worries, she spotted Lady Brumley heading toward her with half the gossips in tow. Her hands grew clammy.

Turning to Ian, she whispered, "Why don't you and Jordan go off somewhere and talk? I can handle this better without you standing there frowning at everyone and convincing them that you are indeed the Devil Incarnate."

That brought a smile to his lips. "Was I frowning?"

"Glowering, more like." She drew her hand from his elbow. "Go on now. Talk to your friend—you'll feel better afterward. I'll be fine."

His gaze bore into hers, serious again. "I love you."

"Good. Keep that thought in mind." Because after what she was about to do, he might want to strangle her. Especially if it didn't work.

Jordan and Ian had scarcely left her for one of the card rooms when Lady Brumley and her entourage were upon them. It was now or never.

"My dear girl!" Lady Brumley exclaimed, eyes bright with pleasure. "So glad to see you here! And married, too! What a shock! We've been hearing the most amazing stories, but as I've told everyone, it's all nonsense."

"Stories? About me?" Felicity asked in her most innocent tone, wondering if she could pull this off.

Sara and Emily shook their heads as if to warn her, but she ignored them. She had to try this. Otherwise, Ian would continue to suffer at the hands of the gossips.

"Some troublemaking creature insists that you're Lord X." Lady Brumley kissed the air on either side of Felicity's cheeks. "I told them it couldn't be true."

"But it *is* true, my dear Lady Brumley," Felicity replied. "Now that I'm married, I see no reason to keep it a secret."

That clearly took everyone by surprise, not so much because it confirmed the gossip, but because she didn't seem disturbed that her identity had been revealed.

"Is Lord St. Clair forcing you to end the column?" someone asked.

"No, indeed." She forced a bright smile to her face. "My husband likes my column, you know. In fact, we discussed it on our way here. I'm thinking of calling it 'Secrets of a Viscountess.' Ian says the title's misleading, since it's not supposed to be *my* secrets, but I think it has a lovely ring. What do you think?"

Lord Jameson, who'd always treated her like a daughter,

said hesitantly, "Your husband doesn't disapprove of your writing?"

"Heavens, no. Why should he?"

The older man looked uncomfortable. "You must admit that you've been . . . rather critical of him in previous columns."

"Oh, *that*. He's quite forgiven me for that. After all, if it hadn't been for my columns about him, we would never have met and fallen in love."

There was an uncomfortable silence. Then Lady Brumley came to her rescue. "These fools have some notion that love had nothing to do with it. That St. Clair blackmailed you into marrying him."

She widened her eyes in bewilderment. "Blackmailed me?"

"Yes. I told them it was utter nonsense, but they'd heard that you found out all your husband's secrets and he married you to keep you silent about them. Some idiot claims that his lordship threatened to ruin you if you didn't marry him."

Ian's uncle had certainly hit close to the truth, hadn't he? Well, she wouldn't let him succeed in this. She wouldn't! Felicity looked at Lord Jameson and the others, who avoided her gaze. Then she burst into deliberate laughter. "It's true, every word of it."

She had their attention now. Shock was written on their faces. Lady Brumley, Emily, and Sara eyed her as if she'd gone mad.

She continued in a dramatic tone, though her knees were knocking beneath her gown. "Lord St. Clair found out I was Lord X, came to my house, and demanded that I stop writing about him. I refused, of course. So he gave me an ultimatum—either marry him or he would ruin me." She paused for effect. "It was a very difficult decision. I mean, what woman wants to marry a rich viscount when she can be a poor nobody writing columns for the newspaper?"

When Sara smiled and Emily joined her, Felicity felt more confident. She tapped her finger against her chin. "I thought about it for . . . oh . . . nearly half a minute. And I decided that while being ruined by a man with such obvious assets could be enjoyable, I'd much prefer to be a wealthy viscountess. That way I could have *all* his assets, if you know what I mean."

For a moment, when her audience continued to gaze at her as if she were mad, she thought she'd made a huge mistake. *Please, God,* she prayed, *let them have a sense of humor.*

Suddenly Lady Brumley chuckled, and a few others tittered as well.

Pressing her advantage, she sighed with great exaggeration. "So here I am, locked into marriage with an attractive and wealthy young man of rank. It's awful, don't you think? Now I can't marry an old lecher or penniless barrister! And I did so have my heart set on that."

There were laughs now. Loud ones.

"He's such a troublesome husband, too," she went on quickly while she had them on her side. "He insists that I buy things, and he *knows* I hate to shop. Who wants all that jewelry and silks and furs cluttering up one's bedchamber? It's really too vexing. And the way he treats my brothers—" She rolled her eyes. "I keep telling him not to spoil them, but he won't listen! He's sending my eldest brother off to a very expensive school, and he constantly buys presents for the other three. I swear, I won't be able to do a thing with them if he doesn't stop it!"

She'd gathered a crowd by now, most of whom were either laughing or asking their neighbors to recount what she was saying.

"What about in the bedroom?" one of the outrageously plainspoken March sisters called out. "Has your husband proven 'troublesome' there as well?"

She didn't have to fake her blush. "Very much so.

mean, would *you* want a man like that in your bed? So tall, virile, and well built? Here I was, hoping for a short bald man with a paunch, and instead I got *that!*" She added with a wink, "And I must complain that when he demands his husbandly rights, he makes me want to behave *most* improperly. . . ."

There wasn't a soul left in the audience who wasn't smiling, and most were laughing. Lady Brumley guffawed so hard she actually had tears in her eyes. And Sara and Emily beamed at her approvingly.

Felicity could already hear a few whispers of, "I knew it all along" and "Don't they make an adorable couple?"

Suddenly all conversation stopped. A woman with a haughty bearing came toward Felicity, the crowd parting before her in awed interest.

The Duchess of Pelham herself.

She stopped before Felicity and swept her with the contemptuous glance Felicity remembered all too well. "This is all very entertaining, Lady St. Clair." She spoke Felicity's title with a sneer. "But you don't fool me with this talk of your husband's good qualities. I've heard he has a history of forcing himself on helpless women. You mentioned one such woman in your column, as I recall. And his own uncle claims that the viscount fled England after abusing his aunt. I'm sure you know what I mean."

A silence fell on the crowd at the duchess's deliberate cruelty. No woman with an ounce of feeling would mention such a terrible accusation about a man to his wife.

For a second, she was back in the Pelham library when the duchess had made those vile accusations to Papa and humiliated her.

But the thought of Ian stiffened her spine. The bitter old witch hated all the women her husband had ever lusted after, whether those women had returned his lust or not. And now she sought to use Ian to degrade Felicity publicly.

She fixed the duchess with a cool gaze. "Ian's uncle? You mean Mr. Lennard?"

"You know who I mean."

Felicity pasted a sympathetic look on her face. "The poor man. Is he still repeating that tale after all these years? It's so sad. He never recovered after his wife's death, you know. I think he blames himself, although it was purely accidental. She fell and hit her head while in his bedchamber. They were arguing—or so his mistress told me."

That took the duchess by surprise. "His mistress?"

"Why, yes." She hoped Miss Greenaway would forgive her for this as long as all names were kept out of it. "That woman I mentioned in the paper, the one on Waltham Street? It turns out I was mistaken about her connection to my husband. He helped her because she'd been Mr. Lennard's mistress for a time and was in dire straits. She'd left Mr. Lennard because she couldn't endure his grief any longer. I talked to her about all of it myself."

"Y-you talked to her?" the duchess stammered.

No woman ever talked to someone presumed to be her husband's mistress, which Felicity prayed would lend credence to her claims. "Yes. I wanted to find out if I could do anything to help dear Mr. Lennard through his grief. He *is* family, after all. Ian and I are both very concerned about him. The poor wretch's mind seems to have snapped." She leaned forward and lowered her voice as if to impart a great secret. "He has some notion that he should have inherited Chesterley instead of my husband. Can you believe it, your grace?"

That started the whispers going, as she'd hoped it would. Such a "notion" offended firmly held beliefs in primogeniture. Besides, everyone assumed that the estate was entailed on Ian's heir. Thus Edgar Lennard's "notion" only proved his madness.

"That doesn't explain why your husband fled England," the duchess persisted.

To Felicity's surprise, Lady Brumley answered that one. "He left to fight in the war, of course. Everyone knows that. His father—wise man that he was—refused to let his heir join the army, but boys will be boys, and Lord St. Clair wanted to serve his country."

"Really, Lady Brumley," the duchess retorted, "do you expect us to believe that a viscount's heir—"

"Just ask Wellington about it," Sara put in. "Only the other day, he mentioned Lord St. Clair's service to my husband. He said England wouldn't have won the war without the Viscount St. Clair."

Though she still looked skeptical, the Duchess of Pelham clearly realized when she was outnumbered. Casting them all a scathing look, she tipped up her chin and walked off.

Felicity nearly collapsed. Good Lord, she hoped she never had to deal with that woman again.

Lady Brumley took one look at her pale face and clasped her arm. "Do come tell me more about your troublesome husband," she said as she dragged her away from the crowd. "I want to know all the details."

With relief, Felicity allowed the woman to lead her along the edge of the dance floor and away from the others. As soon as they were out of earshot, she asked in a low voice, "Do you think they believed me?"

"The ones who don't will keep it to themselves." She patted Felicity's hand. "You did very well, my dear. Now you must leave matters to the rumor mill. Coupled with your obvious affection for St. Clair, your story should gain more credence than Edgar's in time. So relax. You've won."

She dearly hoped that was true. Ian had suffered enough. She cast a quick prayer to the Deity: *Let it work, God, please. I'll never complain again if You'll do this for me. And for him.*

"So tell me, how much of that Banbury tale is true?" Lady Brumley asked.

Felicity's eyes widened. "What? Didn't you believe me?"

Lady Brumley laughed. "Not a word. Well, except for the parts about your husband's qualities. I take it you're well pleased with your 'troublesome husband'?"

A shy smile crept over Felicity's face. "Very pleased."

"I'm glad to hear it. Some young women can't recognize a good man even when he lands in their laps."

She thought of what Ian had told her about his uncle and Lady Brumley. "That's because men—both good *and* bad—hide their characters very well. For example, Edgar Lennard might seem like a good man to some young women. But any woman who escaped marriage to him should consider herself fortunate. From what I understand, he has a temper. A *violent* temper. And a tendency to loose it on women."

Lady Brumley stared at her keenly, and Felicity didn't flinch from her gaze. In that moment, an understanding passed between them.

"I think I already knew that," the marchioness finally said. "Though I sincerely hope his nephew doesn't take after him in that respect."

"Not in the least. But then, you knew that, too, didn't you?" She squeezed Lady Brumley's hand. "Thank you."

The marchioness looked uncomfortable. "For what?"

"For having faith in him when no one else did—not even me."

Lady Brumley gave a little shrug that set the ship's bells on her new headdress tinkling. "You're welcome, Lord X. And if you should ever need someone to write your column for you—"

Felicity laughed. "Don't worry. You're the only person I'd consider."

Heedless of the loud music and the sounds of dancing feet coming from the ballroom, Ian and Jordan stood silently in a deserted card room. Ian had just finished his story, amazed by how much easier it had been to tell it the second time. Encouraged by Felicity's earlier reaction, he'd left nothing out. Besides, it was becoming evident that the truth might emerge shortly, given his uncle's determination to ruin him, and he wanted Jordan to hear it from him, not from Edgar Lennard.

Jordan stared at him a long time. He'd asked questions here and there, but hadn't made any commentary that might reveal what he thought, and that worried Ian.

Finally, his friend sighed. "My God, I wish I'd known about all this long ago. How you must have suffered!"

The reaction stunned him. He'd expected more shock, more revulsion. But apparently his wife was as wise in this as in everything else. His friends cared only about him. And they understood—as she had—that it had been an accident.

"If I'd known, I might have done something to help," Jordan went on.

"There was nothing anyone could do, I'm afraid."

"Still, you could have told me. I'm your oldest friend. Why didn't you say something?"

Ian shrugged. "Shame. Guilt. I hated myself. And I had no reason to believe my friends would feel any differently."

"But something changed that, didn't it?"

A smile crept over his face. "Yes. My wife. She finally made me accept that we all make mistakes. That living with them doesn't have to mean torturing oneself with them. Or bearing them alone."

Jordan gripped Ian's arm, squeezed it briefly in a show of sympathy, then released it. "Your wife is a remarkable woman. Almost as remarkable as mine."

"Yes, I know." To him, she was more remarkable, but he doubted Jordan would agree.

"As for your uncle . . ." Jordan's tone hardened. "You can't let him win this. Even if I'd never known the truth, I would have thought it an abomination for your uncle to gain Chesterley. I wonder why your father ever considered it."

Ian ignored the sudden jolt of pain in his gut. That particular torment wasn't likely to go away soon. "He thought me more unfit for the position than my uncle."

"That's not true." Jordan's eyes narrowed. "If he had, he would have disinherited you entirely, but he didn't. Is it possible he set up that will as a way to make you see your responsibilities? When he died, he had no idea where you were or if you would ever return. Perhaps your father feared you wouldn't return without good reason. And the threat of your uncle inheriting would certainly be a good reason."

Ian had never considered that, but it made sense. It was the sort of test his father would have given him. And it might mean that his father had believed him, after all. It was comforting to think that.

"Perhaps you're right, my friend," he told Jordan. "In any case, we'll never know. Right now, I'm more concerned with making sure Felicity doesn't suffer the same nasty rumors I've endured for the past few years. So I think it's long past time we returned to the ballroom."

"You're right," Jordan said, then headed for the door.

When they entered the ballroom a few minutes later, he instantly noticed a change in the way people regarded him. The coldness that had been there earlier was absent. Some of the women even eyed him with interest.

He wanted only one woman, however. As they joined Gideon beside the punch table, it took Ian a few minutes to spot her standing with Lady Brumley amidst a crowd of matrons. Someone glanced at him, then said something to Felicity that made her laugh and cast him a delighted smile. He smiled back. What the devil was going on?

He didn't have long to wonder. Emily and Sara hurried up to the three of them, out of breath and beside themselves with excitement. "Where on earth have you two been?" Sara asked. "You've missed everything!"

"Oh?" Jordan asked, exchanging glances with Ian.

"Your wife is amazing!" Emily told Ian.

"I'm quite aware of that, believe me. What has she done now?"

"Well, you needn't worry about the gossip your uncle spread anymore," Sara remarked.

It took Emily and Sara several minutes to tell the tale. As they detailed Felicity's blithe parrying of every accusation made by Edgar, Ian's astonishment grew. They were right—Felicity *was* amazing. It would never have occurred to him to attack the problem as she had. Somehow she'd turned all his uncle's lies into compliments to her husband without so much as calling Edgar Lennard a liar. Incredible.

Sara's eyes were bright with mischief as she finished her tale. "I believe she's still complaining about her 'troublesome' husband and how miserable she is married to a man who provides for her brothers, supports her profession, and as she puts it, makes her 'behave most improperly.' She has them all laughing at your uncle's claim that you forced her into marriage. And pitying him for his other accusations."

Ian could scarcely breathe, his throat was so tight with pride and love. She'd said she wouldn't disappoint him, then she'd gone on to surpass all his expectations. How had he gotten so lucky? To find the most wonderful woman in London, when all he'd sought was someone to give him an heir. He didn't care what happened now, as long as he got to keep her.

He looked for her again and spotted her in close conversation with Lord Jameson, another of the notorious gossips. No doubt she was laying further seeds of doubt on the most fertile ground possible.

As if she felt his gaze, she looked up, saw who surrounded him, then flashed him a tentative smile, as if trying to determine if he'd approved of her tactics. He put as much feeling into his answering smile as he could manage, and her face glowed. He felt other eyes on them, but could think only of her. And how badly he wanted to get her home and make her "behave most improperly."

Suddenly he caught sight of someone approaching her, and his smile vanished. Uncle Edgar, damn him. "Excuse me a moment," he murmured to his friends and hurried toward Felicity.

His uncle said something to her and then they both headed out of the ballroom down one of the hallways toward the private rooms. Which was just as well, Ian thought as he followed them. What he had to say to his uncle was not for others' ears.

He found them entering a parlor off the main hall. He hurried toward it, but slowed as he approached the open door and heard his uncle say, "You wouldn't listen to me, would you? You had to take up with him. You had to defend him and make me appear the fool. Well, I hope you enjoyed yourself, Lady St. Clair." He spoke the courtesy title with condescension. "You and your naïveté. When you hear the whole truth—"

"I *know* 'the whole truth,' " she said fiercely. "He's told me all of it. What's more, if I'd wanted to tell 'the whole truth' to the world, I would have made sure you came off sounding like the vermin you are."

Ian paused at the door.

"The fact is," she continued, "I don't want to tell the whole truth—I have no wish to cause my husband further pain. But if you ever reveal what happened that night in that cottage, I won't hesitate to denounce you publicly for the wife-beater you are!"

"That won't prevent my nephew from going to prison for murdering my wife!"

"You might be surprised. I'm sure your former mistress— who detests you, by the way—would be happy to claim that *you* were the one who pushed your wife. I'm also sure any number of your servants could attest to your sordid habits. So go ahead, try accusing Ian of murder. Miss Greenaway and I will make sure you go straight to Newgate for it. I won't let you hurt him anymore!"

"There are other ways I can hurt him," he said in a sly voice that sent a chill down Ian's spine. "I wonder how my nephew would feel to discover me lying with his wife? Shall we find out?"

Ian surged through the door, slamming it so hard against the wall that his uncle whirled around in the process of reaching for Felicity. "Touch her," Ian warned, "and I'll tear you into so many pieces they'll never find you!"

Felicity had never been so happy to see her husband in her life. Though she undoubtedly could have used her knee trick on his uncle, she much preferred to have her husband at her side for this. "There you are, my love! I was just telling your uncle how delighted I am to have joined the Lennard family. But for some reason, he refuses to congratulate me."

"Come here, Felicity," Ian commanded, though his eyes remained on his uncle. "We're expected in the ballroom. Our friends are probably looking for us right now."

"Probably," she said cheerily and joined him at the door. Now that Ian was here, she was beginning to feel quite pleased with herself. She'd made her point with his uncle, and had the distinct impression that he would hesitate to bother them any further.

She laid her hand in the crook of her husband's arm, and he covered it with his, squeezing it. His gaze swept her quickly. "Are you all right?"

"Perfectly all right," she reassured him.

He returned his gaze to his uncle. "I'm warning you, Uncle Edgar—I protect what is mine. If you ever come near my wife again, there won't be enough left of you to bury. Do as you wish with me, but leave her alone. Is that understood?"

His uncle glowered at him. "We're not finished, you and

I. Chesterley may yet be mine. You still have to bear an heir."

"Believe me, I have every intention of it." Ian gazed down at his wife, and there was no mistaking the love in his gaze. "So we'd best get right to it, don't you think, my darling?"

"Oh, certainly," she said, beaming up at him. "We must start on it at once."

They left his uncle behind, cursing them both loudly.

Before they could reach the ballroom, however, Ian whisked her into what looked like a study and shut the door, driving the bolt to.

"What are you doing?" she asked, startled by the sudden thunder in his expression.

"You must promise never to let that man get you alone again. If he'd hurt you, I swear—"

"But he didn't."

"Promise me, Felicity! Or I'll keep you locked up in here until you do. And the Strattons might find that odd in the morning."

"I promise," she said softly. Now that she'd had her say with his uncle, she need never see the wretch again. He visibly relaxed, but when he made no move to leave, she added, "Shouldn't we return to the ballroom now? You said our friends were expecting us."

"I lied. Besides, there's another matter to discuss."

"What's that?"

Eyes gleaming dangerously, he trailed his fingers over her cheek. "I hear that you consider me a most 'troublesome husband.' "

She sucked in a breath. How much had Sara and Emily told him? Could he have disapproved of her methods? Ian *was* a very private person, after all. She deliberately kept her tone light. "Wherever did you hear such a thing?"

"Everyone's talking about it. Apparently you were almost as busy spreading tales about me this evening as m uncle." He hooked his fingers beneath her sleeves and drew them slowly off her shoulders.

Her pulse quickened, for his eyes reflected a decidedly wicked intent. He unfastened her gown. "They're saying I have this annoying habit of making you feel things you shouldn't."

Trust Ian to use her words against her. "It's quite true." She pressed his hand against her breast to feel her heart pounding. "You see? You're doing it now."

"That's what happens when you let a 'tall, virile, and well-built' viscount force you into marriage." He ran his finger beneath the edge of her bodice until it skimmed her nipple, and she sucked in a breath. "Instead of holding out for the 'penniless barrister' you had your 'heart set on.' "

She blushed. "Did they tell you *every* word I said?"

"Sara has an astonishingly good memory."

He clearly wasn't angry. Or if he was, he had an odd way of showing it.

He peeled her gown and chemise from her shoulders, exposing her breasts to his avid gaze. "I especially liked the part about how you find yourself behaving most improperly when I'm around."

She was losing the capacity to breathe. "You mean . . . like this?" Reaching up, she began to untie his cravat.

"Exactly." He reached for her hair.

"Not the hair, Ian!" she protested. "I'll never get it back up properly, and then everyone will know what we've been doing!"

With a dark smile, he began removing the pins. "Good. I must live up to my reputation, after all. I'd hate to make a liar out of my wife." He bent his head to kiss her throat. "Especially when she went to so much trouble to enumerate all my bad qualities."

"I didn't begin to enumerate all of them," she said testily as her hair tumbled down around her shoulders. "I forgot to mention your insistence on having your own way . . .

your arrogance . . . your tendency to choose the most inappropriate times and places for seducing me. Shall I go on?"

"Not now, my darling viscountess," he whispered as he pressed kisses down her breastbone. "Save something for your column. Because right now, I'm planning to illustrate my bad qualities by doing the one thing you find most 'annoying.' "

"Oh? What is that?"

"I believe you called it, 'demanding my husbandly rights.' "

And to her utter delight, her troublesome husband did just that.

Epilogue

Readers will be pleased to learn that Lady St. Clair has borne a son, christened Algernon Jordan Lennard, the heir apparent to her husband, the viscount. Both mother and son are doing well, and no doubt the viscountess will return to authoring this column very soon. The Honorable Mr. Edgar Lennard, the viscount's uncle, has reportedly left England to reside on a plantation he purchased in America. We wish him and his family all the best in their new home.

LADY BRUMLEY, *THE EVENING GAZETTE*,
NOVEMBER 11, 1821 (Martinmas)

Three identical blond heads bent over Felicity as she sat propped up in the huge master bed at Chesterley, cradling her three-day-old son. "Give poor Algernon room to breathe, boys," she admonished as the triplets crowded around her. "You'll have plenty of chances to look at him, I assure you."

"Why is he so wrinkled?" Ansel asked. "He looks like an old man."

"So did you when you were born," she told him. "All babies look like that when they first come out."

"Does he know we're his uncles?" William asked.

"Not yet, but he will. And think how lucky he will be to have four uncles living in the same house with him."

Georgie peered more closely at the baby. "He sleeps an awful lot, don't he?"

"*Doesn't* he," a stern female voice automatically corrected behind him.

"*Doesn't* he," George repeated, with a furtive glance at the woman who towered over him.

Felicity smiled up at Miss Greenaway. "You're making progress, I see."

Miss Greenaway rolled her eyes. "Yes. Now I only have to correct Master George ten times a day instead of twenty."

"I ain't—I'm *not*—all that bad," Georgie grumbled.

Both Felicity and Miss Greenaway burst into laughter. That woke the baby up, who immediately started caterwauling.

Miss Greenaway cast her most governess-like look on the triplets. "Come now, you three, we've got Latin lessons to finish. And your sister needs a rest."

Their chorus of groans didn't deter the young woman, and in seconds she had all three boys marching out of the room like real soldiers. Felicity shook her head in amazement. That had been the best move she'd ever made—asking Miss Greenaway to be the boys' governess. The woman had a natural ability with children, if her work with the triplets was any indication. Miss Greenaway had leapt at the opportunity as well, since a woman with a bastard child would have difficulty finding suitable work.

Lately Felicity had noticed Ian's unmarried man of affairs eyeing Miss Greenaway with something more than idle curiosity. Miss Greenaway had rebuffed his initial attempts at courtship, telling Felicity that a man of his intelligence and position deserved a "pure" woman.

But Felicity knew the man would wear Miss Greenaway down. When the only thing that stood in the way of love was a dark past, the principals in the affair never had a chance. Love would always triumph. She'd wager all her pin money that there'd be another wedding at Chesterley soon.

Little Algernon's mouth was opening and closing like a fish's. She quickly lowered her gown, and he fastened his tiny mouth to her nipple, dragging on it lustily. He was perfect, she thought, surveying the little snip of a nose, the shells of his ears, the still-blue eyes that would probably soon turn black to match the fuzzy raven hair that whorled around the center of his delicate head.

He looked like his father, of course. A little sultan to match the big one. Well, there'd be no harem for her darling boy, if she had anything to say about it. No, he must have a nice, presentable girl . . . some lovely earl's daughter or even a duke's—

She groaned. She'd better watch it, or she'd turn into one of those women she always criticized in her column.

He'd finished suckling and had fallen into a sated sleep against her. Carefully, she drew her gown back up over her breast.

"No need to do that on my account," came a rumbling male voice from the doorway.

She looked up in delight. "Ian! You're back!"

"So I am." With a smile, he entered, then lowered his heated gaze to her now covered breasts. "I see I should have been a few minutes earlier."

"Don't tease me," she warned. "We've got six more weeks, you know, before we can indulge ourselves."

He groaned. "Believe me, my love, I'm well aware of it." He strode to the bed and sat down beside it, reaching out to trace his son's cheek. "He's beautiful, isn't he?"

"Yes," she agreed with maternal pride.

"And now he's the proud heir of an entire estate."

She gazed up at him eagerly. "It's settled then? It's all done?"

He nodded. "Uncle Edgar can't touch us. I think he'd already realized it the night of the Strattons' ball."

Mrs. Box bustled into the room. "His lordship has come and— Oh, there you are, milord! Beat me up here to tell her, I see." She approached the bed, smiling broadly. "Shall I take the little master for you, luv? Looks like he's nappin' again."

Felicity handed the baby to Mrs. Box. The woman had proven an excellent nurse, and Felicity had no doubt she'd continue to be one through many more little Lennards.

As soon as Mrs. Box was gone, Ian stretched out beside her on the bed. "I found something interesting while I was at the solicitor's in London." He drew out a folded sheet of paper. "Apparently, my father had left instructions that I was to be given this if I succeeded in having an heir before the appointed time."

She tried to guess from Ian's expression what it said, but he merely stared at her in that inscrutable manner he still sometimes had. Taking the paper with trembling hands, she opened it and scanned the lines:

> My son, if you are reading this, then you have not disappointed me. No doubt you think my methods extreme. You always did. But I had to be sure that you would care for Chesterley in my absence, and this seemed the best way of forcing you to acknowledge your responsibilities. Forgive me if you can.

Felicity tossed the paper down angrily. "And this is all he wrote? No words of apology for driving you away? No hint that he believed you innocent all along?"

"This *was* his apology, my love—or the closest my father could ever come to one. Jordan once said that if my father had truly believed me unworthy of being his heir, he wouldn't have arranged that strange will. He would simply have left the estate to my uncle. But he didn't—because he wanted to make sure I came back for it."

Noting the resignation in his tone, she took his hand in hers. "You're not angry at him? All those years of torture, of thinking he despised you—"

"I'm more angry at myself than anything. If I'd stayed, we might have worked through our differences. But I let my pride drive me away." He smiled. "Then again, if I'd stayed, I might not have met you."

She grinned. "Oh, I'm sure you would have. You're such a troublesome man, you would eventually have done *something* to merit mention in my column. And then you would have strode into my study and warned me about crossing you—"

"And seduced you and laid the most careful strategy to have you." He squeezed her hand. "You're right, *querida*. It would have made no difference at all. One encounter with you would have been sufficient to make me want you. It certainly was all it took the first time."

"What? You didn't *act* as if you wanted me that day. You acted like a bully."

He raised an eyebrow. "For all the good it did me. You merely continued to write precisely what you wished about me."

"Speaking of which," she said, with a twinkle in her eye, "it's time I went back to writing my column. What do you think should be the subject of my first column since the baby's birth? How the Viscount St. Clair roused a doctor out of bed the moment his wife first complained of birth pains? How the good viscount's notoriously even temper deserted him when the doctor said it might be hours and he should sleep a while longer? How the baby arrived amid the constant advice of a father who seemed to think he knew something about physic when he most decidedly did not?"

"I have a better idea," Ian said with a dangerous smile.

"Why not write a column on the various ways the good viscount intends to torture his wife with pleasure once the doctor approves marital relations?"

"Oh no, I couldn't write about that!" she said in mock horror.

"Too scandalous even for you?"

"Not at all," she said coyly. "Too long. That would take far more than one column."

"I've decided to have a baby."

Caleb swore, and Laurel saw that he'd poured wine on the counter.

"You didn't just tell me you're pregnant."

"No. I told you I'm going to *get* pregnant."

His eyes narrowed. "That usually requires a woman *and* a man."

"You know I can't... I don't want..."

What she thought was anger faded from his face. "I know. So you're—what?—planning to find a donor?"

"I already have." She busied herself dumping noodles into the now boiling water. "You know Matt Baker?"

Caleb's tone was careful, controlled. "Why him?"

It was the last thing she'd expected him to ask. "He's a friend. And smart. He's nice. Healthy..."

"Did you consider asking me?"

From somewhere she found the courage to whisper, "What would you have said if I had asked?"

Dear Reader,

Let's say your best friend is a guy. You want to have a baby. He's smart, nice, has good genes. Why would asking him to father your baby change your relationship at all? I mean, hey—you've been friends forever.

Done laughing? After all, having a baby changed your relationship with your *husband*, right? But in my heroine's defense, she turns to her best friend because of a whole lot of complicated fears and needs. He feels safe to her. Of course, he isn't at all.

First Comes Baby drew together several themes that seem to preoccupy me as a writer: the aftereffects of traumatic life events, the powerful need to have a child and the emotional vulnerability pregnancy brings. Best of all, I finally had a chance to write about the transformation of friendship into passionate love, a process that proved easy— Caleb is one of my all-time-favorite heroes.

I hope you fall in love with him, too!

Best,

Janice